PETER SHANN FORD

THE KEEPER
OF DREAMS

SIMON & SCHUSTER
NEW YORK   LONDON   TORONTO   SYDNEY   SINGAPORE

SIMON & SCHUSTER
Rockefeller Center
1230 Avenue of the Americas
New York, NY 10020

Simon & Schuster and colophon are registered trademarks
of Simon & Schuster, Inc.

Designed by Anne Scatto/PIXEL PRESS

Manufactured in the United States of America

10 9 8 7 6 5 4 3 2 1

LIBRARY OF CONGRESS CATALOGING-IN-PUBLICATION DATA
Ford, Peter Shann.
The keeper of dreams / Peter Shann Ford.
p.   cm.
1. Australian aborigines—Antiquities—Fiction. 2. Archaeological
thefts—Fiction. 3. Australia—Fiction. I. Title.
PS3556.O7127K44 2000
813'.6—dc21   00-040007
ISBN 0-684-87219-6

DEDICATED TO THE STORY KEEPERS

BOOK I

DREAMINGS

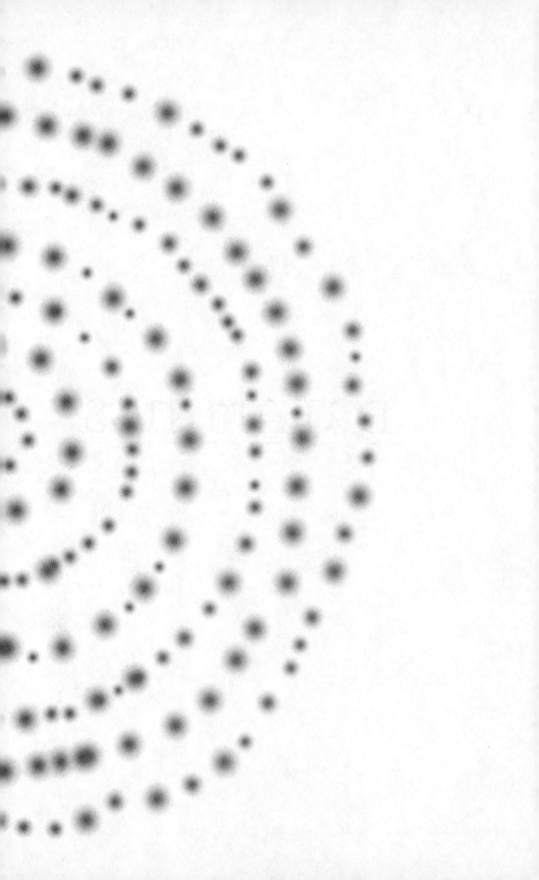

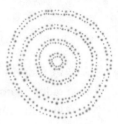

CHAPTER I

THE FIVE OLD WARRIORS came over the desert like tongues of fire, daubed red with ocher, and white with clay that coiled on their black skins in ancient patterns of secret men's business. A hard crossing they had of it, driven by danger beyond comprehension, traveling fast, coming to summon a savior.

They wore only hair strings at their waists, braided in front in protective pubic tassels. One of them carried a smoldering firestick, the others bore ceremonial killing spears, painted and tied with the codes of their spirits. They ignored a searing wind that hissed in from the vast ocean of sand and up the smooth stone escarpments rising around them. They were oblivious of the white wake of a jetliner, cutting a thin high scar of vapor through the stratosphere. They had journeyed far to this secret place, through hidden gaps in the ranges, down echoing gullies, and up to this bowl of pale orange rock, protected by edict and sentence of death on any uninitiated traveler who trespassed within a day's walk of here.

They set leaves and twigs in a charred crevice and ignited them with the firestick. When the flames flared and took hold, the elders covered them with a green eucalyptus branch, raising a thick billow of aromatic smoke. They walked three times through its clouds to purify themselves, then they removed the branch and the fire leapt up again.

Walkalpa, the doctor, watched the smoke eddy up from the great bowl of rock around them. They were surrounded by the geological monuments and mnemonics of all their creation songs and stories, lodged for infinity in curving ridges and stone formations and shifting dunes and buried watercourses radiating from the heart of the continent. Walkalpa curled his misshapen foot beneath him and sat facing the fire, unrolling a supple square of kangaroo skin, revealing the sinister tools and talismans of his profession.

The others took their places around the fire and watched. Walkalpa of the Emu Poison Bush Dreaming was tested and trained from childhood as a ngangkari, with the powers to heal, to lift and lay spells, and to speak to the spirits who travel this world and the country of the dead.

He had been hunting their quarry for nine days and nights since the theft that threatened the existence of every living man, woman, and child of his people. Walkalpa had examined the scene of the crime, assaying evidence concealed upon the ground, and resonating above it. The culprits had used all their powers to hide their way, but Walkalpa barely acknowledged their skillful deceptions. Instead, he cast his awareness over the continent, sensing their furtive echoes of guilt as clearly as any embedded tracks or urgent sounds of escape. He felt two men fleeing, and beyond them an accomplice, and beyond him, one other. With his senses ranging ahead, Walkalpa bore down on them, singing a secret song whose lethal words were timeworn forty thousand years ago. Ahead of him, two quarry felt the first terrifying intuitions of his pursuit. They changed course, seeking shelter within the boundaries of towns and missions. But one by one, Walkalpa was confronting from afar each fugitive with the consequence of his crime: first the two thieves, then their accomplice. The fourth man, however, eluded Walkalpa.

This last quarry was more dangerous, moving with complete indifference to the crime. To secure him, Walkalpa needed an ally.

«A kudaitja,» he said in the dialect of their people, his menacing voice coiling like smoke around the watching elders, «must be made.»

Kudaitja, meaning Changed One. A ritual assassin.

«He will have to travel where we cannot go,» Malu of the Red Kangaroo Dreaming said solemnly. He was nearly sixty years old, with grizzled hair and lined skin, but his scarred chest and arms remained muscular and strong.

«Some of us can go where the thief is,» said Tjitutja. He was a Dingo Dreaming man, in his mid-forties, with the leanness and sharp eyes of the Australian native dog whose name and totem he shared. But on a continent where the life expectancy of an Aboriginal man is forty-eight, Tjitutja was already well aged.

«If the thief hides it in one of his places, we cannot go there,» Lungkata of the Blue-Tongued Lizard Dreaming said. «Not even Tjitutja can go there.» He meant no offense, and Tjitutja the Dingo Dreaming man showed no reaction. Lungkata was merely stating the reality. There were places in their own country where all of them—despite their enormous wisdom and courage and painfully earned respect—were barred from entry.

A coal popped loudly, firing a burst of sparks in the air. The fifth elder had not spoken since he arrived. He had walked in alone from the deep desert, from far beyond the usual hunting range of the Wirruntjatjara, the tribal group to which they all belonged. They were Central Desert men, experienced hunters, warriors, and elders, but the fifth one was distinguished by a character that was at once calmly aloof and dangerously elemental, as if he had been born by wind and lightning from a cave in the farthest reach of the red plains. He was taller than all of them, with gaunt cheekbones and deep-set eyes. Like them, his chest and upper arms bore the ritual scars of initiations through all the levels of manhood. His silver-shot hair and beard were long and groomed, and he smelled of kangaroo grease, smeared over his skin against the sudden cold of desert nights.

They knew him as Kumanara, the name given to dead men. His dignified silence enveloped him like a mantle, and they had waited all day to hear him speak.

He was a Story Keeper, a walking registry of all the creation songs that defined and guided and preserved his people. He listened to the brief debate about the warrior who must be summoned. If the crime was not redressed and punished, all their songs and stories would end, lost in the final outrage of an invasion that in two hundred years had brought genocide to tribal lines once traced in unbroken links back to Creation.

Now, he raised his bearded jaw, quietly assessed them all, and spoke.

«It must be Tjilkamata, of the Spiny Anteater Dreaming.»

The men stared at Kumanara in silence. His suggestion was impossible.

«Tjilkamata is long gone from us,» Tjitutja of the Dingo Dreaming said. «Farther away than we have ever gone. Someone must Sing him back from that place.»

Kumanara turned to Walkalpa of the Emu Poison Bush Dreaming and their eyes met for an instant. Understanding flashed between them like desert lightning. Secrets. Powers beyond power. And a name, unspoken, a flicker of thought: Kalaya. Kumanara relaxed his focus into the middle distance, as if he were already traveling back to the heart of the desert.

PETER SHANN FORD

Walkalpa nodded to himself. Kumanara had been there when Tjilkamata of the Spiny Anteater Dreaming was first taken from his people. And Walkalpa himself had known Tjilkamata at the most profound time in their lives, but it was Kalaya of the Emu Dreaming who had brought Tjilkamata back to his own people. It was Kalaya who knew where Tjilkamata traveled on all his journeys between the desert and the outer world. Kalaya it would be then, who would deliver the summons.

Walkalpa uttered the name of Tjilkamata's place so quietly they barely heard it. It drifted through the last coils of eucalyptus smoke and resonated in whispering echoes around the curving walls of rock, strange, distant, utterly foreign.

"Houston."

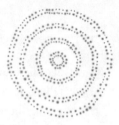

CHAPTER 2

EVERYBODY HELD THEIR BREATH, watching the astronaut's hand reach across the black gap of space. A second astronaut waited, farther back. The live images were so clear it seemed anyone in the room could touch the two space suits glowing in the brilliant sunlight. The gloved hand closed over the hatch handle of the crippled satellite. There was a painful silence, as the handle resisted.

"Got it." The astronaut's voice was triumphant, and the hatch swung open.

The room erupted in applause.

The second astronaut calmly reached through the satellite's hatch, into its heart.

Those watching in the room knew better than most the extraordinary journey the shuttle team had made to chase down the satellite and dock with it. They did not look exceptional, these men and women crowded around the television screen, casually dressed, ranging in age from mid-thirties to early sixties. The most striking thing about them was their quiet confidence. All of them appeared fit, and all of them had the alert look of disciplined intelligence. Many of them wore multi-dialed navigation chronometers or keyboard-buttoned calculator watches, the tools and talismans of pilots and mission specialists. More than half of them had travelled in space, the rest were in training, waiting, watching the grinding interplay of Congressional budgets, available berths on shuttles, and their own diminishing timelines of age and hierarchy. Only one woman could be described as stunning. She was talking to three men at the edge of the crowd. Her dark hair was tied back, baring the rich tan curves of her cheek. Her mouth was sensuous, her eyelashes were thick and black, and her penetrating gaze was lightened now by laughter. She wore a tailored linen skirt and blouse as bright purple as bougainvillea flowers, and lipstick the same color, lush and exotic against her dark skin.

On the other side of the room two men talked quietly together.

"Score one for the humans, Bob," Blake Scanlon said, nodding toward the screen. "Your bugs couldn't do that."

"Not yet," Dr. Robert Erhard agreed.

"You'll never replace us."

"No question about it." Robert smiled at Blake and looked at the screen again. He'd had the same conversation with every astronaut who sought him out at gatherings like this.

Blake drank the last of his Scotch and smiled ruefully. "You want to know the truth?"

"Sure." Robert saw the woman in purple turn to look at them across the crowded room.

"You scare us," Blake said quietly. "We'd never admit it in public. Nothing scares us in public. But your mindless vermin scare us."

"You think they'll hurt someone?"

"Hah! If they did, you think there'd be an official inquiry? You think a robot could be charged with negligence? Or murder?"

"It's just a robot. It's running a program."

"You think they're responsible for their actions?"

"The programmer's always responsible."

"Not the robot?"

"Just executing the program." Robert watched the woman excuse herself from the three men. "They'll never replace humans."

"Better believe it." Blake nodded toward the astronauts on the screen. "You can't beat a trained man on site. Or woman."

"Couldn't agree more."

"Ah, Grace." Blake grinned as the woman in purple came closer. "Tell the good doctor here you agree with me. Mindless vermin'll never replace us skilled professionals."

Grace Morgan appraised the two men.

"Blake, honey, you'll get no argument from me," she said as she slipped her arm around Robert's waist, and his hand closed around hers. "I'll take a skilled professional every time."

꙼

The watch face lit up with a pale green glow, showing a miniature map of the world, and 01:34 hours in the U.S. Central time zone. Robert Erhard released the light button, and his watch went dark again. He pushed his chair back from the computer, spun to face the landscape behind his desk, and gazed thoughtfully at the red desert of the Mars Excursion Mock-up stretching into darkness. The artificial Martian surface was only a hundred feet along each side, but intricate lighting and photo-real murals running around the set gave one the vivid impression of actually looking across a flat, rocky stretch of the Red Planet. Around Robert, workbenches and cubicles ran along the back wall of the large hangar housing the MEM. In their ordered clutter lay arrays of tiny robots in various stages of dismemberment. They ranged in size from a shoebox to a match folder. Most were fitted for six legs, while some had wheels or complex caterpillar tracks. A few stood on the floor, connected by umbilical cables to computers on the benches. Others had infrared or radio control links. They looked like a motley flock of mutated insects, and indeed, the half dozen programmers and electronics engineers who worked on them called them Insectoids. As the fastest developing area of robotics, they attracted, from their inception, universal wonder, scorn, and fear. Others outside the MEM referred to the Insectoids and their engineers as the Nerd Herd, grouping the robots with their builders and keepers.

Designing, assembling and programming herds of small robots to survey and eventually populate the moon and the planets occupied most of Robert's waking hours.

Ever since Rodney Brooks developed the first Insectoids in his Robotics Lab at Massachusetts Institute of Technology in the early 1990s, Robert Erhard had known where his own passion lay. Like Dr. Brooks, Robert earned his master's in science at Flinders University in South Australia, and his doctorate at MIT. Unlike Brooks, Dr. Robert Erhard was a full-blooded Aborigine, born in the desert to tribal parents and adopted, raised, and educated by a white couple. He was of the infamous Stolen Generations of Aboriginal children, but he had turned his adversity to advantage. His education and natural intelligence carried him up pathways denied most Aborigines in Australia, to scholarships and positions first at Flinders, then Stanford, and finally MIT, and the inner sanctum of artificial intelligence and robotics. His speciality was memory compression, making computers store and transmit data faster and better, the sort of abilities needed to let a robot report back from anywhere in the solar system. For Robert, computer programs were like music, to be composed with elegance and harmony.

They were songs he sang to his robots to bring them to life and talk back to him with their experience of the world. When he played his software into them, they became tiny facets of himself, ranging across new country, bound for new worlds.

Insectoids stirred the imagination of everyone except the astronauts. A rocket big enough to reach the Red Planet and return with a crew of two humans, or one of the old Martian surveyors, like Mariner or Voyager—each the size of a Volkswagen—could instead carry more than a hundred Insectoids, land them, and radio home their soil and atmospheric data, and color pictures in stereo. If an astronaut or single lander was disabled, the mission was critically endangered. If one Insectoid, or even fifty, were destroyed, the mission could still proceed with the remainder.

Astronauts hated the Insectoids, and derided them as bugs and MVs, mindless vermin. There was a time when rats and roaches threatened to overrun ancient sailing ships. Now the stroes quietly dreaded the idea of spacecraft venturing beyond Earth's gravitational shores crewed by a Nerd Herd in place of humans. But contractors could read the future. Congressional budget cuts forced NASA to improvise, and the Insectoids answered a host of questions that perplexed its engineers and accountants.

Robert finished his tea, but it did little to stem the tide of weariness that had been draining him for four days. Sleep eluded him, and when it came, it brought graphic dreams that evaded his memory when he awoke, but left him as exhausted as a marathon runner. He stood slowly and put on his VR helmet. It was like a bulky baseball helmet, with circuit boards around the rim, and a closed compartment over the eyes, containing two stereo screens that provided the imagery of virtual reality. A narrow coaxial cable ran from the helmet to a black glove, which Robert slipped onto his right hand.

"BILBO, wake up," Robert said quietly into his mike.

His eyes adjusted automatically to the three-dimensional image inside the VR helmet. He could see the Martian Mock-up surface as clearly as if he'd been standing on the planet. Rocks ranging from the size of marbles to bowl-ing balls were strewn across the plain. Robert raised his gloved hand, made a fist and rolled it forward, like the throttle of a motorcycle. Colored numbers, words, and symbols streamed up the left side of the VR screens.

At once, the three-dimensional image in his headset moved, close to the ground, swaying slightly in a smooth gait. To one side of the mock-up, an Insectoid the size of a milk carton strode carefully on six legs onto the plain ten yards in front of Robert. Its body was covered in green printed circuit boards. On top of it, a small Polhemus tracker controlled the direction of its tiny twin Teleos Research PRISM-3 stereo cameras. Behind them, a minia-ture satellite dish aimed itself at a receiver inside the high roof of the hangar, transmitting the striking images Robert saw in his VR helmet. A small plaque on the rear of the robot read "BILBO" between the logos of NASA Johnson Space Center and the Intelligent Machines Project.

Robert used his glove to guide BILBO toward a large boulder. He intended to order the little robot to probe the rock with a newly fitted hollow drill sensor, testing for bacterial life that may once have lived on Mars. Robert wore sneakers and jeans and a polo shirt. He was just over six feet tall, lean from long-distance running, and lithe and muscular from regular workouts in Johnson's staff gym. He stood with his feet apart on the sand, leaning in con-cert with the movement of the pictures in his helmet. He saw the movement over the Martian plain, the red sand and rocks passing behind BILBO's smooth passage. Then Robert blinked hard. Perhaps what he saw was the product of too little sleep.

On the stereo screens he saw BILBO's images move toward something dark on the sand. He rolled his control glove, and the little Insectoid moved faster. The dark shape came into focus, and BILBO obeyed Robert's glove command to lean back on its spindly legs and track its camera upward. Robert checked the data streaming up the side of his image. There was no indication of any large object in front of BILBO. But in his three-dimensional viewer, Robert watched mutely as the image moved up from the pair of bare feet standing on the red surface far ahead of him.

The feet were black. As Robert watched, one foot rose from the sand and settled comfortably against its opposite knee. The legs were bare, so too were the strong thighs, and the flat belly and broad chest, with its lines of horizon-tal scars. The figure was completely naked, save for a narrow waist string sus-pending a finely knotted pubic tassel. The arms were powerful, crossing the body to where both hands rested lightly along the haft of a long hardwood hunting spear, decorated below its sharp stone tip with the long gray feathers of an adult emu. The image tracked up to the head, with thick black hair pulled back and tied with a leather thong, behind a somber, bearded face, black and grave, which stared straight through the VR screens with deep and sightless eyes.

Robert felt suddenly cold. He tore the VR helmet off and stared back.

Ahead of him BILBO hunkered back on its rear legs, pointing upward toward empty space. But apart from the little Insectoid and the scattered rocks, there were no other shapes or figures to be seen anywhere across the entire Martian landscape.

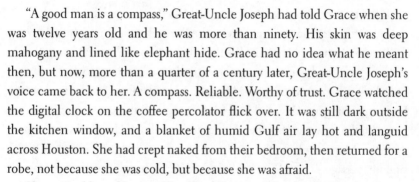

"A good man is a compass," Great-Uncle Joseph had told Grace when she was twelve years old and he was more than ninety. His skin was deep mahogany and lined like elephant hide. Grace had no idea what he meant then, but now, more than a quarter of a century later, Great-Uncle Joseph's voice came back to her. A compass. Reliable. Worthy of trust. Grace watched the digital clock on the coffee percolator flick over. It was still dark outside the kitchen window, and a blanket of humid Gulf air lay hot and languid across Houston. She had crept naked from their bedroom, then returned for a robe, not because she was cold, but because she was afraid.

She poured herself a cup of coffee and tiptoed down to her study. She sat on a large cedar chest, holding the cup with both hands, and closed her eyes.

Great-Uncle Joseph had run away to sea at the age of eleven, more afraid of a lingering death in the drunken desolation of Indiantown than of any perils beyond. He traveled the world on sailing ships, and returned seven years later, lean and hard as a warrior, his hands toughened by swaying rigging and savage fights with men who learned to show him the same respect they accorded whites. He brought home new skills and wisdom acquired on the great wooden ships, and took his mother and baby sister away from Indiantown and set up shop as a carpenter in the village of Milroy, in Amish country, Pennsylvania. There most men valued honest expertise over skin, and Joseph Babbs prospered modestly as a master of wood, from barns to beautifully dovetailed wedding chests. He built the large dowry box his sister, Grace, took to the home of her new husband, a Polish coal miner, at the end of World War I. And he turned his aging hands to one last chest when her daughter, Gretel, a nurse, became engaged at the end of World War II to Dr. Howard Morgan, the first black physician anyone in the central counties could recall seeing. The prejudice that Great-Uncle Joseph and his Cherokee relatives constantly collided with seemed almost trivial compared to the indignities Dr. Morgan endured.

They only abated during the polio epidemic, when the physician and his young wife braved a greater prejudice, directed against anyone suspected of having the disease. Howard and Gretel Morgan ministered to every patient who came to their home, and answered every call to farms and mining towns within a day's drive of Milroy. They named their daughter Grace, and when Dr. Howard Morgan died of polio twelve years later, Great-Uncle Joseph took her on his knee and talked about good men. "A man who takes your trust under false pretenses," he said, "is worse than a thief. A good man will always point true."

She had looked for these good men through school and then at the university, and—among the river of white men who were oblivious to discrimination because it did not touch them, and of black men who seethed with anger they rarely acknowledged—she occasionally found a man she thought might meet Great-Uncle Joseph's standard. But invariably she was disappointed—until she met Robert Erhard at a director's briefing the week she arrived at Johnson. She looked at him closely, through the aura of brilliance that cloaks the best and brightest at the space agency, and examined instead the subtle human signatures she knew identified men as reliably as the radiation spectra she studied on downlinks from Hubble. When Robert Erhard spoke about his family, he reminded Grace of Great-Uncle Joseph. Within the dazzling matrix of technology he navigated and helped build, Robert kept his feet firmly planted in tradition. He was the most comfortable man she knew, and in the year since they had moved in together, she allowed herself to think more about where they were going. After the agency they could both write their own tickets anywhere. Grace never told Robert, but she wrote an algorithm to plot the Mendelian probabilities that any child they had might more closely resemble Great-Uncle Joseph's Cherokee parents, or Howard Morgan's African forebears, or Robert's ancestors, who, like all Aborigines, were black Caucasians. She knew the realities of each possibility. Whatever the outcome, wherever they were going together, Grace Morgan trusted Robert Erhard implicitly. He was a compass she could navigate life with.

Until less than an hour ago, when she had woken next to him, to sounds she did not want to believe. Grace put her coffee cup on the floor and knelt in front of the chest, sliding her fingertips over the dark mahogany so beautifully shaped and fitted by Great-Uncle Joseph's weathered hands. An ornately carved wreath of roses coiled around a raised letter G, worn smooth in the more than seventy years since her grandmother Grace first owned it. She raised the lid smoothly. The interior smelled of cedar. She lifted away a layer of calico and rested the back of her hand on the white satin gown neatly folded beneath it. She shivered, closed the lid, left her coffee cup on the floor, and walked up the hallway to their bedroom.

She did not move silently this time, and he awoke as she entered. He looked tired, and something more, which he tried to cover with a smile.

"You're up early," he said.

"I couldn't sleep." Grace tried to keep her voice steady.

"What's wrong?" Robert sat up, completely alert now.

"You tell me," she said.

He blinked slowly. "I'm fine."

"You were talking in your sleep. And making this moaning sound."

"I don't remember a thing."

"Who," Grace asked softly, "is Carla?"

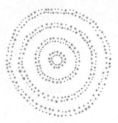

Chapter 3

THE BUFFALO EXPLODED from the trees and swerved onto the killing ground.

Its wide black horns slashed the air like scythes. China Egan and Mick Best raced their stock horses hard behind it, aiming the huge bull down the center of the clearing. They were shouting and whistling wildly, and their stock whips cracked liked rifle fire. The earth rumbled and shook with galloping hooves. Through the tumult and the dust they could hear the furious grunting of the great beast ahead of them, powerful and straining, looking for a break to turn and savage its tormentors. Between China and Mick, Owen Bird spurred his horse up, level with the galloping buffalo's rump. He gripped the reins in his left hand, and reached down for the bull's flailing tail with his right, and his heart beat so hard he feared it would burst.

As his gloved hand closed on the buffalo's tail, Owen Bird felt an avalanche of all the doubts and fears that stalked him just two hours earlier, when the day had begun with such deceptive and soothing peace.

⁂

Picaninny dawn slit the night from hip to hip, a thin incision seeping pink and blue-white fat along the black horizon. The land lay still like a slumbering creature: vast dark surfaces, teeming with life beneath. The thick glittering stream of the Milky Way curved up through an ocean of stars, traversed by winking satellites and space junk. A sudden chill lowered itself on the Top End of Australia's Northern Territory in this last hour of night. They were more than forty miles from the nearest homestead, and one hundred and thirty miles by road from the smallest township.

The calls of waking birds pealed in like random notes of strings and woodwinds, tuning for a symphony. A stock horse snorted softly in the darkness. Its companions stood with their heads down, dozing inside the lashed sapling rails of their camp stockyard. Close by, men slumbered in their swags around a smoldering fire. There were seven of them. Each swag was made of woolen blankets on a slim mattress pad, encased in waterproof canvas.

At the head of one swag stood a splendidly tooled leather steamer trunk, as tall as a man, with a recessed brass spine of piano hinges that allowed it to open smoothly into two vertical halves. The right half was a narrow chest of drawers, beautifully upholstered in leather and latched with polished brass handles, and a bottom compartment big enough to hold three pairs of hand-made riding boots. The left half was a high slim wardrobe containing a full-length Drizabone oilskin riding coat on a wooden hanger, and three high-powered rifles and a 12 gauge pump action shotgun, each in its own leather saddle holster, secured in the trunk with brass-buckled straps. The front of the trunk was engraved and stamped in gold with its owner's name, Owen Carlisle Bird.

Close by the fire and circling swags, three vehicles were parked under a stand of trees. A white portable satellite dish was aimed into space from the roof of the tucker truck, which was tidily packed with rations, supplies, a large freezer, and cooking equipment. Parked next to it was the four-wheel-drive bull catcher, with its roof cut off at the windowsills, a sturdy knock-down bar bolted in front of its engine, roll bars welded over the top, and a steel shooting frame anchored on the back, with rifle rests and handholds for high-speed pursuit over rough and dangerous ground. Beside it stood a horse truck large enough to carry half a dozen mounts, and all the hunting party's riding and camping gear.

Beyond the camp, a Bell 222 high-performance helicopter stood in a small clearing. Its fuselage was streamlined like a killer shark, black and smooth, with smoked portholes along its large passenger cabin. Owen Bird used it to fly between the hunting camp and his twin-jet Gulfstream IV, which was hangared on a mining company airstrip twenty-two miles south of them. His pilot would use the 222 during the hunt, to guide Owen and his wingmen to the biggest buffalo. The helicopter crouched sleek and low beyond the trees like an alien vehicle from another world.

A black coaxial cable snaked down from the satellite dish on the tucker truck, across the roll bars of the bull catcher, and over the steamer trunk, to drop to a telephone in a sturdy metal case on the ground beside Owen Bird.

Owen lay in his swag with his hands behind his head, savoring the smells of horses and bush on the crisp night air. The luminous hands of his gold watch moved toward five o'clock. Two hours to go. He slept in his riding clothes and socks. His sweat-stained Akubra hat lay on top of his boots, next to the satellite phone. Their simple, familiar details reassured him.

A breeze moved in from the plains. There was moisture on it, from shallow sheets of water remaining after The Wet. The monsoon season was over and the land was bursting with fresh grass and scrub where, six months ago, the ground baked and crumbled, and willy-willies wound their spinning columns of searing red dust across dry and brittle earth.

In one of the other swags Owen saw the shadowy figure of Hobson the cook, throwing back his canvas and laboriously sitting up to roll a smoke.

Coffin nails, thought Owen. He'd given up smoking ten years ago. *It won't matter, if I'm dead before the day's out.*

He felt his heart contract, and mentally rehearsed the hunt again, estimating the dangers, making mental corrections for each one. With his eyes closed, he could conjure up the maelstrom of violence he was about to enter, the powerful acceleration of his horse beneath him, and the buffalo's mass of gnarled horn and muscle heaving alongside.

"You should've killed him a hundred times in your head, before you ever see him," Ben Crotty told him. Ben managed Alligator River Downs. They met when one of Owen's companies bought the eight-hundred-thousand-acre cattle station, and its twelve thousand head of beef. It was Ben who introduced Owen to this uniquely dangerous way of hunting buffalo.

"This way, you give the beast an even chance," Ben said.

Owen learned well. That was sixteen years ago. Now it was an annual rite which he approached with growing trepidation each year.

I'm a bloody fool, Owen thought. That too was part of the ritual. The risk made it irresistible, an obsession. Rationally, he knew it was irrational. But his entire life had become rational, calculated, complex. This was different. This was basic. Primitive. Elemental. This stripped away his skins and his wealth. This was honest. The truth. This was him and the beast, and either of them could die.

Owen Bird was about to turn sixty-eight. Most men his age played genteel games of lawn bowls, and dithered over flowerbeds, or dozed beneath a paper. But Owen had no time for mundane diversions. He was a commercial force of nature, a multibillionaire. When he bought his first Australian television network in 1984, *Newsweek* gave him one sentence in an article on the Asian economy. When he took over a trucking and courier conglomerate in Germany the following year, the *Wall Street Journal* gave him a paragraph on page eight. When Owen bought his first newspaper in the United States four years later, *Time* magazine dubbed him Bird of Prey, four U.S. senators lobbied the Departments öf Immigration, Commerce, and State to block his entry into the country, and a major New York daily devoted a front page to his photograph and an editorial on the end of honest journalism. Eighteen months later, Owen owned the daily and three American radio stations, and began bidding on five television stations from Boston to Seattle. He confided to his lawyers that he didn't even like television, but the bargains were too good to miss. He had passed a critical mass, where the gravity of his global fortune began to pull in streams of wealth from around the world. He answered to no law but his own. He was an aging man-of-war, plying the world's oceans, filling his holds with plunder.

But battle scars and deeper wounds had spread like barnacles across his hull, with their subtle drag and whispering vortices. In their gathering chorus below the surface, he heard the fugues of amassing guilt. His wife and only son were long departed, and each year, a mortal loneliness loomed more clearly beyond the terminators of his great sea.

Emotion was a currency he no longer exchanged, confining it to a soundless vault: it once had fueled his father's violence, and was a flaw which Owen refused to inherit, so he banished it. He told himself that only power and wealth were real. He barely noticed that becoming a billionaire was no cure for avarice. He only wanted more, and as soon as it came, it paled, like the brilliant lights that flash and die on the scales of a massive deep-running fish, hauled from the darkness to the surface. For all its lavish trappings, his life was losing its lustre. More and more, his dreams drew him down toward hidden lights, tongues of fire flickering in the blackness of the abyss, beacons of something beyond: a reckoning. They tantalized him with their lethal secrets, taunting him with his own mortality.

Tempting death was all that remained to season a life that denied him no more temptations. There was a time when he had conspired with death. As a young fighter pilot, he had smelled it on others, and waited for it to take them, through lack of focus in dogfights, or in fatal lapses of concentration on sorties. He had never smelled it on himself. It was something he doled out to others, in the shuddering exultation of a cockpit rocked by howling turns and the hammering of his own machine guns. In return, he was rewarded with medals, and national gratitude, and the smug air of immortality that cloaks the young. It all seemed too easy. After Owen came home, the grueling labor of founding and building a company consumed him. As he began to grow rich, he thought he would value death more when he had more to lose. But the idea was smothered by his greed, and his obsessive drive to pave over his past with the laminates of wealth.

He seized every opportunity when it appeared, and created it when it didn't. He had made something of himself, and of everything in the world he touched. As he accrued more power, he found fewer men resisting, and fewer laws restricting. Morality was for those who had no influence. When billionaire Kerry Packer died for seven minutes during a heart attack on a polo field in Sydney, and was revived to report of death, "There's fucking nothing there," Owen Bird had laughed out loud, and hoped that he was right.

But lately, the muted uncertainty was multiplying, and the ripples of doubt soughing over his hull echoed those canons and fugues from the deep, where great scales of light speared down through ice cold oceans, emphasizing with their radiance the completeness of the dark. He knew, as his genes had always known, that there was something there after all—after everything.

Owen came to the bush to shed his scales of wealth, and to confront death. He sought the company of horsemen, who made and risked their lives in the wilderness. Up here, he wanted to believe he was measured only by his courage, galloping a horse at breakneck speed in pursuit of a monstrous beast. Once more, he was wagering everything, because doing it and succeeding exhilarated him beyond measure, and because he was afraid of the day he would not be able to raise the nerve to do it.

Where are you now, old fellow? Owen silently addressed the buffalo. He wanted a worthy beast. He imagined it would be asleep, standing in a thick clump of paper-barked ti trees. He pictured its smooth gray hide, and power-ful, rippling hindquarters, broadening out to huge muscled shoulders hunched above a wide head. He saw the armored bone of its skull, and its thick black horns, turning sharply up and back to the tips, spanning the length of a man from point to point.

Owen heard Hobson kneading damper on a flour-covered board at the tucker truck, his steady wheeze punctuated by the slap of his hands on the white dough. Across the eastern sky, pink and golden light bled into the ebbing night. Owen heard the others stir in their swags. There were horses to feed and water, swags to roll and stow, equipment to rig and set. And there were weapons to be checked for the last time.

"Room service, Owen."

Ben Crotty loomed out of the shadows and crouched beside Owen's swag, holding out a pannikin of steaming black tea.

"Thanks, Ben."

"How'd you sleep?"

"Fair. You?"

"Fine. But I've been out here for a week. First night on the ground's always the worst."

"No argument here." Owen winced. "I'll be fine."

"Been rehearsing?"

"All night."

"Hobson's got breakfast on."

Owen sipped his tea. It was sweet, with black leaf tips swirling in it.

Ben's voice dropped, bearing bad tidings.

"I've been talking to China," he said. China Egan was Ben's Aboriginal head stockman, a splendid horseman, and Owen's lead wingman for the hunt.

"He's all set?"

"All set." Ben nodded. "But there's still no sign of Errol Dingo." Errol Dingo was Owen's other wingman, highly experienced in hunting buffalo.

"It's been a week. He's gone bloody walkabout, hasn't he?"

"China reckons Errol's mob've got some trouble."

"How's he know?" Owen growled, glancing at his satellite phone.

"China? Ah you know blackfellers. They don't need phones. He just knows."

"Fuck."

"I know. But Mick Best is more than up to it. I've had my eye on him for a while, Owen. He's ready."

"What's China think?"

"He agrees with me."

"Who'll drive the bull catcher? That's Mick's job."

"Albert. Jimmy'll be in the back with me, with the 12 gauge."

"All right." Owen threw back the canvas of his swag, and sat up and reached for his boots. "I want to be moving by six-thirty."

"No worries," Ben said.

Owen rolled his swag and strapped it in silence, letting Ben wait for him.

"Errol Dingo," he said finally, taking two of the holstered weapons from his steamer trunk, and placing them with a cleaning kit on the rolled swag. "He's one of mine, isn't he?"

Ben nodded. "Off Clementine Downs. Mostly Pitjantjatjara. Some Yankuntjatjara. A few other mobs. All Ayers Rock people."

"What kind of trouble?"

"China didn't say. Men's business. Must be serious. Errol's generally steady."

"That's a long walk. Seven hundred miles."

"He's had over a week. He'll have hitched rides some of the way."

"Tell Hobson to send breakfast over," Owen's voice turned arctic. He unholstered the Winchester .270 rifle.

"You cleaned them both twice last night, Owen," Ben said quietly.

"I don't want any more fucking surprises."

"The main thing is, keep the buff moving," China Egan said.

"No worries, mate," Mick replied. "As long as the old man can handle it."

"Don't you bloody worry about Mr. Bird," China said, glancing at Owen, working quietly on his weapons on the far side of the camp. "He's been doin' this for yonks."

China and Mick Best squatted together at the horse truck, finishing off Hobson's grilled steak and bacon, fried eggs, and slabs of fresh damper dripping with butter. They sluiced it down with sweet black tea, brewed in a soot-coated one-gallon billycan on the open fire.

Both men wore the uniform of the Australian stockman: denim jeans, elastic-sided R.M. Williams riding boots, a plaited kangaroo skin belt, buckled through double rings and holding a multibladed castrating knife in a leather pouch. The leatherwork on the belts and knife pouches was beautifully crafted, handmade by their owners after work in the stockmen's quarters. The sleeves of their Army surplus shirts were cut off at the shoulders. Tipped back from his forehead, each man wore a sweat-stained Akubra with a plaited kangaroo skin hat band, the wide felt brim rolled up at the sides.

"You don't think he's gettin' past it?" Mick said. He was twenty-four years old, and his face and hands were ruddy from years in the tropical sun. A strip of forehead exposed beneath his hat appeared obscenely white.

China Egan was twenty-nine, with the steady confidence of a man much older. Three centuries ago, long before the British arrived on the continent, a Mongolian ancestor from a Dutch raider came ashore for fresh water, and with a charming smile and a red scarf had seduced a north coast girl, leaving his genes for uncanny balance and reflex to travel through more than fifty generations to China Egan. China had the dark gunmetal blue skin of his Aboriginal family, a distinctly Asian sleekness of eye which earned him his nickname, and a remarkable ability with horses that carried him through the constant tide of discrimination that grinds on every non-white in Australia. China rolled a cigarette, one-handed, into a neat narrow cylinder, ran the tip of his tongue along the glue line, and sealed it.

"Son, Mr. Bird'll eat your bloody boots for breakfast," he said quietly. "Just you keep the buff moving. If it gets a chance to turn, it'll have a go at us. Remember what happened to Gary Waters, on Moroak."

"Too right. Poor bastard." Gary Waters had barely survived. They'd had to shoot his horse. "Anyhow, thanks for the chance."

"Don't thank me, mate." China lit his cigarette with a red plastic lighter. "The boss made the decision."

"Does Mr. Bird know?"

"The boss told him first thing this morning."

"How'd he take it?"

"Wouldn't know. But you're going, eh. Just don't fuck up."

"No worries." Mick shook his head. "Bloody Errol. Should have more sense."

"Don't you worry about Errol. He's got business to attend to. Here. Take care of the plates. I'll get the horses."

China stood up and heaved a saddle onto each shoulder.

"Look at him," Mick said as he nodded in Owen's direction. "All the fuckin' money in the world. Power. Land. Jets 'n' fuckin' helicopters. Big mobs of women. Why would he risk everything with a fuckin' wild buffalo?"

"Beats me, mate," China answered. "You ask me, all you whitefellers are fuckin' mad."

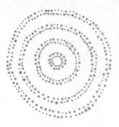

CHAPTER 4

AYERS ROCK REARS FROM the stark flat belly of the continent, up through a searing blue furnace of cloudless sky: a huge, headless, rust-red, round-shouldered, barren mutation of arkosic sandstone. Its sides plummet in coarse eroded folds, riddled with caves and hidden chimneys. Its broad stone summit is grooved and wind-worn, scored by heat, and scarred by lightning.

Two and a quarter miles long, one and a half miles wide, and one thousand, one hundred, and forty-three feet high, it is a geological monstrosity, demanding attention from every horizon. The traveler watches, astonished, as the soaring, time-creased surfaces change color through the day. At dawn, it is pale orange, filling to blood red, like a massive heart, until the sun begins to sink. Then lancing rays that pass unblocked down half a continent cast it through a blazing spectrum of burnt orange, then dark blue, then indigo, then violet, before the last fires of sunset die into the desert. Then the Rock goes dark, drawing the night into it like the gravitational core of a black hole, deep in space.

Visitors in comfortable chairs outside their hotels five miles away watch Ayers Rock move the dying light up through its wavelengths. They nurse drinks that clink and frost with ice while they peer into one of the grand natural mysteries of the planet. But they are only passing through, these outlanders, in cars and planes and air-conditioned buses. The original observers are elsewhere, out on the desert floor. They gather in secret places their ancestors have come to for more than a hundred thousand years. For them, the great desert teems with physical and mystical life, radiating from the monolith. Ayers Rock resonates down their pathways of story and spirit. It is a colossal vortex of creation tracks, from the first great dreamings of the Tjukurpa.

The Aborigines here call themselves Anangu, the People.

They call everyone else Piranypa, the Others.

Anangu have only ever known Ayers Rock as Uluru.

The mercy flight passes north of Uluru, a silver sliver, sliding out of the sunrise. On board, the compressed smells of electronics that saturate light aircraft mix with the thick aroma of strong, sweet tea, poured from a thermos into Styrofoam cups.

"He helped design the bomb," Dr. Tim Kennedy says above the muffled drone of engines.

His pilot, Philip Petrohilos, has the Beechcraft King Air aimed at the Petermann Aboriginal Reserve: seventen hundred square miles of arid plains and dry lake bed in the southwestern corner of the Northern Territory.

Tim glances at his flight nurse, Judy Hall, napping on the stretcher racked along the starboard bulkhead. She is twenty-five years old, a year younger than he. At her head are an electrocardiogram and a defibrillator for heart trauma. Above and below her are latched drawers and spring clips holding emergency care equipment. Stowed farther back are cases and racks of instruments and pharmaceuticals. It is outfitted as thoroughly as any aircraft in the Royal Flying Doctor Service, and more sophisticated than anything dreamed of by Reverend John Flynn. For more than half a century, the famous white and silver planes have spread his Mantle of Safety over nearly two million square miles of the Outback—from Mount Isa and Charleville in the eastern reaches, to the dry backblocks of Western Australia. Ever since John Flynn organized the first medical flights on Qantas biplanes in the 1920s, "Flynn of the Inland" and his Flying Doctors have been household words across the bush, legendary heroes in Australian folklore.

"The atomic bomb?" Petro's voice shows casual interest now.

Tim gazes over Petro's shoulder and through the cockpit windows at the haggard red land sliding far beneath them. It is an hour since they left Alice

Springs, heading west-southwest, twenty thousand feet above the desert. The flat surface rolls relentlessly out to every horizon. For the uninitiated it is a wasteland of biblical adversities, ravaged by towering sandstorms spawning fiery columns of churning red dust, and hammered by staggering heat through droughts that can last a decade. When rain comes, it brings flash floods that thunder down the parched creek lines and riverbeds, sweeping away animals and trees and bursting the banks to spread fast and wide for hundreds of miles across the flat country.

Uluru bulges from the skyline, far south of the mercy flight. West of it, they see the thirty-six squat rock knuckles and fists of the Olgas, which Aborigines call Kata Tjuta, meaning Many Heads. They are the bare, glacier-worn peaks of a buried mountain range, and like Uluru more than four hundred million years old. On the entire desert, these are the only elevated features visible from the aircraft.

The land is dull red, rimmed by veils of dust, combed by waves of sand dunes and veined by scattered lines of hardy spinifex and meandering tracks that run into other roads or simply disappear into the desert. The immigrants who settled this sparsely populated region call it the Dead Heart.

"The hydrogen bomb," Tim replies. "He worked on it at Cambridge, at the Cavendish Laboratory. Showed how it could be done, even before they built the first atomic bomb. Then he worked on the British nuclear tests at Maralinga in South Australia after the war."

"You met him before?"

"Oh yeah. On clinic flights. We overnight at the mission."

"What the hell's he doing out here, if he's so bloody smart?"

"Hard to say, Petro. He came out to Lake Amadeus in the fifties. After he left Maralinga. He's been running the mission there ever since. He runs a school for the Aboriginal kids. He keeps everyone healthy. You won't find a single case of conjunctivitis or malnutrition. That's more than you can say for the government reserves. He studies the tribal histories and stories. Published a few articles on the Pitjantjatjara and Yankuntjatjara people. And he's working with another local mob nobody knows much about. He's taping some of their oral history."

"Is he married?"

"Nope."

"Straight?"

"Oh, yeah. He's certainly that."

"Hah!" Petro barks. "He's a gin jockey, then, ay?"

"No way," Tim says quickly. The idea of the Reverend Brother Mark Hansen sleeping with any of the tribal women on Amadeus is absurd to him. But so what, Tim thinks, if Mark Hansen did take up with an Aboriginal woman? He suspects the missionary would feel it was she, not he, who was stooping below cultural restrictions.

"Well, what is he then?" Petro asks.

"He's a scholar." Tim looked forward to his stay-overs with Mark Hansen on routine clinics at Lake Amadeus. The mission was founded in the early 1920s, by the Church of England Order of the Bush Brotherhood of the Good Shepherd. God only knew why they chose this place. Even its name carries infernal ironies: Lake Amadeus, "For the Love of God," is mostly sand and salt, devoid at first sight of any mote of love, life, or water. It had grown to five wooden buildings, surrounded by the stand of gum trees and gnarled bull oaks that first revealed the presence of an underground spring to surveyors more than a century ago. There was a defiance in this baked oasis that offered Mark Hansen hope for his own existence. The trees' fierce, deep-rooted grip on life in the blistering reserve struck a chord in him. He had come here to save souls, beginning with his own.

He learned well the irresistible pull on the old prophets, wandering into the wilderness, howling for God. And the sheer size and stillness of it never failed them. It focused them on the balance between life and death, between creation and a grain of sand, between God and man. Mark Hansen called the wilderness "God's sounding board." "There are no atheists in the desert," he claimed.

The buildings were small, and well built, painted white, with corrugated iron roofs. The main cottage housed a kitchen and dining room and Mark's study and sleeping quarters. A two-room sick bay stood alongside. There was a radio transceiver, tuned to the Flying Doctor net, and several AM radios in the compound, but no television to threaten those two highly endangered species: books and conversation. After dinner, Mark and Tim usually retired to the veranda with glasses of dark Bundaberg rum and water, to lie back in long canvas squatter's chairs and watch the profusion of constellations and galaxies glittering across the vast desert sky.

"You know, Rev, I reckon if you listen hard enough on a night like this, you can hear the stars," Tim had said on one of those still evenings.

"Aborigines say the stars sing," Mark said, shifting in his chair, with a creak of canvas and wood that sounded comfortably organic. "They were the first real astronomers, y'know. When they traveled at night, to avoid the heat, they learned to navigate by stars. They named all the important ones after their creation spirits. When they look up at Orion and the Pleiades and the rest, all those constellations we know by Greek and Roman names, they see their great Dreamings, the stars of the Kangaroo Dreaming, Emu Dreaming, the Rainbow Serpent, the seven sisters searching for their husbands, all their creation stories. Their stars mark their seasons, when to hunt, and when to move to new water. And they did it a good forty thousand years before the Egyptians or Greeks or Romans named their zodiacs. Life is one great continuous movement for Aborigines, y'see, and all integrated, spiritually and physically. Whereas we've separated those things."

Tim felt confined with the missionary in a starlit vault, with the intimacy and liberation of the confessional. A meteor drew a graceful white curve across the star field and flamed out over the desert. "Did you do astronomy, Rev?" Tim asked.

"Not per se. But we spent a lot of time looking at the transmissions and states of stars. They're all chain reactions. Even during the war, there was still a hard core of determinists, looking for an absolute description of the universe. They thought if they could measure every detail about the universe at any instant, they could predict its next instant, and by virtue of that, they could see the future."

"That's a lot of measurements."

"Certainly. But Einstein liked the idea. And the Marxists and Leninists loved it; it supported their political philosophy—and atheism. Then along came Werner Heisenberg, who found the most you can calculate is the probability that the particle will be at a certain place at a certain time. So, it follows that you can only do the same thing for the universe. It negates any chance of determining the absolute future. Einstein was arguing against Heisenberg's Uncertainty Principle when he said, 'God doesn't play dice with the universe.'"

"And does he, Rev?"

"Does God play dice with us?" Mark made a wincing smile in the darkness. "According to his laws of quantum mechanics, he can if he wants to. There're enough gaps of probability for him to manipulate things."

"Do you believe he does?"

"Ah, well, Tim, that's the dilemma. The physicist says events happen in logical trains. Every effect has a logical cause. Even within the bounds of probability. But the theologian believes in divine intervention, the possibility of miracles." He paused and sighed. "And the cynic believes if the latter is possible, why do we have famines, and abused children, and plagues?"

"And what do you believe?"

In the starlight, Tim saw him slowly shake his head, like a journeyman fighter, hunkered in his corner, waiting for a sad, familiar bell—"I believe, Timmo . . . I believe we should have another rum."

Now, as their aircraft approaches the seared flats of Lake Amadeus, Tim Kennedy considers Petro's question again, and adds, "And he's looking for God."

"He is, ay? Well, if he's a bloody missionary, he should have found Him by now, shouldn't he? How can he sell something if he doesn't know it's there?"

"Oh he's sure. Most of the time. But he keeps trying to test it. He says faith's no good if it hasn't been thrown against the wall a few times. And he believes if God gave him the brains to ask questions, he owes it to God and himself to look for answers. That's his main problem. He reckons, 'God blesses man with intelligence and damns him with intellect.'"

"Sounds like a load of cods to me," Petro said. "He's been out here too long. What he needs is some bearded clam."

"Ah, he has a theory about that too. He says sex gives mankind the swiftest joy, and the slowest grief. He knows. He had a torrid affair with the wife of some Yank in England during the war. Caused this big scandal. He was ready to give up everything for her . . ."

"That's very romantic," says Judy. Tim is surprised to see her sitting up on the stretcher.

"G'day, Jude. We thought you were asleep."

"Did he love her?" she asks.

"Who?"

"The Yank's wife. In the war."

"Yeah," Tim answers. "That was the thing. He fell all the way for her. Bloody stupid really. Her husband was a weapons contractor. She was never going to leave the money."

"That's so sad."

"I suppose so. That's when he went into the Church."

"That's when he should have got back in the saddle," Petro offers. Judy makes a face at him.

"Well, that wasn't the only reason he ended up out here," Tim says.

"You sound like a disciple, Doc."

"It's just that he makes me think. Not much of that with you lot, is there?"

He feels protective, regretting now his reference to the affair. He feels he has betrayed the privilege of the doctor or the priest.

He knows also there is another influence here: Shiva—the mythical Destroyer of Worlds, the baleful saint of nuclear physicists—who still haunts the man whose emergency call they are answering now.

"You've been taking care of him, Millie?" Tim asked as they crowded into the little Lake Amadeus sick bay.

"That's right, Doc."

"How long has it been like this?"

"Three days, Doc." Millie Abbott was a Pitjantjatjara woman in her late fifties. She moved with confidence around the bed despite the fact she was completely blind. She sucked her lips nervously between her teeth, and glanced at the young Aborigine lying motionless under a cotton sheet on the white iron bed. Outside, they could hear Petro trying to joke with the mission Aborigines, but none of them wanted to talk. The plane was parked thirty yards away, where they had taxied across the hard ground from the mission's dirt airstrip.

"What's his name, Millie?"

"Teddy, Doc. Teddy Gidgee. He's Kevin Gidgee's boy, from Clementine Downs." Like many of her people, she pronounced her v's as b's.

Tim turned to Mark Hansen, standing at the foot of the bed. The missionary looked as though he hadn't slept for days.

"What do you think, Rev?"

"Well we've been running a Glasgow coma scale on him every hour since we radioed, as you instructed." His voice was low and deliberate. He had the incongruous physique of a baritone. He was tall, thin, fair-haired, with skin permanently reddened by sun and wind. There were deep rings under his eyes. "He's stayed above twelve throughout the night."

"Not a coma, then," Tim said. "Does he have any friends or relatives?"

"That's them on the veranda," said Millie. "They brung him in from Clementine. They won't come in here, but."

"Did they say what happened?"

"Won't talk about it, Doc."

"What's he eaten?"

"Nothin', Doc. Bit o' soup."

"Water?"

"When I make him," Millie said. "He don't wanta do anything much. Just waitin'."

"For what?"

Millie shrugged and said nothing.

"Has he said anything since he came in?"

"Nothin', Doc. Anybody'd think he's deaf . . . he's not, but."

"All right," Tim nodded to his nurse. "Let's have a look at him, Jude."

He opened his black leather instrument bag beside the patient. He guessed the young man was between nineteen and twenty-five. He looked like a fullblood—they were less prolific in Australia after two centuries of settlement by whites, but still common out here. His skin was dark black, with a sheen of gunmetal blue. His hair was a rich mat of thick black curls.

The eyes were closed. His forehead was broad, sloping back from a wide, hooded brow that beetled over a classically wide nose and thick lips. Like the nomads who first trekked over the Indonesian land bridge and onto the Australian continent before the oceans rose, this young Aborigine was a Caucasian, with the distinctive characteristics of the Dravidians who inhabit the Indian subcontinent, and who in turn trace their roots to the anthropological cradles of Egypt.

Standing, he would have been about five feet eight inches tall. He was well-muscled and lean, with spread feet, unaccustomed to shoes or riding boots.

Tim gently pulled the sheet back to the foot of the bed. The patient wore a pair of green hospital pajama shorts. There were old, shiny scars of scrapes and nicks along his black skin, consistent with the hard life of a working cattle station. But there were other marks that left no doubts about the young man's tribal heritage.

Running horizontally across the dark chest were two long, ridged scars, raised and shiny. They were the cicatrices of ceremonial incisions, made during initiation into manhood. On the bulging deltoid of his right shoulder, there were three short scars, the totem mark of his animal spirit.

Millie stood watching quietly, her right heel on her left knee, one hand on her hip, the other on the headrung of the cot. The heat radiated from the white wooden ceiling. Judy took the patient's pulse.

"Sixty-two," she said, recording it on her clipboard.

Tim put on his stethoscope and listened to the flow of life beneath the dark surface.

"Heart sounds are normal," he said.

"Nothin' you can do, Doc," Millie said. "He knows that."

"Breathing is shallow but steady. Lungs sound clear," he continued, peeling each eyelid back and peering through its uprolled iris with his ophthalmoscope.

"Retinal vessels are normal."

He changed instruments.

"Ears look normal. No lesions." He was beginning to feel an inexplicable foreboding. The familiar routine was suddenly crucial to his sense of equilibrium.

This was Tim's third year as a practicing physician, and his second as a Flying Doctor to the men, women, and children on the far-flung settlements and cattle stations of the Outback. He had treated severed and crushed fingers, toes, and limbs; gore wounds made by wild pigs; snakebites; third-degree burns; and countless broken bones and contusions from accidents with horses, vehicles, and machinery. He had delivered babies—on the ground and in the air—and had correctly diagnosed diverse maladies, from the scurvy-like Barcoo rot to AIDS. He had even pulled the odd tooth on droving camps and cattle stations across the desert. He was rightly confident in his medical skills. Putting them to good use as a Flying Doctor was part of the great experience he sought in the Dead Heart.

But now, in this oven-hot ward, on this isolated mission, at the edge of this lake of sand and salt, he felt a dark premonition that shook all logic and experience.

He struggled to stay calm, and continued his examination until there was no more he could do here.

"What do you think, Timmo?"

"Can't say for sure, Rev." Tim rubbed his chin with the palm of his hand. "Millie, would you go and fetch the pilot, please?"

"Righty-ho, Doc." Millie walked surely out to the veranda.

Tim sat on the edge of the bed watching the young Aborigine stretched out beside him.

"What do you think, Mark?" He didn't take his eyes off his patient.

Mark unfolded and refolded his arms. It was a protective gesture. Like Tim, he wore white shorts and long socks folded back over his calves. His knees were sunburned. He studied the thick ginger hairs growing along the backs of his freckled hands and arms. He sighed quietly.

"Some of the boys say an Old Fellow came through here a week ago," he said. "He camped out at Six Mile Bore."

"Does anyone know him?"

"Some of the boys knew of him. They say he's Wirruntjatjara."

Tim felt the skin along his neck slowly contract into gooseflesh; he had no idea why, but the name deepened his sense of dread.

"What's that?"

"They come from Uluru," Mark said.

"I thought that was Pitjantjatjara country."

"It is. And Yankuntjatjara, among others. Uluru is revered by a host of tribal groups, friend and foe."

"What about this Old Fellow?" Tim said.

Mark's voice dropped. "The boys say he's hunting some people."

"Including this chap here?"

"Possibly."

"But this one's not Wirruntjatjara. The people on Clementine are Pitjantjatjara, right?"

"That's true, Timmo. But the Wirruntjatjara may have a serious score to settle."

"What else do they say?"

"That was it. That he's an Old Fellow." Mark cleared his throat again, and the next words came as if he were forcing them out in a reluctant confession. "A sorcerer."

Tim felt his senses dislocate, as if the room was distorting.

"And he's after more than one person?"

"That's what my boys say," Mark replied.

"Do you believe them?"

"I doubt they'd lie about this sort of thing."

"You, ah . . ." Tim hesitated. "You're talking about Singing?"

"Well now, Tim, I've heard a lot of stories about it, and pointing the bone. So have you, no doubt. I think this sort of thing only works if the victim believes in it." He smiled wanly, trying to camouflage his unease. "That's something it shares with religion."

"That doesn't answer the question, Rev. Do you think he's been Sung?"

There was a long pause, punctuated by the irregular clicking of the hot roof.

"Millie does. The rest of them do."

"But what do you think, Rev?"

Mark raised his eyebrows and shook his head slowly. He felt weak from lack of sleep, and from the fear which slid into him as his resistance flagged. He had sought God in this wilderness. He sought certainty. Instead, his faith was being tested by the pressure of far more ancient beliefs, and their agency over life and death.

He shook his head, and silently looked at the figure on the bed. Ritual Singing was not a possession by devils, susceptible to exorcism in the name of the Father, Son, and Holy Ghost; it was a primitive eviction order. He saw life simply evaporating before them, leaving this dark body defined on the sheet, like ink drying on paper.

"Jude," Tim said quietly, as Mark remained silent, "let's get him started on a Hartman's drip. We're taking him back to the Alice."

"Coming up," Judy said, opening the backpack she'd carried from the aircraft. She had remained quiet during Tim's exam, speaking only to confirm vital signs as she wrote them down. Tim sensed she was initially skeptical, but now he heard a different tone in her voice. It fed his own uneasiness.

"Petro, let's get him loaded."

"No worries," the pilot said, and headed out to the aircraft for the gurney. He was regretting his dig at Mark. Now he felt glad to be away from this place and the disturbing stillness of the Aboriginal men and women waiting outside the sick bay.

Tim folded the sheet up to the patient's chin. He watched the body on the bed, the eyes closed, the breathing gentle.

Gentle people, he thought. *With powerful stories and magic.*

He began repacking his medical bag, looking for comfort in the order and form of his instruments as he slid them into their pouches and loops. But the limp figure on the bed mocked all their intricacy and purpose.

The aircraft leveled off above the desert. Ayers Rock had long disappeared beyond the southern horizon.

"The Alice is on the radio, Doc," Petro called back from the cockpit.

"What do they want?"

"Want to know what's wrong with your patient, so they can warn out the ambulance and hospital."

Tim glanced at the young Aborigine, strapped to the stretcher.

"Tell them exposure and dehydration." He raised his eyebrows at Judy and shrugged, then gazed out the window. If Reverend Brother Hansen was right, somewhere down there on the desert floor, a terrifying Old Fellow was balancing accounts.

Tim had heard whites in the Territory telling the stories. It was a matter for the elders of a tribal group to punish any offense. For crimes deserving more than a ritual beating or spearing, the elders engaged a tribal doctor, a sorcerer. In the event of an extremely serious crime, so the old stories went, the most senior elders summon up a ku_daitja—a spirit-assassin, invested with supernatural powers to hunt and kill. Ku_daitjas were the stuff of legend and nightmare.

Anyone who spent any time in the Outback heard and repeated tales of sorcerers who could Sing their victims to death by chanting their spirits into the next world, directing them on their way by pointing of a piece of human bone.

The courts of common law in Australia had never had to decide whether death by Aboriginal magic was murder. The few Outback doctors and coroners who encountered such cases invariably wrote "heart failure" as cause of death. Few of them had any desire to put his suspicions in writing, or his orthodox reputation in jeopardy.

"Look at that," Petro called back, breaking Tim's reverie. They were less than twenty minutes out of Alice Springs. South of the town, a line of high ridges rose up at the foot of the MacDonnell Ranges like city walls, jagged ramparts the color of dried blood along the skyline. They were flying beside the great north-south highway that bisects the continent from Adelaide, on the Antarctic-chilled waters of the southern coast, to Darwin, squatting on the northern tropical shores of the Arafura Sea. "There goes our tucker for the week."

Far below, they saw a caravan of six enormous trucks, each towing two long refrigerated trailers, threading up the black bitumen highway. Even at this distance, the logos on the sides were unmistakable. The bold red letters, *BIRD*, were blocked eight feet high on the silver metal, the D of each clasped in the talons of a crimson eagle. The familiar fleet colors were emblazoned on hundreds of similar rigs, and scores of cargo jets. The convoy of frozen food was following the same route plied more than a century earlier by camel trains, which carried supplies and water to the center of the continent.

What a bastard of a trip that must have been, Tim thought, imagining the bellowing and grunting camels swaying like luggers across the desert. He could imagine the creaking of harness straps and leather pack saddles and the urging cries of their Afghan drivers. They were strangers in a strangely familiar land, those robed and turbaned migrants. This terrain was redder and flatter than their mountainous deserts of Afghanistan, but it was as stark and as clearly stamped by the divine fist of Allah. Long after those hardy caravanners joined the dust of the Dead Heart, a railroad was built along the route they plied through the Centre. The train that carried supplies and people in their wake was named *"The Ghan"* in their honor, and its original rattling, open-windowed carriages frequently seemed as uncomfortable as the camels they followed.

Now, the Alice had grown accustomed to green irrigated lawns, shopping malls, and satellite television. By day, commercial jets hauled in tourists from around the world, and at night, camouflaged heavy transport jets howled in from U.S. Air Force bases in California and Hawaii with fresh supplies and crews for the intelligence ground station at Pine Gap.

The Dreamtime spirits of Creation were forced to share their land and skies with the invaders' noise and discord. The harmony of the ancient songs was shattered first by explorers on strange animals, then by machines, and now by frenetic, microwave squeals of high-speed data streams from spy satellites over Asia. The landmarks which the creation spirits sang into existence on their first journeys eons ago were now desecrated by the spoor of tires and shoes, and violated by cameras, and the triangulated signals of global positioning satellites. But no technology could infiltrate the primal secrets that shroud the continent.

Tim imagined an unseen matrix of protean forces rippling across the land like synaptic currents. Through his porthole, he looked down on the continent defined by distance and solitude, and thought it seemed more like a single organism, networked by spiritual lines as enigmatic and vital as the essence of life. In his mind, the Dead Heart appeared neither dead nor empty. And if there was a sorcerer down there, far away in space and time, behind that veil of secrets, his influence reached into this aircraft, with its satellite navigation, and long-range radios, and electronic monitors and miracle drugs.

For eons, the Aborigines had endured excruciating hardships and dangers in their perpetual journeys across the continent. They were survivors. Their very existence was testimony to their tenaciousness and resilience.

What is it then, Tim thought, watching his patient, *that can make them give up the ghost like this? Without even a whimper?* Red and black and white wires snaked from the electrocardiograph to contacts attached between the rows of ceremonial scars.

Tim stared at the cruelly ridged flesh with a sudden intensity. Teddy Gidgee may be his name in the white man's world, but those scars bore witness to another life and another name in a parallel world, separated by a yawning gulf.

What did you do, old son? he silently asked his patient. *What did you do to them down there?*

If Teddy Gidgee died, Tim knew he could simply accept it as another of the daunting mysteries of the Dead Heart. But if he was to honor his Hippocratic oath, he would have to fight these arcane forces to save his patient. He realized that the act of acknowledging the challenge across two worlds made his dilemma real. He had thought it into tangible existence as vividly as the old creation spirits had sung the world into being:

Cogito, ergo est: I think, therefore it is.

The discovery came spontaneously, like the transformation of a complex image in a revolving kaleidoscope; and as swiftly and as completely, the uneasiness that had been building in him since they landed at Lake Amadeus Mission filled him with a chilling dread that sank deep into his bones. He glanced through the window again toward the southern horizon and Ayers

Rock, Uluṟu, the biggest of all the features and lives sung into existence so long ago, and the most imposing of all the ganglia of spiritual forces and paths enmeshing the continent.

Uluṟu had slipped beyond the rim of the earth, but in his mind's eye, Dr. Tim Kennedy could see it with penetrating clarity, silent, immense, mysterious, and coursing with power.

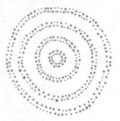

CHAPTER 5

OWEN STRIPPED AND CLEANED the Winchester .270, working methodically to control the time and his nerves. There were two magazines, including a spare; each held five rounds. There would be little time to use the second, but he would carry it for insurance.

All the while, he killed the buffalo in his head, racing in close until his right knee was up against the animal's heaving left rump, and then reaching down with a gloved hand to grip the base of its thick bony tail. At a flat gallop, he would have only one chance to time the throw, for an instant when both the buffalo's hind hooves were off the ground. In that split second, he would have to ram the beast's rump to the right with his horse's shoulder, then haul back on the buff's tail, pitching its hindquarters out from under it.

In his mind, he kept his eyes glued to the crashing bull, as he wheeled the horse, cross-drew the Winchester from its saddle holster, and fired into the brain. The skull would be so thick, he would have to lay the bullet into an eye or ear.

He would have preferred to use the Steyr/Mannlicher. Its .308 Norma magnum cartridges were each as thick and long as a man's middle finger. But the big bolt-action rifle's recoil was so harsh that it cut his reload rate to less than one shot a second: far too slow for insurance. Worse, its magazine only held four rounds. The Winchester gave him one more shot and a faster bolt action. Instead, Ben Crotty would use the big gun to cover him from the bull catcher.

Owen looked up as Ben ambled over.

"All right?"

"All right," Owen said. "Nearly ready."

"No hurry. We've got plenty of time."

Owen clicked a full magazine home, leaving the chamber empty. He pulled on a pair of Wells Lamont cowhide gloves, cut back to expose his trigger finger.

He squeezed the rifle stock hard, to steady his hands. Adrenaline was beginning to make his joints feel lax. He wanted to keep his muscles taut, to work through this feeling of weakness.

"All right." He nodded to Ben. "Ready."

The buffalo was a monster.

They'd been riding through thick scrub and timber, following radio directions from Owen's helicopter pilot, who was hovering five hundred feet above them. The Bell 222 gained altitude and dropped farther back as the horsemen closed in.

They found the bull standing quietly near a tall anthill. His size astounded Owen, but there was no time to think once they sighted it. China and Mick were shouting, whistling, hunting the beast out from the trees. It broke into a trot, then a gallop, crashing through scrub, bulldozing saplings, barreling toward the killing ground.

Owen felt a wall of pressure rise around him, and willed his concentration onto the beast. He felt weight inside his chest and throat, and realized he was yelling, the way he used to in dogfights. He was right behind the beast now, with China on his left and Mick on his right, and through the yelling and volley of stockwhips, he could hear the heaving breath of his galloping horse and the pounding of hooves beneath him, and the fierce grunting of the buffalo in front of him, as it looked for a break to turn and attack. Far off to his left, Owen was aware of the bull catcher roaring through the scrub, pacing them. It was just outside his line of sight but he knew Ben Crotty was braced against the roll bars with the Mannlicher. Jimmy would be wedged beside him, nursing the Browning 12 gauge, as Albert gunned the truck through the scrub, dodging trees and stumps and anthills tall as a man.

"If anything happens," Ben had told Owen, "get clear of the buff and let me take him with the big gun. Nothing lost. Plenty of time for another go later. Just get away from him."

Owen cleared his mind and focused on the animal. They seemed locked together now inside a brutal whirlwind.

His thoughts streamed. *You've got him. Don't fuck up. Don't think negative! Positive. Positive. Positive. Focus on the tail. Grip. Ram. Pull. Turn. Draw. Safe off. Aim. Breathe! Fire. Focus. Focus!*

He kept a tight rein with his left hand, and leaned down with his right, out over his knee, into the storm of violence and speed, forcing his mind to stay clear, barely hearing the wingmen now. His horse was sweating heavily, straining up to the buffalo.

Keep-him-moving-Get-in-tight-Focus-Up-close-Get-his-rump-on-your-boot-On-your- boot!

He eased his left hand up and squeezed with his ankles. His horse surged forward, the two stockmen dropped away, and Owen was alone with the beast. Its rump banged his leg with astonishing force.

His horse kept its feet, gamely hugging the bull's hindquarters like a camp drafter. The hair on the tip of the buff's tail was long and black, but the shaft was stubbled and gray. Owen reached for it. His gloved hand hovered above the spine.

Now! Now! Now!

His fist closed hard around the tail as he took his weight on his right stirrup, saw the buff's rear hooves clear the ground, reefed the reins to the right, felt his horse slam into the gray rump, then heaved back with all his force, feeling the bull fall.

Owen didn't see the snake, uncoiling in front of them as the buffalo went down.

But his galloping horse's eyes flared at the sight of the brilliantly colored scales slithering beneath it. The horse shied violently, as the buffalo's massive left horn plowed into the ground, then slashed up, into the horse's flying hooves. Owen felt the horse crash beneath him, its forelegs shattered. He saw the ground freeze, then rush at him, slamming him into a wall of flashing darkness.

Get up! Get up! His mind raced, slowed, raced, slowed back. *Move your feet!*

He couldn't focus. He was on his back and he couldn't feel his legs. There was no pain. Worse. There was nothing. The ground seemed to roll and he felt sick, and swallowed hard. He couldn't see the buff.

Get clear! His mind floundered, refusing to accept the truth. He hauled himself onto his elbows. A wall of lacerating heat flattened him, erupting in his back and belly, blinding him.

He groaned, and through the haze of pain, he heard another sound, louder, more primal. He turned his head and saw the buffalo behind him, laboring onto its feet. His horse was screaming pitifully, trying to get up, its front legs flopping in bloody splinters. It collapsed on its left side, on the Winchester, firmly sheathed in its saddle holster barely an arm's length away. Owen heard the buffalo rising. He lunged for the rifle, felt his gloved fingers slide off the stock. He lunged again, missed. The buffalo was on its feet, turning for him.

Owen felt death very close, dark wings opening. He raised his shoulders again and straightened his arms, groaning as the pain wracked his belly, trying to haul himself toward the rifle.

Not yet, you bastard. He formed the words, but all that came out was a wrenching groan.

The buffalo seemed to rear up from the ground, unearthly, like a beast from a horrifying dream. Its eyes drilled into his, and he knew it wanted only to kill him. Then the head plunged, and a long black horn smashed into Owen's left arm like a sledgehammer.

A deafening crack ripped the air.

The beast crashed onto him, a brass-jacketed .308 buried behind its ear.

Owen couldn't breathe. The dusty smell of the buffalo filled his nostrils, but he couldn't draw air into his lungs. His heart hammered in his ears. His left arm felt consumed by fire. He couldn't raise the beast's head from his face. It was going to smother him, and take him with it.

Not yet, you bastard. He willed the words to his mouth but he couldn't open it. *Not yet!*

He twisted his head hard to make a space between his face and the soft, hot, suffocating hide. Pain seared through him.

Air! He inhaled the powerful musk of animal and blood.

Agony impaled his chest and belly and back. His left arm crunched sickeningly as he moved.

Not yet, you bastard. He tried to narrow his thoughts into a core, as if by sheer willpower he could keep death at bay. *Not yet, you bastard.*

He felt the animal move. *It's still alive!*

"Get the bloody thing off him!"

He heard Ben Crotty's voice, and realized the stockmen were pulling the dead bull clear.

"Owen! Can you hear me?"

Owen grunted.

"Hang on, mate." Ben's voice was close to his ear. "We're onto the Flying Doctor. You'll be fine."

But Owen felt himself slipping down a long, dark passage. He wanted to resist, but it drew him down. A small part of his mind lazily wondered if he would see his life unravel, playing itself back. Twilight. A hazy image of his son, Andrew, turned away from him into blackness, then a buzzing filled his ears, bearing him into oblivion.

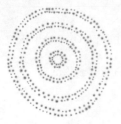

CHAPTER 6

"DR. KENNEDY! YOU'RE NEEDED." The duty nurse appeared out of breath in the doorway. "In the radio room!"

Tim looked up from his hospital admission report on Teddy Gidgee.

"What's the problem?"

"We have a spinal on Alligator River," the duty nurse said, heading back to the radio room, with Tim on her heels. "You wouldn't believe the fuss it's causing."

"Who've we sent?"

"Nobody. They have their own aircraft."

"They have a doctor?"

"Can't say. They called in on a satellite phone. And in no time, we were getting calls from three hospitals in Sydney and two more in Brisbane."

"About the spinal?"

"All offering advice."

"They're over seventeen hundred miles away. Why're they calling?"

They rounded the end of the corridor and into the glassed-in room housing the Royal Flying Doctor Service Base radio. The duty operator was on the telephone, speaking calmly, but his patience was clearly strained.

"The spinal's at a droving camp." The nurse lowered her voice. "Has his own helicopter, and his own Jordan Frame, if you please."

"What's his story?"

"It's Owen Bird."

"He's the spinal?" Tim let out his breath.

"Somebody phoned here less than five minutes ago," the nurse said, nodding, "from the camp. Says Mr. Bird came off a horse."

"Where's the lesion?"

"He reports no feeling below the waist," she replied. "And he has a broken arm."

"What's the plan?"

"Tim." The radio operator turned to him, hanging up the phone. "That was the head of neurology at Royal North Shore Hospital in Sydney. I've had more specialists call in the last few minutes than I've talked to in ten years."

"And we're not sending a plane?" Tim asked.

"Nowhere to land nearby," the operator said. "No need, apparently. They have their own helicopter fitted up like an air ambulance. Bell 222."

"Medics?"

"Their pilot's ex-rescue. He says he knows how to fit a Jordan Frame."

"Hope he's right," Tim said, going to the operations wall map. "Where are we meeting the chopper?"

"We're not. They're taking him to this Continental Mining strip." The radio operator pointed on the map to a World War II bomber strip, resealed and rebuilt for survey aircraft. "He has a Gulfstream IV waiting to fly him to Sydney."

"Nice for some," the nurse said.

"Have they got methylprednisolone?" Tim asked.

"On the jet? I'll have to ask them. What is it?"

"Pure magic for spinal injuries," Tim said. "When was he injured?"

"Less than fifteen minutes ago," the operator said, checking his log.

"You need to get methylprednisolone in within four hours of an injury."

"It's five hours from there to Sydney. Nearly six by the time he's delivered."

"And four hours to fly up from here in a prop. They'll have to bring him here themselves." Tim was firm. "Their jet can make it in three hours."

"What is this methyl . . . ?" the operator asked.

"Methylprednisolone. It can make the difference between being paralyzed and walking out of here."

"You talk to them," the operator said, and handed Tim the radio mike, raising his eyebrows. "Owen Bird . . ."

"If they don't fit the frame properly," Tim said, "it won't matter who he is."

Owen drifted in and out of darkness, still lying where he had fallen. His pilot set the alloy tubes of the Jordan Frame around him on the ground, then showed Ben Crotty how to fit the flat plastic slats, lengthwise and crosswise. Each slat was slid under Owen's body without moving him. Owen was barely conscious when they locked the slats on to the surrounding tubes, to complete the construction of the emergency stretcher underneath him, all the time keeping his spine immobile. The pilot fitted a padded stiff-neck collar around Owen's throat, and lightly secured straps down the length of the stretcher to stop him rolling. They worked slowly, taking more than a quarter of an hour before they felt confident that he was stable enough to lift. Owen felt nausea take him again as they raised him on the frame and carried him to the helicopter.

They locked down the frame in its latches in the passenger cabin, and the pilot took off so smoothly that Ben and the three stockmen sitting around Owen barely felt it moving. Twelve minutes later, they were touching down gently next to the Gulfstream IV. The jet's two pilots were waiting with the hatch open and stairs down. They eased Owen on board, keeping the frame horizontal, and harnessed it onto the double bed in his private wardroom.

"You fellows sit along each side," the chief pilot said. "The mattress should cushion him when we land in the Alice."

Owen opened his eyes as the twin jets powered up for takeoff.

"Give me some water."

"No water, I'm sorry Owen," Ben said. "Flying Doctor says no fluids, no food."

"I can't move my legs."

Ben shook his head. "You'll be right, Owen. Just hang on."

"Put a fucking bullet in me."

"You'll be right, mate. Hold on."

"Fuck that." Owen groaned in pain as the bones in his left arm grated. "Where are they taking me?"

"Alice Springs."

"Call Agnes in Sydney. Tell her. And no leaks, or I'll have the bastard responsible." He winced again and gritted his teeth.

"We'll take care of it in the Alice, Owen."

"No we fuckin' won't." Owen felt the darkness rising around him again. "Do it now. Call Agnes. Use the satellite . . ." Then darkness again.

The heart monitor alarm shrieked through the men's ward, and brought the day nurse running. She pressed the intercom as she reached the bed, her eyes on the glowing screen and its lifeless, flat line.

"I need the crash trolley," she shouted above the shrill alarm, "in Main Men's! Bed seven. Now!"

She killed the alarm, and began external heart massage with the heels of her hands, counting off the beats. Patients around her peered silently from their beds. She pulled away the patient's oxygen trickler tube, and replaced it with the full nose and mouth mask at the head of the bed. Her hands looked unnaturally white against the scarred black skin.

The crash trolley banged the ward doors open, pushed by a doctor and two nurses unraveling cables and the paddles of a defibrillator. The team were well rehearsed.

The doctor set the paddles on the patient's chest and nodded to the nearest nurse.

"Clear!"

The team stood back, and the patient's body arced off the bed. The doctor checked the heart monitor.

"Again. Clear!"

The patient shuddered, but the heart monitor's trace remained flat.

The doctor took out a penlight and peeled back each eyelid.

"One more time," she said. "Clear."

The burst of current flexed the patient's back off the bed again, but the heart line continued straight across the center of the screen.

The crash team disconnected the cables and leads.

The doctor checked her watch and made an entry on Teddy Gidgee's chart.

"Time of death, one-sixteen P.M.," she said. "Cause of death — heart failure. Confirmation to be obtained by postmortem exam."

One floor below, the plastic doors of the emergency room were thumped open by an ambulance gurney pushed by two paramedics and surrounded by three nurses and two doctors. Owen Bird's chest was bared and wired, with leads to the portable heart monitor mounted over him on the gurney.

"Stay sharp, people," the casualty resident ordered. "We've got a lot of blood here. How much methylprednisolone has he had?"

"Three hundred mils," Judy Hall answered. "As soon as we got him off the jet."

"Thank you, nurse. Good call, Tim." The resident peeled back Owen's eyelids. "Mr. Bird? Owen Bird! You're in Alice Springs Hospital. Can you hear me?"

Owen remained still.

The resident ran through a checklist for neurological damage, his voice still calm.

"Cut his boots off. Shears. And the rest of his shirt. This isn't all his blood is it, Tim?"

"Buffalo," Tim said. "He was hunting."

"Beautiful. Let's get him wired."

A nurse removed the portable leads, and attached contacts from a hospital monitor. Owen's head rolled and he opened his eyes, then closed them.

"Mr. Bird? I'm Dr. Walker. You're in Alice Springs Hospital. Can you hear me?"

A nurse with a clipboard turned to Judy Hall. "I'll need a list of everything he's been given."

"Two Hartmann bags, according to his pilot," Judy said. "Point nine percent sodium chloride, five percent dextrose."

"Got it."

"Call X-ray," the resident said. "I want a full spinal and a good look at that arm."

A second nurse said, "I'm switching his IV to the Gemini pump."

Owen opened his eyes again. He saw the team working around him, but the buzzing still filled his ears, and he barely heard them talking.

At the foot of his gurney, behind the nurse who was cutting away his boots, he saw a young Aboriginal man staring at him. Owen tried to focus. The Aborigine's scarred chest was bare, he wore only hospital pajama shorts, and his eyes seemed open and closed at the same time, staring straight through Owen.

"Who the fuck are you!" Owen growled.

"Mr. Bird?" The resident switched on his penlight again and shone it into Owen's eyes. "It's all right, Mr. Bird. You're in Alice Springs Hospital. Can you hear me?"

"Who the fuck are you?" Owen's voice was stronger, as he tried to point at the Aborigine. The nurse with the surgical shears hesitated, stared behind her, then continued cutting away his boots.

"I'm Dr. Walker, Mister Bird."

"Fuck off!" Owen snarled at the Aborigine.

"Mr. Bird," the resident said firmly. "It's all right. We're taking good care of you."

Owen saw the people in white leaning in over him, but his eyes were locked on the black specter of the staring Aborigine at the foot of the gurney. He felt cold, as if the Aborigine was drawing off all his body heat. Owen felt himself shake violently. Fear slid in with long icy tendrils that seemed to burn through every vein in his body. He wondered why, if his legs were paralyzed, this terrible cold scalded his feet and legs and belly and chest.

"Fuck off!" His voice faded.

"Calm yourself, Mr. Bird. You're going to be all right." The resident watched Owen's pulse climb on the monitor. "Mr. Bird, please keep still. You'll only do more damage. Keep your arm still."

Owen fought to point at the dark, silent figure staring at him, draining his heat. There was a familiarity about him that cut Owen's defenses like acid.

"Fuck off, you black bastard."

The resident's eyes flashed from Owen to each of his team. All of them were white. The only black person in the ward was a patient in a cubicle, out of sight behind a curtain.

Owen felt the nurses and resident struggling to restrain him, their hands felt hot, but deep inside, chilling currents coursed up his back and chest and into his throat. He felt he was drowning, and tried to shout for help, but the cold had him now, freezing his throat, and he saw the darkness moving around him again like a baleful presence, embracing the specter, until all Owen could see were those hideous unblinking eyes sunk in a black void.

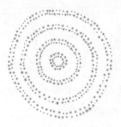

CHAPTER 7

A TRICKLE OF BLOOD FOLLOWED the smooth black path curving down through a layer of white foam. Robert Erhard didn't feel the razor bite into his cheek. He didn't see the blood in his shaving mirror. His eyes were riveted beyond his own naked reflection, to the figure of a scarred Wirruntjatjara warrior who materialized behind him. The man wore the totem paint of the Emu Dreaming spirit, Kalaya. The figure seemed shrouded in shadows within the mirror, though Robert's bathroom was well lit. The elder stood silently holding a ceremonial killing spear, cruelly barbed and decorated with long gray emu feathers.

The figure beckoned to Robert, with a raised hand, decorated at the wrist with more soft gray feathers. Robert's heart pounded and he felt the breath sapped from his lungs. He spun around to confront the Emu Dreaming man and saw only white-tiled walls, glaring back at him. He turned back to the mirror, and for the first time noticed the small stream of blood running down his face and dropping in red splatters on his white bath mat. Behind his reflection was only the bare wall. He wiped his hand across his cheek, smearing blood through the shaving foam. His hands were shaking. He told himself it was lack of sleep. He told himself it was the argument with Grace. They hated fighting with each other. But that only drove home the cause of his insomnia. For six nights, he had resisted Kalaya's ominous invitation to follow him. He had worked at the Mars Mock-up far into each night, trying to out-last the darkness, napping at intervals, but the moment his eyes weighed shut, the Emu Dreaming man emerged from the darkness. The late nights only made Grace more suspicious and unhappy.

In the lab, surrounded by robots running rehearsals for a planetary mission, Robert talked to the overnight crews, refined software, and tried to focus on anything that pushed the Emu Dreaming man out of his mind. He watched the data streams from his Insectoids, running through their routines on the mock-up and around the lab, moving to the music of their loaded codes. He gazed at the live survey satellite images, traveling for twenty-two minutes across the solar system from Mars to the monitors around his lab. When his Insectoids reached the Red Planet they would have to think for themselves during those long pauses, exercising free will, and following their own rituals, sending their data aloft like prayers, waiting in silence for commands and answers to cross heaven. Robert and his teams would send each new instruction the way he sent signals to BILBO in the Mars Mock-up, appearing in the tiny robots' awareness like apparitions from another existence. In the heart of his lab, Robert was insulated by walls of computers, and glowing screens, and fantastic machines.

But whenever his eyes strayed to the red sand of the mock-up, or simply slowly rolled shut from mounting exhaustion, the dark warrior was there, waving him back to an existence he had left long ago.

Robert watched the trickle of blood drawn by gravity down the curve of his cheek. He looked away from the mirror and hurled the razor across the bathroom. It shattered on the wall tiles, clattering in splinters to the floor around him. He leaned against the basin, and groaned. It was the same sound he had made in his sleep, when he had spoken the name Kalaya. With the rolled r beneath the l it would have sounded to Grace like "Carla." Another woman. Robert wished it were so simple. He had denied everything, and told her nothing, which made him dread even more what he was about to do to her. He stared again into the mirror, but there was no sign of Kalaya of the Emu Dreaming. There was no longer any need. Robert Erhard was beyond resistance.

"Take all the time you need." The director was earnest and reassuring when Robert asked for compassionate leave to return to Australia. "I've got you a berth on a T-38 into LAX, so you can make the next connection home.

Blake Scanlon's flying out to Edwards to ferry the *Endeavor* back to Kennedy. He'll drop you off on his way."

"That's very kind of you."

"Hey, Robert, family's priority one." The director's smile became conspiratorial. "Besides, we always take care of our people." His voice dropped. "I sure hope your folks are gonna be okay, Robert. Y'all give 'em our best, hear?"

$$\approx$$

"A bogeyman!" Grace paced the kitchen, her eyes locked on Robert. "You expect me to believe all this is about some bogeyman?"

"It's not a bogeyman, darling." Robert kept his voice calm. "He's real."

"Right. Let me see if I understand this now," she said as she spun to face him, stabbing the air with her finger. "You want to drop everything here, everything you've worked for, everything you've worked harder for than anyone else, worked harder for than anyone else who's not black, not to mention everything we've worked for together, everything we've planned together—if there's anything we've got together that I can trust anymore—you want to drop all that, and just go back to the end of the world, and maybe not come back, ever, turn your back on the rest of your life, turn your back on me, all because you've had a nightmare about some guy named Carla who says you have to go home. Did I get all that right?"

"Kalaya," Robert said, aware the flood was only beginning, "not Carla. Kalaya."

"You know how hard it is . . ." Grace closed her eyes for a second. ". . . to get to where you are. You know how hard it is for a black man to get anywhere near where you are. You know what they'll do here if they ever, ever get wind of why you're going away. You know how gunshy they are of anyone who doesn't toe the line, anyone who could give Congress any excuse for more cutbacks. I just can't believe you'd do this, Robert. To yourself. To the agency. To everything you've worked for. And most of all to me. What do I do while you're off following Carla, Carly, Kalaya to the end of the world. Wait? What am I waiting for, Robert? The chance to maybe see you come home, to maybe get used to you being here again, to maybe learn to trust you again, just to have you get another dreamland visit from this here Carla, and disappear again? Is that it? Is that it, Robert? You think I want to sit around here, waiting for you to go native again?"

His eyes widened, and she stopped dead, recoiling from her own words.

"You know what I mean," she pressed on, but more gently. "You know what I mean."

"You knew where I came from right from the start, darling," he said quietly.

"And I know how far you've come. You want to give all that up?"

"It's not about where I've come. It's about where I'm from. It's who I am."

"I almost wish it was another woman. It would be easier."

"You know that wouldn't happen. I wouldn't do that to you."

"A compass." She passed her hand over her brow. "I thought I had a compass."

"I beg your pardon?"

"Nothing." She sank onto the cedar chest. "I want to understand, Rob. But I don't want to see you throw everything away just because you're homesick."

"It's not about that."

"You really believe you saw him. Not just a dream?"

"Yes."

"And so you have to go home?"

"Yes."

"But you don't know for how long?"

"No."

"Do you know what he wants?"

Robert sat beside her and stroked her hair, and tried to push the image of the Kalaya man out of his mind. He felt Grace relax against him. There was no one he had met since he left home whom he loved more. He could not imagine being without her. An image of his own image in the mirror returned, the red trickle curving down his black skin between the rows of white foam, obeying a force beyond understanding.

"No," he lied.

څ

The NASA T-38 Talon carved a thin white jet trail high over the Colorado River, into California. Robert slid down the glare shield on his helmet against the full blast of the lowering sun that painted the desert dark red below them. He remembered the family farewell party for him before he first left Australia to take up his scholarship to Stanford, when he was twenty-one.

"I'm so proud of you, darling," Giselle said.

"I know, Mum," Robert answered softly. He put his arms around her and kissed her blond hair. "You shouldn't worry about me."

"I'm afraid you won't want to come home."

"I'll always come home, Mother."

Home. Mother. Family.

"Looks like Mars, doesn't it." Blake Scanlon's voice on the headphones broke the permutations coiling through Robert's memories. "Your bugs would get a real good workout down there."

"They're up for it," Robert said. "They really scare you that much?"

"Nah, Bob. I'm more afraid of some middle manager screwing up and covering his ass. Challenger wasn't the first, and it won't be the last. But your vermin, why, they're just too pretty for the accountants to ignore. We're afraid they're going to wind up bumping us off a mission. Used to be you had to be a test pilot to fly a mission. Then just an engineer. Pretty soon, you'll only have to be an engine."

"That's pretty poetic for a bonehead."

"You get my point. But you still can't beat a trained human on site."

Robert smiled grimly in the confines of his helmet, and the image of the Kalaya Emu Dreaming man came clearly into his mind, bearing his irresistible summons.

"No argument from me, Blake," he said wearily.

The Qantas 747 climbed out of Los Angeles and began its long slide down the arc of the globe. Robert felt himself drifting into his first sound sleep in a week, but this time there was no apprehension about closing his eyes. There would be no grim Kalaya man to stalk him in the shadows of sleep now. Instead, he dreamed of great wheels rolling smoothly along steel tracks, stretching toward the horizon of a vast red plain. Above the sound of the wheels came the voice of an Aboriginal woman he had not heard in an age, familiar and loving, embracing him deep inside his dream, until tears welled beneath his sleeping mask, and slid slowly down the smooth curve of his cheek.

BOOK II

THE KEEPER
OF DREAMS

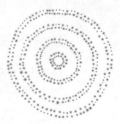

CHAPTER 8

THE ABORIGINAL WOMAN'S VOICE slid through Robert's mind as smoothly as a key in a lock, tumbling connections to memories long sealed, opening a labyrinth that snaked back along narrowing paths to the moment of conception, when all codes were loaded, all definitions set, all journeys begun.

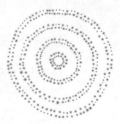

The baby howled above the church font as the pastor marked the sign of the cross with water on his forehead and renamed, redefined, and baptized him Robert Heinrich Erhard. Tears curved over his tiny cheeks, framed in white christening lace that swaddled him from head to toe. The ceremony cut Robert's last recorded connection with his birth family and their tribal country deep in the desert far north of his new home city.

Friends of Pastor Heinrich Erhard and his wife, Giselle, were alarmed that—after all they had both endured in the war barely five years earlier—they wanted to take on the problems of raising an Aboriginal child. The government had long cited chronic racial violence in the United States to enforce a White Australia Policy, barring immigrants who weren't white or well educated. Inside Australia, Aborigines had no vote, few rights, and little hope of surviving in their traditional tribal existence. In the past they were hunted and shot like wild animals. Genocidal operations a century earlier were recalled in history classes as brave expeditions by white pioneers. Shootings still occurred. Aborigines were regarded as savages who must be civilized to survive. Anthropologists soberly noted that Aborigines were Caucasian, not Negroid like Africans: there were no persistent genes that could produce a black baby several generations after its ancestors mated with whites. Outback pioneers once joked about "fucking them white."

By the end of World War II, the federal government had settled on what it called a more educated solution, and encouraged white families to adopt babies from tribal communities, and raise them as their own. White couples with the best intentions complied. Few of them knew that Aboriginal mothers were told they should give up their children to a better life than the one they were born to in impoverished settlements or iniquitous camps on the edges of towns and cities. The white couples were frequently told they were adopting a black child whose parents were dead, and repeated the story as their ward grew up. Other couples were not so ingenuous, but Heinrich and Giselle Erhard could have no children of their own, and earnestly believed they were providing a home, education, and love to an outcast who faced a life of discrimination and degradation without them. After the torment he survived in the war, Heinrich simply wanted to save and raise one baby, with a passion bordering on desperation.

Giselle felt no obligation to explain any of this to her friends, and they knew argument was futile once her mind was set. The baby's adoption occurred with remarkable speed. He was three months old when he was delivered to them from a mission in the Central Desert. The nursing sister who brought him to Adelaide met the Erhards in the office of a government lawyer, who saw the papers were signed before tea was poured.

"The father drank," the lawyer said gravely, unable to keep his gaze away from Heinrich's hands. "Abandoned his wife and child. These people are primitives. No laws. No rules. She fell ill and passed away. You're doing a wonderful thing."

The nurse silently handed the child to Giselle.

It was love at first sight.

Robert Erhard was a darling child. Giselle's only regret in the first weeks they had him was that she could not nurse him herself. When Heinrich came into their bedroom one evening he found her sitting up in the double bed, her nightdress unbuttoned to her waist, and the baby quietly suckling at a breast. Giselle was crying silently. He sat on the bed, and put his arms around her.

"I heard that women can make milk for a baby even if it's not theirs," she said. He dried her face with a corner of the bedsheet. "I so wish I could feed him."

"You're giving him everything he needs, liebe," Heinrich replied gently. "You look so beautiful together."

He held her for a long time, listening to the baby stirring in her arms, lulled by a sense of contentment that bound the three of them safely away from the world. The feeling returned often to Heinrich as Robert grew. The boy was taller than most of the children his age and he was developing a dignity that drew them to him. Any fear that the chronicled drunkenness and dissolution of his birth parents could influence his own nature soon disappeared. He made friends easily and Heinrich and Giselle were relieved and delighted when he began bringing a train of friends home from around their neighborhood. White friends.

Heinrich tried to spend time with his son every evening before bedtime. At first, he simply held him on his lap and rocked him. Giselle frequently found him in the bedroom they furnished as a nursery, reciting from memory long tracts of poetry and the Psalms. She occasionally heard him singing while the baby watched him quietly. She realized she often cried, but that it was from love for her husband and child. It made her sharply aware of time, and their mortality. As Robert learned to say his first words, it was Heinrich who began reading to him at night from children's books, pointing to all the details of each illustration. Sitting on his father's lap, the boy slapped the pictures with delight and ran his fingers along their outlines. His favorites were from Beatrix Potter's storybooks and the cover of a children's anthology of Greek legends, showing Medea riding into the sky in her chariot, pulled by a brilliant long-tailed dragon, like a great colorful flying snake.

Sundays were workdays for Heinrich, with morning services at the church, and visits to hospitals and congregants confined to their homes in the afternoon. Giselle taught a Sunday School class for older children, and Robert entered the class for preschoolers. On Saturdays, they both took Robert to visit friends, or into the Mount Lofty Range above Adelaide on picnics. Heinrich began teaching Robert the names of trees and birds and insects. The bush teemed with animals, and frequently they would see a kangaroo or wallaby break from the bush and hop across the road in front of their car.

"Kangaroo!" Robert called, pointing from his vantage on Giselle's lap.

"Good boy!" Heinrich saw the excitement in their son's eyes as he watched the animal bound away through the trees.

There was so much he wanted the child to learn. Most of all they wanted him to be well prepared and confident when he entered school, and the inevitable ocean of racial bigotry that permeated the country.

He was confronted on his first day at school. A boy from the seventh grade came with three of his cronies during the lunch break, looking for Robert.

"My dad reckons Abos should all be rounded up and shot," the kid said. At the age of five and a half, Robert was more robust than most of his classmates. The seventh-grader wasn't much bigger than Robert, but he had his three cronies backing him up.

Robert stood still and looked the boy in the eyes. The boy expected some response, but Robert merely watched him with an unsettling sense of calm. The bully's expression shifted from a sneer to an uncertain glare. Robert waited, his gaze steady and penetrating. The three cronies looked at their leader to see what he would do. The bully's tone changed, and he cleared his throat before he spoke again. "Did you hear me?"

"And what do you reckon?" Robert said quietly, making the confrontation personal, excluding the three confederates and the bully's father. The older boy blinked. Then he broke eye contact and looked down.

Robert waited.

"I reckon you're all right by me," the bully said to his friends' astonishment. "Me name's Russell Gunther. What's yours?"

"Robert Erhard."

"Good on yer, Robert," Russell Gunther said and held out his hand. He seemed relieved when Robert shook it. "You're all right for a blackfeller, I reckon." Robert watched silently as the bully led his three mates away across the playground. The encounter disturbed them. It seemed perfectly natural to Robert: by the time he was four, he had discovered an ability to remain completely centered and stare down neighborhood dogs. The animals recoiled from the boy's stillness. Now he realized the ability was transferable to humans. There appeared to be nothing supernatural about it, but if the four white boys had been asked about it, they would have been at a loss to explain it. It was entirely beyond their comprehension.

Heinrich taught Robert the basics of cricket and football, and took him to watch the Adelaide teams play on weekend afternoons. Heinrich and Giselle both helped him with his homework, and he learned swiftly. They began setting him more difficult assignments, to stop him getting bored. His teachers reported that he was a quick and able student, with a gift for mathematics, and as accomplished in the classroom as he was on the playing fields.

"He will always have to be better," Heinrich said, "to be accepted as an equal."

Robert seemed too good to be true.

By the time he was ready to complete fourth grade, Heinrich and Giselle no longer marveled at their son's abilities. The friends who originally cautioned them against adopting a black child no longer remembered their own warnings. Young Robert Erhard was an exceptional child, they all agreed, a perfect example of environment triumphing over breeding, of nurture taming nature.

The Erhards, their friends said, had brought a baby savage out of the desert, and raised him as a civilized white child—a model for the way all Aborigines could be assimilated. Heinrich and Giselle privately cringed when their friends talked this way. Instead they thanked God that Robert was blessed with such remarkable natural grace and talents. Few of their friends knew that as well as learning from his parents about the deeds and adventures of civilizations from the ancient Greeks to the first European settlers in Australia, Robert was also learning the most rudimentary Aboriginal legends of the Central Desert. Heinrich had a book called *Native Australian Myths*, little more than children's stories illustrated by artists who rendered the wilderness and its inhabitants and animals in a distinctly English style. But Robert listened to each of them intently.

"I don't know all the details, Robbie," Heinrich told him. "One day, you'll be able to find out for yourself. But for now, I'll teach you what I can."

Robert loved Heinrich as his own father, and he adored Giselle. He called them Dad and Mum ever since he began to speak, at fourteen months. In the final term of his fourth year at elementary school, when he was nine and a half years old and ready for the year-end tests, his teacher considered having him jump a year, because he was doing so well. It was October, the end of the Australian spring, and there was a month to prepare for the November exams and the end of the school year. Robert had been scoring As in all his term tests. Heinrich and Giselle had no doubt he would do the same in the year-end exams.

Then Robert vanished.

67

Heinrich had only one clue to Robert's disappearance.

A district police sergeant who was in Heinrich's congregation assured the Erhards that their boy had probably just run away from home and would be back by sundown. Robert did not return that night. The following morning, the sergeant sent a missing persons telegram to every police station within a hundred miles, with a description of Robert, noting clearly that he was the adopted son of a Lutheran pastor, and that the police were concerned for the boy's welfare.

"Pastor Erhard's a war hero. I don't want them treating the boy," the sergeant said piously, "like another bloody Abo."

"You know, he's been having nightmares all week," Heinrich said to Giselle as they sat alone in their kitchen late the next night. The sergeant and a constable had politely asked if the boy had been disciplined recently or had trouble at school, or if he was worried about the exams next month. They had assured the police there had been no crises in Robert's life before he left.

Both policemen had sons who were schoolmates of Robert's and he came to their homes after school. As soon as the last class was out, the kids kicked off their shoes and played barefoot through the schoolyards and neighborhood. Their feet acquired calluses that let them walk unharmed over rough ground oblivious to prickles and thorny bindi-eyes. The boys traveled in loud, mischievous packs, like flocks of Noisy Mynah birds, descending on each other's houses for something to eat, then tearing off into the parks and nearby bush, peeling off along creeks to float leaves and makeshift boats, falling into teams for football or slipping away to smoke or build treehouses.

"Robbie's a bloody whitefeller," the sergeant told his colleague in the car as they left Heinrich and Giselle, meaning it as a compliment.

When the police had gone, Giselle made tea and sat at the kitchen table with Heinrich, praying the phone would ring, expecting to look up and see her son coming through the door, grinning.

"He never said anything about nightmares," Giselle said, hurt that her son had secrets with Heinrich. He was only nine years old. He was still her little boy.

"He didn't want to tell me," Heinrich said. "I found him sitting up in bed when I walked past his room. I thought the moon must have woken him up. It was quite light in his room. I asked him if he was all right, and he said he couldn't sleep. He said he had been unable to sleep for a few nights. He said he was having some bad dreams. I asked him what were they about, and he said, 'The bird man.' He couldn't tell me who that was. He just kept dreaming about the bird man. I asked him if he wanted to pray with me, and he did. So we said a short prayer, and he lay down and when I came back from the toilet, he seemed to be sleeping."

"What is this bird man?"

"I don't know, liebe. He couldn't say. Or wouldn't. I really don't know."

"Do you suppose he's gone"—Giselle had formed the sentence in her mind, and did not want to say it—"native?" It was what gave them pause when their friends talked about the influence of environment over breeding. They worried that while their son was being raised as a young white man, he was still a fullblooded Aborigine. They did not know what forces flowed beneath his surface, or if they were strong enough to draw him away on the Aboriginal journeys called walkabout.

"I don't know, liebe. I don't know. I'm sure we'll hear something in the morning. The best thing we can do is leave the lights on for him, and get some rest."

"You know how I used to dread waiting."

"I know, liebe."

He stroked her hair, and she reached up and took his scarred hands in hers and kissed them.

"I couldn't bear to wait like that again."

"I know."

They spent the next night the same way. And the next. And the following one, for a week, then two, until days and nights became a chain of kitchen lights and cups of tea and distracted chores and disturbed sleep, broken in starts at the slightest noise through the constantly lit house.

The bird man didn't scare Robert in his dreams. But he described them as nightmares when Heinrich asked him that night, because he couldn't think of a better explanation. Robert saw the bird man standing on a wide red plain. He had long thin legs, and wispy brown and gray feathers on his body and head. There was no mistaking the form of an Australian emu, taller than a man, and like its distant relative the ostrich, able to run incredibly fast, but unable to fly. The boy had wanted to tell his father the bird man was an emu, but something stopped him. The emu man danced in one place as he looked at Robert across the dream, his feet hitting the ground lightly and propelling him upward with enormous power. There were no words, but Robert felt the man drawing him away onto the red plain with him. That was what made him describe the dreams as bad. He felt a frightening urge to go with the emu man.

For five nights, with the moon waxing full, then waning through his bedroom window, he dreamed of meeting the emu man on the plain. Each time, the long legs carried the man swiftly away toward the dark red horizon, then brought him back to stand before Robert, beckoning.

Robert felt there was a part of him missing, and that the emu man knew where that part was. On the fifth night, he could no longer resist. He slipped out of bed and pulled on a pair of shorts and his red football jersey. Tiptoeing barefoot across the floorboards, he followed the image of the emu man out of the darkened house and onto the grassy footpath. The packed-dirt street was deserted save for a brand-new 1959 Holden sedan, gleaming under a street lamp.

The emu man led him out of the neighborhood and down to the train yards. Robert couldn't actually see the man, but he knew he was just ahead, crossing a maze of steel tracks. A short way off were large square railway sheds and workshops. Robert walked beside a line of passenger carriages and flatbeds and boxcars, standing silent and still on their rails, like great animals sleeping in the moonlight. He sensed the emu man was inside one of them. They smelled of dusty freight and machinery grease, looming up against the stars, their high wooden sides painted dark red. A sliding cargo door was ajar on the rearmost boxcar. Robert stared up at it, daunted by its silence and the darkness inside. He was certain the emu man was up there. Fear of the unknown made him hesitate, but a stronger force urged him to reach up and haul himself through the door. In the darkness, he could make out sacks of grain and wooden crates. Some steel oxyacetylene welding cylinders were chained securely to the floor. In the corner, he found a stack of empty sacks. He no longer felt any fear: instead when he sat down on the sacks, he realized he was very tired. This time, the emu man let him sleep soundly.

No noise or dream stirred him. The irritated grumbling of a stout Aboriginal woman, heaving herself into the boxcar and sliding the door shut, failed to waken him. She settled into a far corner, arranging herself between some sacks. Robert didn't hear the dull steel clanking of the carriages as a locomotive far ahead shunted back and coupled with the train. He was oblivious to the painful creaking of wood and steel as the engine built steam and began easing the wagons out to the main line. The movement of the wheels along the steel soothed him like a river as they made their way out of the city and through the Flinders Ranges and north, toward the red desert.

The train was called *The Ghan*. It steamed slowly north, an irritable caravan of creaking railway cars and grumbling passengers. The regulars called it the *Rattler*, because of the noise that assailed them in their carriages for three days and nights on the trek from Adelaide to Alice Springs. Sometimes, if rains sent flash floods across the plains and washed out the line, the journey could take three months. There were train drivers who'd had to shoot game to feed their passengers, stranded between flooded stretches of track, hundreds of miles from the nearest town. But on this journey, the skies remained clear, blazing by day, flooded by moonlight at night. Curled up in the boxcar, Robert dozed throughout the morning. He woke in the late afternoon, refreshed, but thirsty and hungry.

«Good! You are awake!» a woman's voice said in the dialect of the Wirruntjatjara people.

Robert was so startled to hear another voice, he didn't realize the woman was speaking a foreign language. She was sitting on the floor near him with her legs straight out in front of her and her hands in her lap. She was wearing a wool cardigan over a weathered cotton dress. She had a purple cotton scarf rolled into a bandanna and tied around her forehead. Her feet were bare and callused, and her toes were splayed from rarely having been inside shoes. Her arms and legs were slim, though she had a round belly and plump cheeks. She appeared to be in her late thirties, but she had the pretty flirtatious smile of a young girl.

«You call me Maureen,» she said in Wirruntjatjara, showing her small teeth and a greenish chewing wad of bush tobacco as she grinned broadly.

Robert look bewildered.

«You don't understand me?» the woman said. Robert did not, but he heard clearly the mild disgust in her voice. "You don't understand your own language?" she said in English.

"Of course I understand," Robert said, his voice small, still startled.

«What's your name, young fellow?» she demanded in Wirruntjatjara.

Robert looked blankly at her.

«You say you understand your own language?» She sounded irritated now.

Robert could make no sense of the words she was saying.

"You say you understand your own language?" she repeated in English.

"Of course," Robert said.

"English is your own language?" Her voice mocked him.

"Yes." Robert sounded confused.

"Wirruntjatjara is your own language," she pronounced.

"My language is English," he answered. Her eyes sparkled at his defiance.

"English is the Piranypa language," she said. "You are Wirruntjatjara."

"I'm Australian," he said, more firmly.

"What do they call you, boy?" she asked.

"Robert."

"That is a Piranypa name," she said. "A whitefeller word. Are you a white-feller?"

In the shadowy daylight of the boxcar, her pretty smile had a sly lift to it now. Robert felt a cold shock of excitement slither up his spine. His mind shot back to Heinrich and Giselle, telling him how he had been brought to them by God, and reminding him over and over how much they loved him.

"I am Robert Heinrich Erhard," he said confidently.

Maureen thought about this, then nodded slowly.

"And who is your father?" she asked.

"His name is Heinrich Erhard."

"That is a Piranypa name," she said. "You are not a Piranypa."

Robert stared at her.

"Look at your hands," she ordered, holding her own up.

Robert examined his hands, first the pink palms and finger pads, then the skin on their backs, dark as gunmetal.

"Are they Piranypa hands?" she asked.

"They're my hands," he replied.

"They're Anangu hands." The name Anangu came easily off the back of her tongue, pronounced with a rolled r into the n, and making a soft, palatal ng without a hard g in the second syllable, so that she made the sound "arn-ung-oo." She said it again, "Anangu. The People. Piranypa call us Aborigines. We are Anangu. The People. Piranypa are not. We Anangu were here a long, long, long time before the Piranypa came. You have Anangu hands. You are Anangu. And your language is Wirruntjatjara." She paused to see if he understood.

He could not speak.

"What is your father's name?" she asked again, and waited silently for his answer.

"Heinrich Erhard," he said at last.

"What kind of hands does he have?"

He had seen people look at Heinrich's hands, trying not to stare, but constantly drawn back to them. Was that what she was talking about? Robert cleared his throat.

"They were in the war," he said in a small voice.

She appeared puzzled by his answer.

"What color are they?"

"White," he said.

"What color are yours?"

He looked at his hands in the shadowy light.

"Black."

"What kind of hands does he have?"

"Piranypa," Robert said quietly. He feared he was committing an act of betrayal.

"That is right," Maureen answered soberly. "How can he be your father?"

"I was brought to him by God."

Maureen's eyebrows rose.

"By God, eh?"

"God brought me to my mother and father and they love me."

She nodded slowly. "They told you that?"

"It's true." His voice was indignant, but he was confused, as if the floor had opened into a wide lattice, no longer safe and solid, filled with gaps through which he could fall.

"Who is your father?" she asked.

"I told you! Heinrich Erhard."

"Who is your father?"

"I told you," Robert cried, as if he was clinging to the idea in a turbulent current.

"Who are you?"

"I am Robert Erhard."

"Who are you?"

"Robert! Robert Heinrich Erhard!"

"Why are you here?"

Robert hesitated, then answered, "The emu man brought me."

"What did he look like, this emu man?"

"He had long legs and feathers on him like an emu."

"That is the Kalaya man. The Emu Dreaming spirit. You dreamed him." She said it as a matter of fact.

"Yes." He looked at her with new interest. Could she read his mind? His dreams?

"If he led you here, you must have dreamed him," she said. "How long have you dreamed him?"

"All week."

"How many nights?"

"Five. Five nights."

"Munkorpa kutjara," she said. "That is how we say five. Watch me closely, young Robert." He watched.

"Kutju," she began, holding up one finger. "You say it."

"Kutju." The new word felt good in his mouth.

"Kutju," she said again, motioning him to hold up a finger.

"Kutju," he repeated, raising his forefinger. A flicker of excitement stirred inside him.

"Kutjara." She raised two fingers.

"Kutjara." He copied her.

"Munkorpa." She held up three fingers.

"Munkorpa." He mirrored her hand with his.

"Now we add the numbers to make bigger ones," she said. "Kutjara kutjara," she showed him four fingers.

"Kutjara kutjara," he responded, the excitement stronger in him now as he showed four fingers.

Silently, she extended all the fingers and thumb of her hand and waited for him with a questioning look. The words already felt familiar as he spoke them. The answer slipped into place unconsciously and he held up his own open hand.

"Munkorpa kutjara," he said quietly, but she saw triumph in his eyes.

She laughed with delight. She wasn't like any other adult he knew. She had a childlike joy. Still, she was an adult, and behind her laughter, he sensed a watchfulness that seemed both protective and dangerous, and for no reason he could understand, he remembered the beautiful cover of the book Heinrich read to him, showing Medea and her brilliant winged snake, rising into the sky.

"You saw the Emu Dreaming man munkorpa kutjara nights, five nights," she said.

He nodded.

"You were awake when you saw him?" Maureen asked.

"Yes I was."

"Our dreaming is not like whitefellers' dreaming," she said gently. "A Piranypa only dreams when he is asleep. That is the only time the Piranypa can see their spirits. Anangu dreaming is all the time. All the time, we can hear our spirits and see them. All the time they can talk to us." She laughed again, a sweet cascading glissando. "All of us have our own birth-dreaming spirit. Soon you will know yours." She lowered her voice. "That is men's business."

She said it ominously. He felt part of something he could not see, something great and timeless, beyond his boy's vocabulary. But he imagined the latticework below him closing again, becoming the solid wooden floor of the boxcar, secure, moving along the steel onto the red plain.

"Drink some water." Maureen held out the water bag she carried and he took the top off and tipped it up to his mouth, smelling the sweet freshness of moisture evaporating off the canvas as he drank.

"Good," she said, reaching into her paper bag of fruit. "Eat this."

She gave him a banana and he peeled it and ate it in silence. He wondered what else she knew about him. She sat peacefully next to him, occasionally looking at him with her thoughtful smile. He felt no need to talk to her while he ate and she offered no conversation of her own. It was as if she had stopped using energy and had becalmed her muscles and bones.

"Now, young Robert," she said when he finished eating, "you lie down again and sleep." She patted her lap, and he obediently lay his head there, and she stroked his hair and sang to him, a tonal chant whose rising and falling course dulled the clatter of the rails until he drifted into sleep again. He had long forgotten the aromas of his birth mother. Giselle always smelled of fresh soap and lavender water perfume, and he connected those smells with safety and love and an unconscious sexuality. Now, as he slept with his head on Maureen's lap, his memory recognized older smells from his infancy: the pheromones of an Anangu woman, the redolent imprints of cuddling and suckling and love and security. They reached him across a river of time, from his first days and weeks of life, soothing him. He felt that he belonged here in these smells. As the train rolled farther north across the plain, Robert had no sense of leaving Giselle and Heinrich; only of moving to another place that felt as familiar as home.

He woke a little after noon. The air in the boxcar had grown hot.

"You know why you are here?" Maureen's voice greeted him above the loud creaking of the train. He sat up beside her and stretched.

"The Kalaya man led me here," he said.

"Do you know why?"

"No."

"Are you afraid?"

He hesitated. "No."

"I see. I will tell you a story, Robert."

"What about?"

"It is how the world was made."

"I know how it was made."

"Eh? You do, eh? How was that?" She seemed amused.

"God made the light and the sky and the stars and the earth. Then he made men."

"He did, eh?"

"And then he made the animals."

"How do you know that?"

"My father told me. He talks to God."

"He does, eh? Your Piranypa father?"

"My father," he said firmly.

"Mm."

The train clattered on. Maureen fell silent. Robert wondered if he had offended her. Years later, he would still shudder when he realized what she was offering him.

"What is the story?" he asked her finally.

She looked at him shrewdly.

"This is the story your Anangu father learned." His body went tense.

"My Anangu father?"

"Your Anangu father. Not your Piranypa father who talks to God. Your Wirruntjatjara father. Listen properly."

"Where is he?"

"He is gone," Maureen said quietly. Robert felt something enormous moving through him, given to him and at once taken away again. He felt terribly lonely.

"He's dead?"

"I cannot tell you."

"And my mother?"

"She died some years ago. I am very sorry, little fellow. But you have family. All waiting to see you."

She patted the wooden floor in front of her, motioning him there. He felt dazed. She patted the floor again. He sat cross-legged near her feet.

"We go back," Maureen said, fixing Robert's eyes with hers. Her voice blanked out the sounds of the train. "We go back and back. And we go and we go and we go. And we go back before that. And we go and we go and we go before that. We go back to the time when everything was spirits. The time before men and animals and rocks and plants. We Anangu call this time the Tjukurpa. The creation time. It was then. It is now. This is still the creation time. And before all the spirits, there was one spirit. We call her Wanampi, the Rainbow Serpent." She pronounced it wahr-nampi, rolling her tongue again into an r sound on the n.

"Wanampi made all things. She made the stars and the night and she made the sun and the fire and the day. She made the ground and the air. But she was all by herself, and she was very lonely. Wanampi was so lonely that she began to cry, and her tears fell from the sky and made the rain and the water. Then she went into the ground, into her burrow. And the earth and rock she pushed up as she dug made a big, big mound. And she named that mound Uluru. And the rain kept falling, and filled up the entrance to her burrow beneath Uluru, and made a water hole on top of the rock. And that water hole on top of Uluru is called Uluru too.

"Then Wanampi came back up from the great rock called Uluru, and up out of the water hole on top, called Uluru. Then she made all the spirits so she wouldn't be lonely anymore. All the spirits of the Tjukurpa, she made them. And the spirits were the ancestors of all things. They were the spirits of the emu and the kangaroo and the parrot and the python and the goanna and the eagle. And she made the spirits of the spiny anteater, that the Piranypa call the echidna, and she made the fish and the dingo and the witchetty grub. She made all these spirits and all the other spirits. And she sent the spirits out on the ground around her and they walked out on the ground from Uluru. And they walked and they walked and they walked.

"And when each spirit walked, he sang about where he walked. And the singing was his dreaming. And when he sang about a hill, the hill appeared there. The hill was his dreaming. And when he sang about a creek, the creek appeared there and the creek became part of his singing. And if he was Kalaya, the Emu Dreaming spirit, he sang the emu and the emu appeared on the land. And the emu was Kalaya, and the emu became part of his singing. And his song made a track across the land, and this was his creation track. His dreaming track. If you walk along his dreaming track and know his song, it will tell you everything about each rock and tree and water hole and animal there. And it will tell you how to talk to the spirits along the dreaming track. It will tell you how to find food and water on the dreaming track and how to prepare it. And it will tell you the Law for living there. All the spirits sang about the hills and the rocks and the creeks and the rock holes and the sand dunes along their creation tracks. They sang all the animals. And then they sang men and women. All of the spirits made their dreaming tracks across the land. And when each of them were finished, they went into the ground, or they went into the sky. And where they went into the ground, they became a hill or a tree or a rock or a water hole, where that spirit lives today. And where they went into the sky, they became a star, where they live today.

"And that is how the world was made, Robert. That is the Tjukurpa. The Creation and The Law."

Robert was silent for some time, surrounded by the shadows and noise of the boxcar, but seeing instead the glory of Wanampi, and the creation spirits of the Tjukurpa heading out on their journeys.

"What happened to Wanampi?" he asked finally.

"Wanampi's dreaming made all the spirits and all life. Then she went back into the water hole on top of Uluru. But she is always traveling. Whenever it rains, you know she is weeping. And when the rain is gone, you can see her, the beautiful Rainbow Serpent, coming through the clouds. She lives in the rain and in all the water holes. That's why when we come to a water hole, we call out to Wanampi to tell her we're coming and ask her to use her water."

"My father says God is a he, not a she."

"Mm. Has your father seen this God?"

"He talks to him."

"So you said. Has he seen this he God?"

"Have you seen Wanampi?"

"Of course. All the time." Her voice became stern. "I told you to listen properly. You can see Wanampi in the clouds after it rains."

"That's a rainbow."

"That is Waṉampi," Maureen said, as if there was no further argument.

"I have a question."

She heard the new respect sliding into his voice, the tone used to address an elder.

"What is it?"

"When I met you, you said Robert is my Piṟanypa name. But you said your name is Maureen. That is a Piṟanypa name."

Maureen chuckled, and gave him a slow penetrating look. "You are a cheeky one, Robert. Maureen is the name the Piṟanypa gave me."

"What is your Aṉangu name?"

"You will learn it when we get there."

"Where are we going?"

"Home."

Robert felt as if the floor were opening into a lattice again.

"My home is in Adelaide," he said.

Maureen's voice became gentle.

"I will tell you why the Kaḻaya man brought you here," she said. "Where was he when you dreamed him?"

"He was standing in the bush, on a plain. Looking at me. Then he ran away. Very fast. Like an emu." He became thoughtful, recalling the first dream. "I was very sad. I wanted to go with him."

"Where did you want to go?"

"Where he was going."

"Do you know where that is, Robert?"

"No."

"You were dreaming you want to go home. To the place where you were born. To your birth ground. To your spirit home." She saw his lip tremble.

"Are you afraid, Robert?"

He nodded, feeling ashamed to admit it.

"Good. A proper journey should always begin with fear."

Narrow slivers of sunlight lanced in through cracks in the doors and walls of the boxcar, making shiny blades through the haze of fine dust that hung in the air. He didn't trust himself to speak.

"You are afraid, Robert, because you don't know where your home is. You have been a little boy in one home, with your Piṟanypa parents. Soon you will not be a little boy anymore, and you will know where your true home is. Do you love your Piṟanypa parents?"

He answered without hesitation. "Yes."

"Good," Maureen said. "But you also have another family. You have another home. You know you want to go there."

Robert's face contorted in protest, but she raised a hand to silence him. "That was why the Kalaya man came to you, Robert. It goes on when you are asleep and when you are awake. He is always with you, eh. He comes from inside you. He is part of you, like your belly and your face." Her fingertip touched his navel, then his nose, and he giggled. Her voice remained grave. "When you wanted to go home, your dreaming showed you the way. Trust your dreaming, Robert. All the time, all the time, trust your dreaming."

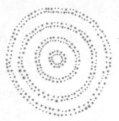

CHAPTER 9

HEINRICH FELT GISELLE'S ARM go heavy on his chest. They had talked late into the night, meandering over memories of Robert, falling into a mournful silence after each recollection. Heinrich felt powerless and angry, though he was familiar with walkabout, and suspected why Robert had run away. Groups of Aborigines from towns and cattle stations would disappear overnight, with no warning, and could be gone for weeks. They would return without a word about where they had been. Whites often thought walkabouts were arbitrary whims that moved Aborigines at random.

But over years on Outback missions and camps, Heinrich Erhard learned of the great spiritual tides that carry Aborigines through ritual timetables of conception, birth, initiation, and death. Ever since Robert was a baby, Heinrich accepted the possibility those ancient currents may reach through the safe walls of their suburban home in the Adelaide hills and ebb back toward the Central Desert, taking their child with them.

Giselle's breathing became regular and relaxed. It was after midnight. The kitchen light still burned constantly, and on the veranda encircling the house, bulbs glowed inside clouds of white moths. Heinrich remembered other nights he had waited for the return of men whose instincts for escape outweighed any thought of the consequences to themselves or to those left behind. He resisted the memory, but too late to stop the horror surging up from the past, plunging him back to the POW camp on Singapore Island, and into the hands of the sadist who controlled it.

"I have enormous patience," Captain Ashima had said pleasantly, his features smooth and fat, facing Heinrich across a wooden table. It was mid-morning and already blazing hot. A humid breeze stirred five beautifully folded paper herons on the tabletop between them. They both sat on the veranda outside Ashima's office, in clear view of the parade ground where the prisoners were drawn into ranks to watch. The men's uniforms were ragged and their bones and ulcers bore witness to the malnutrition and brutality they had suffered for more than a year since the Japanese invasion.

"However, Chaplain Erhard," Ashima made his voice carry to the prisoners, "I am afraid you are running out of . . . bargaining chips." He was amused by his clever allusion, and mastery of English.

He appraised Heinrich, hunched on a wooden stool, wounded hands cradled to his chest. A pair of fencing pliers lay near the paper birds, their ridged steel jaws slicked with blood and quick. On the dark wood next to them were five ugly slivers of keratin—three fingernails from Heinrich's left hand, and two from the right, their tips pale and grimy and their roots still wet and red where skin and cuticle remained attached.

"Where did they go?" Captain Ashima asked again. The watching prisoners knew even if Heinrich did not betray the four escapees, they faced daunting odds. The Japanese controlled the island. But every prisoner wanted to believe there was a chance of escape, of salvation. Hope was survival, and Heinrich held it on the tips of his fingers.

Ashima's hands were squat and fat, but moved gracefully, sliding a square of white paper from his imperial officer's notebook. Heinrich cringed. He tried not to watch, but his eyes betrayed him, drawn irrevocably to the paper. Ashima's fingernails were clipped with military precision, straight and strong, and filed smooth.

"You have until the heron opens its wings, Chaplain," Ashima said. Once more, a powerful tide of dread ebbed through the prisoners, sapping them of hope, leaving only their despair for Heinrich.

He prayed like St. Francis of Assisi, to forget all else but the words of his prayer, but his eyes would not release their focus on the paper, moving lightly in Ashima's fingers. Heinrich prayed like Jesus for God to not forsake him, to let the cup pass from his hands, but he saw no sign of God, and only the bloody ruin of his fingers. Time slowed, smoothed itself, and realigned to the ordered rituals of origami.

Ashima folded it first from one corner to its opposite, into a triangle, firmly running his thumbnail along the crease to make it sharp. Each movement had its own form and pace, measuring precisely the changing dimensions, and the fleeing of time. He folded the triangle in half again, once more creasing the edge with a firm stroke of his thumbnail. Heinrich winced at each fold, as if it were made in his own bones and sinews. He could clearly hear the small dragging sound of Ashima's nail running along each new edge, as the paper took shape, into smaller triangles which, with a series of delicate folds, became long, elegant spires. Every fold absorbed more of the precious seconds that separated Heinrich from the next cycle of torture. Time slipped away, along the new angles and edges of paper.

Heinrich prayed for strength to resist betraying the four men fleeing through the jungle. He prayed for deliverance. He prayed for Ashima, and for the power to love his enemy.

As if in answer, Ashima smiled. He raised the paper shape to his lips, and blew a sharp burst of air into the base. The paper puffed at the center. Then with his manicured fingertips, Ashima pulled two of the paper spires apart, opening them into a slim, white heron, its wings outspread in the palm of his hand. The small bird was beautiful, and the sight of it, complete and exquisitely formed, filled Heinrich with terror.

"Your time, Chaplain Erhard," Ashima said, setting it next to the five other paper birds, "has once again come."

A guard gripped Heinrich's shoulders and another seized his wrist, slamming it on the table, spattering blood across the six beautiful birds. Captain Ashima's powerful hands pried Heinrich's fingers open. He felt the terrible intimacy of Ashima's grip, a familiarity that promised the omnipotent devil facing him could protect him when God had so clearly abandoned him. He had an urge to surrender himself to Ashima, to give in to the devil and his overwhelming power. Heinrich prayed for courage. Then the pliers bit down, and he was engulfed by excruciating heat, the sensation of something deep inside his nerves tearing apart, and the sound of his own screaming.

He jerked awake, bathed in sweat.

Giselle woke with him. "You're safe." She spoke close to his ear, drying his face with the sheet. "You're safe, darling. You're safe."

He nodded, blinked hard, and nodded again.

She kissed his brutally scarred hands, a fingertip at a time, while his pulse settled and his breathing calmed. All the while she crooned her litany, "You're safe, darling, safe."

He lay in silence, wondering why, if he was strong enough to save four men he barely knew, he could not save his only son, whom he so desperately loved.

☙

Robert awoke, his head no longer on Maureen's lap. The train swayed and rattled around him. He sat up sleepily and saw the plain sliding past them, in bright moonlight. Maureen had pulled the near-side door of the boxcar partly open. She had her dress hitched up around her waist, and was holding with both hands on to each side of the doorway as she hung herself outside to pee. The train clattered over the rails. Robert was embarrassed and aroused by what he saw and the two emotions seemed to feed each other. She half squatted in the doorway looking serenely at some point on the opposite door of the boxcar.

"You have to do it properly or the wind blows it back," she said cheerfully as she finished, casually pulling herself upright, and smoothing her dress down into place with prim dignity. She left the door open, and came back and sat next to him. Moonlight faintly lit his face.

"You didn't sleep much good, did you?" she said, ignoring his embarrassment.

"No."

"You dreamed, eh?"

He nodded.

"What did you see?"

"The plain," he answered, pointing toward the door.

"What did you see?"

"Just the plain."

"Don't you worry 'bout that, eh Robert," she assured him. "You will see properly good, soon."

"How much longer do we have to stay here?"

"Kutjara," she answered holding up two fingers. "Two nights more. We have to stay out of sight until then. They find us here, the train fellers give us a proper good boot up the bum. Maybe worse. You want some food?"

"No."

"You want a drink of water?"

"No."

"You want to make water?"

"Yes."

She raised her chin in the direction of the door. He hesitated, then stood up and went over to it. The train was moving at a sedate thirty miles an hour, and a warm breeze eddied around him. He hitched up a leg of his shorts and felt the air sliding over his skin. It felt as if the desert were breathing on him, an excitingly intimate caress. He imagined Waṉampi's breath flowing over him, making him safe, joining him with her. As he peed into the void, in a long arc in the moonlight, he felt he was returning a part of himself into the plain. When he finished, he came back to Maureen and lay again with his head on her lap. Sometime later, he felt Maureen get up and close the door. Then he felt the softness of her thighs under his cheek again, and her powerful smells lulled him back into the depths of sleep.

The *Ghan* made four stops at remote sidings during the day, but no one came back to the boxcar. It was hot and dry inside. The waterbag was less than a third full by late afternoon. Occasionally they ate some fruit from the bag. The train rattled on north, and the country became wider and drier.

It seemed they had always been on the train. Sometimes Robert napped, hearing the sound of the train creaking and the rails clacking below, the constant voice of their closed universe. As Maureen recounted the stories of the Tjukurpa, the warm, dark boxcar became a rumbling womb, filled with images of creation spirits, striding across the land with their powerful words and songs, conjuring men and animals into existence, laying down the laws for birth and life and conflict and peace and death. Robert felt his blood flowing with spirits of his ancestors, moving him deeper and deeper into the world of his own people.

The sun moved down to the horizon and painted the red plains with fire all the way in to the railway line. It was unfenced, running straight across the open country, and when Maureen opened the door and they sat with the rails rumbling below them to watch the sunset, there wasn't another soul or building or man-made object in sight. She gave him the last of the fruit, a sweet pear whose juice ran down his chin. He wiped it off with his sleeve.

"Don't waste that," she said sternly. "Use everything. Water. Juice. Nectar from bushes."

When the juice ran down his chin again, he wiped it up with the back of his hand and then licked it clean. Maureen nodded approval. He ate the pear and the core, then lay down again and listened to her singing. He felt her fingers stroking his hair and inhaled her familiar smells until he was fast asleep.

When he awoke, it was night once more, and the train was slowing to a stop with a painful chorus of squealing brakes and clanking fenders.

"We get off here," Maureen said quietly. He sat up, alert. The moon was up, bathing the plain around them. She slid open the off-side door. The *Ghan* hissed and moaned to a stop on the main line. There was nothing else to see through a crack in the near-side door except a tiny building the size of an outhouse. A white sign next to it announced they were at Rumbalara. They had entered the Northern Territory.

A short conductor with thinning black hair and a stout beer belly went down a near-side step to the packed-dirt platform. There was no lock on the door of the small building and he shone the yellow beam of his lantern on the handle and opened it and put the mailbag he was carrying inside. Then he shut the door, set his lantern glass to green, and swung it slowly to signal the engine driver. Robert and Maureen watched him silently. Their boxcar was thirty yards back. While the conductor was climbing back on board, they slipped off the train and crouched beside the rails. In the moonlight, any movement across the open ground could be seen from the locomotive. They waited in the eerie shadow of the boxcar, until the *Ghan* clunked and squealed and slowly pulled out. The big steel wheels rolled so close beside them that Robert could smell the thick grease on their axle sleeves. He feared the conductor or the engine crew might look back and see them. They remained motionless until the rear guard's van shrank away down the track. Silence lowered itself around them as the last sounds of the train disappeared. When it was gone, they stood up.

"Good," Maureen said. "Now. You have been living in the big smoke too long. Too many Piranypa there. Too many buildings. Too much noise. Out here, you listen and you look. Listen and look."

He saw only a vast moonlit emptiness. He felt the packed stones of the rail bed beneath his bare feet. Maureen stood still and looked westward across tracks and over the plain. The stars were dimmed by moonlight. She waited.

He began to hear the silence. It seemed to have a noise of its own. He was conditioned to the constant voice of the city, which Maureen called the big smoke. Even in a quiet suburb there was a cacophony of background noise; of cars and trucks and radios and lawn mowers and refrigerators and doors and adults and children and dogs, and above them the constant scatter of birds, and the occasional high drone of propellers. His brain was used to filtering them out. Now it confronted no more of those sounds: instead it heard their absence. Robert listened to the silence, feeling the softness and stillness of it, and a minute hissing that was the natural tension of his eardrums. Then he began to notice other sounds.

There was the boo-book call of an owl, swooping across the desert for insects. Then came the click and chirr of insects, and nearby, the sound of something small being dragged over the sand. The dragging stopped, then started again. Robert peered into the shadows, trying to identify it.

A long sorrowful wail rose out of the night, and set his skin into ridges of goose bumps. He heard the dragging sound abruptly joined by a fast patter, like small feet pounding over the sand, then a cascading giggle, as Maureen shook with laughter.

"That old curlew properly scare you, eh, young Robert?"

Robert couldn't speak. He felt his skin still crawling, and the hair follicles on his neck tingling.

"You properly scared that goanna too, eh. You see him take off there?"

He shook his head. He had not seen the goanna—the big yellow lizard must have been at least four feet long to make so much noise. Robert had only heard its tail being pulled through the sand, then the pad of its four clawed feet flying over the ground in alarm—not at the call of the night bird, but at the startled jump Robert made when the curlew's call frightened him. He could see Maureen's small teeth against the shadows of her face.

"You didn't see him? He was just next to us. I tell you something, Robert. You want to see a thing at night, you don't look at it. You look next to it and you will see it. You have your daytime eyes and you have your nighttime eyes. Your daytime eyes look straight at a thing to see it. Your nighttime eyes look next to it to see it. You see that clump over there?"

He saw her raise her arm and point to a large shadowy mass just across the tracks.

"Look straight at it," she told him. He did, and still could see only a mass of shadows.

"Now look next to it. The side of it and the top and the bottom."

He did as she said and his face broke into a wide grin. The moment he looked at a point near the clump, instead of directly at it, he could see it clearly, at the edge of his vision. It was a wide ring of spinifex grass, more than six feet across. As Robert looked around its outline, the details of its stiff grassy stalks became clear in the darkness.

Many years later, far from that remote desert, Robert would recall that night as his second birth. By then he no longer defined Maureen physically, as a fat middle-aged Aboriginal woman with splayed bare feet and a soggy wad of bush tobacco rolling permanently on the corner of her lip. Instead he learned to see her—as she taught him to see in the dark—with different eyes, as a powerful and benevolent descendant of the mighty entities of the Tjukurpa. By then, he saw only a glorious and wise woman, whose strength reached from deep within the land to the outer reaches of the great dreamings.

"We will sleep there tonight," she said, pointing toward the small shed. He thought she meant they would stay inside it, but instead, she crossed the line and sat down on the leeward side of it, and began scooping a shallow hole in the sand, about eight inches across. Then she reached around her for bits of dried spinifex and laid it in the hole.

"Get me some of that dead mulga there," she commanded, pointing to some brittle branches lying a few yards away.

"Are you going to rub two sticks together?" Robert asked. The dry branches he fetched were thin and snapped easily into twigs. He was excited by the idea as he watched her place a dozen pieces of the mulga kindling on top of the grass.

"I'm going to rub one stick together," she said slyly, reaching into her pocket and taking out a small box of wooden matches. She struck a flame and held it to the spinifex. It flared briskly, and she blew on it gently, raising it into a small blaze that crackled up through the mulga twigs.

"Piranypa always make their fires too big," she said. "They waste all the wood and heat. This fire is all you need. Keep warm, big enough to cook a goanna. No waste."

She lay on the ground beside the fire.

"Where are we?"

"We are in Kuniya's country. This is my country. Kuniya is the Python Dreaming spirit, a big powerful spirit. She is my dreaming spirit. Bigger than that train. She came here from Uluru in the Tjukurpa." Her voice carried a tone of warning. "And near here is where she made her dreaming track back to Uluru to have her babies. She left here joyful that she had so many eggs. She wanted to give birth to them at Uluru, because that was where her dreaming began. The place of a baby's birth makes its country and its totem, and Uluru is the most powerful place of all. That is where Kuniya wanted her babies to be born. But a terrible thing was about to happen to Kuniya." She paused, and saw Robert's eyes widen in the firelight.

"What? What happened? Tell me."

Maureen chuckled and made herself comfortable on the ground, folding an arm under her head.

"Tomorrow."

"Maureen! What happened to her?"

"I will tell you tomorrow."

He imagined Kuniya, the giant python, so happy with all her unborn babies, beginning her journey home. He wanted to know the terrible thing waiting for her and her children. Was it still there, out in the night?

"Tell me now," he blurted. "Please."

"I cannot tell you tonight what happened. To learn the story, we must follow Kuniya's dreaming track. It will tell us what happened to her and to all her children."

Robert looked forlornly into the fire. Maureen knew it was not because he was thinking of Kuniya and the doom that threatened her and her children.

"You miss your Piranypa mother," she said.

He nodded.

"And your Piranypa father?"

He nodded again.

"I know it is hard for you, Robert." She patted her lap. "Come here, eh."

He shook his head angrily and stared into the fire. He suddenly resented Maureen. He wanted to blame her—not the Kalaya man he had followed to the train, not his own instincts—for separating him from Heinrich and Giselle. He didn't question the strange way her path intersected with his. It seemed to happen so naturally that he didn't consider it.

Maureen watched him silently. He stared into the fire, with his bottom lip pushed out and tears welling in his eyes. He was annoyed at himself: boys his age didn't cry. But with the night wrapped around them, and the sound of the train gone, he was aware of how isolated their long journey had made them. The fire had destroyed his night vision and he could hardly see the railway tracks behind him anymore.

They had traveled nearly eight hundred miles north from Adelaide. The steel tracks were his last connection with the only home he could remember: family, love, friends, school, his bed. All of them had disappeared into the darkness. He felt desolate and afraid.

"When Wanampi made the spirits at Uluru and sent them out on their dreaming, she cried because she was lonely again," Maureen said. She looked into the fire, but she could see him, lit by its glow, in the corner of her eyes. "She cried because she was so lonely." She smiled at him gently. "You will go back to your Piṟanypa family, Robert."

He felt relief flood through him, but he kept staring grimly at the fire, his mouth pouting and his eyes glistening.

"Tomorrow," Maureen said, "we follow Kuniya's dreaming, back to where she came from. It will take us home, Robert. To Uluṟu."

She patted her thighs. He came over to her and sat on her lap. She rocked slowly, talking into his hair.

"You are here to come back to your people. Your Wirruṉtjatjara people. You are Wirruṉtjatjara. That is who you are."

He let her rock him until he grew sleepy. Then she lay on the ground and he snuggled with his back to her round belly, feeling the security of her bulk behind him and the warmth of the small fire in front. White ash peeled off the glowing mulga coals and fell onto the sand. He fell asleep listening to the night birds out on the plain, and insects and a small lizard rustling through the maze of stiff grass stalks in the spinifex.

He was woken twice by the faraway howl of a dingo, but each time he felt Maureen's hand on his shoulder, and he fell back to sleep.

Along the edge of the desert, dawn slipped into the darkness with a change in the bird calls. The night birds moved back into their nests and shelters and the day feeders began waking with the first pink light in the east. The new calls were clear musical notes in the dark air, floating gracefully across the surface as the earliest risers flew out for food.

Robert saw the Kaḻaya man turn and walk swiftly off to the west, then he woke up. He felt the cold breeze that blew up ahead of the rising sun, and nestled closer to Maureen. It seemed to grow darker just before first light, then in a few minutes, the sounds and images changed. He felt her stir behind him and sit up. She casually scooped a handful of sand over the coals.

"Got to get some tucker," she said. "You hungry?"

He rubbed his face and nodded.

"You want a drink?"

He nodded again, looking at the water bag. He thought she would offer it to him, but instead, she picked it up and ambled toward the west, away from the railway tracks. He followed her, feeling the coldness of the air now, and seeing the sky begin to light softly in the east.

He looked back once and saw the silhouette of the little railway shed. He saw a flash of faint light off the steel of the tracks. Robert watched the lines thoughtfully, then he turned away from them and walked quickly to catch up to Maureen. When he glanced back again, the shed and rails had disappeared.

The sun was still below the horizon, but already he could see far out over the plain in the soft, clean light that was moving onto the desert.

She stood motionless, waiting for him.

"What do you see?" she asked.

He looked around him.

"Sand. Spinifex. Birds."

"What do you see?"

He didn't know what she wanted, but craned his neck, to show he was looking.

"Be still," she said quietly. "Let the country show you."

He stood still, letting his body relax the way hers did. They stood that way for some time, and as they had the night before, sounds and images began to emerge separately on the desert floor. The sun was clearing the horizon, and their long soft shadows stretched over the land. The ground was hard, with loose red sand sliding over it and there seemed to be no trees anywhere. Instead, there were mulga bushes, some low to the ground, some higher than a man, each with dozens of slender black stems spreading up from a narrow, knotted base, with thin green hardy leaves and bright yellow flowers.

"Look. Listen," Maureen said. She pointed at a brown wedge-tailed eagle circling nearly five hundred feet above them.

"He is looking for snakes. Lizards. Hopping mice. Small birds." She pointed to a variety of birds that had been out foraging since first light. Things seemed to materialize in front of Robert as she pointed out each new animal. She explained the different ways they moved, from the circling glide of the patrolling eagle, to the squalling rush of a small flock of wild pink galahs, filling the air with their screeches and beating gray wings.

"See where the galahs come from?" Maureen asked him. "Don't see where they go. See where they come from." She pointed to the northwest and set off in that direction. "They sleep near water. They show us where water is."

She walked with a relaxed, slouching gait, expending the least amount of energy necessary to carry her across the sand. Robert fell into step beside her.

"You walk too hard," she told him. "You make too much work." She carried the water bag by its canvas handle. It was nearly empty. "Walk more easy."

He tried to understand what she meant, and watched her moving beside him, until he felt his shoulders settling and his arms swinging through smaller arcs.

They walked in silence for more than a mile and a half. A pair of small green mulga parrots burst from the scrub with a flurry of wings, and flew off to the north. Maureen froze and listened. Robert stopped beside her. She tipped her head to one side, with her mouth slightly open. Robert tilted his head and opened his mouth: the sounds seemed clearer, and easier to detect. He closed his mouth. The sounds faded. He opened it again, and felt the same kind of excitement as when Maureen showed him how to see at night.

Three tiny willie wagtails fluttered busily along the ground near them. Robert heard their calls clearly, sounding like "sweet pretty creature" in English.

"They are Tjintirtjintirpa," Maureen said, indicating the little black and white birds. "Little gossipers those ones. They listen to some people, then they fly over and tell some other people. Their dreaming place is at Uluru." She began walking again, and Robert stayed beside her, imitating her slouch and gait, but walking faster to keep pace.

"Where is Uluru?"

"That way," she said, pointing to the west. "Where the Kalaya man told you in your dreaming. It is a properly long way from here. Place of big spirits. That is where you come from. Where you were born. It is your country. That is where you will find your totem."

The three willie wagtails were feeding on insects that jumped in small arcs from the sand. When people sat on the ground, as they did in camps, they disturbed the insects, attracting the wagtails. When another group of people sat nearby, they startled new insects, and the wagtails flew over to eat them. Anangu were accustomed to the wagtails' movement from one group of humans to another, and accused the little birds of spreading rumors. If there were no people around, the wagtails flew low to the ground and flushed insects out with their wing beats.

Maureen stopped abruptly and began clapping her hands. Robert looked at her in surprise.

"Wai, Wanampi!" she said. "'Wai' is 'hello there!' We have to tell her we are coming. I told you last night. Sometimes Wanampi stays in the water holes. She guards them. You come up to a water hole, you have to warn Wanampi you are coming. Show respect for her." She emphasized her words with loud clapping.

Robert began clapping his hands. The childlike smack of his palms countered the sturdy slap of Maureen's, as he peered cautiously ahead.

"Good," Maureen said. "You tell her we are coming."

They approached the clump of mulga, clapping and calling out.

"Wai, Wanampi!" Robert shouted. "Here we are!" Calling out to the Rainbow Serpent made her spirit real and alive. When he prayed to God, as Heinrich and Giselle taught him, he had no sense of the entity, but as he shouted and clapped his hands now with Maureen, he became certain that Wanampi was there. He expected to see her rearing up from the mulga, towering above them, filling the sky with her tears and rainbow light.

Robert realized that Maureen had found water, but he couldn't see it. Then they climbed a small rise and behind it he saw a dry, narrow gully, glutted with sand.

"This is where Kuniya came through," Maureen said as she pointed at the gully's curving slash across the desert.

There were small animal tracks running into it. Robert recognized bird prints like those he and his mates found along the creek near home—the Erhards' home. He felt a pang of sadness when he thought of it. He bent over with his hands on his knees and looked at the patch of ground Maureen was pointing to.

"What do you see, Robert?"

"That's a bird."

She nodded, unimpressed.

"I don't know," he admitted.

She pointed to scuff marks on the sand behind each small pair of trident-shaped claw prints. "His tail feathers make that mark," she said. "He lands on the ground and he goes up and down like this." She made a bobbing motion with her upper body, imitating a Richard's pipit, a small beige-colored bird. "He came in here to drink."

She led him along the sandy floor of the gully to a solitary river red gum, which she called apara. Its white-barked trunk was twisted and stunted. At the base of the gum, where its scarred roots met the gully bed, animal tracks converged on a large puddle of water in the sand.

Robert saw only a bewildering a maze of paw and claw prints, but Maureen patiently pointed out each animal spoor. She described dozens of birds, their tracks all trident-shaped, save for the in-turned toes of the pigeons, and the curved Xs of the parrots. Under Maureen's gentle urging, he began to distinguish the elongated toes and small outer toes of a family of kangaroos, and on top of them, having arrived to drink much later, the squat pug marks of two dingoes.

"You see the heel pad and the four toe pads on each foot? That fellow is a dingo. We call him Papa."

Robert grinned, and Maureen looked at him keenly until he explained.

"Papa is Piṟanypa for father."

"Here," she replied sternly, "it is dingo. He is also called Tjiṯutja." Robert fell silent. "See, this fellow is bigger than that one," Maureen continued, pointing to the two sets of dog tracks. "This small one is the bitch, I think. And this," she added slyly, "is papa Papa."

Robert beamed at her and studiously examined the ground.

"You heard them last night. They mostly go in packs." She held up the fingers of both hands. "But this is breeding season. This old fellow brings his girlfriend here."

The idea of the tracks having a romantic story made them more significant, more personal. The desert was becoming alive and vivid around him: no longer a daunting wilderness.

"And this fellow here is probably your old friend from last night. The one you frightened off." She was leaning over the spoor of a goanna.

The sun was above the horizon now, and the air was rapidly warming. Robert looked at the brown water in the soak beneath the gum tree. He couldn't imagine drinking from it.

Maureen gestured for him to follow her a few yards up the gully. There, she dropped to her knees and began scooping out a hole in the sand. All her movements were economical, using the least energy needed to dig. After a few minutes, she stopped and motioned to him.

"You do it."

Robert obediently knelt on the other side of the small hole and began scooping. He was beginning to sweat by the time he had dug a foot down.

"Don't dig hard, Robert. You waste your water. Dig easy."

He dug more slowly, falling into a rhythm. As he approached a depth of two feet he was beginning to lean farther into the hole, until his head rested on the sand on the other side when he reached down to scoop more out. He widened the hole, moving more sedately now, making the sides slope gently down so the sand wouldn't cave in. At two feet, he had to sit down in the hole to reach the bottom, with his feet braced against the other side. A few inches more and he was raising out handfuls of cool sand that slopped water. At two and a half feet, a small puddle of clear water formed.

"Good," Maureen said, peering down at the hole. "Drink some water."

He dipped his head in respect. "You drink before me."

"No," she said, approving. "You dug it."

He had to lie on his belly with his head down in the hole. The air inside smelled of clean wet sand. He blew on the puddle to clear the film of floating particles, then sipped sweet water. Maureen watched him silently, with his head deep inside the cavity he had made in Kuniya's dreaming track. He had the sign of the Piṟanypa big smoke all over him: it was not just his clothes, it was in his habits, and his blindness and deafness to the Tjukurpa. But he was a ready student, and as he lay inside Kuniya's ground, suckling her water, Maureen could see the scales of his other world shedding, exposing the unformed Aṉangu boy inside.

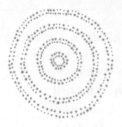

CHAPTER 10

MAUREEN AND ROBERT WALKED in the morning and late afternoon, resting through midday in the shade of mulga and desert oaks. For three days, they followed Kuniya's dreaming track, due west. Each new landmark they passed was a mnemonic for a library of stories in Kuniya's songline, containing directions for finding food and water, and warnings about rituals to be observed and dangers to be avoided. From the time she was a little girl, Maureen was brought along this creation track, learning first the most elementary stories, the children's tales, reciting them until she proved to the elder women who brought her that she could recall every word in the correct order, with the proper information and knowledge stored in it. As she grew older, and retraced again and again the journey with the elder Kuniya Dreaming women, she was given more stories in greater detail, proving on each initiation passage her responsibility and readiness to learn, to hold in safe trust far more than the children's tales of the track. She had become a guardian of all the secret women's business conducted along it; a story keeper of the Kuniya Dreaming.

When she saw each landmark, from a curve in a creek bed to a boulder split in a certain way, Maureen remembered its associated creation tale, and the journey on which she had learned it. The stories she passed on to Robert were only the most basic children's tales, but they were enough to begin his education in survival and respect.

Maureen showed him how to drink nectar-sweet water from the large yellow flower pods of honey grevilleas; how to break edible seeds out of the flat pods lying beneath mulga; and how to dig for protein-rich witchetty grubs tunneling inside the roots of ilkuwara bushes. The grubs were soft white moth larvae, the size of a man's middle finger, and—raw or lightly roasted on fire-heated sand—tasted like the yolks of fresh bird's eggs. With each new lesson, Robert saw the desert change from a barren, lifeless wilderness to a versatile storehouse of food and water.

"Some things you must not take or kill or eat," Maureen told him. "My dreaming is Kuniya, the Python Dreaming spirit. I will never kill or eat python."

The desert assumed another series of laminations too, as he began to learn the songs and taboos that governed his people's existence.

Robert became the keeper of the fire.

Throughout each night, he woke to feed it dry branches. Maureen taught him to look for kurkara, the desert oak. Its wood was rich with resin and made the best firesticks. Before they set off each morning, he stripped a kurkara branch, and ignited the tip, before covering their abandoned fire with sand. He swung the firestick with the rhythm of his walking, to keep the glowing end of it burning with a faint hissing, as the resin fed the flame.

On the third day of their crossing, before it became too hot, they chased a yellow sand goanna up a tree and killed it with rocks. The lizard was about three feet long, with plump shoulders and legs. Maureen buried it in cool sand, in the shade of a mulga, while they napped through the midday heat. When they set off in the afternoon, she drove a small stake through a palm of the goanna's forepaw, and used its protruding ends like a handle to carry the carcass.

She set an easy pace, unfolding the song of Kuniya's dreaming track, so instead of being aware of distance, Robert saw their journey as the stages of a long, epic story.

Late in the day, they came to the road that ran from Adelaide, up through Alice Springs, to Darwin on the northern coast. The road was one lane wide and sealed with bitumen. After three days of walking across open desert, it appeared to Robert like an obscene invader, slicing straight across Kuniya's dreaming track. On the other side of the road was a lone and dilapidated wooden building and two fuel pumps. A weathered Ampol Petrol sign hung above the pumps, and another rusting green sign near the door advertised an Adelaide beer, Emu Lager. There were no other buildings in any direction for another eighty miles. They had reached Erldunda, the turnoff to Ayers Rock, Uluru. In three days, they had trekked nearly seventy-five miles.

"We will wait here," Maureen said. "Someone will be coming."

She sat beneath a tree, casually reaching for kindling on the ground. Robert scooped a small hole in the dirt and set the wood, then slid his fire-stick into it. Maureen watched Robert kneeling over it, nursing its coal into flames, while she rolled her bush tobacco around the corner of her lip with quiet satisfaction. They rested while the fire blazed, then slowly burned down to glowing coals. Maureen pinched the skin around the goanna's anus between her thumb and forefinger, kneading it out, until its rectum and bowel began to turn inside out, and hang down behind it. She pinched it off, and discarded its waste. The goanna lay with its insides cleaned, but with no incisions or cuts in its hide. Maureen lay it next to the fire and used a stick to scoop a layer of scalding sand and coals over it. As the big lizard began to cook, she tested Robert.

He tried to concentrate, but his mouth watered with the aroma of baking meat and fat, spattering and bubbling beneath the hot earth. When the goanna was cooked, Maureen used her stone flake to carve it according to custom, saving the best organs and pockets of fat for herself, and giving Robert portions of meat from the tail and legs. While they ate, she continued to question him and nodded approval as he provided each answer.

He is a good learner, this one, she thought. *He needs to be. He will need to be properly prepared when the men come for him.*

They came before dawn, driving a battered Holden utility that grumbled and clattered over the gravel and brought Maureen and Robert awake with a start. He huddled into her as they watched the headlights swing off the road toward them. The tires made loud popping sounds over the stones. The car stopped and the headlights went off. Springs creaked, doors slammed. Four men climbed out of the vehicle, along with three pureblood dingoes. The men loomed into the firelight. They were Anangu, with very black skin, and wearing an assortment of old shirts and trousers. One had on low-cut elastic-sided riding boots without socks. The others were barefoot. The driver was a large man, muscular, barely thirty. Robert felt something deeply wild and unsettling about them. They had a sense of purpose he had never seen in city Aborigines down in Adelaide. One of the dingoes came over and looked at him with an acutely intelligent expression. Robert held its gaze, and it stared steadily back at him. Then it craned up and licked Robert's mouth and nose, and turned and trotted away. The driver stood watching the boy and the woman, while the other men took a freshly killed kangaroo out of the back of the vehicle and walked off a short distance to make their own camp.

The driver came around the fire and towered in front of Robert, noting that the boy looked him directly in the eye, before dropping his gaze. The child smelled and looked of Piṟanypa.

«Does he speak our language, Kuniya?» he asked Maureen in Wirruṉtjat-jara, keeping his eyes on Robert.

«No, Maḻu,» she answered. «But he is ready to learn.»

«Does he know who I am?»

«No, Maḻu. He only knows a Kaḻaya dreaming man brought him here.»

«What do they call him?» Maḻu asked.

«His Piṟanypa name is Robert.»

Robert's eyes sharpened when he heard his name. They widened when the big Aṉangu man crouched in front of him, but Robert stood his ground. The man had a pungent smell that was not unpleasant. Nevertheless, Robert felt afraid when the man looked at him. He didn't notice Maureen walking off into the darkness.

«Do you know who I am, boy?» Maḻu asked him in Wirruṉtjatjara.

Robert couldn't speak. The three other men materialized around him. One carried a eucalyptus branch, and threw it on the small fire, making it smoke thickly. The four men waited. Robert cleared his throat and tried again.

"Wai," Robert responded as Maureen had taught him: *Greetings. You are well?* "Nyuntu palya?"

The men smiled, one of them laughed softly, and Robert felt his fear ebb away.

«I am well,» Maḻu replied with the Wirruṉtjatjara word "palya," then asked, «You speak your people's language?»

Robert looked blank, unable to understand the question. He looked around for Maureen, but she had disappeared.

«You'll have to learn quickly, then,» the man said, then continued in English, "I am Maḻu, of the Red Kangaroo Dreaming. Your mother's brother.»

Robert stared at him. A blood relative!

"Malu," Robert said, his voice small.

The men stood silently, watching the firelight play across the small boy.

"When a baby is born," Malu said, his voice low, "its mother and father know its birth dreaming. His birth dreaming is the name he will be known by. He is shown to his people and they say his name for the first time. When you were born, you were taken away. Now the Kalaya dreaming man has brought you back, and we will say your name for the first time. Your birth dreaming is Tjilkamata, the Spiny Anteater Dreaming. You are Tjilkamata."

Robert felt himself crossing a barrier.

"Tjilkamata," Robert said, testing the feel of it on his tongue and palate.

"Tjilkamata," Malu repeated, and nodded. "Palya."

"Tjilkamata," Robert said.

"That is your birth name," Malu said.

"Who is Tjilkamata?" Robert asked.

"The spiny anteater," Malu answered, describing the Australian echidna which looks like a small porcupine. "Tjilkamata is a Story Keeper. A powerful dreaming spirit. You will learn about him."

Robert felt excited and fearful at the same time, but he remained silent. Malu placed his hands on the boy's shoulders and bent down close to his face. He reached out and scooped smoke around Robert with his hands.

"Wai, Tjilkamata of the Spiny Anteater Dreaming. I am Malu."

Robert responded, "Wai, Malu."

Malu guided him to the man on his right. Great hands fell gently on his head and shoulders, and scooped smoke around him.

"Wai, Tjilkamata, I am Lungkata of the Blue-Tongued Lizard Dreaming."

"Wai, Lungkata," Robert replied, and was passed to the next elder, until he had circled the fire three times, purified by smoke, and introduced by touch and word to his four relatives and guides. When he returned to his uncle for the third time, he stopped. Lungkata took the eucalyptus branch from the fire.

"When we tell you something," Malu said, "you tell no one else. It is men's business. No women, no other boys. You understand?"

"Yes, Malu," Robert replied.

The men turned to leave for their own camp. Robert saw Maureen emerge from the darkness.

"Learn well, Tjilkamata," Malu said, with a parting order. "You stay with Kuniya. She is your father's sister. Listen to all she tells you."

"We're organizing a manhunt," the police sergeant said, pleased with himself for making it happen so quickly.

"No!" Heinrich was appalled.

The sergeant was expecting gratitude, praise. He blinked. "We're mobilizing men from Adelaide to Alice Springs. The mounted boys are going to help in the desert. Horses, camels, the lot."

"No," Giselle said, watching her husband face the policeman across her kitchen table. "We're very grateful, Sergeant, but no. No manhunt."

"If they've taken him, Mrs. Erhard, it's kidnapping. We've already lost three weeks."

"A manhunt will traumatize them," Heinrich said. "Their old people remember. They associate manhunts with chains, and shootings, and bodies burned and buried in the desert. The moment they hear of it, they'll disappear. We'll never find him."

"What do you suggest?" the sergeant snapped, unable to conceal his frustration.

"We would like an enormous favor of you," Giselle said quietly, feeling Heinrich's fingers close around her hands.

"Provided it's legal," the sergeant replied, his voice softening.

"Robbie's birth records are sealed," Heinrich said slowly. "The government solicitor who arranged his adoption won't open them without a warrant."

"That's a tall order," the sergeant said looking from Heinrich to Giselle and back.

"It's the only way we can find where he came from." Giselle's voice was pleading.

"We think he's originally from a mission," Heinrich said. "If we knew which one . . ."

" . . . then you could call them and ask if Robbie's come back—" the sergeant said.

"No," Giselle broke in. "He's our son. We would go there and find him."

"I'll go, liebe," Heinrich said gently. "You'll have to stay, in case he comes back."

The sergeant looked steadily at them both, glancing at Heinrich's fingers, gently clasping Giselle's hands.

"I can't promise anything," the sergeant said. "But I'll do what I can."

"That is Atila," Maureen said, pointing to a solitary tabletop mountain, far south of the road. Its sides were dark vertical cliffs, and looked black and menacing in the distance. "It is an evil place. Bad spirits there." Despite the hot air buffeting over them in the back of the utility, Robert felt a shiver through his bones.

The old Holden utility rattled along the dirt road, raising a huge flume of red dust that drifted across the desert. Maureen and Robert sat in the back with two of the men and the three dogs. She had to shout over the noise. Robert watched the sinister shape of Atila slide past them to the south. Halfway down its steep sides, an apron of schist and finely broken rock sloped outward to the ground at a steep angle. Whitefellers call it Mount Connor.

They drove through the day, until Maureen nudged Robert awake. She pointed ahead, and Robert stood up into the wind over the cabin. They were driving into the sun, and he had to shield his eyes to see.

Rising out of the plain far ahead was the small, round-shouldered shape of Uluru. Robert expected to see something striking. But with the sun dropping behind it, it only seemed to be an innocuous rock, barely breaking the monotonous line of the horizon. He was disappointed. He didn't realize they were still thirty miles from it. It disappeared behind waves of red sand dunes, lying in low swells on the desert floor.

Steadily, Uluru loomed larger for another hour, and now it seemed to be filling his mind, as it filled the sky. There was no sudden impact of discovery. But its presence began to dominate Robert's view of the world, as if everything that existed was focused on this place, anchored to the earth by it.

"The great python spirit came to the gagarara, the east part of Uluru, and made a camp at a place called Taputji," Maureen said. Her voice became harsh, ominous. "Then something very bad happened."

Robert listened, but could not take his eyes off the rock. It was growing redder as the sun fell.

"Kuniya was attacked by Liru poison snake men. They wanted to kill her and her babies. She fought them and fought them, all along the south of

Uluru. You can see the holes up the sides of Uluru, where her spears hit. You can see the bodies of the Liru warriors she killed, all turned into boulders. But she could not kill all of them, and they attacked her babies and slaughtered them. Kuniya wept and wept and wept, and where her tears landed, poisonous plants grow now. She came back to her first camp, and went into the ground at a place called Kuniya Piti, where her piti, her wooden dish, is still lying on the ground. Poor Kuniya. She came so far to bring her children here, then she lost them all."

Maureen looked sadly at Robert, then turned to watch the sunset, bathing Uluru the color of blood.

Brother Mark Hansen noticed the first signs near the end of October. They began as a subtle restlessness through the outlying camps, like gentle puffs of breeze lifting flurries of dust, far ahead of a storm. The children responded to the new energy, playing more noisily, laughing louder, scampering through the camps faster, as if they could wear down their growing nervousness. Through nine years at the mission, Mark gradually assumed the spiritual cycles of the Anangu. When he first arrived, the Anangu staff listened politely to his plans for efficiency. They nodded solemnly when he made up work schedules and rosters, and a calendar of projects for the year ahead. Nothing changed. Soon he found himself falling into the rhythms of the desert, rising an hour before dawn and working until late morning, when the temperature became oppressive and everyone found shade and slept until late afternoon, when the heat began to ease. It was the beginning of a slow conversion. Once, he and his colleagues at Cambridge searched for a Grand Unification Theory, to elegantly link all the nuclear and gravitational forces in existence. Their talk of light cones, representing the universal singularity at the instant of creation, moved away from the vocabulary of Big Bang and into the region of Mens Absoluta, absolute intent, meaning the purpose of creation, implying the mind of a creator, the complete overview of existence. Now, at the farthest corner of the planet, on the oldest ground, Mark believed he had found a metaphor for such a unity in the closed cycles of life and death in the Tjukurpa.

He had come to expect this great stirring through the camps toward the end of spring, when the October nights lengthened in the Southern Hemisphere, and men began to drift away from the mission. "Gone walkabout," young Millie would say in Mark's first years at the mission. As he gained their trust, the Anangu revealed to him a little of the nature of "men's business."

From the veranda outside his office, Mark could see the low outline of Ayers Rock on the horizon. He learned that this annual stirring through the Anangu was associated with the Rock. Soon he too was calling it Uluru, with a reverence for the monolith that reflected theirs. As spring rolled into summer, Mark prepared for the change in workload that would come as the Anangu left for Uluru's secret places. It was during such a change in 1959 that he received a message from Pastor Heinrich Erhard, who had arrived at the little fuel station at Erldunda, and was asking to come out to the mission on a matter of urgency. There was no telephone at the mission, and Heinrich had to call the Royal Flying Doctor Service Base in Alice Springs, and have the message relayed to Mark by radio. Mark Hansen agreed. It would take Pastor Erhard more than a day to drive the nearly one hundred and forty miles of hazardous dirt road from Erldunda to Lake Amadeus Mission, enough time for Mark Hansen to learn what he could from the Anangu about Pastor Erhard's request.

The first three weeks Robert spent with Maureen and the Wirruntjatjara were among the happiest he would ever recall. The community of little more than fifty men, women, and children was spread through three camps, along a dry creek line. Robert lived with Maureen in the family camp. There were no buildings, only a few wiltjas—lean-to shelters made of mulga branches—scattered through stands of river red gums. He slept with Maureen, between their sleeping fire and a yuu, a small windbreak Maureen made from stacked mulga.

The adults addressed Robert as Tjilkamata, and the children copied them. When he was alone, Robert practiced the sound of it, rolling his tongue over the l, learning the feel of it. It gave him a profound sense of belonging. Steadily, he began to learn to speak Wirruntjatjara. Occasionally a man or woman would come up to him and say something on the order of, «Tjilkamata, I am your father's wife's sister» or «I am your father's brother's wife's brother,» specifying their relationship. He could not recall his Anangu parents. He remembered only the Kalaya man of his dream, leading him across the red plain.

Like all the children, he lived naked. Maureen had rolled his clothes into a bundle and stowed them in a wiltja. The weather was mild and growing warmer, and Robert no longer thought about wearing them. Maureen—like all the women—lived naked, save for her waist string and pubic tassels. Robert had Maureen all to himself. Her husband was a stockman on a cattle station northwest of Alice Springs. Their two sons were seventeen and eighteen, initiated but not yet old enough to take wives, and so had to live and sleep in the men's camp. It was located farther down the creek line from the family camp. It was a place of mystery and fear, and was forbidden to women and children. Lately, all the husbands had begun moving out of the family camp to the men's compound. Through the night, distant catches of chanting and click sticks could be heard, far out on the desert.

With the men away from the family camp, the women were noticeably more relaxed. Dinner was a communal event. On this night, there was good meat, kuka. The women had chased a perentie lizard they called ngintaka up a gum tree earlier in the day, and stoned it to death. They gutted it, curled it into a circle, and covered it with baking sand from the fire. They were joined by marriageable girls from the women's camp, segregated far away from the family and men's camps. After dinner, the girls and their chaperones would return to their seclusion, but now they sat around the fire with the other women, talking and laughing as they prepared the food. There were curved half cylinders of bark containing grass roots and yams and fat witchetty grubs gathered during the day. Someone had collected more than a dozen bird's eggs, delicate, dirty white, and speckled with navy blue dots. Another gathered dozens of honey ants, twisted off their bitter heads, and served the sweet bodies in the thick carved half-shell of an emu egg, black-green on the outside and the size of a man's two cupped hands. Others had cooked delicious flat, round cakes made from wungunu grass seed flour, hand milled between two grinding stones.

Occasionally an unweaned child would toddle up to its mother, suckle at her breasts, then wander off again to play. The meal was punctuated by gales of laughter. There were good-natured arguments over the best parts of the big lizard, with the choice pockets of rib fat and delicacies from the tail and legs going to the senior female elders, including Maureen. In Wirruntjatjara, Robert now addressed her as Kuniya. She continued to teach him day and night, but he sensed there were important things she was withholding.

The women shared a joyful affection for each other and their children.

But though the children returned their love, even the youngest soon discovered that women had little standing among the men: the camp dogs were treated as more valuable utilities. After dinner, the women sang and told stories, sitting in a circle around the fire, tapping intricate rhythms on click sticks to their high-throated chanting. Perhaps because he had not been conditioned since birth to disregard them, Robert was fascinated by the women and their tales. In their stories of intrigue and death, he heard secrets of survival and life. He sensed these women, especially Maureen, knew far more than they shared with the men.

At first sight, the children seemed to belong to everyone. They tumbled out onto the plain in the morning with the women, looking for mirga—the grass seeds and roots and wild pods and small fruit that provided the community's vegetables. It was time-consuming work. It took three women three hours to gather less than five pounds of seeds for flour. It took them another two hours to grind the seeds on their flour stones, winnow off the husks, and bake them in small flat cakes on the hot sand of a fire hole, from which the coals had been scooped away. The women moved slowly across the country, rarely walking more than a mile from the camp, always watchful for food. They were able to read the smallest details of plant and animal life and climate as they foraged. Processions of tiny ants told them about the location of water, certain flowers, coming drought or rain. Thin cracks in the red dirt beneath yellow-flowering ilkuwara showed them where to dig for succulent maku, witchetty grubs. The women conserved their energy, instinctively rationing it, so the food they prepared always provided more calories than they expended gathering it. Many of the women were nursing infants, often carrying their baby on one hip and their digging sticks and piti on the other. The piti were oval wooden bowls, curved up at the sides to form open-ended dishes. The women used them to winnow seeds and carry food.

The children's games seemed endless. When Maureen brought Robert into the camp, he was welcomed with the characteristic warmth and generosity of the Anangu. The children were already aware of his place in the complex web of relationships that governed them all, but they remained wary of this new outsider, testing him the way their counterparts around the world put all new arrivals on trial.

Malu made Robert two short spears from mulga wood, straightened and hardened over coals, and also gave him a small throwing club, called a tjutin, and a spear launcher, called a miru, both carved from roots, using sharpened stone slivers.

«Next time, Tjilkamata,» Malu said, «you will make your own.»

The boys showed Robert their own practice spears, and some disks made of bark. The aim was to roll the disk along the ground and spear it before it stopped moving. Robert learned the subtle differences between both his spears as he threw them at the rolling bark targets.

Once a boy mastered the art of throwing a spear by hand, he learned to use his miru, the spear launcher. It was flat and narrow, the length of the elbow to the fingertips. It had a dull barb of wood bound to one end of it that notched into the base of the spear, which then lay along the length of the miru. The other end of the miru was carved to fit the hand, and the thrower gripped this part and the haft of the spear together to make his launch. The spearman extended the miru and notched spear at full length behind him and hurled it forward, holding on to the miru and releasing the spear at the instant of maximum power. It was difficult to master, and ungainly to use, but in the hands of a skilled and accurate spearman, the miru provided lethal additional range and power. In a perfect launch, the miru's barb, notched into the base of the spear, described a pure arc in the air, and the missile departed from the launcher on a tangent that set its trajectory straight to the target. Like the smooth aerodynamic curves on the aerofoil arms of a kali, which Piranypa call a boomerang, the miru carved a locus of form and technological perfection that would dominate the age of aviation and space travel, tens of thousands of years after its first use by Aborigines at the beginning of the Tjukurpa.

Robert learned the new skills swiftly until he rarely missed a target.

From first light, the boys tracked animal spoor over the hard ground, chattering and laughing about which creature had been this way, and where it was going. They played the way Robert and his friends used to, racing through the bush after school, except that here in the desert, every game honed the skills of survival.

When the women left early to pick food, the men moved out to hunt for meat, kuka. During the seasons of men's business, they took with them boys who had begun their rituals and trials of manhood. When the men came back into camp with freshly killed kuka, the boys imitated the way they carried their big hunting spears and miru, affecting the same casual ease with their own practice weapons.

Maureen and the women made kiṯi, the sticky black resin that oozed from the roots of spinifex plants when they were warmed over a fire. They gathered the kiṯi on the end of a short stick, until it formed a fat black ball, sometimes half the size of their fists. They used it as an all-purpose glue. It could be heated to caulk cracks in wooden dishes and implements. It was used to secure stone axes and blades to their handles, and to cement sharpened stone flake points and wooden barbs into the heads of hunting spears. Every man and woman carried their own kiṯi, and Robert and the boys copied them.

One of the first children Robert met, when he arrived in the camp, was the only son of Maḻu. Their first encounter petrified Robert. He was playing near Maureen early in the morning when he looked up and saw Maḻu standing over him with a boy about Robert's age next to him. Robert began to smile in greeting when he saw Maḻu, but in the same instant he felt his skin go cold. When Robert looked into the boy's face, he saw the eyes of a terrifying old man. Robert's mouth opened, then closed again. He tore his eyes away, lowering them, and felt a second shock. The boy's right foot was cruelly deformed, clubbed inward, but he betrayed no sense of self-consciousness about it. Instead he maintained his silent, terrible gaze on Robert, as if he could see far inside him, into dark places no mortal dared travel.

"This is Walkalpa," Maḻu said. "My son. The son of your mother's brother."

"Wai, Walkalpa," Robert said, his voice quavering. "Nyuntu palya?"

"Palya, Tjiḻkamaṯa," Walkalpa said. And for the first time, he smiled, a quiet conspiratorial smile, warm, with no trace of terror in it, and welcoming, as if he had been waiting for Robert.

"Walkalpa is of the Emu Poison Bush Dreaming," Maḻu said. "Now, you both go and play."

Robert became fast friends with Walkalpa. They may have been drawn to each other by a sense of being outcast, or by their blood relationship, but they swiftly discovered each balanced the other's limitations with his own strengths. Where Robert was lithe and fast, Walkalpa had remarkably good eyesight and powerful intuition, but when his gaze grew intensely focused and penetrating, children shrank away in fear. In time, Robert's initial shock was replaced by a deep respect for Walkalpa's obvious powers, and the beginning of a lasting friendship. He helped Walkalpa practice throwing a spear, mimicking the way they saw the men grip, aim, and throw with a smooth roll of the shoulder. He rolled out bark disks as targets, until Walkalpa could hit them three times out of five. And he coached Walkalpa until he could accurately hurl a kali, making it hiss through a long flat curve above the ground and return gracefully to his hands, passing through a designated point in the air that would one day be a targeted bird, or the head of a small animal. In turn, Walkalpa taught Robert to watch and listen, to temper his reflexes with patience and judgment. Walkalpa had an uncanny ability to go still and sense things before they came into view. Robert tried to imitate it, but invariably Walkalpa would point to a place on the plain well before an animal emerged from cover, or before an elder returning from the hunt appeared over a sky-line. It seemed natural for Robert to become Walkalpa's physical protector. It was less obvious that Walkalpa was also teaching Robert more subtle skills of guardianship and custody.

Walkalpa's mother was a skilled string maker. For amusement, the women tied a two-foot length of possum hair string into a circle and manipulated its loops between their fingers to make a mesmerizing array of shapes and out-lines. Walkalpa became adept at forming the loops into the outlines of ani-mals, or of the tracks they made. It was one of the skills Robert could never seem to master.

Together they made a formidable hunting team. Walkalpa could spot a goanna and its ground hole long before Robert did. He blocked the entrance while Robert chased the animal until it ran up a tree or bush. The goanna could easily outpace both boys over a short distance, but Robert could even-tually run it down and spear it or stone it to death.

Robert barely noticed his transition into the world of his blood and spirit. He became immersed in the language and codes of the Wirruntjatjara. The world of the Piranypa seemed to no longer exist. The only clue was an occa-sional glimpse of the battered Holden utility, sitting in the trees beyond the forbidden ground of the men's camp, an alien vehicle from another world.

It was the time when women and older children whispered fearfully about "men's business." At night, they heard loud, mournful moaning across the desert. The women whispered it was the voice of spirits, of monsters who stole young boys away to make them into men.

Throughout the month, strangers began appearing in the camp, all of them Wirruntjatjara men who arrived wearing the clothes of stockmen and station workers, before they disappeared down to the men's camp. At night, with the stars crowding brilliantly overhead, the women and children listened in terror to the monsters moaning and howling out on the desert. They knew the deep groaning voices by the name Wirrun. Their bloodcurdling sounds came through the darkness and petrified the listeners in the family and women's camps. Robert huddled into Maureen, and felt her lying awake and tense behind him, as if she was waiting for something awful. The spirit monsters moaned across the desert for three nights. Robert barely slept.

On the fourth night, they came for him.

The monsters burst in from the darkness, surrounding the slumbering women and children, shouting fiercely and banging their wooden clubs and shields. Their bodies were painted with white clay and red ocher patterns, and covered with feathers, glued to their skin with kiti. The air filled with the screams of women and children. The spirit monsters moved swiftly, seizing boys and hoisting them off the ground. The women wailed and cried, pleading with the spirits to release their children. Some of the boys could barely whimper, others shrieked hysterically. Robert screamed as a monster swept him up with brutal force. He saw Maureen clutching for him, crying his name. He howled, kicking and writhing to escape, but the painted spirit shook him violently, then plunged into the night with him.

Crashing through the darkness, the moaning of the spirits grew louder, frightening off the last of the women who tried to follow. Robert felt branches smack into him, and heard the wails of other boys close by, and the deafening roar of the spirits, booming in from the desert around them, coming closer.

Heinrich made Lake Amadeus Mission in five days of hard driving from Adelaide. Mark Hansen was ready for him. The message Heinrich telephoned from Erldunda to the Royal Flying Doctor Base in Alice Springs was relayed on the ten o'clock "galah session" on the RFDS radio network, along with nearly two dozen other messages to people on remote cattle stations and missions and settlements across the Inland. In 1959, some of the outstations had acquired diesel electric power units, but many others still had their original Traeger pedal radios designed thirty years earlier for the Flying Doctors, with a generator driven by bicycle pedals mounted beneath the operator's chair. The motley assortment of radio transceivers across the Inland reached into the ether and drew together the isolated souls like ghosts gathering for comfort in the heart of the void. The disembodied voices, crackling out of thin air into kitchens and radio rooms, assured their faith in another life beyond their isolation. The radio network spared no one's privacy, and the messages to Mark Hansen and the others became community property the moment they were transmitted, savored by each eavesdropping listener as a touch from a hand, stretched fleetingly across a chasm, then withdrawn again, back to the world outside.

Heinrich arrived at Lake Amadeus Mission at sundown, overwhelmed by the size of the country into which he was convinced his adopted son had disappeared. Mark carried Heinrich's battered leather suitcase along the creaking veranda.

"Any news?" Heinrich asked, when they reached the small guest room, with its enameled iron bed and wash stand, and a low bookcase lined with dusty rows of Everyman paperbacks. An Albert Namatjira watercolor hung above the bed, a scene of ghost gums on sandy ground that ran back to blue-shouldered ranges of red stone.

"We may have something," Mark said cautiously. "But I'm afraid I have to warn you, Heinrich. The news may not be what you want."

"He's dead?"

"No. No. No. If my information is correct, if it is young Robert, he's alive and well. But I'm afraid by the time you see him, you may not know him."

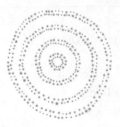

CHAPTER 11

THE SPIRIT MONSTERS RACED through the darkness with the boys over their shoulders. The children grunted and moaned, disoriented, their heads upside down, screaming. A mile from the camp, the runners stopped and dumped the boys on the sand. They lay there, peering up at the ghostly patterns looming above them like creatures from Creation, white-clay totem figures hovering against the stars.

A kick drove Robert to his feet. He heard other boys wailing and being forced up again. The monster shoved him forward. Robert began running, sobbing as he went. He tried to see into the night, the way Maureen had taught him, but everything remained vague dark shapes rushing under his feet. His joints felt weak with fear, and he stumbled and careened into scrub that lashed his face and body.

The boys were fit from their constant ranging over the desert, but terror sapped them and they were soon out of breath. The spirit monsters drove them on. They ran and trotted for more than fifteen miles. Their lungs burned and their feet bled. They ran with their eyes to the ground, trying to see obstacles before they crashed over them. Always, they heard the feet of the monsters pounding behind them, and away to each side, the hidden spirits droning fearfully, like giant dingoes hounding prey.

Then the spirit monsters halted. They had been traveling for almost three hours. The boys instinctively huddled together as their abductors milled around them in the darkness. There seemed to be a dozen or more painted bodies floating in the gloom. The monsters closed into a cordon around them, packing the boys in shoulder to shoulder, frail and small and helpless in the circle of painted giants. Robert counted five other boys. Then the circle opened, and Walkalpa was thrust into the group.

From the moment the spirit monsters had burst in on them, Walkalpa had refused to cry out. He had clenched his mouth tight as his kidnapper carried him like a dead wallaby over his shoulder. When he had been dropped on the ground and forced to run, Walkalpa had closed his ears to the wailing of the boys around him, and strove to keep up with them. Every time he fell, his captor drove him roughly to his feet. He knew his deformed foot was wounded, but he kept running on, with his limping gait. When the pack finally stopped, he had fallen a few hundred yards behind, with his tormentor goading him on. He saw the wall of men part to admit him, for already he realized the spirit monsters were elders, and that their deception was part of the ordeal. The men closed in around him, forcing the boys to walk at a shuffle, unable to see anything now but the painted shapes packed around them. They traveled another two hundred yards like this, smelling the paint and ocher on the men's skin, and other smells, mixed with sweat.

They saw the legs of the men beginning to glow and flicker as if they were moving into flames. Then the wall of bodies parted, revealing a large fire that instantly blinded the boys' night vision. Men threw green bloodwood branches onto the flames, and drove the boys into the dense smoke, guiding them through it three times. The branches were pulled away and the fire sprang into bright flames again. The men forced the boys onto the ground, facing the fire. The children huddled together, wide-eyed, as the unearthly sound of an enormous beast rose from the darkness. Chanting voices joined it, and the beat of throwing sticks clapped together. The song grew louder, and the boys saw a line of intricately painted men move into the firelight, circling around the blaze like a long gaudily patterned snake.

Robert did not feel himself sliding into a trance state induced by the mesmerizing chanting and the rhythm of the click sticks and the terrible moan of the unseen creature beyond the fire. But one by one, all the boys stopped crying, and stared in awe as the dancers replayed the first acts of Creation, and the beginning of the dazzling parade of spirits teeming down the ancient paths of the Tjukurpa.

"I must know what Robbie's facing," Heinrich said firmly. His voice dropped. "I hardly think there's any ordeal he might face that would shock me."

Mark resisted the urge to stare at Heinrich's hands. He cleared his throat. "Was Robert circumcised as a child?"

"No." Heinrich's shoulders dropped. "He was already two months old when he was brought to us." He fell silent for some time.

Mark drank his tea, and waited.

"Is there no way to find him?"

"We could go to the camp in the morning and look for him," Mark said.

"Why not tonight?"

"If they've already taken him away for initiation, we'd never find him. If he is still in the camp, yes, certainly, we could bring him back." Mark paused, examining his hands, then looking silently at Heinrich.

"You're thinking that would be unwise," Heinrich said, his voice very tired, lowering a barrier, letting the words empty from him. "You're right, of course. I've had this conversation with myself many, many times. He's a full-blood. All this sanctimonious preaching about nurture and nature, heredity and environment, is farcical. Robbie is certainly an unusual child. Gifted. Potentially brilliant. But . . . he's still a fullblood. There's still a . . . a rawness, a primitiveness to him. It's not visible. And he's such a gentle child. But I see it. He has no control over it. It's part of him. It is him. And as for the superstitions. I keep an open mind. My ancestors believed in the spirits and ghosts of the Black Forest. It's as if we all have a fundamental hunger to connect ourselves with all the heroes and demons of our mythology. We want to believe we're a part of something larger, older. Durable."

There was a water jug on the table. Mark turned in his chair and fetched a bottle of Bundaberg rum and glasses from the cedar sideboard behind him.

"Until we see God," Mark said quietly, "actually looking back at us from the heart of the abyss, we're all working on blind faith."

"I've known for a long time," Heinrich said as Mark sat down again, "that I would have to let Robbie go, let his nature take its course."

Mark doled out rum and water. They silently raised their glasses to each other and drank. Heinrich put his glass down. He examined his hands.

"Tell me, Mark," he said finally, "what happens."

"The men raid the women's camp at night, and take the boys to the north side of Ayers Rock. The men's side. There's a network of caves there. For several days and nights, they are kept awake with dancing and ceremonies. The boys are told what totem they will be as men. The men give each boy a secret name. They teach him secret words. Men's business. Each boy is assigned his own elder throughout the ceremony, usually the boy's future father-in-law . . ."

Heinrich looked up sharply. He had reconciled himself to accepting Robbie's initiation, but mention of an arranged marriage suddenly projected the chain of events far into the future. He was familiar with betrothal at birth, though a boy would only take up with his wife several years after his initiation into manhood. Until then, he was bound to provide gifts of food and weapons for her family. He became the protector and avenger for his future mother-in-law. Heinrich felt himself drifting away and pulled his mind back to Mark's voice.

" . . . they give them the full treatment. It goes on for several days and nights without a break."

"Sleep deprivation," Heinrich said. "I imagine it creates a hypnotic effect while they're learning the corroborees."

Mark nodded. "The Aborigines knew about it thousands of years before the Chinese started using it on our fellows in Korea. The boys begin to hallucinate. The dances and stories become real."

Heinrich stared at his glass, trying to conceive what Robbie was going through. He imagined the eerie chanting, the sounds of great spirits striding the land, the beat of the click sticks around the fire, and dust lifting from the bare feet of painted dancers, glowing against the flames and mingling with the smoke rising into treetops that seemed alive with firelight and shadows.

"When do they return to the camp?"

"After about eight or nine days. Then they are no longer children. From that time until they take up with their wives, they live in the men's camps. They can visit their mothers and sisters, but they can't touch them, or eat with them. Their mothers provide their food, but can only leave it out for the men to take back to their camp."

"So, the transition from boy to man is irreversible," Heinrich said, trying not to imagine the inevitable cut and the sea of pain that would engulf his nine-year-old son.

"There's no going back," Mark said. "He has left his mother. He is no longer a boy. He must speak a restricted language with a refined vocabulary. Altered forms of speech used only by his initiation brothers and elders. There will be certain words he can no longer use. He will not be allowed to look at or speak to certain members of his community, and he will live now in the men's camp. He will be separated by his transformation, and distinguished by it. But, he will know exactly who he is, and where he came from. He will know his absolute role in the universe. Whatever happens to him after, nothing will ever shake his sense of identity."

The old man addressed Robert. «What is your birth country?»

«Uluṟu is my birth country.»

«What is your birth spirit?»

«Tjiḻkamaṯa is my birth spirit.»

«What is your name?»

«My name is Tjiḻkamaṯa, the Story Keeper. Tjiḻkamaṯa guards the songs, and the beginnings of all the dreaming tracks.»

The old man nodded solemnly. Tjiḻkamaṯa is a powerful spirit and his totem confers great strength and knowledge. But they come with great responsibilities. It is rare for more than one child in a generation to be born to his totem.

«You are the Dreaming Keeper. Our stories are our past and future. Our songs are our life and security. Who is your father, Tjiḻkamaṯa?»

Robert hesitated. His elder had revealed the truth about his father during the three days of ceremonies. The revelation seemed part of the waking dream of spirits and pain that attended his initiation. But now he was fully conscious, his voice trembled when he answered the question.

«My father was of the Emu Dreaming,» he said. «A Kaḻaya Dreaming man.»

The elder understood the boy's turmoil. «The Kaḻaya Dreaming spirit brought you home, Tjiḻkamaṯa,» he said, more gently. «When a boy becomes a man, he is taken on a journey through his country, the country of his fathers and their fathers. You must make this journey. But your dreaming will also take you far from here, beyond your fathers' journeys. Others will go with you on these journeys, and you must learn things you cannot learn here. But Uluṟu will always be your country. You will always come back here. When the Kaḻaya Dreaming spirit calls you, you must listen. You must trust it. Always trust your dreaming, Tjiḻkamaṯa.»

Two weeks later, an old Aboriginal man came to the mission and asked to speak to Mark and Heinrich. He introduced himself as Malu, Robert's uncle. The three men sat on the ground below the veranda and talked through the afternoon and into the night.

In the morning, Mark and Heinrich drove out to the Wirruntjatjara country to collect Robert. They left the car and walked together to the men's camp, and found Malu waiting for them with Robert, who was dressed in the clothes he wore when he ran away from home.

Heinrich had rehearsed his greeting a hundred times in the two weeks of waiting at the mission for word of his son to arrive. Waiting had been torture. He knew he had no alternative but to wait, talking to Mark each night on the starlit veranda. He had radioed a message to Giselle, relayed through Alice Springs, saying he knew all was well, but not over. He remembered the toll that waiting had taken on Giselle during the war, when officers and chaplains came to visit her with sketchy reports about Heinrich, imprisoned by the Japanese somewhere on Singapore Island. She recognized in their kind words and sad eyes that they were hiding something terrible from her, but she was a war wife, and she tried to grasp at the slim hopes they offered her. When she saw what they had done to her husband, she felt she would go mad. They nursed each other back from the war, soothing each other in the long watches of the night when nightmares wracked their sleep and brought them gasping awake in a cloak of sweat. Heinrich did not want his wife to go through that again. He did not think she would see that this ordeal their child was enduring had a purpose, a structure, unlike the malicious violence Heinrich had suffered. He was afraid she would see only scars and agony. So he resolved to protect her, to join the silence of secret men's business. Heinrich forced himself to be patient, to wait for whomever had taken their son, to surrender to their alien rhythms. Now that the time was finally here, the words escaped him.

He smiled at Robert.

"Son."

"G'day, Dad," Robert said, and the English words felt strange on his tongue.

"Hello, Robbie."

Heinrich had brought a dozen five-pound bags of flour, half a dozen Army blankets, an eight-ounce packet of tobacco, a dozen jars of jam. He offered the gifts to Malu, who took them without comment.

"Thank you," Heinrich said, unable to say exactly why he felt such gratitude. For returning his adopted son? For leading the boy along a path that Heinrich was unable to negotiate? For letting him go? They were standing fifty yards from the men's camp. Farther off, they could make out the outlines of the family camp. The men did not see Maureen sitting on the ground there, surrounded by the other women, weeping silently as if her own son was being taken from her.

«May I go now?» Robert said to Malu.

Heinrich stared in silence when he heard his son speaking dialect.

Malu smiled faintly, with a gracious tilt of his head. Heinrich thought he saw quiet pride in the man's eyes, tempered with deep sadness.

«Journey well, Tjilkamata,» Malu said. «Remember your dreaming.»

Robert nodded solemnly, and looked up at Heinrich and Mark.

"I am ready to come back with you," he said to Heinrich.

Heinrich was embarrassed to feel tears stinging his eyes. He blinked hard once. He had too much to ask, and nothing to say. Instead, he nodded slowly toward the two elders, put his hand on Robert's shoulder, and led him to the car.

They drove back to the mission in silence, each weighing and measuring his own thoughts. When they arrived, Heinrich was eager to be off. But as soon as he headed the car down the road from the mission, with Robert sitting quietly in the passenger seat, Heinrich felt cast on a foreign sea. He silently rehearsed things he could say to his son, that would let them resume their relationship where it had so abruptly been suspended more than a month ago. He discarded each one as stilted, and unnatural. He tried to recall the stories he had taught Robert, to look for something in each of them that could mark the beginning of this new relationship. For it felt new, as if he were meeting his son for the first time.

He gripped the steering wheel in exasperation at his own ineptness. This was after all a nine-year-old boy. His boy. Heinrich stopped the car.

"Do you have any pain, Robbie?" he asked gently.

"Not anymore," Robert said, and thought carefully. "But sometimes the memory hurts." He looked across at his father, and Heinrich saw the boy's face transformed by a maturity beyond his years. Robert reached over and rested his small fingers on the brutal scars on Heinrich's hands. "You know what that's like, don't you, Dad."

Their eyes locked for an instant, sharing the language of pain and ordeal, bridging the chasms of age and race and time.

"Ah, son," he said as he held his arms out, and Robert came into them and hugged him. "My son, my son, my son. Yes, I do. I do know."

BOOK III

BIRDS
OF PREY

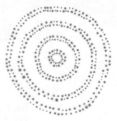

CHAPTER 12

THE CAMERAMAN KNEW this Horstmann woman was deliberately intimidating him. He'd covered wars and riots and the most powerful people in the country. But Agnes Horstmann made him feel like a quaking novice. Ever since she summoned him with his soundman and a makeup lady, and had them flown more than a thousand miles to Alice Springs on a BIRD corporate jet, she'd kept the pressure on them—spiriting them in from the airport in an ambulance, undetected through the gauntlet of reporters and camera crews staking out the hospital, swearing the three of them to secrecy, implying dire consequences beyond their imagination if anyone leaked the truth. The cameraman put his eye to the viewfinder again, and checked focus. In his headphones he heard the network producer, fifteen hundred miles away, counting him down. He cleared his throat, avoided Agnes Horstmann's imperious gaze, heard the producer's cue, then called, "Twenty seconds!"

Agnes Horstmann raked the room with her eyes. Unconsciously, the orthopedic surgeon stepped back a pace, embarrassed by this reaction to her. He felt his shoe sink into two dozen roses lying on the floor. The room was lined with flowers in open boxes and vases, on tables, stools, and chairs, stacked on the carpet, and propped against walls. Two computer workstations stood on a wide work desk, beside a fax machine, four telephones, and Agnes Horstmann's large leather document case. Three nurses stood nearby, surrounded by flowers. Usually, they feared no one except matron and the chief of surgery, but they hugged the wall nevertheless, trying to avoid Agnes

Horstmann's attention. The physiotherapist and her consulting neurologist watched from a prudent distance near the door. A television monitor revealed the national morning program host in her studio in Sydney, and two other screens showed the man in the cameraman's viewfinder.

Owen Bird's head and shoulders were impeccably groomed, from the gray Sulka banker's tie knotted neatly in the collar of a handmade Egyptian cotton shirt, to the beautifully tailored Zegna jacket with a subtle gray pinstripe. His hair and thick mustache were freshly trimmed, and the makeup lady was doing a final pass over his forehead with a powder brush. Owen's image glowed with health and vitality.

"Ten seconds!"

The cameraman saw the makeup lady move out of his shot, and Owen appeared framed in front of a cobalt blue curtain.

"Four," the cameraman called, "three, two." He fell silent for the final seconds, then the morning host in Sydney came out of a commercial break, and introduced a smiling, fiercely confident Owen Bird by asking him how he was.

"Couldn't be better," Owen boomed, turning the soundman's readouts red.

For three minutes he answered her questions earnestly and directly. He was up and active, he assured her, with no ill effects whatsoever from his riding accident, no matter what lies the tabloids on the coast were printing. The only reason he was still in Alice Springs, he said, was because his doctors demanded he stay over for routine observation. "They're just covering their tails," he said wryly, grinning fiercely into the camera. His staff had flown out here with him, to set up a command post at the hospital. He was firmly in the saddle, just look at him, he urged. He'd be out in a day or so, and if stockholders had any niggling doubts after reading the newspapers or listening to gossip, he was here now live and in color, brimming with energy, to set them straight as they ate their breakfasts and faced the day around the country.

"My pleasure," they heard Owen say, when the interviewer thanked and farewelled him.

"We're clear!" the cameraman called.

Agnes Horstmann shot a final warning look around the room, confirmed the red camera light was off, then strode to the hospital bed, where Owen was sagging perceptibly into the pillows stacked behind the blue curtain. He winced, and used his good hand to shift the fiberglass arm cast that protruded from a long slit in the sleeve of his jacket.

He felt cold sweat break over his face, and the makeup woman leaned over to wipe it away. It was an innocent gesture, but in that instant, Owen remembered a freezing night more than half a century earlier, watching his mother wipe sweat away, amid the obscene sounds and smells of violent death.

🦎

Corporal Frank Bird came home a hero from World War I. He'd left his job as a laborer on a wheat property in 1914, more than happy to escape the grueling life of the ax and plow for adventure in the name of God, King, and Country. He returned four years later, a wounded veteran of the bloody hills and beaches of Gallipoli, where the Australian and New Zealand Army Corps established the legend of ANZAC. He was the first soldier to return safely to Doctor's Crossing, and the town of thirteen hundred and fifty-four welcomed him home to its bosom with speeches and bunting and a dinner, and Nellie Trent, the girl he left behind. A photographer was hired to record Nellie in her bridal gown and crocheted Catholic veil, virginal and smiling next to Frank, the epitome of the tall, bronzed ANZAC soldier in his pressed corporal's uniform, his gaze assured in the knowledge he had earned his place of honor in a nation the politicians promised would be a "home for heroes."

Frank had declined a job with his father-in-law as an apprentice at Trent's Butcher Shop, and signed on instead with the state government railway as a fettler, laying and repairing track.

"A man has security with the government," he told Nellie in his ponderous drawl. "Lifetime security." They moved into a three-room cottage, provided as married quarters by the State Railways, near the station.

A year after they were married, their newborn son died in the influenza epidemic of 1919. Nellie was devastated. Frank went down to the local pub and was drunk for two days. He sobered up to the monotony of marriage in a small country town, and the petty tedium of labor on the railways. The steel rails defined his life like the bars of a prison. Nellie mourned her baby's death for nearly a year, and two more years passed before she became pregnant again. The priest at Doctor's Crossing christened the baby Owen Carlisle Bird. Nellie swamped the boy with affection and attention. Frank stayed longer at the pub after work, and frequently came home supported by drunken mates.

That was how he arrived one night when Owen was barely four years old.

Frank staggered into the kitchen looking for his dinner, and found Nellie reading to their son from a children's book of fairy tales.

"Look at the sight of you." She turned her nose up at Frank in disgust. "It's a disgraceful example for the boy."

Owen was sitting on top of two pillows at the kitchen table, running his fingers over the pictures in the book.

"Disgraceful, eh?" Frank bellowed. "By God, he should be grateful I work so hard to feed him. It's a man's right to have a drink at the end of the day."

"Don't blaspheme in front of the boy." Nellie's voice rose. Owen stared at them both in alarm, then burst into tears.

"Ah look," Frank sneered. "We've made him cry. Don't be a bloody sissy!"

Owen wailed louder and lurched off the chair and into his mother's arms. Frank crossed the kitchen in three strides and leaned over the child. "Stop that bawling now, you little sissy, or I'll give you something to bawl about!"

"Don't," Nellie hissed, "you threaten my child!"

"Your child, is he?" Frank's face grew livid. "That'd be bloody right! I know you've turned against me, woman. But you won't turn him!"

Owen clung to her leg and howled. Without thinking about it, Frank slapped him, open-handed across the top of his head. Owen screamed.

"Stop your bloody bawling!" he yelled above the cries of his wife and child. "I'm not raising a bloody girl!"

"Get out!" Nellie shrieked. "Get out of this house! You're a disgrace!"

Frank glared at her, and she thought he was going to hit her too. Instead, he lowered his hand and stepped back.

"You're a real pair, you two," he said, his voice low as he headed for the door. "A real pair of bloody girls."

Frank Bird felt his household sink into a conspiracy against him. Nevertheless, when his vacation came up seven months later, he seemed glad to take them both to Brisbane to visit his brother, on the free rail passes that came with his holiday pay.

"A change'll do us a world of good, old girl," he told her with a warmth Nellie had nearly forgotten. "We might see Smithy land."

Charles Kingsford Smith and his co-pilot, C.T.P. Ulm, and two Americans, navigator H.W. Lyon and radioman Jim Warner, had taken off from Oakland, California, on Wednesday, May 31, 1928, in a Fokker trimotor, Southern Cross, to attempt the first flight across the Pacific. Smithy was more famous south of the Equator than Charles Lindbergh.

Families across America and Australia pored over newspapers and crowded around radios to follow their course, first to Wheeler Field in Honolulu, then far across the Equator to the landing field on Naselai Beach, in Fiji, then down the map on their most hazardous leg into Brisbane. Young Owen had a collection of newspaper photographs of Smithy pasted in a brown paper scrapbook Nellie stitched together. At his uncle's house in Brisbane, he collected every photograph of the plane and crew he could find in the newspaper and magazine accounts of the epic flight, and pasted them in with a homemade glue of flour and water.

"You wouldn't believe it," his aunt said, watching the little boy. "Four years old, and mad about planes."

Radios reported the aircraft bucked and fell four hundred feet in wild turbulence off Fiji. The air was so cold none of the crew could hold a pen to write up the flight log. America and Australia waited breathless for news of their four sons.

June 9, 1928, fell on a Saturday.

At Brisbane's Eagle Farm Aerodrome, police on horseback and foot jostled to keep the crowds back from the grassy runway. Frank Bird and his brother brought their families early. Owen was perched high on Frank's shoulders, when the first shout went up. "I hear it!" "Listen!" Eyes searched the sky. "There they are!" The roar of the crowd drowned the drone of engines as Southern Cross circled the landing field twice, then made her final approach onto the far end of the grassy runway. Smithy lowered her into a smooth, showy three-point landing. The crowd surged toward the plane as it taxied to a stop, surrounded by a cordon of police.

Owen struggled to get down and Frank, irritated by his fidgeting, lifted him off his shoulders. The boy disappeared into a maze of legs, weaving like a terrier through the crowd, dodging through the line of police and darting toward the aircraft. He heard the constables shouting behind him, and a few surprised laughs as the crowd watched him sprint over the grass. Some of them cheered him on. The pilots and crew were ringed by a small welcoming committee.

Owen raced into the group and pulled up in front of the two pilots. He knew Smithy's face as well as his own father's.

"Geez, Smithy," Owen said loudly. "That was beaut!"

Ulm and the surrounding dignitaries laughed and Smithy swung Owen up onto his hip.

"And who are you, young feller?" he said, thinking the boy belonged to one of the VIPs.

"I'm Owen Bird. I'm four years and eleven months old. And I'm going to be a pilot like you." There was a patter of laughter from the VIPs. He felt safe there on the pilot's hip. He felt the worn surface of the sheepskin flying jacket and smelled aviation fuel and oil and sweat, and adventure and security. The pilot put him down and patted his head.

"You'd better find your Mum and Dad, son," he said.

"G'bye, Smithy." Owen looked sad.

"Just a sec, son," the pilot said. He reached into his flying jacket and took out a small leather-bound pilot's log and a fountain pen. He wrote something on a back page and tore it out, and handed it to Owen. The boy watched the blue ink, still wet and glistening on the lined white paper.

"Thanks, Smithy," he said, beaming, unable to read the writing.

"Hooroo, son," the pilot said, waving to him, and turned back to the welcoming party.

That night everyone sat around the table after dinner, poring over the special editions on the landing. The page from Smithy's notebook, with its characteristic one-word signature, was passed reverently from hand to hand and read out loud by each relative, until Owen, who couldn't read, knew the inscription by heart.

"To Owen Bird, Future Pilot, CKingsfordSmith."

"We'll put this in the scrapbook for you, darling," Nellie told him. "It's a piece of history."

For several weeks after they returned to Doctor's Crossing, Frank Bird regaled his mates about how his boy had met Smithy. But like the glory of the war, the novelty faded, and he found himself back in his cycle of boredom, and frustration, and drinking, completely oblivious of how or why he arrived there. Toiling on the railway line, driving spikes in blistering heat, on long lonely lengths of steel spanning horizon to horizon, he felt a bewildering sense of betrayal, of failing dreams, passing like trains, from places he'd never been to destinations beyond his imagination.

Frank Bird came home each night hated and feared by his wife and son. He responded with escalating violence until the night Owen discovered a devastating weapon. Frank had staggered into the house, gripping a tall bottle of beer in a paper bag.

"I hear y'got in a fight today," Frank said amiably. It was Owen's first year in school. He was growing into a stocky fellow, with a quiet, determined air. He nodded from his seat at the kitchen table, wary of Frank's attempt to be friendly. He had no idea his father was relieved to find something they could both talk about, father to son. Fighting was a right of passage that Frank Bird understood.

"What happened, Owen?" Frank asked, leaning for support against the kitchen sink while Nellie took his dinner from the oven.

"He put dirt in my sandwich."

"So, you gave him a hiding, eh? Good for you, son." Frank couldn't resist adding, "It's a good thing you did. Otherwise, you'd have to go back tomorrow and take him on again until you did, eh."

"When I'm grown up," Owen said quietly, "I'm going to take you on too."

"What'd you say?" Frank swayed upright, the blood rushing to his face.

"He didn't say anything," Nellie said quickly. "Here, Frank. Eat your dinner. I've kept the lid on, to stop it drying out in the oven . . ."

" . . . Yes he bloody did. Cheeky little bugger. What did you say, boy?"

"I said when I'm grown up, I'm going to take you on too."

"You are, eh?" Frank's hands flew to his leather belt. It was thick cowhide, three inches wide, with a solid brass buckle. He hauled the belt violently from his trouser loops. The end slapped loudly as it came out. "We'll see about that, sonny boy."

He lurched around the kitchen table.

Nellie rushed in front of him, shouting.

"Don't you touch the child!"

Frank pushed her away. She crashed over a chair and onto the floor. Owen ran to her, but Frank caught him by the shoulder and spun him around.

"Take me on, eh?" he shouted. The belt hissed savagely onto Owen's legs. The pain shocked him. His vision went blank for an instant, then the belt swung down again, and again, and Owen heard himself screaming, a high-pitched desperate wail that frightened him more than the pain. He didn't want to cry. He tried to stop screaming, but the violence of the belting was raising angry red bruises from his ribs to his ankles. He heard Nellie shrieking at her husband, trying to put herself between them, but again Frank shoved her away, and she collided with the wooden dinnerware cabinet, knocking down plates with a fusillade of shattering china.

"Take me on, ay, you little bastard?" Frank leaned down until his face was over Owen's. The boy could smell stale beer and tobacco smoke on his breath, and the intangible reek of nameless hate and impotence. "You'll never be half the man I am," Frank shouted. "You'll never amount to anything when you grow up, you hear me? All this bloody hero-worshipping of Charles bloody Kingsford Smith and the rest." His rage gave way to a sly leer. His eyes raked the room like tracer, until they trained on the kitchen table and found what he was looking for, lying under Owen's schoolbooks. In two strides, Frank crossed the room and snatched up Owen's scrapbook, sending the other books spinning to the floor. He draped his belt across his forearm and slowly and deliberately tore the scrapbook into halves, then quarters, then, with difficulty now, into eighths.

"You'll never be a pilot." Frank's voice came hissing from the depths of his belly. "You'll never be anything, hear me? Nobody! That's what you'll be. A bloody nobody!"

Owen stood with his body slumped, his eyes and nose running, saliva slicking his swollen lips as he looked down at the pieces of his scrapbook fluttering to the floor.

"Like you?" he sobbed. Frank bellowed and reared back, raising the belt behind his shoulder, but this time Owen clenched his jaws tight and stopped struggling. The belt lashed into his shoulders, drawing beads of blood along a scalding welt, but Owen did not make a sound. The belt rose and hissed down again, and still the boy remained silent. Frank straightened up, and glared. Tears were streaming down Owen's cheeks, but he kept his mouth clamped tight. He realized his silence was a weapon and felt a sudden surge of triumph.

He noticed Nellie, still lying on the floor sobbing, gasping for breath. Owen ran to his mother. He helped her sit up and stroked her shoulders and hair until she stopped crying. She put her arms around him and hugged him, patting his back and legs. She felt the hard angry welts that ridged his skin. Her fingers froze. They were wet and slippery.

"Blood! You brute!" She held her hands up to Frank, her fingertips smeared with Owen's blood. "Look!"

"He didn't hurt me," Owen said defiantly. He glared at his father. "You can't hurt me." Despite his bruises, and the pain burning through the wounds on his body, he felt his voice become firmer and clearer. "You can't hurt me. You can't hurt me."

Owen saw the fury in Frank's eyes go out like a snuffed flame. He knew he had won an irrevocable victory against his father. His legs and ribs throbbed as the bruises swelled tight. But he could bear the pain. He knew he could bear anything, to see the effect he had on his father. He didn't want to be thrashed again, but he would never let go of that sense of power. He knew he could tolerate anything now, and not be afraid anymore.

The scorching southern summer of 1929 relented to a gusty dry autumn in March, then the westerlies blew up from the inland plains in late June with the first chilling snap of winter. It was dark and bitterly cold outside when Nellie woke Frank.

"Bert's at the door," she said.

Frank sat upright. The luminous bedside clock showed eleven twenty-four. Frank pulled on his dressing gown and padded barefoot across cold floorboards to the front door where Bert Woolcott, the railway stationmaster, huddled against the cold.

"Sorry to wake yer, Frank," Bert said. He had an Army greatcoat pulled tight around him and his breath came out in thick clouds.

"Come inside, mate," Frank offered.

"Evenin', Nellie," Bert said, stepping into the house. "We need a hand, Frank. Bluey Murphy's feelin' crook. I reckon he's got the flu." Bert kept a straight face, but Frank knew better. Bluey, the station porter who perversely earned his nickname because of his red hair, was most likely drunk. "The goods train from Brisbane's due in a quarter of an hour. I wouldn't wake yer, Frank, but it's droppin' off a flatbed, and we need another hand for the shunting." Bert paused, and added, "Of course, you'd get Bluey's shift allowance. I'll square it with the union."

"No worries, cobber," Frank said. "Gimme a mo' to get me boots on."

"Good on yer, Frank." He waited near the door, his hands deep in his pockets, while Frank went back into the bedroom to dress, pulling on his hobnailed leather work boots and his old Army greatcoat and Digger hat. Frank and Nellie's cottage was next to the railway tracks, and it was only a short walk to the station. The night sky was brittle and bright with stars, and their breath came out in white bursts as Frank and Bert strode down together. Frank felt the cold air clearing his hangover.

Charlie Bowers, the junior porter, was waiting in the station office, warming his hands over a potbellied wood stove. Frank thought, without irony, young Charlie was a lout, a mug lair, desperately in need of the discipline the Army gave a man. *Like all these young mugs who never went to the war,* Frank told himself.

The train pulled in punctually at twelve minutes to midnight, and the three men walked down the station platform to the adjoining goods yard to uncouple the flatbed wagon. There were seventeen cars on the train, including fuel tankers, a string of boxcars, and several flatbed wagons. The flatbed they had to take off was the second to last wagon in the train, coupled in front of the red guard's van. Chained securely on its flat wooden top was a new combine wheat harvester.

Bert Woolcott walked up the track beside the engine, to talk to the driver. Steam hissed steadily from the big polished pistons above the drive wheels.

Bert stayed on the ground beside the engine as Charlie manned the track switch to the branch line, and Frank waited to unhook the guard's van. The driver nodded to Bert and called, "Ready."

"Unhook it!" Bert yelled down the train.

Frank Bird hopped up onto the round steel fenders that served as bumpers between the cars. He leaned down to release the coupling between the guard's van and the flatbed wagon in front of it. The coupling was made of heavy steel, blackened by grease and dust and soot and cinders. A night wind hissed over the train, chilling them all. Frank shivered and felt the coldness of the metal through his thick canvas work gloves as he raised the release ring. He jumped down from the steel fenders of the guard's van and cupped his hands toward the engine.

"Free!" he called. An overhead light cast him in a yellow glow.

There was a loud staccato chuffing from the locomotive and a chorus of squeals and clunks of fenders along the train as the power of the steam engine was transferred through the couplings of each car in succession, and they slowly began rolling. Each wagon weighed forty to sixty tons and the smallest movement created a massive momentum. The train clanked steadily forward, past the track switch.

When the flatbed was safely uncoupled and parked, the train shunted back to the main line. Charlie Bowers reset the track switch for the final shunt back to the guard's van. Bert was walking beside the engine, still guiding the driver. Frank Bird waited back at the guard's van, to check the couplings when the train reconnected. Charlie Bowers jogged back in the semidarkness, after he'd reset the track switch to the main line. He grinned at Frank across the track, near the front of the guard's van.

"Piece of piss," Charlie said cockily.

Frank and Charlie waited beside the guard's van as the train backed toward them. Charlie was jogging in place, stamping his boots, trying to keep warm. His energy and confidence were infectious. Frank found himself envying it, remembering how he once felt so vital, back in the war, the real war, long before the enervating skirmishing he lived with at home.

The train was about thirty feet away from the guard's van when Charlie suddenly jumped onto the tracks.

"What the bloody hell are you doing?" Frank said.

"Relax, mate," Charlie said, grinning broadly. With an easy movement, he climbed up onto the fenders of the guard's van. The train was twenty feet away now. Charlie was about to turn around so that his back would be against the guard's van and he could face the train as it recoupled.

"Shit, Charlie!" Frank hissed. "Y'stupid bugger!"

Charlie stepped lightly onto the coupling to turn around. Perhaps it was the cold that made his leather hobnail boots stiffer, with less traction. Perhaps there was more grease than normal on the coupling. Charlie's boot skidded off it and he crashed onto a fender, grunting as he hit the icy steel, cracking three ribs high up under his right shoulder.

"Shit!" He gasped for air, feeling fire lance through his ribs and lungs. His right arm had gone numb and hung limp across the fender. "Give me a hand here, Frank! Quick!"

Frank saw the train fifteen feet away now. He knew there was no time for the driver to stop the eight-hundred-ton train, even at this low shunting speed.

Frank leaped onto the tracks and grabbed Charlie's shoulders. He tried to pull him free of the fender, but his legs were hooked over the coupling. Frank reached up and pulled the legs clear, then caught Charlie's shoulders again and heaved him away from the fender. Charlie cried out in pain. Frank was straining to lift him off when he glanced behind him and saw the train looming over them. The last thing he remembered was dropping Charlie, letting him fall safely to the track bed beneath the cars.

A staggering force hit Frank in the belly. He felt as if he had been crunched in half. He saw blackness, then his body went numb. The two fenders gripped him, front and back, like the jaws of a vise.

He heard the heavy double clank beside him of the coupling reengaging between the guard's van and the train, locking the jaws together. He couldn't move. He expected pain, but there was only a massive pressure driving the air from his lungs, and a deadness in all his limbs. He didn't want to look down. He wanted this all to be a terrible nightmare. He looked down. He didn't believe what he saw.

The fender of the guard's van was pressed deep into his belly. He knew the coupling had engaged. He knew the fenders crashed together as the cars coupled. His brain knew he had been crushed between the two steel fenders and locked, but his mind fought to shroud the knowledge. His brain flooded his body with endorphins, drugging him, shutting down circulation to his outer vessels, harboring blood and oxygen for his most vital organs. He felt terribly cold and realized he was listing to one side. His hat had fallen off and the wind whipped icy fingers around his head.

His body was held up by the steel face plates that had crunched his spine and compressed his belly and muscles and pelvis until the tissue and bone exploded.

He tried to breathe, but could only manage a shallow gasp that ended in a bubbling rattle. There was a rush near him of someone running, then an acetylene flashlight lit his face.

Frank couldn't speak. A trickle of blood erupted in his mouth and ran over his lips.

Bert Woolcott took in the sight and exhaled slowly. On the ground Charlie Bowers was crawling out from the track bed.

"Bert!" Charlie called. "He's trapped! Get him out! Unhook the car!"

Frank vomited, and in the pale blue light of the acetylene lamp Bert Woolcott could see blood in it.

Bert heard the driver running back from his locomotive.

"Unhook the car!" Charlie shouted, groaning with the pain in his ribs, and looking desperately from Frank to Bert.

"Shut up, Charlie," Bert said.

The engine driver ran up to them and looked at Frank, and sighed under his breath, "Ah fuck. Ah fuck." The driver dragged the palm of his hand over his face. "Ah fuck. Ah fuck. Ah fuck." He looked at Bert sadly. Bert shook his head.

"What are you bloody waiting for!" Charlie shouted. "Get him down!"

"We can't do that," Bert said quietly.

"He's right," the driver said.

"Why the fuck not?" Charlie demanded.

Bert took off his greatcoat and placed it around Frank's shoulders. Through the stink of vomit came a smell of excrement and urine. Frank's legs were bent at unnatural angles below his mangled trunk. Streams of warm fluid overflowed his boots and seeped into the cold track bed.

"Why the fuck not?" Charlie was crying now.

Bert waved him back from Frank, and the driver steered Charlie away, out of earshot.

"He's done for, mate," the driver said quietly. "Seen it before. Twice. Bloke gets crushed like this, he's finished. As soon as you pull the cars apart, everything runs out and he bleeds to death in a couple of seconds. There's nothing we can do for him. There a doctor in town?"

Charlie shook his head.

"Does he have a family?"

"Wife," Charlie said dully. "And a kid."

"Ah fuck," the driver muttered. "Ah fuck, fuck, fuck."

"Charlie," Bert said. "Frank's Catholic. Get up to the church and tell 'em. You, mate," he said to the driver, "you're going to have to stay with him for a bit. I'll have to get his wife."

Frank was mired in a dark, throbbing river. Shapes and lights moved vaguely around his blurred field of vision. He had no sense of time. Coldness filled his bones and marrow. The shapes and light came closer.

He heard Nellie's voice, a muffled cry. She didn't want to recognize the shape beneath the greatcoat, clamped in steel.

"Why's he still there?" Nellie cried. "Let him out." Bert Woolcott held her shoulders firmly and whispered in her ear.

"He's in a bad way, Nell," he said gently. "Very bad. If we pull the train apart and free him, he'll bleed to death before we can help him. I'm sorry. He's been asking for you. There's not much time, Nell." The driver had fetched a blanket and a first-aid box from the engine. He gently pulled the blanket around Frank, over the greatcoat. There was nothing in the first-aid box he could think to use.

Nellie stared at her husband. She had grown up with the sight of butchered carcasses in her father's shop. But nothing prepared her for this ghastly vision of someone she once loved with all her heart; and loved even still.

She touched his cheek. It was cold and unearthly in the pale light of the lamps.

"Frank, I'm here, love."

His eyelids barely lifted, but he tried to focus on her. He struggled to breathe. "G'day, love."

She couldn't remember the last time he had called her that. There was a time when he said it constantly, with great tenderness.

"Oh, Frank. Oh, love. I'm so sorry."

"I'm through, Nell. Funny. I really thought . . . me number . . . was up at Gallipoli."

"Don't try to talk, Frank."

"No time, Nell. Lot to say. Been a real bastard."

"Oh no, Frank."

"A real bastard . . . to you and Owen."

"Ah, Frank. He loves you, you know that."

"I made him hate me."

"Don't say that, Frank. I mothered him too much. I'm sorry, Frank."

"Don't be, love. You're a good old girl."

Nellie wondered how he could speak at all.

"Wish I could have it back. This is punishment."

"Ah, Frank, you did your best. I know that. Owen knows that." She wanted to feed her own life into him, feed the flame she saw fading from him.

There was a commotion behind her but she didn't want to look away.

"Bloody hell!" Bert Woolcott muttered. "It's their boy."

They saw Owen walking beside the train in his pajamas and dressing gown, looking for his mother.

"Frank, love," Nellie whispered in desperation. "Owen's here."

Bert picked the boy up and passed him to Nell. She held him on her hip.

"Owen's here, Frank," she sobbed. "Say hello to your dad, darling."

Owen said nothing.

"Say hello, darling. Owen," Nellie sobbed. "Say hello to your dad."

She put her right arm around her husband's shoulders, bringing man and boy face-to-face.

Owen stared silently at Frank. He watched his mother use her handkerchief to wipe the sweat and blood and vomit from Frank's face.

Frank raised his head. His face was drawn in the rictus of shock. His eyes flickered open and strained to focus on his son. He peered at Owen and grunted and raised his right arm, groaning with the pain of it. His hand fell large and cold on Owen's shoulder. The boy recoiled.

"Forgive me," Frank whispered. Owen smelled the carnage on his father's breath. "Forgive me, son."

"Oh, he does, love," Nellie cried. "Don't you, darling? Tell your father. Please, Owen. Tell him you forgive him. Tell him you love him."

Frank's hand slid from Owen's shoulder. His eyes were losing focus again, and a look of desperation passed across them.

"Forgive . . ."

But Owen didn't make a sound. His silence was a weapon he refused to yield.

Frank's breath bubbled up from his chest, and his hand fell to his side. Nellie heard the life rattling out of him like a long chain running over its couplings. Behind her, the priest hurried toward them, his pajama pants showing below his hastily donned cassock. Nellie stroked Frank's cheek. It felt deathly cold, and then his mouth went slack and she clasped his face to hers, with Owen still slung on her hip watching mute, as the chain ran all the way out and fell into silence.

Frank Bird was finally free of the rails.

꙳

Flight Lieutenant Owen Bird came home a hero from World War II. His old boarding school in Brisbane invited him to be guest speaker at a morning assembly, chaired by the Monsignor himself.

"I came to this great school as a scholarship student, by the grace of God, and the generosity of Holy Mother Church . . ." Owen began, resplendent in his dress blue uniform with its rows of campaign ribbons. Every boy in the school knew the stories behind those medals: of how as a newly commissioned pilot officer, Owen had joined 3rd Squadron, RAAF, in Libya, flying Tomahawk fighters against the Germans over Tobruk; of how he had won the Distinguished Flying Cross after landing in the desert to pick up a comrade forced down by enemy fire, bringing them both safely back, with the rescued flier crammed in the pilot's seat and Owen sitting in his lap flying the plane; of how Owen had been forced down with half a wing shot away, and had taxied across the stony desert for twenty-six miles to his home base, to be met by his flight engineer with the immortal welcome, "If I'd known yez wanted t' bloody drive, sir, I'd have given y' the CO's car"; of how he had been captured in Syria, transported to a German Stalag Luft in northern Italy, and had escaped in a vegetable cart with two POWs who fled with him to Switzerland.

". . . but I came back to this hallowed place today," he continued, "by the grace of de Havilland, Pratt & Whitney, and Browning."

The boys roared. The names of the makers of warplanes and engines and guns were as familiar as their sports heroes.

After a morning tea with the staff and prefects, the Monsignor eased Owen aside.

"A very amusing speech," the cleric said with the smooth hushed tone that Owen associated since boyhood with real authority. "Ye've done Mother Church proud, my son."

"The Church was more than generous to my mother and me when we needed it, Father. I plan to return the favor, as the Bible told it: 'pressed down and overflowing.'"

"Do y' now? Well, well, well. A worthy intention. And I've a mind you're the one to do it. How old are y' now?"

"Twenty-two, Father."

"Aye." The old man nodded thoughtfully. "And already a full lifetime behind y'. And tell me, Owen, what are y' plans for the future, now ye've returned safely to this home for heroes?"

Owen brushed his thickening black mustache thoughtfully, looking for a hint of irony in the Monsignor's face.

"Well, the Americans here are dumping everything they can, now it's all over. They can't wait to get home. I plan to pick up a couple of Army trucks and start a transport business. It doesn't matter what the country does in the next ten years, Father, people will want to move things, and I plan to be there to move them. And, as soon as I have the capital, I want to buy a plane." He spoke with quiet conviction, matching the Monsignor's hushed tone of confidence. But he couldn't resist adding, "And if you'll forgive the expression, Father, it's been my experience in the past that if heroes want a home worth returning to, they'll have to build the bloody thing themselves."

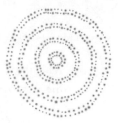

CHAPTER 13

A JETLINER DESCENDED onto Alice Springs airport, its engines howling and wind screaming over its open air brakes and flaps.

"Nice timing," the sound technician said below his breath, coiling up Owen's microphone, as the aircraft roared over the hospital, and landed beyond the town. He didn't want the old man or Miss Horstmann blaming him for a noisy soundtrack, and he was relieved the breakfast show interview was over before the morning planes arrived from the coast.

In the first class cabin of the jet, Robert Erhard watched the red spine of the MacDonnell Ranges slide up beneath them, like a great prehistoric reptile slumbering full length on the pale orange plain. This region was north of his country, but he knew some of the secret stories of the range below, when creation spirits descended shrieking from the skies and sang this part of the world into existence. River red gum trees grew in loose forests along its base, where the Todd River bed crossed the range through a cleft called Simpson's Gap. Droughts lasted years, and for most of the time the Todd river line was only a winding stretch of white sand where gum trees grew down from the banks to its center, forming shaded campsites for scores of Aborigines who came to Alice Springs because this was their country, and who stayed for the occasional work, and regular welfare checks. They called their government dole "sitting down money" and bought canned food and beer and cheap wine with it, and sat beneath the shade in the dry bed of the Todd River, aware of the town bordering their corridor of trees, but immersed in the invisible currents that flowed in from the desert and through them all as powerfully as their old river when it rose in full flood.

Grace Morgan knelt in front of the cedar chest and ran her hands over the carved roses on its lid. "A good man is a compass." She remembered Great-Uncle Joseph's gentle weathered hands, and the soft rumble of his voice when he held her on his lap. She opened the lid and folded back the calico and ran her fingertips over the smooth white satin beneath. Grandmother Grace and her Polish husband were appalled when their daughter, Gretel, wanted to marry Dr. Howard Morgan. They both knew firsthand the constant corrosion of discrimination, and physician or not, Howard Morgan and his family would always be treated as black. Grandmother Grace surprised everyone when her granddaughter, Grace, grew up pale enough to pass as white. "The Morgan women are color-struck," she told young Grace, "and they'd love for you to pass. It's your decision, girl. But you ask me, you are who you are, you are your blood, and you dishonor all your ancestors by being anything but proud of them. I'm proud of you, darling, and I'm as proud of your daddy as I am of my own daughter. We are who we are."

Grace gently lifted the white satin from the chest and let it drop out to its full length. Grandmother Grace wore it once, on her wedding day, and her daughter, Gretel, wore it once, on hers. Both of them wanted young Grace to do the same. She held it against her and turned to face the mirror. She had never put it on, but she knew it would fit. She was embarrassed that it meant so much to her. Everything she had become, all she had studied and worked for, her degrees and doctorate, her selection to NASA, her rise to equal and surpass the men who a generation ago would have kept her at home, raising babies, all of these things made her blush to think this dress meant so much to her.

"A compass you can trust," Great-Uncle Joseph had said. "There are places on the ocean where compasses spin in all directions. But once you're past them, the needle swings back on North again, and holds steady. Trust your compass, little darling. And when it swings wild, trust your instinct. Between them, you'll never go wrong."

Grace closed her eyes, holding the dress against her, sliding her hands over its cool surface. "You are your blood." She folded the dress carefully and set it back in the trunk and spread the calico over it again and smelled the clean sharp aroma of the cedar as she closed the lid. "Trust your instinct."

She had spoken to Robert's parents by phone when she began dating him, and frequently since they moved in together. They had exchanged photographs and birthday cards. It took her less than seven minutes online to the American Airlines Web site to work out an itinerary and book a ticket.

When she leaned back from the screen, she expected to feel excitement, even trepidation, fear. Instead she felt calm, steady, like a needle settling back on its proper bearing.

ᾀᴗ

An ambulance rolled along the sandy bed of the Todd River and through the trees, and stopped next to a police Land Cruiser.

A constable was waiting for them. Near him, a young Aborigine sat with his back to a gum tree, staring out along the long dry riverbed. The constable noted the man was well dressed in stockman's clothes, a red R.M. Williams western shirt, new boots, and tipped jauntily back on his head, a neatly blocked Akubra hat with a brilliantly colored parrot's feather in the plaited leather band. The young man's hair was neatly cut, and he appeared in excellent health. There were no signs of violence on him, as far as the constable could see. A driver's license identified the young man as Russell King, living on Clementine Downs.

The young man's eyes seemed clear and focused, staring into the distance.

But there was no doubt in the constable's mind that Russell King, sitting so peacefully along the Todd River, had been dead for some time.

ᾀᴗ

Robert caught a cab from the airport in to Alice Springs, letting the dry, hot air through the window wash over him. The driver didn't speak to him, suspicious of an Aborigine whose jeans and shirt and sneakers looked to be new and designer label. The cabbie was just as suspicious of Aborigines whose clothes were hard-worn. Either way, he maintained, they were on the government tit, and squandering the earnings of hardworking taxpayers like himself. Robert ignored the silent hostility in the front seat, and looked across the flat country into town.

His country around Uluru was three hundred miles south, but still he felt the resonance of his own story lines, and of the creation songs of the spirits who came this way. He moved through both dimensions, into the town with its ordered streets and shopping strips, and outcast Aborigines down on the river sand, and into the distant music from his own country, rising across the central red plains, carrying the clear singing of the Kalaya Dreaming man.

Elsie Cosgrove knew smells. For more than forty years of marriage, she had ridden with her husband, Conrad, along thousands of miles of stock routes, droving cattle across Australia. She'd smelled drovers who'd lived in the saddle for more than two weeks on end without a bath. She'd shared a swag at night with Conrad, after he'd eaten more than a pound of steak and washed it down with half a bottle of Bundaberg rum. She'd smelled cattle and horses and sheep rotting in muddy bogs and drought-parched paddocks alongside heavily trafficked roads. She knew the smell of a stillborn calf, with its carcass shrouded in glistening placenta. She cherished the smells of warm damper, and hot scones, and billy tea, and eucalyptus fires, and newly picked flowers, and freshly bathed babies. And she knew the unmistakably cloying smell of decaying sweetness that had begun drifting from her neighbor's house.

She watched a Northern Territory police four-wheel-drive roll into the dirt driveway to her wooden cottage. She was waiting on the front veranda, in the squatter's chair where Conrad had spent most of his retirement before he died, drinking rum and spinning stories with his mates.

"I noticed it first thing this morning," she told the policewoman as they crossed her unfenced yard to the house next door.

"Was he home last night?" Constable Janice Monroe asked. She was sure the old lady kept a good eye on her neighbors.

"That's the thing," Elsie said, wrapping her dressing gown tighter. She was wearing slippers shaped like floppy-eared rabbits, a gift from her teenaged granddaughter. "The last I saw of him was two days ago. He come home from the Post Office looking like he'd just won the Lotto. Went inside. Didn't come out yesterday, or last night."

"Did you talk to him?"

"No. I just happened to notice him from the kitchen when he come home."

"What time was that, do you know?"

"Two twenty-five," Elsie said at once. "Somewhere around there."

They were approaching the neighbor's front door, and the smell was much stronger.

"I think you'd better wait in your house, dear," Constable Monroe told her.

"Not on yer life, lovie!" Elsie said, planting herself at the front steps. "There's nothin' in there I haven't seen before."

The policewoman gave her an appraising look. She knew dozens of oldies like Elsie living in Alice Springs: men and women in their seventies and eighties, some past ninety, who'd retired to town after arduous lives on cattle stations and stock routes across the Territory. They were the last of the pioneers, independent, single-minded, and tough.

"I wouldn't doubt it," Constable Monroe said gently. She rapped on the door and waited. Elsie watched with sharp, astute eyes that reminded the policewoman of an old cockatoo, missing nothing. The smell was turning the policewoman's stomach. She knocked again, then unclipped her radio and called her dispatcher.

Elsie was back in her kitchen with a fresh mug of tea when she saw the government contractors arrive next door in their black hearse. There were already two more police vehicles parked outside. One of them had delivered a forensic photographer. Elsie watched the whole drama, until the two contractors emerged from the house with a stretcher, covered by a black plastic sheet.

She knew Oscar Woolie was under it. The old art dealer lived alone, and Elsie knew the comings and goings of everyone who visited him: his Aboriginal relatives and friends who came over for a drink; the occasional client who wanted to conduct business away from his gallery; and the occasional woman who stayed the night. But nobody had visited Oscar in two days, of that Elsie was certain. It had to be him being slid, none too gently, into the back of the hearse. Her nose was never wrong.

Robert paid the cab driver, and stood in the sunlight with his bag, feeling the weight of the morning heat, and the nearness of his prey. It would take no more effort to get to him now than it did to ride in from the airport.

But the Law required the proper rituals, to be performed in the proper place and time. The crime that brought him home to the place of his birth and dreaming cut across a host of story lines, and the Law required he return to their origins, to allow justice to literally follow the correct course from its beginning. He would have to journey south now, for three hundred miles, into the heart of his own country.

Robert stared off into the center of Alice Springs for some time.

Then he turned and carried his bag across the station platform to the waiting splendor of *The Ghan*.

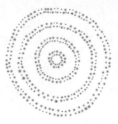

CHAPTER 14

"VERY GOOD, WONDERFUL." Agnes Horstmann beamed at Owen.

"Think it worked?" he asked.

"I don't see why not," she said as she helped him out of his jacket and tie. "You answered every question, no darting eyes, no hesitation, all straight answers."

"What about the crew?"

"No one," her voice became flat, "will talk."

Agnes unbuttoned his shirt. Across the room, the cameraman looked up from breaking down his gear and saw Agnes helping Owen into a silk dressing gown. The cameraman didn't want to stare, but he couldn't look away, astonished by the transformation. For a brief moment, Agnes no longer looked like the legendary harridan who for more than forty years had been Owen Bird's manager, confidante, and temple dog, the formidable "Iron Maiden" to titans and minions alike who came into her orbit and who muttered the title well behind her back. When men who knew her said publicly they respected her, they invariably meant that at some time they had experienced the scrotum-tightening chill of her gaze, backed by the full weight and influence of the BIRD corporations and their founder, and what they really meant was that of all the women they knew, she was the one they came closest to fearing. She was married to her job, and nobody would separate them. But in that fleeting glimpse, the cameraman saw Agnes Horstmann in the role of someone she might have been in another time and place, a loving and devoted wife.

☙

Owen Bird had done far more by the time he was twenty-five than he promised the Monsignor. In the three years since his speech to his old school, he had parlayed his pair of U.S. Army trucks into a growing fleet of semi-trailers and intercity delivery trucks. In the third year, he convinced his bank to back the purchase of another U.S. disposal, a Douglas DC-3. The old *Biscuit Bomber,* which had last dropped supplies to commandos in New Guinea in 1945, was refitted for passenger service, and carried mail on a healthy Post Office contract. On its tailplane, Owen had painted a red eagle clutching in its talons the bold letters BIRD. A year later, he had six aircraft, and his bank offered him his first seven-figure line of credit to lease more.

He bought a large Georgian sandstone home overlooking Sydney Harbour. But he spent fewer nights in the great cedar bed on its top floor, and far more on the leather couch in his office, a glassed-in command post above the BIRD Transport terminal where his trucks came in for maintenance, and his drivers checked in from long-haul routes across the country and from door-to-door runs in the city. Like a good bishop, Owen paid attention to their gossip: they were his intelligence network, growing steadily. The man who was eyed by city matrons as a most eligible bachelor, and by bankers and investors as a most secure bet, lived in sleep-creased clothes, smelled faintly of sweat and diesel fuel, and catnapped to the music of trucks being serviced one floor beneath him, and aircraft engines overhead, plying the city's airport two miles away. Ground staff at BIRD Aviation were accustomed to the founder barreling in at dawn, unshaven, unkempt and ready to help load cargo onto aircraft, or carry passengers' bags across the tarmac. Few of the travelers realized their disheveled young porter owned the airline. A few did.

"Thank you, Mr. Bird." Owen heard a female voice behind him as he unloaded a large suitcase and a leather man's valise from an arriving morning flight. Owen glanced up to see a woman in her late twenties, tall, straight-backed, slim, attractive in an austere way, in a navy skirt suit and matching felt hat.

"This must be yours," Owen said, indicating the large suitcase.

"No." She reached for the briefcase. "This is. And you are a mess, aren't you?"

Owen stared at her, then at his rumpled clothes.

"You need someone to look after you, Mr. Bird."

Owen's eyes hooded.

"You mean a wife?" he said, his voice harsh.

"No, I mean an office manager."

"Ah. A secretary."

"Don't ever confuse me with a secretary, Mr. Bird. If you think the place won't run without you, you obviously need an office manager. And if you must sleep there overnight, you could at least install a bath and wardrobe." She appraised him from his grease-streaked shoes to his stubbled face and sleep-spiked hair.

"And where, madam," his voice hardened further, "would I find this paragon of efficiency?"

"Freshly matriculated from business college, Mr. Bird. And it's not madam. It's Miss. Miss Horstmann. And if you're planning to buy me breakfast, you should at least comb your hair."

Owen still spent more nights sleeping at the truck terminal than at home, but now his office had a private suite with a bathroom and a clothes closet and a single bed. He had a new administrative office downstairs, which ran smoothly under the stern and unforgiving eye of Agnes Horstmann. She worked the same long hours as Owen. She hired office staff, supervised the building additions, and surprised him with a plan for improving turnaround times on the maintenance floor. When the chief mechanic objected to taking advice from a woman, Owen fired him. The new man answered to Agnes. In the year since he first bought her breakfast, Owen's fortunes multiplied. On New Year's Day, 1950, he was ready to buy five new Lockheeds with options on ten more. He was also nursing a staggering hangover, and sitting up in a bed that wasn't his. Six weeks later, Agnes faced him across his desk.

"Pregnant," he snarled. His voice was tired, hard.

"What do you plan to do about it, Owen?" she sounded as tired, paving over her emotions with a stony expression.

"What do you take me for, Agnes?"

"You don't have to worry. I can take care of everything."

"That's illegal, Agnes, apart from anything else."

"That's a nice Catholic response."

"It's the simple truth."

"You'd have to pay for everything."

He shrugged impatiently, accepting the obvious.

"We both know who can do it," she said. "He's very good and very discreet."

Owen stared past her, bitterly remembering that morning, in that bed.

"I can't let you do it, Agnes," he said after a long pause.

"And what do you propose instead?" she asked, already afraid of the answer.

He breathed in slowly and looked directly at her.

"Marriage," he said.

Her eyes welled and she looked down, angry at her lapse of control. She could barely find her voice.

"No."

"I could do worse." His eyebrows went up wistfully, then his voice became businesslike. "It's time someone made an honest man of me."

Again her eyes welled, and she clenched her jaw until it passed.

"You're certain?" she asked.

He nodded.

"I see," Agnes said quietly. She sat up straight, squared her shoulders, and looked him in the eye. "And who is she, Owen?"

"Isabel Macquarie."

Agnes remained motionless, in control now.

"Does her father know?" she asked, all pain erased from her voice.

"Nobody knows, apart from you, Agnes." He looked wistfully at her, unaware of how much worse he was making it. "You're the only one I could tell."

Sir Andrew Macquarie made the best of it, partly consoled that the young scoundrel's wealth and ambition overshadowed his miserable origins. He fumed at his daughter, then underwrote a spectacular cathedral wedding, a lavish reception on his four-acre estate, overlooking both the Harbour and Owen Bird's eminently respectable two-story sandstone, and saw to it that his newspapers in every city covered the celebrations, and that his national women's magazine gave over a six-page spread to it. Owen and Isabel Bird left for Europe on a four-week flying honeymoon. Agnes Horstmann cabled daily management reports to their hotels.

When they returned, Owen spent the first month sleeping with his bride in the sandstone's great bed upstairs. In the second month, he found it necessary to spend a few nights at the office. By the sixth month, it was two or three nights a week. In the eighth month, Sir Andrew's newspapers and magazine announced the joyful birth of a boy, to Owen and Isabel, six weeks premature, but as healthy as a full-term baby, praise be to God. He was christened in the cathedral, Andrew Trent Bird.

Sir Andrew appointed Owen to the boards of two newspapers. BIRD Aviation bought its first Lockheed Super Constellations, and began international service to Hong Kong and London. BIRD Transport bought its one hundredth truck, extending its flying eagles from the nation's largest city, in the southeast, to its biggest mining site, in the far northwest. He assayed his drivers' reports from around the continent and began buying mining and grazing property. BIRD Communications bought a country newspaper, and joined it with a rural radio station. Owen and Agnes spent more time at his regional offices. Isabel spent more time and money restoring the sandstone. When Andrew turned six, she began hiring tutors. Over the next five years, Andrew acquired a piano teacher, an art master, and a ballroom dance instructor. He saw more of his father in newspaper articles than at home. When Owen was at home, Andrew fell asleep at night to the muffled sounds of arguing from the great bedroom.

And when Owen was at home, he badgered his son to excel at everything a young man needed to make his way in the world: football, rowing, boxing.

"I don't want a bloody sissy for a son!" he shouted to the faithfully refurbished oak beams high above the sandstone's ground-floor ballroom, unaware of the weekend dance lessons there.

When Andrew turned twelve, Owen sent him off to boarding school. Admission was smooth. The Monsignor had risen to Bishop and was glad to help the son of such a generous Old Boy of the school.

"Rub shoulders with the young men you'll be doing business with," Owen told him. "You can't trust them if you don't know them. And don't take any bullshit, son. If you lose a fight, go back until you win. I don't want a bloody sissy for a son."

Isabel visited Andrew on weekends. His friends thought she was incredibly glamorous. Andrew thought she looked tired, and something else. Lonely. She was there for all his football matches, and his regattas. She never watched him box, but dutifully admired his trophies. Presents came from Owen after each success, bought and delivered by Agnes. Money arrived on birthdays with a note from Owen on how to invest it. Owen appeared once a year on Speech Night, shook hands with his son, and sat with the Bishop on stage. Andrew's grandmother Nellie wrote every week from Doctor's Crossing, and pinned a single banknote to every letter. She had declined Owen's offers to buy her a house in the city, and only reluctantly took possession of the brick home he built her on the main street of Doctor's Crossing, at the opposite end from the railway station.

In Andrew's senior year, Nellie died. Owen flew with Isabel and Andrew to the tiny town for the funeral. Her will was clear: she wanted to lie beside her dear late husband, Frank. Owen sat beside her coffin in the church, but refused to go to the cemetery for the burial. He left Isabel and Andrew at the airport and flew on to Los Angeles and New York to visit movie and television studios.

"I so miss Nellie," Isabel told Andrew on the way back to school. She pressed the switch to close the privacy glass behind the driver. "Now all I have is you. And you're so distant."

"Survival, Mother. I've been kept at a distance since I was twelve."

"Never by me, darling. Never." She settled a gloved hand on his arm. "Don't make me cry now. I'll look a wreck."

"You always look beautiful, Mother."

"If only your father thought so."

Owen expected Andrew to go straight from school to university. He wanted to bring his son in on the ground floor in four years, and onto his first board in six. BIRD Communications now owned a controlling share in Sir Andrew Macquarie's publishing chain. They were bidding on their third television license. BIRD Transport had subsidiaries in Britain and Europe. The airline's new Boeing 707s plied the Pacific and Atlantic daily. At home, BIRD Holdings owned eleven thousand square miles of mining leases, and three million acres of grazing country on cattle stations in the Northern Territory and horse and merino studs near the east coast. Owen expected his son to start earning his way. Andrew's announcement midway through his course hit Owen like a steel hammer.

"I'm signing up."

"Don't be a bloody idiot, Andrew. You're getting your degree. The war'll be over by the time you graduate."

"I want to go."

"What the fuck for? Even if your number comes up you'll be deferred."

"I'm going in this week."

Owen glared at him. At nineteen, Andrew was leaner and taller than his father, with rower's shoulders and the alert stillness of a middleweight. For the first time, Owen realized how little he knew his son. He saw traces of Nellie and Sir Andrew and lines he refused to acknowledge were Frank's.

"Drink?" Owen poured two glasses of Glenlivet from a Baccarat decanter and held one out to Andrew.

They raised their glasses and drank in silence.

"You're not even old enough, Andrew."

"You were nineteen."

"That was a different war. Things were clearer then. We had no choice."

"Neither do I."

"You can come onto the fucking board. You're more valuable here."

"Bit of a sissy reason, don't you think?"

Owen smiled bitterly. "How long have you been saving that up?"

"I want to go."

"I could stop you until you're twenty-one."

"No you won't. Telling you's just a formality."

"Have you told your mother?"

"That's part of the formality. I want you to be here when I tell her. And I want you to be here with her while I'm gone. Agnes can take up the slack."

"I've no idea why you want to do it, Andrew." Owen shook his head and emptied his glass. "But you wouldn't be my son if you didn't want to go."

"You'll stay around here, then?"

Owen nodded.

"Your word on that?"

"All right." Owen snarled. "You don't trust me?"

"I don't know you well enough."

Eight gunships hammered off the pad beyond the perimeter and turned north toward Xuan Loc, tailing each other over the jungle like fat green dragonflies armed with rockets and machine guns. In the tent lines someone was playing a saxophone, a long lazy blues run to the fading beat of the Hueys. The insect sounds of transistor radios hung on the muggy air, barely audible through the coughs and hacking of Jeeps and half-ton trucks and the rumble of a pump vehicle moving down the perimeter line, spraying defoliant on weeds and new scrub. Sweat soaked Andrew Bird's uniform and slicked the wooden stock of his assault rifle as he picked up his pace to match Captain Rayner Posner's. The two men were no longer conscious of the thin chemical stink from the pump truck, or the amalgam of dust and oil and fuel and cooking smoke that were the constant companions of the most pervasive smell in the country, the rich coagulant aroma of fertile soil, redolent of cycles of rain and rot and life and death.

"No way, Andrew." Rayner Posner waved his hand irritably. "No how."

"The stuff's too good, Rayner. My boss doesn't trust it."

"What do you mean?"

Posner stopped in his tracks. Small rings of sweat marked the armpits of his carefully creased uniform, replete with his U.S. Marine captain's bars and corps insignia and two rows of service ribbons, none of which involved actual combat. Rayner Posner liked to think he used his head not his feet to win the war. He stood with one hand on his hip, the other on the holster of his service Colt .45 pistol. Rifles, as far as he was concerned, were for grunts like Lieutenant Bird here.

"I mean," Andrew said, stopping to face him steadily, "it's too clean. It makes him nervous."

"What the fuck does that mean?" Rayner turned and stalked into his office, in a mobile home in the intelligence complex known as the Intel Shop. "Coffee or coke?"

"Both."

Rayner grinned and tossed a can from his refrigerator without looking. Andrew caught it neatly, feeling condensation popping across the cold metal as he snapped it open. Rayner spooned Bolivian coffee into a percolator and dropped into the leather chair behind his desk. Andrew took one of the plastic chairs in front, cleared his rifle and rested it with the magazine out against the wall beside him. They faced each other across the desk.

"What's to be nervous about?" Rayner swung a patent leather shoe onto his desk. "It's A-grade shit. You Aussies are getting everything we get, Andy."

Andrew knew that was a blatant lie. The only reason the Americans were sharing intelligence was to keep their meager allies in prominent view on the evening news. The White House wanted body counts and international collaboration. Rayner offered him a Camel and Andrew lit it with his Zippo, engraved with the Australian Task Force coat of arms.

"No sign of ambush. No bullet holes. No frag marks." Andrew blew a smoke ring and aimed his forefinger through it. "No blood."

"You think this stuff came from Cordon and Search ops?"

"That, or your blokes are running the tidiest ambushes in country."

"Got you guessin', eh?" Rayner grinned smugly. "Let me tell you, buddy. Some of these grunts couldn't cordon and search their own fuckin' dicks. Shit, I Corps lost eleven KIA outside Xuan Loc before breakfast this morning. Eleven! A third of a fuckin' platoon! They were supposed to be doing a recon patrol up there. Charlie waxed 'em while they were havin' breakfast."

"They were in a night harbor?"

"Fuckin' A. Dug in. Shellscrapes, sentries. By the book. Charlie had 'em cold. They knew exactly where they were."

"Are you surprised?"

"They sure as shit were. What are you gettin' at?"

"Nothing, mate."

"Don't shit me, Andy. What's your point?"

"You already know, mate. Let me guess. They got choppered in yesterday afternoon, they went into a night harbor, fired a couple of hundred rounds into the bush around their perimeter and went to sleep?"

"You got it. Reconnaissance by Fire, man. Put out a Wall of Steel. This war's all about firepower."

"Mate, a recce by fire doesn't hit anything but trees and dirt. Charlie just lies in dead ground and waits for it to end. All you're doing is telling him where you are. If you want to secure your perimeter, you've got to put out clearing patrols. You've got to put men out there to cover all the dead ground on foot."

"Yeah? Well you're such a fuckin' expert, how come you're not leading your own fuckin' platoon out there, eh?"

Andrew felt blood rush to his face. Rayner chuckled and held up both hands.

"Hey, no offense, Andy, y'know? I don't even know why you're out here. If I had your daddy, I'd be chasin' pussy in King's Cross or wherever, not gooks."

"You don't chase gooks, Rayner." Andrew's voice was quiet, savage. "You sit here and make coffee."

"Okay. Foul ball. I'm sorry. Me, I wouldn't be caught dead out there. People like us use our brains. Out there's for grunts. Redneck farm boys and hippies. Half of 'em are so hopped up on grass and heroin, they'll shoot 'emselves before they even see Charlie. Let 'em have it, I say." He saw Andrew was still fuming, and changed tack. "Listen, you want to know where this stuff's coming from?"

Andrew took a long breath, willing his blood pressure down. "I'll bite," he said.

"I'll tell you," Rayner replied, his face blank. "Does G-String mean anything to you?"

Andrew mentally ran through the list of code words and ciphers on his daily classified briefing sheets. The term meant nothing to him. He shrugged. "A new unit?"

"Nope. Never heard it before? G-String?"

"Not unless you've got B girls doing recon." He sipped his coffee.

Rayner smiled lazily. "You'll never guess it. Forget about briefings. You didn't see it there. It's not even an official code name. But this is strictly Cosmic, got that?"

Andrew nodded, putting his mug slowly back on the trestle table.

"It's one of our guys here."

"One bloke? All this stuff came from one man?"

Rayner nodded.

"How's he getting it?"

"He goes for long walks at night," Rayner said. He held his lower lip with his upper teeth and moved his jaw from side to side.

"By himself?"

Rayner nodded. "At least that's what he says. Nobody ever sees him come or go. And remember, Andy, we got major light around the perimeter. Enough to light up Yankee Stadium. And nobody, but nobody's seen him go out through the sentries. No breaks in the wire. Nothing from the K-9 patrols. Diddlysquat."

"What is he?" Andrew pressed. "Berets? Lurp?"

"None of the above. He couldn't pass the physical for the Berets. Long Range Reconnaissance wouldn't have him."

"What's his problem?"

"He's a total wacko, Andy. Looney tunes. Buuuut," he held his hands open, "he's our wacko."

"He's a collector."

Rayner raised both eyebrows in feigned amusement.

"Ears?" Andrew had seen the type coming in from patrols with dried bloody ears hanging off their dog tag chains.

Rayner shook his head. "Worse." He grinned.

"Go on."

"Heads."

"Say again?"

"He collects their heads."

Andrew watched the smoke coil from his cigarette, damp with sweat from his fingers.

"I'm not kiddin'," Rayner said. "He brings them back most every other morning. He's walkin' fuckin' death."

"What's he doing here?"

"He was a company commander with Airborne. Did great. But they figured he was gettin' too spooky. Used to go off by himself at night when they were out on ops. Always came back with something useful. But then he started collecting heads. They sent him back here for," he emphasized each syllable, "psychiatric evaluation."

"And?"

"Our shrink says he's perfectly normal. Shows you the high caliber of mental health care we give our fighting men out here. Then while he's being evaluated, he starts taking little walks at night. We'd find him in the morning, sleeping like a baby with a burlap sack full of heads under his cot. Well, not full. One or two, maybe three. But he had this wonderful fuckin' Int on him. VC cadre lists. Targets. Maps. O Group notes. Troop movements. All the shit-hot stuff we've been sending you guys. So." He shrugged, palms upward. "The brass get a hard-on, look the other way, and he stays on 'between postings.' As long as he doesn't hurt anyone, he's ours. He's our best asset."

"As long as he doesn't hurt anyone but Charlie," Andrew amended.

"Shit. He can wax all the gooks he can get his hands on. It's cool with us. More bodies for Tricky Dick to lie about back home."

"Any chance of meeting him?"

"Why?" Rayner's voice hardened. "You want to debrief him yourself?"

"No, no, mate. He's your boy. We appreciate you sharing. But you know how my boss is. The more he knows about his sources the better he sleeps at night."

"I dunno, Andy."

"Sounds like the word's already out on him. Shit, Ray, how many blokes keep a bag of heads under the bed, and stay a secret? Fancy code names or not."

Rayner stared hard at him for a moment. Andrew could see in his eyes a turmoil of bravado and caution. Then Rayner sucked violently on the last of his cigarette, igniting the tobacco down to the filter in a cloud of acrid smoke.

"Sure," he said, holding the smoke in his lungs. "Why the fuck not?"

Andrew slowly drained his coffee and examined the inside of the mug. He felt a door opening in the darkness, and a need that he was incapable of identifying or understanding.

"Ready when you are," he said to Rayner, stubbing out his cigarette.

"Great. It's, what, oh six-forty. He should be having breakfast. He eats in his tent. He's a vegetarian. Likes to do his own food. C'mon."

"What's his name?"

"Bliss. Captain Keith Bliss. Cute name, eh?" Rayner said. "Bliss. Motherfucker. C'mon."

They headed down through the lines, rows of tents ranked back from the perimeter, and joined by duckboard walkways. They passed a handful of enlisted men lifting weights in an outdoor gym.

"Guys," Posner called as they passed.

"Hey, Rayner," one of them called. Andrew cringed inwardly at the familiarity. "Eight and a wakie."

"No shit," Posner answered cheerfully. "What you gonna do?"

"Me? Shit. Nine days, man, I'm gonna hit beautiful downtown Fort Lauderdale. Gonna buy me a red T-bird convertible, eat some pussy."

"Your lips to God's ears, man."

"Red, Rayner. It's gonna be candyass red."

"Angry color for pussy, man." Posner waved, and kept walking.

They walked on and found Bliss's tent at the far end of the row, closest to the perimeter, in the most dangerous location in the lines, closest to Charlie on the outside, and the softest target for fraggers on the inside. Adrian Cronauer's voice crackled on transistor radios tuned to Armed Forces Radio Service Vietnam, then "I'm gonna wait till the midnight hour" blared along the lines. The tent flaps were all open to catch any breeze that moved. Some had mosquito netting. When they reached the end tent, they heard the voices of two women singing.

"Keith?" Rayner Posner called from outside.

"Come in, Rayner." Posner looked at Andrew with raised eyebrows, then lifted the mesh flap and entered.

Andrew stared. Captain Keith Bliss was not what he expected. He looked frail. He was wearing black-lensed wraparound sunglasses that hugged his face. He was sitting cross-legged on a canvas folding cot in an olive green tank top and baggy khaki shorts that showed off thin arms and legs and sagging shoulders. In front of him were a bag of dried apricots, a hand of five bananas, and a green plastic water canteen. A Grundig reel-to-reel tape recorder stood on a wooden card table in the middle of the tent. The reels turned slowly, as the haunting soprano duet from Delibes's opera *Lakmé* flowed from the speakers.

Keith Bliss swayed like a charmed creature to the ethereal voices, smiling in a way that struck Andrew as distinctly angelic. He found himself glancing from Bliss to the floor of the tent, for signs of a burlap sack seeping ominously on the ground.

"Keith, I want you to meet someone . . ."

" . . . Hey, an Aussie," Bliss said softly, smiling broadly at Andrew, examining his uniform through his heavy shades. "Joan Sutherland, La Stupenda. Australia's gift to the world. Divine. Robert Helpmann. Such a sensitive dancer. And dear Chips Rafferty. What a marvelous actor. In Hollywood, he would have rivaled Coop. You look like a Chips Rafferty, sir. Oh I think so, yes, Chips, Lieutenant, whaddya think? You mind if I call you Lieutenant Chips? Mr. Chips? Mate?"

"Whatever, Captain," Andrew said. Bliss's complete sense of ease magnified his menace. Andrew held out his hand, and Bliss shook it with a boneless grip. "Pleased to meet you."

"And I'm very pleased to meet you, Mr. Chips." His laugh was barely audible. "Beautiful, aren't they?" Bliss said, indicating the tape recorder and the two soprano voices.

"Yeah. Just great," Rayner said.

"It's a barcarole," Bliss said. "Lakmé's the daughter of an Indian priest. A Brahmin. She's taking a bath in the river with her servant girl, Mallika. It's night, and they're singing together about the beauty of the stars and the perfume of the flowers along the river. They're talking about running away together. It's too beautiful, don't you think?"

"They sound like a pair of fuckin' lesbos," Rayner said.

Bliss appeared to have not heard him. He was swaying again, lost in the duet, and Andrew and Rayner saw tears trickle under his sunglasses and down his cheeks. Bliss laughed and removed his glasses. His eyes were closed tightly and he rubbed them with the palms of his hands. He kept his eyes shut until his sunglasses were in place again. "Rayner doesn't have much in the way of cultural tastes, Mr. Chips. You like opera?"

"I've never been a big fan, Captain. But I like this."

"An honest answer," Bliss said soberly, nodding his head, "from an honest man."

He snapped a banana off the bunch and peeled it with a meticulous care that was neither feminine nor delicate, but something in between. He ate quickly, chewing in jerky bites and swigging water from the canteen after each mouthful. Andrew was reminded of a flying fox, the large black fruit bat that descends in clouds on ripening trees along the north Australian coasts. Under different circumstances, he would never have noticed Keith Bliss. He was the scrawny face in a crowd that one sees fleetingly and recalls only as a vague shape. But the knowledge of his night missions made him macabrely unforgettable.

"I'd offer you something, but you've already had breakfast," Bliss said, still chewing.

Rayner instinctively looked down, checking his uniform for spilled food.

"You smell of ham and eggs and coffee, Rayner. And those disgusting cigarettes. And you, Mr. Chips, had something sweet. Thick and cloying. Condensed milk?"

Andrew grinned. "How did you know that?" He turned to Rayner. "C-rats. I had a cereal block. With condensed milk. Beats that powdered shit."

"You also had bacon and eggs and a soda, Coca-Cola. And coffee," Bliss said. "Not very nutritional. And like my erudite friend Rayner, you're a smoker."

"No shit, Sherlock," Rayner said. "I guess I didn't see you in the club at breakfast."

"I wasn't there," Bliss said gently. "I can smell it on you. You both smell like carnivores." He put a dried apricot in his mouth and chewed quickly.

"You're a piece of work, Keith," Rayner said chuckling. "You mind if we sit down?"

"Please. Be my guests."

Rayner sat on the other cot in the tent. Andrew pointed to the footlocker at the bottom of Bliss's cot and said, "Do you mind?" Bliss waved grandly with a flick of the wrist.

"Andy wants to know why you're called G-String," Rayner said.

Keith Bliss smiled slowly behind his sunglasses, like a cheeky blind kid.

"You're not a shrink, are you Mr. Chips? You're carrying something inside, I think. The kind of inner resentment that drives so many malleable minds to psychology."

"No," Rayner interrupted. "He's one of us, Keith. He's an IO with the Aussies."

"Bird. Australian. It's a big country but a small population. Relative of Owen Bird, the mill"—Bliss stretched out the word, smiling around it, and neither Rayner nor Andrew could see where he was looking behind his sunglasses—"yonaire?"

"His only, dearly beloved son," Rayner said. "Can you believe it? He wants to be here. Fuckin' volunteered."

"Did you now, Mr. Chips. And what kind of score are you hoping to settle over here?"

"I believe in the war, Captain."

"Ahh," Bliss said, rocking slowly back and forward. "Young Rayner, I can understand, Mr. Chips. He comes here because he needs to be with his tribe, the Corps. Needs their blood rituals. Semper Fidelis. Always faithful. But you, Mr. Chips, are not I think a tribal animal. I suspect you have another agenda here." He stopped rocking and smiled faintly. "Want to kill Daddy?"

Rayner laughed out loud. "You're a fuckin' piece of work, Keith."

Bliss remained silent.

"You meant do I want to kill people instead of my old man? In place of him?"

"Well done, Mr. Chips."

"He's a desk jockey," Rayner said. "Like me."

"Then why is he here, Rayner?" Bliss said quietly.

"He wants to know why your stuff's so clean."

"He could have asked you, Rayner. Ne c'est pas, Monsieur Chip?"

"A hunch, Captain. I had a feeling I had to meet you."

"Healthy thing, instinct, Mr. Chips. I live by it. And call me Keith. We're all brother officers here. I'm not being formal. I just like the sound of 'Mr. Chips.' But, you know, if the truth be known, you remind me more of Fletcher Christian, the mutineer. Have a little trouble accepting authority, Mr. Chips? Is that why you're doing intelligence, not commanding a platoon?"

Bliss began whistling. It sounded vaguely familiar, but Andrew couldn't identify it. He knew Bliss was deliberately needling him. Bliss smiled and whistled the same bars again.

"No?" he said, and Andrew shook his head. "Bach's Air on a G-String, Mr. Chips. Recognize it?"

"I've heard it before," Andrew said. "But I wouldn't have had a clue what it is."

"What it is, is a clue," Bliss said blandly.

Rayner giggled from the other cot.

"Beats me," Andrew said.

"Show him, Keith. He'll never guess."

Bliss reached into a pocket of his baggy shorts and pulled out a clear, tough plastic bag, the sort used to pack C-rations. He tipped its contents onto his cot, next to the canteen and fruit. There were two stubby cylinders of wood, and the gray spherical shapes of a couple of one-ounce lead fishing sinkers. Andrew recognized what they were attached to, and then he knew.

"Piano wire," Andrew said.

"Have a cigar, Mr. Chips."

"What's the sinker for?" Andrew asked.

In a long graceful movement like a ballet passage, Keith Bliss slid off the bed with a wire coil and one of its handles in his right hand, arcing from left to right, toward Andrew's throat. The wire curved outward, pulled by the sinker and wooden handle at the other end, and whipped twice around Andrew's neck before Bliss caught the wood neatly in his left hand. As his fist closed around the handle, he braced his right knee against Andrew's chest and placed just enough tension on the noose to make a thin indentation around the skin. In that instant, Andrew felt the absolute presence of death, separated by no more than a few ounces of pressure on the wire, enough to slice through skin and vessels and cartilage with a soft pop and sink down to the bone of his spine. Bliss lowered his knee and with a flick of his left wrist unfurled the wire smoothly and coiled it into his right hand. Andrew stood stock-still, paralyzed by the swiftness of the attack and the absolute control of it. He felt completely invaded by the lightning presence that had come inside his defenses with such speed and precision.

"No fuss, no muss," Bliss said, smiling behind his sunglasses and returning like a wraith to his cot, to sit once again cross-legged, munching dried apricots.

Rayner and Andrew were silent. Andrew ran his finger around the angry line where the wire noose had tightened on his throat. There was no sign of blood.

"Fuckin' unbelievable," Rayner muttered.

Instead of fear, Andrew felt excitement. He was unable to connect it to the anger that had lived in the deepest caves of his psyche since he was a child, the separation and emptiness that bred a lethal detatchment from life and worth. All he knew was that what he had just seen electrified him.

"May I see it?" he asked, indicating the coil of wire tossed back on the cot.

"Of course," Bliss said, holding the device out.

Andrew leaned over and felt his fingers tingle with anticipation the second before they closed around the garrote. He picked it up and held it between his fingertips and thumbs.

"Have you used that one yet?" Rayner asked slyly, and before Bliss answered, Andrew felt a hot flicker through his fingers as he studied the wire for evidence of blood or flesh.

"Nah," Bliss said. "I keep the used ones in my footlocker. With the heads."

Andrew's glance shot from the coil of wire to the footlocker beneath him and back to Bliss, and was met by a beatific smile. Rayner was giggling slowly.

"A fuckin' piece of work, Keith," he said. "Whattaya think, Andy?"

Andrew looked over at him but didn't answer. Instead he turned to Bliss. "May I ask you some questions, Keith?"

"Nothing too personal, I trust, Mr. Chips?"

"How do you collect the int?"

"I just go out and listen." He took another dried apricot from the bag, but instead of eating it, he began systematically shredding it in his fingers.

"Where do you go?"

"Out. I go out beyond the perimeter and I sit somewhere and listen. Then I go somewhere else and listen. If I hear something, I go and see what it is."

"How do you get around at night?"

Bliss laughed, a child's laugh, completely free of artifice. "I use the base as a reference. You know how much noise and light this place puts out at night? It's like a lighthouse. You can hear it a mile out. And you can see it five miles out."

"That explains the sunglasses," Andrew said. "Keeping night vision."

"Very good, Mr. Chips. I'd rather stay in total darkness. But it's too hot to keep the tent closed. And I'm afraid it's getting too dangerous to wear a sleeping mask all day. You never know who'll drop by with a little fragging on their mind."

"How do you find Charlie?" Andrew asked.

"Don't you listen? I go out there and listen. You Aussies are good at that. Silent patrols. Sign language. Our guys are taught it, of course, but these draftees have little heart for discipline. Too much booze and drugs and disrespect. But even you Aussies make noise when you get to platoon strength. Charlie's the same. You go out far enough, and sit nice and still long enough, and you'll hear everyone moving around. Sometimes when Charlie's shifting his regiments, it's like Times Square. A veritable stampede. And give him his due, Charlie is good. Very professional."

"How do you tell the difference between Charlie and Friendlies?"

"That's the easiest part, Mr. Chips. Our good old boys stink. I can smell a hamburger fart half a click away. Charlie eats rice and fish. He doesn't fart as much and he doesn't stink. His great vice is cigarettes. Chinese mostly. You know the Chinese produce more tobacco than the rest of the world combined? Nearly five times as much as the US of A? And their cigarettes stink more. The Russians are the worst, though. Floor sweepings. You can always smell the Soviet advisers. You'd think they'd buy American when they got here, wouldn't you?"

"Why do you take their heads?" Rayner asked.

"Fatal immodesty." Bliss grinned serenely. Then his expression and voice became contemptuous. "Anyone can collect ears from a corpse. Very childish. But you take the head, and you take your enemy's identity. His soul. You make it personal. And it scares the piss out of his comrades. Besides—his face became angelic again—I love it so."

"I have another question for you, Keith," Andrew said. He heard his words as he spoke them, and he felt a fullness in his ears, as if his blood pressure had risen, as if he were underwater. He wanted to ask the question before he had time to contemplate the consequences. He felt a momentum from some unrecognizable force deep within him. "Would you let me come with you?"

Rayner stared at him.

Keith Bliss swung his head slowly toward Andrew, smiling in a way that no longer looked angelic. The sunglasses no longer made him seem blind. Instead, they appeared to make him all-seeing. He watched Andrew silently, resembling a malevolent entity who has discovered a corruptible soul. He turned the request over in his mind, and examined Andrew's face. Finally, he lifted his head, and his smile became more placid.

"It would be my pleasure," Bliss said.

"Fuckin' unbelievable," Rayner breathed. "He's never taken anyone with him before."

"No one's ever asked so honestly, Rayner," Bliss said simply. Then to Andrew, he said, "There are some conditions, Mr. Chips."

Andrew's pulse soared the moment he began asking his question. It pounded when he heard Bliss agree. He still felt the influence of some foreign part of himself, turning with anticipation.

"Firstly," Keith Bliss said, "give up meat and cigarettes for two weeks. And no alcohol. Nothing. Drink a gallon of water a day. Piss out the toxins. We have to purify ourselves."

Rayner watched them both, slowly shaking his head in disbelief, as Bliss ran his fingertips tenderly around the coil of wire.

"As for this," he said, "you have to make your own. It has to be a part of you, an extension of your being. Go into town, and find the Fah Tsoi Music Store. And contrary to Rayner's quaint folklore, this is not a G string. Top A is finer and stronger, the highest note on the piano, beyond even La Stupenda's range. You'll need half a dozen, I suggest. Ask for Mr. Ky. He's an old friend. A great connoisseur of opera."

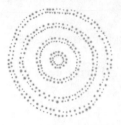

CHAPTER 15

CALAF, LUCIANO PAVAROTTI'S unknown prince, at last revealed his secret identity to Joan Sutherland's Turandot, placing his life in her hands, filling the cabin of the aircraft with their duet as Grace Morgan watched Sydney Harbour rise toward her. A flight attendant's voice broke through the opera with instructions about seat belts and tray tables and announcing local time, seven twenty-six in the morning. Grace had crossed nine time zones. The four-hour flight from Houston to Los Angeles, and the thirteen-hour marathon across the Pacific left her exhausted, and she still had a three-hour connecting flight to Adelaide ahead of her. She surveyed the country outside the porthole, feeling foreign above these unfamiliar red tile roofs and alien trees and small cars, the iconic Opera House and Bridge on the long blue harbor, and beyond them, low dark mountains, guarding the remote plains that ran on to the red desert. Her heart and stomach shifted, and she wondered again if she was on a ridiculous, humiliating mission. "Trust your compass, little darling. And when it swings wild, trust your instinct." She closed her eyes and waited for the jet to land at Sir Charles Kingsford Smith International Airport.

⁂

Owen opened his eyes and saw the ceiling of his hospital room, spread with shadows from the night light. He felt wrapped in a cocoon, unable to move. He felt unaccountably afraid of something in the darkened room, but he couldn't move his head to see. The sense of grave danger grew with each attempt to turn his head. It niggled urgently through his legs and belly. Then he was able to see down the length of his body to the foot of the bed. In the half light he saw three black figures staring at him with empty eye sockets. Owen tried to call out but his mouth wouldn't open. He recognized the youngest as the man he had seen in the emergency room when he was brought in from the hunt. The second was about the same age as the first, with similar thin scars across his chest. Owen forced himself to look at the third man, older, stouter, with no tribal markings, but the same ghastly empty eyes that stared steadily through him.

He tried to look for the duty nurse stationed at a desk near the foot of his bed, but his head remained as paralyzed as the rest of his body. He felt himself suffocating, unable to breathe fast enough to feed his racing heart. He wondered why the cardiac monitor wasn't registering his hammering pulse. He felt the cold clammy grip of death, and tried again to call out, but his body refused to obey him. As he watched, the three men raised their fingers to their mouths and with gusts of air, like ocher blowers, spat their teeth into their hands. Owen saw the red spray blast around their fingers. The specters stared through him and he felt his own eyes go cold as if all his body heat was being drained into what he saw.

The three figures raised their bloody hands and hurled their teeth onto the bed in a shower of red-streaked enamel that clattered loudly on the sheet. Owen gasped for air, still unable to move. Then as the three ghosts looked up at him again, he saw in the shadows behind them a fourth figure, turning slowly toward him. Owen could not take his eyes away, riveted by a terror he had never felt—never imagined possible—before. He desperately tried to look away, certain that the moment he saw this fourth face clearly he would die. The figure rotated steadily toward him, and Owen focused the last of his fleeting strength on his throat, willing himself to call out. Sweat broke out along his forehead, and down the length of his immobile body, and his heart pounded faster, pushing the cardiac readout past one hundred, and triggering the monitor's shrill alarm.

Owen heard a chair pushed back harshly, as the duty nurse dropped her book and ran toward the bed. He was able to see her coming into his view, reaching out to switch off the alarm, as more footsteps hurried through the door. He was freezing, and still unable to move his body, but he could turn his head back to look down the length of the bed. Of the four dark figures and the bloody teeth that had clattered like bullets onto his sheet there was no trace.

ꙮ

Dr. Alistair Steele loved the orderly quietness of his morgue. He was a methodical, calm, thoughtful medical examiner. No matter how a body arrived, whether brutally murdered or profoundly decomposed, Dr. Steele examined it with a balance of clinical detachment and human compassion, but never before with the sense of foreboding that he felt now.

Not when the first of the bodies came in.

Nor even the second.

But the third body also yielded a small document that caused him to put down his instruments, remove his heavy latex gloves, and sit, staring at it.

The third body was identified in its postmortem report as Oscar Woolie, an art dealer, and the autopsy appeared routine, requiring a superficial exam from head to toes, and the removal of the crown of the skull, to reveal a healthy brain with no gross indication of drug or alcohol abuse. The flesh and bone of the head were unmarked by violent cuts or bruising. There was no blood on the hair. The teeth and gums exhibited plaque, wear, and puffy tissue consistent with an unhealthy diet, but not malnutrition. In fact, Oscar Woolie ate too much, exercised too little, and was a habitual smoker, as evidenced by his tar-tainted lungs, exhibiting cellular signatures of developing emphysema. But for now, along with mild accretion of plaque in his coronary arteries, Oscar would not have experienced much more than moderate breathlessness during exertion. His stomach, intestinal and urinary tracts, and bladder revealed that before death he had most recently dined on barbecued steak, fried bread, no vegetables, and what measured out to be four pints of beer. There were no inflammations, new lesions, or superficial organic signs of poisoning in the tracts, a finding confirmed by Pathology.

So when Dr. Alistair Steele wrote on Oscar Woolie's postmortem report, "Heart failure," and signed it and stamped it with his official seal, he should have been satisfied that he had completed an exhaustive and proper exam. But the piece of paper he had found in Oscar's pocket made him deeply suspicious as he gazed again at the shrouded bodies of the two younger men nearby. He would have to turn it in with his report, and imagined the furor it would cause.

He heard a knock at the double doors.

"Mark! Come in!"

"Hello, Alistair," Reverend Mark Hansen said and shook his hand warmly. "You look dreadful. They working you to death?"

Dr. Steele grimaced at the old joke, ushered Mark to a chair, and slid open one of the unoccupied body drawers in the wall.

"Long morning. Drink?"

"Bit early for me," Mark answered, curious.

"I'm having a heart starter. Sure?"

Mark didn't want to, but he heard the tension in his friend's voice, and nodded. Dr. Steele took out a bottle of Bundaberg rum and two glasses.

"Ice?"

"Just water thanks, Alistair."

Mark watched him retrieve a plastic gallon jug of water from the cold air of the body drawer, pour two glasses of rum, and dilute both with a splash of water.

"Cheers."

"Cheers."

They drank, and Mark waited.

"Those're your lads over there," Dr. Steele said, indicating the bodies of Teddy Gidgee and Russell King beneath green plastic sheets. "Got their release papers?"

"Tomorrow morning."

"Good. They'll be ready when you are."

"Thanks. I'd like to pick them up early, before it gets hot."

"What are you driving?"

"Land Rover."

"You've got air-conditioning?"

"Oh yes."

"Then they'll be fine for eight hours out of the fridge. The body bags are well sealed."

"I'll have them home in six, barring anything unforeseen."

"Right you are, then."

"Right."

"Another rum?"

"I'll nurse this one, thanks, Alistair."

"Right."

"Everything all right?"

"Of course."

"Alistair."

"Really. I'm all right."

"What did you find?"

"Heart failure."

"Which one?"

"All of them."

"But Teddy and Russell were only in their twenties."

"All three of them."

"Who's the other one?"

"Oscar Woolie." Dr. Steele pointed to the third covered body. "Art dealer in town. Aged fifty-three, but no sign of heart disease. In fact Teddy was the only one with any apparent symptoms. Oscar simply keeled over in his home. No sign of trauma, not even heart trauma. Russell King just sat down under a tree in the Todd and expired."

"Teddy and Russell are both off Clementine. What's their connection to this Woolie fellow?"

"He was Pitjantjatjara mob," Dr. Steele said. "Not fullblood like Teddy and Russell, but identifiably Pitjantjatjara."

"I see."

"What's going on, Mark?"

Mark Hansen looked into his glass and slowly took another sip of the rum. He cleared his throat.

"Our mission people think Teddy was Sung by an Old Fellow."

"Why?"

"He stole a tjurunga from the Wirruntjatjara. Their most valuable one."

Dr. Steele let out his breath. "And Russell King was in on it?"

"It would seem so. The Wirruntjatjara believe their people will die if they don't get it back."

"Then they will all certainly die, if they believe it," Dr. Steele said. "Enter the Old Fellow."

"I just don't understand what induced the boys to steal it. You saw their scars. They're both Pitjantjatjara initiates. They knew the consequences."

"Think it's payback for something? A quarrel with the Wirruntjatjara?"

"I haven't heard anything to indicate that."

"Maybe they just decided to steal it. Maybe they stumbled on it and thought they'd get something for it."

"I doubt it. They'd have too much respect for the Law."

"These young bucks have lost respect for their Law. Too much grog. Too much petrol sniffing. I've done autopsies on kids of twelve whose brains are mush from sniffing petrol. They're lost. Their elders don't have the clout anymore. Anyhow," Dr. Steele said carefully, "maybe the boys had an extra incentive."

"I can't imagine what that would be. You think Oscar here was in on it?"

"I do. A neighbor of Oscar's apparently identified Teddy Gidgee and Russell King from photographs," Dr. Steele continued. "She says they were at Oscar's house a few weeks ago, and again a couple of days before he turned up dead."

"They killed him?"

"That's what the police'd like to think. It'd make it nice and tidy for them. They don't like to strain too much, especially around blackfellers."

"But you don't think Teddy and Russell did it."

"I don't think they killed him, no."

"What do you think then?"

"When I examined Oscar, I found this in his trouser pocket."

Mark reached out and took the paper from his friend's hand. It was a check made out to Oscar Woolie, and Mark's eyes widened perceptibly as he read the amount, and the signature.

"Back of the left thigh," Owen said, with his eyes closed. He lay on the bed with his knees up, and the hospital gown bunched around his flanks.

"Good." The neurologist moved the cap of his pen along Owen's leg. "Now?"

"Right calf. Knee to heel."

"Good. Now?"

"Right foot. Along the top."

"This?"

"Front of the left thigh. I've got pins and needles there. Like it's gone to sleep."

"On the contrary, it's waking up. This?"

"Top of the left foot."

"Excellent. You can open your eyes now." Dr. Toby Andrews put his fountain pen back in his jacket.

"What's the verdict?" Owen growled.

"Remarkable progress, Mr. Bird," Dr. Andrews said. "It can happen like this with a spinal contusion. The methylprednisolone certainly helped. As soon as the swelling eases, the pressure comes off the spinal cord, and recovery can be quite fast. Can you move your toes for me?"

He watched Owen's feet, as the tips of the toes stirred.

"Excellent." Andrews glanced at his physiotherapist, who was making notes.

"When can I get up?" Owen's gruffness eased.

"Soon. I don't want you jumping the gun." He directed his warning as well to Agnes, who was watching beside the bed. "Try to do too much too soon, and you could end back up where you started. Or worse. We'll take this one step at a time, literally."

"Spare me the fucking disclaimer, Toby."

The surgeon's eyes narrowed.

"You get up, Mr. Bird, when I say so."

"I can get a second bloody opinion."

"I'd encourage it," the doctor said quietly. "But you're getting the best opinion in the country. And my opinion is you follow my advice and be patient."

There was a deathly silence as Owen Bird's face went dark. Agnes saw the physiotherapist hold her breath. Owen was used to obedience from everyone in his orbit, and he had the power to make and break the career, or worse, of anyone who resisted him. His face creased, and he gave a short, sharp laugh.

"You're a bastard, Toby."

"I'll take that as a compliment."

"When, then?"

"We'll schedule more physio this morning. If your neurological signs keep improving, you can try standing tomorrow. We'll take it from there."

"You're the witch doctor."

"I'd still like to recommend a sedative."

"Forget it. I'm fine."

"We thought you were having a heart attack. The duty nurse thought she'd lost you."

"It was just a nightmare. Nothing else, Toby. I'm fine."

Agnes Horstmann watched him closely, unconvinced by Owen's cheerfulness. She turned at a knock at the door, and a nurse put her head in.

"It's a priest," she said, "to see Mr. Bird."

"I don't need a fucking chaplain." Owen watched his physiotherapist finishing her notes. "Let's get on with it," he said to her, banishing any thought of the visitor.

"He says he's from Lake Amadeus Mission," the nurse persisted.

Owen looked up sharply, then relaxed, but Agnes knew him too well to be deceived.

"What's he want?" Owen asked casually.

"He says he has to talk to you, Mr. Bird. Name's Reverend Hansen."

Owen looked at Agnes and tilted his head toward the door and she left silently.

He turned back to his physiotherapist. "Let's get on with it."

Mark saw the nurse stand aside to let an elegant woman in her sixties emerge from Owen Bird's private ward. She surveyed the hallway with a sharp, alert gaze.

"Reverend Hansen." She came toward him with her hand gracefully extended and a warm smile lighting her face. "I'm Agnes Horstmann. It's so nice to meet you. Security didn't give you any trouble?"

She said it conspiratorially, apologetically, but Mark suspected Owen's private guards would be reprimanded for letting in anyone uninvited.

"I came up from the morgue," he said, shaking her hand. "Through the staff entrance."

"Owen will be delighted you've come to see him," Agnes Horstmann said smoothly. "You've come such a long way. You must have such a lot to talk about."

Mark ignored the implied question.

"I have to speak to him."

"It's so nice of you to make the effort."

"Is he free?"

"He's in conference with his doctors at present. He's been so busy, you know. I know he'd hate to keep you waiting."

"I don't mind," he said.

"May I get you something? We've brought our own chef." He could feel her herding him away. "They've given us our own dining room downstairs. A little small"—she became conspiratorial again—"but you'll be comfortable there."

"That's very kind of you," he said. "But I'll wait."

"Very well then. I'll come for you as soon as he's free."

"Thank you."

Mark sat in a vinyl chair and read a magazine, old, dog-eared, irrelevant.

After a quarter of an hour, a nurse came out, passed him in the hallway, and returned to Owen's ward a few minutes later. Twenty minutes after that, the same nurse made the same journey. Fifteen minutes later, Agnes Horstmann reappeared, warm, consoling, her curiosity about Mark's visit, and Owen's acquiescence to it, completely hidden.

"I'm so sorry you've had to wait so long. He'll see you now."

Owen was sitting back in an elaborate adjustable electric armchair, designed for back injuries. Three other leather armchairs stood with it, around a coffee table. Owen was dressed in slacks and shoes and an open-necked business shirt. He was on one of three telephones on the table, taking notes on a legal pad with his good hand. His left arm rested in its fiberglass cast, inserted with magnetic strips to accelerate healing. Owen put his pen down and held his hand out to Mark, as he continued to talk on the phone, without getting up. They shook hands firmly and Owen waved Mark to one of the other armchairs. Mark took in the telecommunications equipment, the walls of fresh flowers, the sole bed, tidily made up. He sat opposite Owen, and Agnes took a chair facing them. Owen hung up the telephone.

"Padre! Good to see you! How's Amadeus?"

"Hello, Owen. Still there."

"What's it been, a year? Two?"

"Something like that."

"You've met Agnes?"

"Yes."

"Mark and I," Owen turned to Agnes, "met years ago when I bought Clementine Downs. He's done amazing things for the natives on Lake Amadeus."

"How fascinating. It must be so fulfilling."

"Did Agnes offer you tea? Coffee. Rum?"

"I'm fine, thank you," Mark said.

"Good of you to come and visit," Owen said warmly, then waved his good hand toward the flowers around the room. "I can't tell if it looks more like an undertaker's or a fuckin' brothel. I still haven't read half the cards on 'em yet. Most of the Cabinet sent something, and half the Opposition."

"Very nice," Mark said.

"Let me tell you, Padre, the only politician you can trust is the one in your pocket. But, they're still cheaper than fucking lawyers. This"—Owen stabbed his good forefinger at Mark like a pistol—"is all protected of course by the supplicant-priest relationship."

Mark thought the last thing that Owen Bird resembled was a supplicant, and wondered if it was a slip of the tongue, a ripple from a deeper current of concern or guilt.

"It looks like you've been in the wars, Owen."

"Oh, I'll be fine. These bloody drugs are fucking up my sleep. But I'm lucky the buff didn't break my back. Young Flying Doctor saved my arse. Tim Kennedy, know him?"

"He's been out to the mission on clinics."

"They keep telling me how lucky I am. I could be dead, they reckon. Or worse."

"What could be worse?"

"Hah!" Owen stroked his mustache. "Tell me, what brings you out of the bush?"

"I came to collect a young fellow who was brought in here," Mark said.

"Taking him home, eh?"

"Yes. Along with a mate of his."

"Ah good."

"They're both off Clementine."

"Are they now? Behaving themselves?"

"They're both dead."

"I'm sorry to hear it." Owen showed no emotion. "I heard something was going on down there. Know a blackfeller called Errol Dingo?"

Mark shook his head.

"He was supposed to be my wingman on the hunt. Off Clementine. Blew through on me. Maybe if he hadn't, I wouldn't be here . . ."

Mark looked steadily at Owen, searching for something. Owen held his gaze until Mark looked away.

"How'd your boys die?"

"The coroner says heart failure," Mark answered.

"Happens," Owen said. "That's how they all die in jail, isn't it. Poor bastards."

"Perhaps."

It became quiet in the ward. They could hear the far-off trill of a magpie in one of the gum trees below. The carrion call of a crow through the window made the air sound dry and still. Mark was acutely aware of it. Of all the sounds in the bush, the crow's long, falling note most clearly defined the emptiness and enormousness of the Outback, and the arc from life to death.

"You don't sound convinced," Owen said.

"They may have been Sung."

"Ben Crotty told me about a Mungera buck off my place up on 'Alligator River.' Ran off with a young lubra. The girl'd been promised to one of the elders. The buck raped her, then killed her. Tried to burn the body. They called in this Old Fellow from King River to point the bone at the killer. Two weeks later the young buck turns up dead on Roper River Station. They reckon he starved to death."

Mark waited.

"It was possible," Owen continued. "The thing was, Ben said, they found him camped on a riverbank. Plenty of water, and crawling with fish and ducks, and big mobs of animals. Bloody blackfellers. Who knows? Your boys must have pissed somebody off."

"They may have stolen something from the Wirruntjatjara."

Owen exhaled softly. His face seemed to grow haggard. He saw mental flashes of black hands throwing teeth onto white sheets. He drove the unknown fear back into darkness. Outside, on a high branch of a gum tree, the magpie was flaring its wings and smoothing its feathers as it sang. It seemed blissfully happy. Owen tried to concentrate on Mark, and cleared his throat twice.

"You believe that stuff, Padre?"

"I've learned not to be dogmatic."

"You believe they were Sung?"

"If they broke the Law. Anangu Law."

"The Law," Owen said bitterly. "You should know better, Padre. Their Law is a pile of superstition and old men's yarns. In another twenty, thirty years, they'll all be gone. There won't be any bloody Law. There won't be any full-bloods. It's all over for them. It was all over the day the whitefellers landed."

"Things are changing out here, Owen. There's a resurgence of interest in the Law. A lot more young fellows are going through the manhood ceremonies."

"A resurgence of interest, eh. If you ask me, that has more to do with land rights and government handouts than any interest in the Law."

"You might be surprised."

"Come off it, Padre. These fellers wouldn't know sacred land if it bit 'em on the arse. The only land they're interested in is a free cattle station, courtesy of the poor bloody taxpayer. That and a welfare check. You know how much the bloody government threw away on Aboriginal and Torres Strait Island Affairs last year? Eight hundred million dollars. A total bloody waste. Most of it went to buy Toyota Land Cruisers and refrigerators for a few ATSIC bastards on the take. Fuck-all got to the poor bloody blackfellers on the ground. They ought to take the Lands Council out and shoot the lot of 'em."

"I see age has mellowed you."

"Don't try to flatter me, Padre. Why are you really here?"

"I came to warn you."

"Really." Owen's voice turned cold.

"There was a third death this week," Mark said quietly.

"Go on."

"An art dealer. From Alice Springs." Mark felt a stillness settle on the room. The magpie chortled through the trees. "Oscar Woolie."

Owen's eyes didn't leave Mark's.

"Never heard of him, Padre."

Mark reached into his jacket and took out a photocopy and unfolded it.

"This shows a check made out to Oscar Woolie," Mark said. "For five hundred thousand dollars, U.S."

Owen took the paper, and looked at it. His eyes met Mark's, then returned to the photocopy of the check.

It was signed by Agnes Horstmann.

Robert Erhard paused on the Alice Springs rail platform and looked along the full length of *The Ghan*. She was magnificent; a thing of beauty, gleaming new, and freshly painted. He stepped inside the first class section and saw wood-grained panels and doors, and glowing brass fittings. He leaned out a window, and surveyed the platform, remembering his first journey north from Adelaide, with Maureen, on the ancient ancestor of this *Ghan*. He could almost smell the dust of that old boxcar, and hear the dry moaning of the hot wind through the cargo door, and the persistent, mesmerizing rattle of the wheels over the rails.

The conductor unlocked the door to Robert's compartment. Inside, a long plush seat ran along the bulkhead from the door to a wide panoramic window. An inner door led to a private shower and toilet.

"Nice and comfy, Dr. Erhard," the conductor said, glancing again from Robert's face to the name on his ticket. "Now then, if you need anything, just ask me. Would you like tea or coffee, when I wake you in the morning? We get into Adelaide at exactly seven-forty, right after breakfast."

"No thanks."

"I see." The conductor seemed disappointed. "Well. Dinner's in two sittings this evening, first is at six-thirty, second is at seven-thirty. Which would you like to reserve?"

"I won't be having dinner."

"Are you sure, Doctor? The dining car's beautiful. Antique glass, silver and linen service, stunning views of the sunset . . ."

"No. Thank you."

"Well. Suit yourself, Doctor. Anyhow, if you need anything, don't hesitate to call."

"Thank you. I will." Robert tipped him a five and the conductor took it, but reluctantly, as if he hadn't done enough for it, and it was all Robert's fault.

Robert closed the door and stood alone at the window looking out at the platform smiling quietly to himself. He remembered the way the light had played in dangerous lattices in that squealing, sweltering boxcar clattering over the rails so long ago with Maureen guiding him on his first journey on the old *Ghan*. Now, classical music played softly from a speaker above him, and air-conditioning silently cooled his cabin. He felt *The Ghan* begin to pull smoothly out of the station with barely a sound on the new steel line. It was exactly one o'clock in the afternoon.

He closed the window blinds and looked at his image in the full-length door mirror, at his gray slacks and polished black leather shoes, the white cotton button-down shirt, and the well-cut navy sports coat. He took off his jacket, and hung it in the closet. Then he discarded his shirt. Across his chest were three straight ridges of ceremonial scars. He looked at them in the mirror, then into his own eyes. His ancestors had been shot, poisoned, infected, jailed, beaten, dispossessed, and forgotten by the Piranypa. Even now, he knew he was invisible to most of them, another black face in a faceless, landless populace. The conductor's tone had revealed as much when he read "Dr. Erhard" from the ticket, as if it were improbable for an Aborigine to be traveling first class, let alone to have the title of Doctor.

But Dr. Robert Erhard knew exactly who he was. He was Tjilkamata, of the Spiny Anteater Dreaming. He was a Wirruntjatjara elder, and he could trace his unbroken story line back across eons to the time of Creation. He knew who he was, and where he was from, and no man or woman, black, white, or otherwise, could deny him his identity or his birthright.

Owen woke wracked with a coldness that made his body feel dead, his bones and muscles frozen rigid. He opened his mouth to call out, but could make no noise. His night nurse sat across the room, oblivious, reading, surrounded by shadows in the pool of light from her desk lamp.

At the foot of his bed, Owen saw the same three black figures watching him silently, their images splitting and joining, moving in and out of focus. Lazily, their hands moved to their mouths, and even before it happened Owen knew what they were about to do. Again he tried to call out, but his throat was lifeless.

Together, the dark figures spat their teeth into their hands and hurled them onto Owen's bed. He heard the clatter of bloodied enamel stumps hitting together, bouncing, streaking red tendrils across the white sheet. He struggled to breathe. He stared desperately at his night nurse and tried to make a noise, to raise his head or his hand, but his body refused to respond. The men at the foot of the bed watched dispassionately, their mouths empty black holes in their gunmetal skin. Behind them, he sensed another ghostly figure, hazy, terrifying, hobbling in the dark boundaries.

Owen felt his life draining into them. His heart pounded so loudly he could hear his blood coursing within his ears. He saw pale light dimming over the men, as they melted into dark shadows around the room, the fourth specter still faceless, more horrifying than any of the others.

Owen opened his eyes, gasping for air. He heard the alarm on his cardiac monitor go off, as the night nurse threw down her book, hit the red emergency button for the crash team, and rushed across the room to his bed.

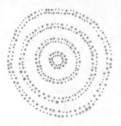

CHAPTER 16

ROOSTER WILSON HAD BEGUN PASSING BLOOD in his urine, not enough to be dangerous he told himself, but a serious sign that he'd taken too many rattlers. He was driving hard through the night with a seven-hundred-mile round-trip ahead, and he knew he couldn't do it without taking more of the little white pills.

His powerful spotlights, four mounted on the steel bull bar on the nose of his Mack, and four more on the roof, bored a blazing tunnel through the darkness of the highway. The raw, hard rhythm of Midnight Oil blasted out of his speakers, above the steady roar of the engine, and the whine of his road train's thirty-eight wheels. He was pulling three large freezer vans, bound for the Docker River settlement, three hundred and sixty miles away. Now the radio reports were warning of rain in the next two days.

"Unfuckingbelievable!" Rooster shouted above the noise

It hadn't rained out here in seven years. This single food delivery would cover a month's loan payment on his rig, but he would have to race a storm to earn it. He'd been on the road for six days straight, sleeping little more than three hours a day. The rattlers kept him awake and alert, but they were eating a hole in his bladder. He'd noticed the blood the last time he stopped for fuel. His hemorrhoids ached, and his body pleaded for sleep. He saw the flicker of a taillight a mile ahead, and unclipped the CB microphone.

"Mad Dog. Rooster. I'm behind you."

He dimmed his spotlights, and his field of light shortened at once from a mile and a half to five hundred yards.

"I seen ya," the reply crackled through his speaker.

Rooster changed down through the gears, easing the road train back from eighty miles an hour. He peered ahead to assure himself there was only one motorcycle parked beside the highway. He was cautious, but Rooster was only hauling frozen food and fifty cases of beer—too small for a biker gang that smuggled three million dollars of amphetamines a year.

He saw the glitter of chrome on the Harley-Davidson, and the dark shape of its rider leaning against it. He hated dealing with the gang, he hated seeing blood whenever he took a leak, and like hundreds of long-haul drivers around the continent, he hated the mill of bank interest, taxes, fuel bills, and maintenance overheads that drove him to break so many laws and take so many risks just to stay in business.

It took nearly a mile of highway to slow his sixty-ton rig down, but he rolled to a stop within a few feet of the dealer. Rooster Wilson grinned smugly to himself, and locked on the air brakes. He might be rattling like a maniac, he thought to himself, but he was still driving like a champion.

Mark Hansen reached Owen's ward as the cardiac team were packing their gear back on the crash trolley.

"Thank you for coming so quickly," Agnes Horstmann said as she met him at the door. "We thought it was a heart attack. Now they say it was stress."

"Padre!" Owen called from his bed. "What are you doing here?"

"I called him," Agnes said.

"What the fuck for? It's three o'clock in the morning. Go home, Padre."

"Looks like you've had a tough night, Owen."

"I'm fine. These bloody painkillers are giving me nightmares."

"What kind of nightmares?"

"Nothing, Padre. Go back to bed. Sorry you were dragged out."

"He dreamed about the men who died," Agnes said, "throwing their teeth."

"Give him a break, Agnes," Owen said. "He hasn't got a bloody clue what you're talking about. It was nothing, Padre."

"One of them was Oscar Woolie."

"Agnes! Shut the fuck up."

The crash team doctors and nurses stopped packing their equipment. For two days Agnes Horstmann had dominated everyone around her. Now they saw her flush with humiliation. Owen fumed, dismissing the crash team and duty nurse with a curt lift of his chin. The duty nurse went last, reluctantly, leaving Mark with Owen and Agnes, and the door ajar.

"Agnes, I'm sorry. But you shouldn't have shot your bloody mouth off."

"Nobody's ever spoken to me like that. Least of all you."

"I apologize."

Agnes drew herself up straight, her eyes closed.

"The teeth?" Mark asked quietly.

"Nothing," Owen said.

"They threw them at him."

"It was just a fucking bad dream. I'm sorry I told you, woman."

"It's about the check." Agnes opened her eyes and looked at Mark. He saw her struggling to keep her composure. "We told you there was no connection. But that wasn't quite true."

"Agnes, shut . . . up."

"Anangu believe that when you lose your teeth, you die," Mark began, "because you can't eat. Old people survive by eating food their children chew for them. Mothers chew food for their infants. When parents lose their teeth, their children return the favor. Otherwise they'll starve."

"Very interesting, Padre. It means fuck-all to me."

"It's about the stone, isn't it?" Agnes said, all steel gone from her voice.

"Agnes, let it go. She doesn't know what the check was for, Padre. I was buying some art, that's all. She signs everything I tell her to."

"Tell me about the stone," Agnes said.

"It was stolen," Mark replied.

"Any Tom, Dick, or Harry could have found it," Owen said, "the way tourists crawl all over everything now. You know that. Buses, four-wheel-drives. German hikers, Japanese loners on trail bikes, nothing's sacred anymore. If the blackfellers get it back, they'll just stick it in some hole in the desert for the next tourist to find. It's a damn sight safer in a vault."

"Yours?" Mark said.

"I've got the finest collection in the world, and you know it. Climate control, security, it's safe as a bank. That's where an artifact like that belongs."

"Is that why it was stolen? For your collection?"

"I didn't steal it, Padre. I bought it fair and square. You saw the check. It's not my problem Oscar Woolie didn't cash it."

"They'll do anything to get it back."

"What do you mean?" Agnes asked.

"They've already accounted for three men," Mark said.

Owen's face gave nothing away. He appeared uninterested.

"How?" Agnes wanted to know.

"Teddy Gidgee and Russell King most likely took it from its hiding place," Mark said, "and sold it to Oscar Woolie. All three of them are dead. They're below us now, in the morgue."

"How did Oscar Woolie die?" Agnes wanted to know.

"Heart failure," Mark answered. "Same as the boys."

"You think that's what happened to Owen?" Agnes asked. "Heart failure?"

"It was tachycardia," Owen growled. "Nothing more. It's just the fucking drugs."

"What exactly did you see?" Mark asked.

"Fucking nothing."

"He says there were four men near his bed. They threw their teeth at him."

"Do you know who they were, Owen?"

"Three." Owen cleared his throat. "Three of them did it. The other one was off in the background."

"You remember it clearly?"

"Fucking hell, Padre! What do you want me to say? It sent the fucking heart monitor off. Of course I remember."

"And it frightened you."

"I don't get frightened. It pissed me off."

"So it made you angry."

"My fuckin' oath it did."

"I see."

Owen let out a long breath, and shook his head tiredly.

"You know, Padre," he said. "I saw my father killed by a train when I was a kid. That should have been traumatic. But it didn't scare me. I was relieved he was gone. I remember being scared in the war. We all were. The man who says he wasn't is a liar. But it was the fear of the moment. Some feller was trying to kill you, and you had to take him first. That was good fear. You had some control in a dogfight. Big mobs of adrenaline, and the relief of still being alive afterward. Churchill was right about the exhilaration of being shot at and missed. But these past two days, I've felt fear unlike anything I'd ever thought possible. You've heard of being scared to death? Well that's what set the monitor off. That kind of fear." He inhaled steadily, striving for control.

"But fuck 'em! I'm still alive. In the cold light of day, it's all bullshit. I never knew a nightmare that survived sunup."

"They won't stop until they get it back, Owen."

"What are they going to bloody do, Padre. More dreams? Come off it."

"You described a fourth fellow," Mark said.

"Where?"

"In your dream."

"Ah. I don't remember."

"First they send a ngangkari out. A sorcerer. He Sings the culprits to death."

"And I'm still alive and breathing, Padre. And tomorrow night, I'll still be alive and kicking too." Owen moved his feet under the sheets. "See?"

"There are worse things than Singing, Owen."

"More heresy, Padre? Black magic? Superstition? I'm surprised at you. You're starting to sound like a bloody Catholic." Owen gave a hollow laugh. "Where's your faith?"

"If they're still not successful," Mark pressed on, "they'll call up a kudaitja."

"Another fucking fairy tale. You think that scares me, Padre? If I backed off every time someone threatened me, I'd still be driving a fucking delivery truck. Flesh and blood I can handle anyday. Bloody blackfellers. If it wasn't for men like me, they'd have nothing. There'd be no welfare. Where do you think the fucking government gets it from? People like me. We made this country what it is. Bloody blackfellers lie around in the shade waiting for their fucking sitting down money. We're out there making it for them. You ever see a blackfeller clear a paddock, or dig a mine, or build a road, or an airline? You ever see a blackfeller put up a building, or a bridge, or a park? Men like me did something with this country. We started with nothing and made something out of nothing. Black-fellers sit around staring off at the horizon. We got off our arses and pulled the wealth out of it, so everyone can share it. Then we went off to war to fight for it. I earned everything I have. They reckon men like me are heroes. I wouldn't say so. All the heroes I know were killed in the war. But I've always paid my way, Padre. I've never stolen a damn thing in my life. I'm not a fucking thief."

Mark waited, then he said, "I take it then, you have the tjurunga."

"Of course I've fucking got it. Paid for in full. You saw that. Proof positive. Signed, sealed, and delivered."

"Why?"

"I told you. It's safer in my collection. Safer than any cave in the desert."

"Why, Owen?"

"I fucking told you, Padre. I have the best collection of Aboriginal artifacts in the world. None better. I'm doing them a favor, keeping it all safe."

"They'll die without it, Owen."

"Putting their stone in safekeeping ought to guarantee they'll survive."

"I don't believe you."

"You calling me a liar?"

"I think you know how valuable it is."

"Of course. Finest tjurunga I've ever seen. Worth every cent."

"I think you know the stakes."

"What the fuck are you talking about?"

"It's what this is all about, isn't it, Owen?"

"Get it off your chest, Padre."

"It goes to the heart of everything you've been talking about. You've taken everything you can out of this country. You've got cattle stations and mining leases from one side to the other. You have real estate. You have wealth, power, fame. People could argue that you've got everything. I don't think that's the case. You find yourself with everything in the world, everything they no longer have. But you've got no soul. Wealth doesn't do it for you anymore, does it, Owen. Or power. You see them with nothing but the one thing you don't have. They know who they are, and what their lives mean. Not the ones in the towns. The ones in the desert. They know exactly who they are. You own everything, but you've lost sight of who you are. You're defined now by what you own, not by who you are. You've gone past the critical mass of wealth and power, and now it owns you, doesn't it? That's why you want something like the tjurunga. You think you can own their soul too."

"That's the greatest load of bullshit I've ever heard, Padre."

"Then give it back."

"Or what?"

Mark shrugged. "I'm not in the business of passing threats, Owen. I've told you everything I know, and I've probably spoken out of turn about you personally. I'm sorry. But if they don't get it back, they do believe they'll die. They can't let that happen."

"It's far too late for either of us, Padre. The sun'll be up soon. Get some sleep. I can take care of myself."

"They will send someone, Owen. You can count on it."

"We've all heard the stories, Padre. Fairy tales."

"I know you know better than that, Owen."

"I'll be fine, Padre. I've had people come after me before. I'm still here. They're not. I've got a full-time security company out there. Even if they did send someone, he wouldn't get through."

"He won't be any ordinary man, Owen. He'll stop at nothing to get to you."

"They're fucking desert blackfellers, Padre. They'd be hard pressed to find their way past the nearest pub."

"Even you know better than that, Owen. You are in real danger."

"I'll be fine."

Mark shrugged tiredly. He glanced at Agnes. "You're sentencing them to death if you don't return it."

"Make your mind up, Padre. You trying to scare me off or save them?"

"Both. I've done my best to warn you. I don't know what else to say."

"There's nothing more to say, Padre. Get some sleep."

"We'll be gone in a few days, anyway," Agnes said.

Mark looked from her to Owen.

"I'm not running away, Padre. I'll be ready to travel in a day or two, that's all."

"Once we're back in Sydney, none of this will matter," Agnes said.

"If they send a kudaitja," Mark said, "it won't matter where you go. Anangu believe he can find anyone and bring them to judgment."

"Nobody's bringing me anywhere, Padre. Certainly not a mob of black-fellers."

"You've already had a near fatal accident." Mark's voice was low, deliberate. "Now you're dreaming things that give you heart seizures. What if they're not coincidence? What if it's not just the painkillers?"

"All right, Padre. That's enough. I've told you, it's all bullshit. I don't believe any of it."

"There's too much at stake." Mark exhaled slowly. "Send it back, Owen. Please. If nothing else, the Wirruntjatjara truly believe they'll die if they don't get it back."

"Don't tell me what to do, Padre." Owen's voice was low, menacing. "Thank you for coming."

Mark appeared about to say more, but the dismissal was clear. He held Owen's steady glare, then nodded silently to Agnes, and left the room.

"I wish you'd reconsider, Owen," Agnes said quietly.

"And what? Turn tail because of some blackfeller superstition? Not fucking likely."

"I know you, Owen. Something's frightened you—no, don't look at me like that. I don't doubt your courage for a second, you know better than that, but I do know you."

"I'm perfectly fine."

"Look, now that Oscar's dead, the check won't be cashed. You haven't lost anything. Why not consider returning—"

"No!"

"Is it that important to you?"

"Now it is. Before this, I might have reconsidered. It's still the most valuable artifact to come out of the desert. The Getty'd pay three times what I did, if they knew about it. But now, there's no way I'm returning it. Nobody threatens me."

"And what if they do send someone?"

"We can handle anyone."

"You heard what Mark said . . ."

"Mark's been out there too long. Forty years. He's as bad as the bloody blackfellers."

"Let me call someone. In case they do try to send one of these . . . hunters after you."

"Who'd you have in mind?"

"You know who."

"No."

"He'll know how to handle this."

"Not a fucking chance. Anyhow, he wouldn't come."

"Of course he would. You're his father."

"That's why he won't come."

"Blood's thicker than water, Owen."

"No."

"Yes, Owen." Agnes leaned over him so her eyes were inches from his. "There's nobody better trained for this."

"You have to get inside them," Captain Keith Bliss had said gently. He sat cross-legged on his cot, facing the young lieutenant sitting opposite him. The two of them were alone in the tent, the flaps closed. "You have to reach out with your mind and feeeeel theirs, Mr. Chips, harmonize with their being. You're like a virus, sliding into their system without setting off the alarms. You're in them before they know you're even near. You invade them with your mind, so their body becomes yours for that final moment. You meld with them, become their shadow, their breath." He paused, smiling. Andrew Bird couldn't see his eyes through the black glasses, but he imagined Keith Bliss had closed them for a moment in what seemed like a long, silent sigh of rapture. "Their death becomes a part of your death," he barely whispered. "A petit mort."

Andrew had not lit a cigarette in the week since Rayner Posner introduced him to Keith Bliss. He bathed his feet in methylated spirits three times a day to toughen them, and began building calluses on his soles by pounding them for half an hour each night on a board wrapped with burlap sacking. He had stopped eating meat, and instead stocked up on rice and strips of dried fish and fresh fruit from the Vietnamese street market outside the base.

"Find your harmony with the earth," Bliss intoned. "Greet the life you pass through: the trees, the ground, the leaves and grass, the air, flowing water. Feel the life in it and become part of it. Become invisible." Bliss showed him how to make his first wire, and carry it in a loop around his neck, uncoiling it and noosing a target pole in a smooth sweep of his arm that became organic. At the end of the first week, Bliss said, "Tonight. Dummy run."

They went out through the wire an hour after sundown, Bliss leading. Nobody saw them go. They were out all night. Bliss moved like air.

There were extended moments that night when Andrew felt as if everything around him had spontaneously altered, when he felt a smoothness in his movement through the bush, so that despite the weight of his pack and harness and assault rifle, he seemed to float in a current of life flowing in the jungle leaves and vines and trunks and ground and air. Then the perception vanished, and he became aware again of sweat pouring off his skin, making the heavy wooden stock of his SLR slippery, soaking into the olive green fabric of his uniform. His cloth giggle hat soaked most of the perspiration from his forehead, but still enough ran into his eyes to sting. He smelled mosquito repellent and rifle oil, and in the humid air of vegetation and damp earth, the faint stench of corruption rising from his skin and breath.

"I keep losing it," Andrew said after they came in through the wire unseen in the last hour before dawn, and back to Bliss's tent. He was tired but exhilarated, still alert, coursing with adrenaline.

"You know why?"

"It's like holding mercury. I have it for a couple of minutes, then it—" He released a sharp puff of air from his lips.

"Focus, my friend. Float with the life force around you."

"Too many distractions."

Bliss smiled behind his sunglasses, and reached without looking for the bag of dried apricots beside him on the cot. "Go on."

"We stink. We carry stuff that stinks. We wear that fuckin' insect repellent . . ."

"Language, Mr. Chips." Bliss's voice was suddenly harsh. "Very bad wah. I will not tolerate it." He put a dried apricot in his mouth and chewed quickly. "Tell me about the stink."

"You know what I'm talking about. We stink. And our gear. All the gear we carry doesn't just have its own smell. It . . . gets in the way of everything. It sounds weird saying this, but, it gets in the way of feeling the bush."

Bliss smiled serenely, his chin raised.

"And what do you think we should do about that, Mr. Chips?"

Andrew felt scales falling from his eyes. "What do you usually take with you?"

"What would you take?"

Andrew felt poised on a threshold between all his conditioning and training to go out as heavily armed and well equipped as possible, and a new, still ill-defined insight. "As little as possible," he said finally. "Maybe black pajamas, like Charlie's." He looked at Bliss for a cue, but saw only an inscrutable smile, and the black band of the sunglasses.

"Perhaps," Bliss said. "How are your feet coming along?"

"No more blisters. The metho's working." Andrew shook his head at the implications. "Even Charlie wears sandals. Nobody goes barefoot out there."

"I do, Mr. Chips. Now. Show me how you're coming along with your wires."

A week later Bliss said, "Tomorrow."

Cao Giap watched the white tape on Ban's backpack float ahead of him in the darkness. It was the only clue he could see of his comrade. There was no sign of Vo, who was traveling on point ahead of Ban. Occasionally, Cao heard a low hiss of breath as Ban, or Vo, bumped into a root snaking out of the leaf-covered earth, or a thorny creeper hanging low enough to snag a cheek or lip.

They had been traveling in silence since dawn, staying away from tracks to avoid ambushes. More than the threat of the Uktoloi ambushes and mines and night bombing missions, Cao dreaded the restless spirits who remained trapped between the place of their death, and the world of the afterlife. They were everywhere, legions of them now, swelling alarmingly since the American War brought its blanket bombing and napalm and gunships. Cao and his comrades felt them as they traveled down the Ho Chi Minh Trail and into the southern provinces. The spirits hovered alone, or in pairs or threes around village cemeteries, and gathered in macabre hordes around the blasted ground of battlefields and bombing sites. At night when he slept, the ghosts infiltrated his dreams, showing their mutilated bodies, and howling mournfully down the wide tunnels of sleep. Ban and Vo confessed to similar nightmares near the killing grounds.

The slope became less steep as they approached the top of the ridgeline, turning left to stay just below it. The three of them were exhausted. They had traveled forty miles in two days, a grueling journey through thick, hilly country. Cao looked forward to the hot rice and vegetables he knew would be simmering on Nguyen's stove. He eased up the shoulder straps of his pack with his thumbs. The legs grew strong over these long marches, but the shoulders never grew accustomed to all the straps. His AK-47 was wrapped in strips of burlap for camouflage, and to stop the sling rings rattling. He had a rice bag slung on a rope across his body from one shoulder, and the leather dispatch bag across the other. In half an hour, he could hand that over, and get a quick meal before sinking into a long, untroubled sleep. The ghosts rarely entered the villages.

Cao watched the white tape on Ban's pack floating through the darkness. A cold chill crept up his spine, as if he were no longer alone. He peered into the darkness around him. Nothing. He saw Ban's tape moving steadily ahead, and slightly uphill from him. Cao increased his pace, still moving lightly over the ground, but now he could feel the ghost around him. He felt the ghost on his skin, as if it was matching him, step for step. He inhaled a breath, willing himself to look around, to confront the spirit, but his mind wouldn't work, and there was a thin intense heat on his throat, and he heard a small popping sound, but it didn't mean anything to him, because all the nerves and muscles and vessels and cartilage in his neck were already severed with that sound as the steel A string passed through, tightening on his spinal cord, as his body slid to the ground with barely a sound, save for a soft exhalation of air, sliding out of his lungs, through the wide gash beneath his chin.

Andrew lowered the body with its head downhill, to stop the blood soaking the dispatch bag. He emptied the contents into his own satchel, strapped tight around his waist. He uncoiled his wire from the courier's throat and cleaned it on the dead man's shirt. Ahead of him, Bliss moved like a ghost, lowering the body of the next courier to the ground, cleaning out his dispatch bag, then deftly feeling for the junction of the second and third cervical vertebrae and sliding his wire between them, severing the head. He cleaned his wire on the man's shirt, removed it, and tied the head inside it, slinging it up by the sleeves and moving back past Andrew without a sound. They passed back into the jungle, silent, camouflaged from head to toe with stripes of mud and charcoal that turned their naked bodies into invisible wraiths of shadow.

"I think it's time you went home, Mr. Chips."

Andrew stared at Bliss.

"Right."

"I'm quite serious."

"I don't understand."

"You're getting to like it too much. In three months, I have seen the change in you."

"You like it as much as I do."

"Ah, yes, but I know what I am, Mr. Chips."

"And what's that?"

"I am the truth. I am the secret weapon every nation needs but does not want to know about. I am a righteous cleaner, I return things to harmony. And I am valuable to them," Bliss said, rocking back and forward on his cot, "as long as the war lasts, which will not be very long now. Nixon is desperate and Kissinger wants his Nobel. Game's nearly over. When it is, they will classify me as a common psychopath, bound for one of their hospitals. I do not intend to go."

"Yes?"

"I will go away. I will manage. But you. You have a world to go back to."

"I could do this."

"Professionally?"

"Isn't that what we're doing now?"

"No. This is just government work. Public service. They let us do it. Free enterprise is a world away from this, and I do not think you have the heart for it. True assassins are born to it, Mr. Chips. They grow up believing in their own righteousness. The rest fail. Don't mistake me. You have shown great courage and talent in what we do. But you do not truly believe in it as I do. One day out there in the outer world, it would catch you up. You would be doing a task, and you would think about it instead of feeling your way through it, and you would hesitate for a second, and that would be the end of it, Mr. Chips. You have to believe. There is no room out there for hesitation."

"So."

"Exactly. So. You are not like me."

"But I haven't made any mistakes. I've brought back as much good material as you."

"Not quite."

"Name one thing."

"You're not a collector." Bliss sounded sad.

"The heads. We're out there to collect int, not heads."

"You do not have it in you, and that is your saving grace, your path to salvation. You must stop now. Go home, Mr. Chips. I'll have Rayner Posner arrange it with your people. You've acquitted yourself admirably as far as they're concerned."

"What if I refuse to go?"

"Well, Mr. Chips. You've come to a pass. The hunger is upon you, you see. The hunger for power over life and death. Do you succumb to the darkness, the dark creature of the heart, the purified evil we sense in all of us, which you have brought awake and dangerously alive? Or do you walk away; into the light? You alone must decide. Now. I will tell you this, now you have the taste for it, if you harbor any doubt, even though that doubt remains your path to salvation, you will be working at a grave disadvantage out there. You will begin to lose focus. You will be putting us both at risk."

"I see."

"Stop now, Mr. Chips. You can't unknow what you know. You can't unknow your dark beast. But"—Bliss raised his shoulders slowly and lowered them, in a gesture that seemed deeply wistful—"you still have time to drive it back into its labyrinth. If you are prudent, and leave now, you may be able to leave it there, until the hunger becomes a memory."

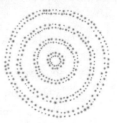

CHAPTER 17

HIGH CLOUDS ALONG THE EDGE of the Simpson Desert were beginning to turn pale pink and gold when the conductor knocked on Robert's cabin door.

"White and two sugars, Doctor," he said, holding a tray of tea and chocolate wafers. "Sure you won't be having dinner? Chef's got Tasmanian salmon and some positively sinful desserts."

Robert smiled and took the tray.

"No, thanks anyway."

"Right you are then. No stops until Adelaide tomorrow morning, though. If you need anything else, just call me, all right?"

Robert thanked him again and closed the door. He took the tray to the window and set it on the side table. Mulga scrub and plains of spinifex swept past at eighty miles an hour. Throughout the afternoon, as the *Ghan* ran south, drawing closer to the center of the continent, it crossed more and more creation tracks radiating from Uluṟu. Off to the west, the monolith lay below the horizon like a massive terminus. Ahead, he could feel the resonance of Kuniya's dreaming track, where the Python Spirit traveled west toward Uluṟu, cradling on her head the eggs she would soon lose so cruelly. He felt his eyes welling, and thought of his own mother being told she had to give up her baby to a white family. Like thousands of Aboriginal parents, she would never see her child again. The Stolen Generations of children who had grown to adulthood were frequently told their parents were dead, or beyond reach. They wandered the audit trails of adoption agencies, and government records offices, searching for paths that would lead them home to their own people, to their own country. Their families, depleted by forced abductions for more than a century, lost track of their children and frequently of their own way. The government's conceit to elevate tribal children to white education and culture sank a multitude into the depths of alienation and depression, into a mire of drugs and alcohol and petrol fumes and suicide. Robert grew up to learn how exceptional his experience was. He sought to make the best of both the worlds he walked in. He accepted that both his birth parents were long dead, but he knew if there was a choice, he had only one true path. He remembered his first night at Rumbalara with Maureen, when she led him off the train and taught him how to find his way home to the heart of the desert.

He felt the convergence of songlines reverberating in a great murmuring symphony of voices across the desert. A quarter of an hour earlier, *The Ghan* had crossed the long low bridge spans over the Finke River, the oldest watercourse on earth, running along channels geologically dated back to three hundred million years, in Piranypa time. In Anangu time, its songline preceded that age all the way back to Creation. Robert had watched the dry riverbed pass beneath him, listening to its harmonies deep inside him, and another voice coming closer.

The Ghan was twenty miles south of the Finke River now, and like a soloist rising through the voices of the choir, the clear chanting of Kalaya, the Emu Dreaming spirit, grew louder, racing in across the red plain.

Robert looked down at his cup and saucer. He was holding them level, but the tea seemed to defy gravity, eerily tilting up to one side in the cup, as *The Ghan* suddenly decelerated.

Carl Duffel blinked hard and craned forward in the driver's seat. He had reached over to tap *The Ghan*'s electronic Vigilance Control, as he did every sixty seconds to tell the locomotive's computers that he was awake, when he first saw the cloud spearing toward them.

"Wally!" he barked to his co-driver.

The steel tracks ran in from the southern horizon, unraveling their concrete railroad ties like rungs, growing larger and faster until they were a blur flying beneath the train. High clouds flared like fire from the west above the dropping sun but clear daylight still lit the plains ahead. They were traveling at just over seventy-five miles an hour. Carl strained to make out the long thin cloud of dust moving in fast across the desert from the east.

"What the bloody hell is that?"

Walter Parkinson looked up from his horse racing guide and put down his mug of tea and stared outside.

"I'll be buggered!" Walter squinted, not believing what he saw. "Stampede?" The line of dust was traveling at phenomenal speed, like a lance arcing in on a perfect intercept with the train. He activated the air horns mounted on the roof, loud enough to be heard for miles across the desert. Their long shattering wail blasted over the cloud, but it didn't waver from its course.

"'Roos?" Carl said, his hand reaching for the throttle.

"Can't tell, mate." Walter strained to see, hitting the air horns again, with no visible effect. "But if we don't bloody stop, we'll hit 'em."

Carl rotated the throttle down to zero, and smoothly applied the brakes. The line of dust streaked closer across the plain. Wally kept the air horns blaring, but the cloud continued on. Carl watched the speedometer unwind, down through sixty miles an hour. Frames of a train driver's worst nightmare flicked through his brain—racing toward a collision with the brakes clamped in a full service application, and nothing to do but wait helplessly for the impact. There were drivers who spent the rest of their days haunted by the eyes of people in cars stalled on level crossings, staring up in horror as the train crashed over them in a long scream of brakes and steel. Fifty-five. Fifty.

"We're running out of road, Carl!"

"Come on, girl," Carl crooned. Forty-five.

"We're gonna hit!" Walter's voice rose sharply. The dust cloud was less than six hundred yards ahead now, to the right of the track, but closing on a collision course. "They're bloody emus! Must be hundreds!"

"Come on, lovely." Carl's eyes flicked from the speedometer to the racing animals. "Gooood girl." Thirty.

They could clearly see the shapes in the huge flock now, long legs flying, dust billowing around the gray feathers covering their bodies, stubby flightless wings clamped tight against their ribs, a forest of long rearing necks, swaying forward and back with the power of their stride. Twenty-five.

Carl saw the needle drop through twenty miles an hour and eased his hand back, jiffying the brake valve to bleed off air, watching the enormous birds pour across the tracks beneath the driver's cabin. Fifteen miles an hour.

The emus swerved wildly around the big diesel as it rolled to a stop in a shuddering clank of couplings and hissing air lines. Carl brought the brakes back on and slumped in his seat, watching the forest of long necks streaming past the cabin, the eyes fixed on some distant point, the thick stubby beaks gaping silently, dust swirling over the windshield. The cabin filled with the muffled thunder of feet pounding the ground as the birds raced past.

Along the line of carriages, conductors leaned out their doors, staring in astonishment. Passengers crowded around them, chattering, cameras clicking and whirring.

In the first class sleeping car, the conductor felt a hand on his shoulder and leaned back inside the door.

"Never seen anything like this, eh, Doc?" The conductor grinned, shouting above the rumble of feet.

"Thanks for taking care of me." Robert pressed a twenty into the man's hand.

"Geez. Lovely. No worries, Doc."

"This is where I get off."

The conductor started, and gave a short laugh. "Y'must be joking. This is the middle of bloody nowhere!"

Robert picked up his suitcase and went down the steps.

"I can't let y'get off here, Doc."

"Of course you can. The ticket's paid to Adelaide. There's no law against getting off early. Besides"—Robert smiled up at him from the ground—"I'm off."

The last great gray bird sprinted across the line behind two large chicks in zigzag black-and-white striped feathers. The dust began to settle. A single gray feather spun slowly in the air in front of the locomotive and settled onto the track. Walter Parkinson checked down the train for the all-clear from the conductors. When it came, Carl released the brakes and eased the throttle on. The *Ghan's* great drive wheels slowly began to turn. Far off now, the great flock raced westward, vanishing beyond their own dust cloud.

Robert watched the train draw away. The air shimmered in the fading heat, distorting the skyline to the west, and less than twenty miles away, the tall signs and low roofline of the Erldunda gas station. He felt the rhythms flowing powerfully through him now, in the air and in the earth beneath him, the singing of Kuniya the Python Dreaming spirit, and Kalaya of the Emu Dreaming. He hefted his suitcase and set off toward the dropping sun.

A child's bare foot came into view attached to a severed leg, blackened at the stump, bent at the knee, and lying more than a yard from its body. The corpses lay so closely packed in the ravine they were simply a drift of tattered clothes, with twisted limbs and lifeless faces at odd angles. But the small naked leg with its bare toes and charred knee, pointing toward the mass of bodies, was riveting, eloquent, imploring the eye to slow and stop and count. The image zoomed tighter, then held steady on the bare toes.

"It's a bitch we can't say 'pools of their own blood and shit and piss,'" the editor muttered. They were both sitting at a flyaway edit deck in the inside corner of the hotel room, away from the window and its sporadic shrapnel and sniper fire. "Tell the viewers the truth for a change. Tell 'em what murdered kids and women smell like. Vomit and shit and farts and fear. Fuck their tender sensibilities. Why don't you tell 'em that? Tape's rolling."

"In three, two . . ." The correspondent held his microphone to one side and began reading from his notebook. "'The smells of death are overpowering—villagers say these decomposing bodies have been lying here for eight days, but they were too afraid to come and bury them. Witnesses say the families—more than twenty people—were herded down here at dawn. Cut to the first witness under voice track of the interpreter.' Out cue is, 'screaming, then the shots.' Wide shot of second witness pointing to the bodies. Voice-over continues in three, two . . . 'This man asks how can the world watch and do nothing. Tonight, as they have every night since the new offensive began, the survivors will hide in homes with no power, no fresh water, and no help in sight.' Sound bite of forensic investigator. His out cue is, 'going on like this for centuries.' Voice-over continues. Three, two—"

A mobile phone rang shrilly and the correspondent put down his script and microphone and dug the handset out of his field jacket.

"Bird."

"Andrew?"

"Speaking."

"This is Agnes."

Andrew's voice went cold. "What can I do for you."

"Your father's had an accident."

"Is he dead?"

"No. He came off a horse. He's injured, but he's going to be all right."

"Fine. Goodbye."

"Andrew, please. He's asking for you."

"What's he want?"

"Nothing. He'd like to see you."

"He's dying?"

"No."

"I'm pretty tied up right now."

"Andrew, he needs to see you. It's rather urgent."

"He hasn't needed to see me in forty years. This is a novelty."

"I wouldn't ask you if it wasn't so urgent. You'll appreciate that at least."

"What's he want?"

"As I said, he'd like to see you."

"For a chat?"

"No. Much more urgent than that."

"Are you going to tell me?"

"Not on this phone."

"Send me an e-mail then. You can encrypt it."

"We're going to send a jet from London. It should reach Sarajevo in about six hours from now."

"They'll try to shoot it down. It's in all the newspapers."

"We've been watching your reports. Your father's very proud of what you're doing. But I have to say, just now you're sounding a little petty, Andrew. Will you come?"

"Agnes, I can't just take off when I feel like it."

"We've talked to Atlanta. They're sending your replacement on the jet."

"What'd you do? Buy CNN? It's still a fucking game to him isn't it."

"Not this time, Andrew. You'll understand when we see you."

"I'm on a deadline, Agnes. Nice talking to you."

"Will you come?"

"Get the jet to carry enough fuel to get straight on from here to Rome. Tell the pilots when they land to taxi straight to the bunkers in front of the main terminal, and keep their engines running till I get on. It'll be a rolling turnaround. And tell the crew to wear flak jackets. This is not a drill."

"Thank, you Andrew. Owen thanks you too."

"This better be good. Goodbye, Agnes."

"Grace. It's so wonderful to meet you at last," Giselle Erhard said as she hugged her warmly and kissed her on each cheek. "You're so much lovelier than your photographs."

"So are you." Grace Morgan took in the blond hair, graying in streaks, braided up in a coil that crowned Giselle's face, tanned and lined with age, but beautiful still, softened by a warm smile that seemed genuinely kind, and too familiar with deep suffering. Still, it was the face of a white person, and Grace felt the same distrust that always rose from deep inside her with each new one she met. They were capable of such cruelty, mostly unconscious, mostly trivial, executed with a throwaway line or a blithely ill-considered observation about any of a million things that reminded her she was not like them, and would never be truly accepted by them solely for the content of her character. Nobody, she told herself, black or white, was ever truly color-blind. Grace told herself to get over it and kissed Heinrich on both cheeks. She thought he too seemed truly kind at first sight. She knew what was done to him as a prisoner of war, and for a moment all her reservations disappeared.

"We've been worried you'd be exhausted by the trip," he said. "We usually put Robbie to bed as soon as we get him home."

"You've seen him?" Grace's voice rose urgently.

"No, no, darling," Giselle, said. "He hasn't come here this time. We don't know where he is."

"He didn't contact us this time," Heinrich said. "Sometimes he calls us on the way back."

"Back from where? You know where he is?"

"No," Heinrich said gently. "As I said on the phone, I don't know exactly where he is."

"We've put you in his room." Giselle slipped her hand through Grace's elbow and they walked through the airport to the baggage carousel. "We want you to feel at home here."

Throughout the drive up into the Adelaide Hills to the Erhards' home, Grace felt vaguely dislocated. It wasn't only because she had no idea where Robert was or what he was doing, or because she still harbored doubts about her own journey to find him, or even because of the slightly familiar but slightly foreign feel of the city of Adelaide, with its old Georgian buildings and forests of church spires and treed parks and wide streets: rather it was because of the complete familiarity with which Heinrich and Giselle welcomed her, as if not only had they known her all their lives but also felt she was part of their family, one of them. White people never behaved in such a genuinely easy, intimate way with her. Grace turned over the irony of her own reaction to what she had always considered an impossible ideal: whites who behaved as if they truly were color-blind—it disturbed her. The car turned from a tree-lined street into a circular gravel driveway and stopped in front of a modest English style two-story sandstone, standing behind a large beautiful flower garden.

"We've kept it almost exactly the way it was when he lived here," Giselle said when they showed her Robert's room. Grace stood in the doorway and peered into Robert's past. The walls were hung with athletics pennants for the five hundred meters and marathon events from university back to high school, and photographs of cricket and football teams ranging back to second grade. A beautifully detailed Spitfire, hand-modeled from balsa wood and doped cloth, in the colors of the RAF hung from a stout fishing line in a far corner. The bookcases were filled with fiction and textbooks, and biographies of scientists and mathematicians. Old models of the famous Lunar Excursion Module that lifted astronauts off the moon, and a small Viking lander, and a Voyager satellite with a broken solar panel were scattered along bookshelves. She saw a photograph of Robert barely in his teens with Heinrich and Giselle. It was a glamorous portrait of a very happy family. Near it stood another, of Robert in his school uniform standing next to an Aboriginal woman who was dressed beautifully in a cotton summer frock and matching shoes and a pretty straw hat. She seemed uncomfortable in the shoes, and perhaps self-conscious about the hat, but all Grace could see was the overwhelming love with which Robert and the woman beamed at each other.

"I think I'll go and make us all some tea," Giselle said, leaving Heinrich to wait silently while Grace walked around the room, running her fingertips over the counterpane on the single bed beneath a window, touching the aging wings of the Spitfire, returning again to stare at the photograph of the woman in the straw hat.

"That's Maureen," Heinrich said. "She found him when he first ran away. Did he tell you?"

"He said you let him go back to his people whenever he needed to."

Heinrich smiled and leaned in the doorway. Grace sat down on the edge of the bed, pressing her hands into the counterpane.

"What else did he tell you?"

"That he loves you both. That you both raised him as your own son. That you knew how important his story was."

"His story?"

"Where he came from. Where he really came from."

"Ah. He taught us that, that the most important thing anyone has is their own story. Who they are. Who their people are. Where they're from. We all need to know our own story. Robert wanted to know his ever since he was a child. That's why he ran away, I think, the first time."

"Is that where he is now?"

"I can't say."

"You don't know?"

"I can't say, Grace."

"Did he tell you?"

"He's told us how much he loves you. We can see how much you love him. He's a rare man, and you're an exceptional woman. He's told us some of your story too."

"I . . . I think I'm afraid of his secrets."

"Everyone has secrets."

"I'm afraid of the secrets that brought him back here. I'm afraid for him. I'm . . . I'm afraid of being afraid of him."

"He would never hurt you, Grace. Never."

"Would he hurt anyone else? Is that why he didn't want to come back? I had this feeling in Houston. Intuition." She shook her head. "Silly. Probably."

Heinrich looked at her sadly, then he sat next to her on the bed with his hands extended, palms downward on his knees.

"Robbie told you about these?"

She nodded. "He said that you were incredibly brave, to save some men."

"I couldn't save all of them. But I would do the same thing again, under the same circumstances."

"Why?"

"Duty. Honor. Sacrifice. They're words people scoff at nowadays. But they are important. They always will be, no matter what they cost. They're certainly important to Robbie." He breathed slowly, with his eyes closed. "Sometimes there is simply no choice. Did he tell you what happened after?"

"To you? After the war?"

"After"—Heinrich slowly held his hands up, splaying the ugly scars where his fingernails should have been—

Grace hesitated, then reached up and gently took his hands in hers.

"Tell me."

The thumbnail had been the worst. Captain Ashima had torn at it with his pliers until Heinrich's joints cracked, the tendons strained against the hideous force, and the flesh ripped away. Heinrich could no longer scream, his voice was hoarse, and agony became another dimension in which he took up sole residence, cut off from all other humans except this monstrous entity who sat across the table, calmly demanding he betray his comrades. The prisoners on the parade ground remained at rigid attention as the sun moved overhead and the temperature passed above the century.

It was the only way left to them to honor Heinrich's courage on the veranda. His terrible endurance shamed them. They saw his face become grotesque with pain. They heard his breathing become labored, weeping convulsions. They saw him retching long after there was nothing left in his stomach. And still he withheld the information that Captain Ashima sought with increasingly desperate savagery. Heinrich's heroism transformed them. The sun bit into their faces and arms and clenched fists, but they braced themselves, fighting the heat and fatigue and thirst and their impotence to save him. Nothing they endured on the parade ground could approach Heinrich's suffering. His bravery galvanized them and gave them a sense of dignity they had thought was lost to them.

What began as an exercise in torture and control over the captives of Seletar prisoner of war camp had become a passage of honor. It took Captain Ashima some time to realize he had conspired to traverse it with them; a collaborator in his own disgrace.

Heinrich's refusal to reveal where the escapees were heading cost Ashima enormous face in front of the prisoners and guards. The realization came to him as he wiped his sweat off the steel handles of the pliers. He had hoped to break the clergyman and turn him into a traitor in front of the camp. Instead, the wounded man was humiliating him. Ashima grasped Heinrich's wrist in one hand, and held the pliers poised in the other. He was about to repeat the question he had asked persistently for nearly two hours. He opened his mouth to speak. He saw Heinrich slowly look up from the table at him. Ashima was struck by the expression in the chaplain's eyes. He had expected defiance. Instead he saw a sense of peace, of sacrificial grace that seemed impossible in the vortex of pain that wracked his victim.

Ashima stared, as he began to understand. He released Heinrich's wrist and quietly put the pliers on the table. He rose from his canvas chair, and came to attention. Then he bowed to Heinrich: not the cursory nod reserved for the merest observance of etiquette, but a deep, respectful bow from the waist, holding it for a moment with his eyes down before straightening to attention again. He spoke rapidly in Japanese to the two soldiers guarding Heinrich. They were surprised, but came to brisk attention and helped their prisoner up from his stool and carried him down the front stairs of the veranda, past the astonished prisoners and back to the wooden hut that served as a crude sick bay.

The men listened to Ashima's boots slam along the veranda and through the door into his office. He remained there for the rest of the day, long after the prisoners had been marched off the baking parade ground and dismissed to their quarters. They went silently, buoyed by a dawning sense of triumph, but deeply humbled by the price paid for it.

Heinrich entered a different ordeal. For days, then weeks, then months, his body struggled to heal the grisly wounds where six of his nails had been. The prisoners went to dangerous lengths to help him. They shared precious caches of food—not the foul gruel served up by the guards, but the minute quantities of precious bread and biscuits and fruit that were smuggled and bartered inside the camp. They scrounged clean cloth for his dressings. There were no western medicines, but a Malay rice carter brought them a poultice of boiled vine leaves that he promised would reduce the pain and promote healing. Someone delivered a bar as valuable as gold—a piece of soap the size of a man's thumb.

One afternoon, a Japanese patrol returned with the decomposing body of one of the escapees, slung on a pole the way local hunters carried dead prey. The men in the patrol considered themselves samurai. They called themselves Knights of Bushido. One of them had gouged out the eyes of the dead escapee with his bayonet. Captain Ashima observed the gaping sockets in the putrefying body and saw in them a sounding of the depths to which his army and his people had descended. He had come to Singapore as a warrior.

Instead he had become a jailer of men who lacked the dignity to choose death over capture.

But this chaplain had shown him true honor, and caused him to shame himself by revealing his own barbarity. It was a disease that was infecting his men as surely as the maggots in the body swinging from the pole. The war was becoming a plague that was turning the glory of the Japanese Imperial forces to the sickly color of gangrene, and Ashima knew there was no way of altering its course. He smelled the odor of inner defeat as clearly as the stink of death rising from the corpse.

Heinrich lost nearly sixty pounds. His bones stretched his skin into skeletal nubs and lines. But the sense of peace never left his eyes. It was always there, haunting Ashima when Heinrich interceded for prisoners facing severe punishment. Breaking an ax or a shovel handle on a work detail earned the offender one day in the dog box—a corrugated iron cube three feet to a side. There were five dog boxes on the edge of the parade ground. In the blazing sun, when the metal walls clicked in the heat and blistered the skin, a man locked inside could lose ten pounds between dawn and dusk. Most of the men weighed close to one hundred pounds. The loss of five pounds through sweating and diarrhea was frequently fatal. Losing a tool on a work detail cost two days in the dog box. Hoarding food earned three. Only one in three prisoners survived three days in there.

Heinrich became the constant advocate for prisoners about to be punished. In the past, Ashima would have had such a representative beaten senseless. The prisoners cautioned Heinrich not to press the commandant. He ignored them. Often, Ashima in turn ignored him. But when a prisoner was accused of a crime that would clearly cost him a dangerous sentence, or the ultimate penalty of beheading, Heinrich was relentless, risking Ashima's fury to press for clemency. The entire camp expected the commandant to execute the chaplain at any moment out of sheer exasperation. But Heinrich seemed to know exactly how far he could push Ashima.

It became a deadly ebb and neap of emotional tides.

News of the bombing of Hiroshima reached the camp—first as a rumor carried by Bumaputra natives from outside, then as urgent overheard whispering among the guards. Reports of the destruction of Nagasaki filtered in like a delayed aftershock. The guards heard the news on a Japanese language broadcast by General Macarthur's Pacific Armed Forces Radio. It reached the prisoners on August 13, 1945, four days after the event. Their jubilation was tempered by a dreadful anxiety. They had witnessed innumerable atrocities by their Japanese captors at Seletar, and heard accounts of many more at nearby Changi. There was a small circle of packed earth at one corner of the parade ground, stained red, and frequently damp for several days. It was here that the prisoners were assembled in ranks during beheadings. Very often it was Ashima who drew his laminated steel katana and performed the ritual of execution. It was here that young prison officers drew lots to blood their own virgin katanas, anxious to sever the neck cleanly between the second and third cervical vertebrae rather than dishonor their blades and themselves with a clumsy stroke.

News of the Japanese surrender on the 14th of August reached Seletar the next day. It flew through the camp with the uncanny speed of rumor, bringing a chilling pall of doom to the prisoners. They were certain the guards would destroy all evidence—and witnesses—of their brutality. When two soldiers came for Heinrich shortly before midday, the prisoners nearest him made a brave and futile attempt to protect him, but Heinrich waved them aside.

Captain Ashima was standing behind his desk when the guards brought Heinrich in. He dismissed them both. There was a peculiar silence in the camp, as if everyone else had already departed, leaving Heinrich alone with his captor. The walls were clean and the room sparsely furnished. There was a map of Singapore Island on one, a photograph of the Emperor's palace gardens on another, and on a third a silk scroll with four black Kanji characters done with a broad brush quoting the Shinto proverb: "Be as water on stone." On the floor beside the desk lay a woven tatami mat with two black cushions and a polished wooden box on it. Ashima was wearing parade khakis, with highly polished boots, swordbelt, and shoulder strap, from which hung his lethal katana, sheathed in its black lacquer scabbard. He bowed solemnly to Heinrich and motioned him to the stool on the other side of the desk. The parallel to their earlier confrontation, across the table on the veranda, escaped neither of them.

"You are a man of great honor, Captain Erhard." It was the first time Ashima had used Heinrich's rank. The Japanese considered the commissioning of clergymen to the level of officers an affront. Ashima spoke as softly as he had when he had begun interrogating Heinrich on the veranda.

"I express my gratitude to you," he said slowly, "for reminding me that a man's dignity can never be taken away. It can only be lost."

Heinrich sat very still. He was not afraid to die, and he had long made and paid for his peace with his God. But he was fearful of doing or saying anything now that could jeopardize the lives of the prisoners. His expression was respectful as he listened to his jailer.

"The war is over, Captain," Ashima continued. "The Allies have won." He paused, looking directly into Heinrich's eyes. "You have won."

Heinrich felt his neck prickle with a dread sense of premonition.

"I have informed Squadron Leader Taylor that as senior ranking prisoner, he is to see to the welfare of his men. My men have been ordered to leave here at noon. They have strict orders that no prisoner is to be harmed. You have the word of an officer of His Majesty's Imperial Armed Forces." He emphasized his words, speaking from his belly so his voice resonated around the office. It magnified the silence beyond the walls.

"There is one thing left for me to do, Captain Erhard." Ashima moved around the desk and stood over him. Then his hands grasped the hilt of his sword and drew it from its sheath. Heinrich watched the razor edge of the blade sliding smoothly out above him. Ashima held the katana in a double-handed kendo stance level with Heinrich's eyes.

He placed the sword softly on the desk, with the hilt toward Heinrich. Then without a word, he went to the tatami mat and knelt on one of the cushions. He raised the lid of the wooden box and removed a white cloth and a shorter version of his katana, with a six-inch blade sheathed in a black lacquer scabbard.

"My grandfather sent me this blade, Captain Erhard. He was a vice admiral. Victorious in the North Chinese campaign of 1894. At the treaty ceremony at Shimonoseki, he was presented with two blades, one great and one small, said to be made by Nagamitsu of Bizen." Ashima shrugged self-consciously. "I am sorry to burden you with this story, Captain Erhard, but it is my purpose to put my actions into some . . . perspective." Heinrich struggled to keep his face impassive. His heart pounded against his gaunt ribs.

"As a youth, I was unable"—Ashima's voice faltered, and he cleared his throat—"to pass the entrance exams for the naval academy. My younger brother did. To him, my grandfather personally presented his great sword. When I was able to enter the military academy"—his voice dropped, with the weight of an old, ineludible pain—"he sent me this." He placed the sheathed seppuku blade on the mat at his knees, with a mixture of reverence and melancholy. "I strove to bring honor to my family as an officer of the Emperor. You will be unable to understand, Captain Erhard, my disappointment at finding myself in charge of an installation for prisoners of war. Men I believed had shamed themselves by not choosing death before dishonor. They shamed themselves, and they shamed me. And I allowed my shame to infect me. Your courage helped me lance that infection, Captain Erhard." Heinrich blinked slowly, and in the instant his eyes were closed, he prayed for guidance.

When he opened them again, Ashima was unbuttoning his right epaulet and slipping off the strap that looped over his shoulder to his swordbelt. It was an eerily sensuous movement. He unbuttoned his jacket and the white shirt beneath, baring his belly. Methodically, he picked up the small seppuku sword, unsheathed it, folded the cloth around the handle and held it in front of him in both hands with the blade downward.

"If you will honor me, Captain Erhard." Ashima's voice was steady. Heinrich shook his head in disbelief. Ashima's voice rose with concern.

"Captain Erhard, I must recover my own honor. You are the only one who can attend me in this."

He pointed, with the polished butt of the seppuku sword, toward the katana on his desk. "You must wait until I have completed my stroke. Then you must make the, the"—the term seemed to evade him for a moment—"the stroke of grace. The coup de grâce." He gave a thin smile of satisfaction, masking his concern that Heinrich's gesture of disbelief was a refusal. Heinrich rose from his stool, still unable to speak.

"If you please, Captain Erhard. Pick it up."

Heinrich shook his head again.

"You must stand here beside me. Hold it with both hands. Raise it above your head, and wait for my stroke. Then bring it down here." He bent his head forward and touched the straight line his close-cropped hair made across his neck. Ashima raised his head again, and smiled faintly. "You have seen me do it often enough. Now." The smile disappeared. "If you please."

Ashima's eyes burned into his, willing him to pick up the katana. Heinrich stared at him, shaking his head slowly. He had a sense of seeing a great train in motion, which he had no power to divert or stop. But he was being given a choice to let his torturer die hideously, or to end his agony quickly. Heinrich found his hands closing around the lacquered hilt, feeling the corrugations of the fine gold bullion cordwork on his palms. His body was so debilitated by ill treatment and malnutrition that he had to muster all his strength to lift it.

"It is not a Nagamitsu, Captain Erhard," Ashima sounded relieved that Heinrich had made his decision. "But it is a good blade. You will not need

great exertion. Bring it down cleanly, and it will complete the stroke itself."
Heinrich felt the same perverse intimacy with Ashima now that he had experienced on the veranda. He heard his feet shuffling across the dry tatami mat, positioning themselves beside Ashima.

"I have one last request, Captain Erhard." Heinrich hardly heard the words, as if they were coming down a long tunnel that absorbed and muffled their sound. He stared silently at the kneeling figure, looking calmly up at him.

"I ask that you forgive me."

The katana rested on its beveled tip on the mat. Heinrich looked at his cruelly scarred hands, wrapped around the hilt. He looked at Ashima and slowly nodded, once, twice, three times.

"Thank you, Captain Erhard."

Ashima's shoulders dropped, he inhaled, paused, then drove the blade into the left side of his belly.

He grunted with the impact. His face swelled red as he dragged the edge sideways, carving it through his flesh with a noisy eruption of vessels and entrails. His mind fought to focus, to extend his neck for the stroke. None came. Ashima looked up, his eyes bulging in pain and filling with alarm when he saw Heinrich had not moved to raise the katana. Heinrich watched his tormentor's body hunch forward in a stench of blood and intestines. Ashima's hands still gripped the haft of the sword, drenched now, but held securely with the cloth. His teeth were clenched tightly to stifle any cry. Still Heinrich hesitated. Thou shalt not kill. Then an image of Pontius Pilate washing his hands flashed through his mind. Heinrich's disfigured hands raised the katana.

Ashima saw the movement, grinding his teeth to keep himself mute, turning his face down again, straining to keep his neck exposed. If he waited long enough, Heinrich knew Ashima would bleed to death. It would take several agonizing minutes. Ashima had tortured him for hours. Fleeting images flashed into his mind of the origami cranes, buffeted on the veranda table, their delicate white paper flecked with his blood. He remembered how he had prayed then for his tormentor, for the wisdom to love his enemy. He felt his mind sliding again, as if he were entering Ashima's soul, bound inextricably by the sharing of pain and control. Heinrich raised the katana higher, and with a cry of despair, struck the head from its body.

BOOK IV

THE
CHANGED
ONE

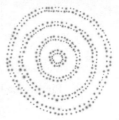

CHAPTER 18

ROBERT'S HEART ROSE when he saw the men waiting for him beneath the eucalyptus trees. They leaned against their old Toyota Land Cruiser, and watched him silently.

"Wai, Tjilpi Malu," he greeted Malu, of the Red Kangaroo Dreaming, using the respectful title for elder, and placing the palm of his hand on Malu's chest. "Nyuntu palya?"

"Palya, Tjilkamata," Malu responded, resting his own hand on Robert's chest. "Good to see you."

Malu's battered stockman's hat was cocked on the back of his head and Robert could see the thick hair had long turned gray. But he was still muscular and healthy, and as gentle as Robert remembered him the day long ago when Malu handed him his first set of spears and miru, his wad of chewing bush tobacco still rolling in a ball at the corner of his lip, and his eyes creasing warmly in welcome. Malu's smile faded at once. It was twelve days since the great crime and all of them felt the sentence of death hanging over them.

Robert was solemnly greeted by Tjitutja of the Dingo Dreaming, and Lungkata the Blue-Tongued Lizard man.

The fourth elder waited inside the Land Cruiser. Robert went back to the rear passenger door and looked in through the window.

The man sitting inside smelled strongly of goanna fat, smeared over his skin. More disturbing was the aura of dreadful energy that cloaked him. He was dressed in an old plaid wool shirt and ill-fitting black trousers, with no belt or shoes. The clothing was a rude disguise, for the benefit of any Piranypa who might stray too close to the vehicle. It failed to camouflage the power emanating from him, or the intensity of his distant stare.

«Walkalpa,» Robert addressed his old friend quietly. «It is very good to see you.»

The sorcerer's penetrating stare softened and a faint smile transformed his features, reminding Robert again of the gentle, frail boy he had protected when they were both children in the desert. Walkalpa, of the Emu Poison Bush Dreaming, examined him through the window.

«Tjilkamata. I am pleased you came.»

«You and Kalaya have been disturbing my sleep, Walkalpa.»

The sorcerer nodded. «He's a persistent one, Kalaya.»

«He stopped the train on time,» Robert said dryly.

«He is a powerful dreaming man.»

Robert surveyed the elders. «What has happened here?»

Walkalpa's smile faded like a single cloud blown apart high over the desert. «We will talk about everything on the way to Uluru. We are running out of time.»

Malu climbed in behind the wheel and Robert sat next to him. Three lean dingoes loped in across the stony ground and jumped into the rear of the Land Cruiser. The two other men rode on each side of Walkalpa. The sun was low on the horizon now. They were parked beside the highway and were about to turn onto it when they heard the roar of a road train approaching from the south, its Dynotard engine brake grumbling loudly as the driver changed down and slowed to turn into the Erldunda gas station. The massive welded steel bull bar across its nose was fixed with powerful spotlights. Its three big freezer vans towered above the highway, behind their Mack prime mover.

Rooster Wilson barely noticed the battered old Land Cruiser pulling onto the highway as he eased the road train up to the diesel pumps. He was certainly unaware of the penetrating gaze directed toward him by one of the five Aborigines inside it as they turned down the trunk of the T-junction, and headed west along Lasseter Highway, into the desert toward Ayers Rock.

Rooster locked on the air brakes, killed the diesel, and leaned on the steering wheel, staring over the Mack's broad nose. The rig hissed and clicked like a beast settling itself onto the concrete. He felt the amphetamines prickling through his system, making everything he saw disjointed, both sharply focused and unnaturally displaced, as if he were peering into the boundary between the real world and something in his dreams. He shook his head wearily and climbed down from the cabin. Out to the west, he saw small banks of cloud, lit by fire from the disappearing sun. He shuddered from exhaustion. He planned to fill the Mack's two long-range fuel tanks, then order a pot of tea and some sandwiches in the cafeteria and pop another rattler just to be sure.

＊

The morgue loading dock was bathed in eerie light, midway between the worlds of night and day, from the blue neon of the cold room where bodies were stored, to the last rays of daylight lancing across the hospital and down the entry ramp. The old woman stood at the top of the ramp, afraid to enter. All her instincts told her this was no place to be in broad daylight, let alone at nightfall. She felt death down there, unnatural death, and this was as close as she dared come, so she sat on the concrete and waited for someone to notice her.

Some time after sundown, a hospital orderly told Dr. Alistair Steele that the woman wanted to speak to the feller in charge, and some time after that Mark Hansen arrived in his Land Rover, bathing the old woman in his headlights when he pulled up at the entrance ramp.

"This is Nancy Ilpara," Dr. Steele told Mark, as he climbed down from the vehicle. "She has something to ask you."

"How do you do, Nancy," Mark said. "How can I help you?"

The old woman looked down, struggling to put her thoughts into the kind of direct question the Piranypa used. She was accustomed to the timeless circle of conversation Anangu used to approach a delicate subject. But the Piranypa never seemed to have time for such politeness. They always asked hard, pointed questions.

"Nancy is a cousin of Oscar Woolie," Dr. Steele explained to Mark, and the old woman cringed at the sound of her dead relative's name. That was another thing Piranypa didn't understand. When an Anangu person died, their name was no longer spoken. Instead another name was used to indicate they were dead.

"I'm very sorry, Nancy," Mark said.

"Oscar's ground is in Pitjantjatjara country," Alistair Steele continued. "His people want to bury him in his own country."

"Ah." Mark was beginning to understand. "She'd like me to take him back."

"You have room for three coffins?" Alistair Steele asked, glancing toward the back of the Land Rover.

"If we stack them, and tie them down."

"All right. Very good. What about that then, eh, Nancy?"

The old woman pursed her lips, and nodded solemnly, satisfied with the result. She still could not bring herself to speak. This was all Sorry Business, and she was extremely uncomfortable in this place with these two Piranypa men, but she had a duty to see her mother's sister's son returned properly to his own country. Now it was done, she wanted to be far away from here.

"Thank you, Doctor. Thank you, Reveren'."

"You're very welcome, Nancy," Mark replied. "Would you like a lift anywhere tonight?"

The old woman tried to hide her horror at the idea of traveling in the same vehicle that would carry her dead cousin. She shook her head.

"No, thank you," she managed, then turned and walked away into the lowering night.

The two men watched her disappear into the dark.

"You realize you'll have to wait here another day," Alistair Steele said. "I won't be able to get release papers for Oscar till lunchtime tomorrow. Too hot to drive then."

"No problem." Mark sighed, and shrugged his shoulders. "I have a feeling we're moving onto a different timetable."

"What do you mean?"

"Call it a hunch. Instinct."

"You've been out here too long, Mark. The Territory's getting you."

Mark grinned in the glow of the headlights.

"That happened a long time ago."

"I think you're converting me to tea," Grace Morgan said. "This is so elegant."

They were in Heinrich and Giselle's sitting room. A tall silver teapot stood with its matching milk jug and sugar bowl and ornate strainer and stand on their large tray on a cedar coffee table, surrounded by a two-tiered silver stand packed with petit fours, and a large Black Forest chocolate cake on a Wedgwood dish that matched the finely patterned cups and saucers. She examined the details of the porcelain and the heavy chased silver border on the tea service tray, as if concentrating on these refinements could help block out the horrors Heinrich had related to her in Robert's bedroom less than half an hour ago.

"Oh, you could get tired of it very quickly, dear," Giselle said. "This is a daily ritual, though we usually have afternoon tea much earlier, around three. You probably think it's impossibly old-fashioned."

"No, no, I love it." She was certain that Heinrich had a specific reason for recounting his execution of Captain Ashima and she suspected it was to do with Robert. She did not want to contemplate the possibilities and so was enormously relieved when Giselle came into the bedroom and announced afternoon tea was ready.

"Perhaps Grace needs something stronger, after all this talk," Heinrich said.

"Tea is perfect," Grace said.

"Then we'll get you to bed," Giselle promised.

"I'm sure I'll sleep like a baby," Grace replied. "But first I need to know where Rob's gone."

Giselle picked up the silver cake knife and involved herself with slowly cutting another slice.

"We wouldn't know where to start," Heinrich said.

Grace lowered her cup to its saucer with a loud click. Giselle looked up from the cake. Heinrich blinked slowly.

"I mean to find him," she said softly. "You may think I'm just another pushy American. You may think I'm pursuing Rob when I shouldn't. You may have good reasons for not telling me where he is. But I do mean to find him, with or without your help. I don't want to get in his way, and I don't want to offend you. But I want him to know I want to be with him no matter where his . . . his dreaming takes him."

"Do you understand what his dreaming is?" Heinrich asked.

"Yes. No. He tells me things that sound like children's stories. But I'm sure he didn't come out here because of a children's story."

"Has he ever talked about men's business?"

"He's joked about it. Just to rib me. Look, I'm not some militant feminist, but I do believe if we're going to share our lives together we need to share everything. And not every gory detail of what we did and who we did it with before we knew each other. I think we do need to know all about everything that's going to affect our life together. And I think it's reasonable that something that brings him halfway around the world after he's lost a week of sleep resisting it is important enough for him to share with me. If that violates men's business then that's tough. I'm going to find Rob whether you help me or not."

Heinrich put his cup and saucer on the table. Giselle lowered the cake knife, smoothed her skirt over her knees, and looked at her husband.

"I quite know how you feel, Grace," Giselle said, her eyes still on Heinrich's. "Not knowing is hell."

Heinrich patted his wife's knee.

"There's someone who may be able to help," he said. "An old friend of ours. He helped us the first time Robbie went missing. His name is Mark Hansen."

"Why is there time, Dad?"

"If we didn't have time, Robbie," Heinrich said, "everything would all happen at once."

Robert considered that, and appeared satisfied with it. He was fourteen at the time, and would live half that many years again before he began to comprehend the flexible fabric and matrices of space-time. But at fourteen, the world was opening up in neat progressions of Newtonian space and a distinct linear flow of time and events. It was his life that was developing in two complex threads: his Piṟanypa family—Heinrich and Giselle and their closest relatives and friends—gave him their unconditional love and imbued him with the languages and nuances of clothing and houses, and straight lines and hard artificial surfaces, and harshly defined hierarchies of social strata, infused with religions that preached equality but practiced blatant discrimination; his Aṉangu family—Walkalpa his friend, his guide Maureen of the Kuniya Python Dreaming, Maḻu his elder, Ilyi of the Rock Fig Dreaming, who while still a baby girl was betrothed to him in the week he was born, and all their people—gave him their unconditional love and taught by example the languages of the universe and the spirits that streamed through it. They opened his eyes to the latticework of life and plants and spoor and tracks and weather, and the irregular natural topography of sand and gullies and trees and hills, and the strictly observed distinctions of totem and skin and dreaming, practiced with humility and dignity toward every living thing.

The stories and laws of the Tjukurpa materialized with every new lesson he learned by instruction from Malu and the men, or by discovery with Maureen and the women. The events and deeds of the creation time lived in the present with all of them. The Tjukurpa was real, extant, not an abstract philosophy or theology to be chosen or rejected. The past lived simultaneously in their present.

By the time he earned his bachelor's degree, Robert Erhard could comprehend the universal speed limit of light, and the peculiar habits of mass as it approached that velocity. He understood both of Einstein's most famous theories, and could visualize the bend and bow of the space-time continuum around large and small gravitational obstacles, and he believed in the inevitable discovery of the Holy Grail of theoretical physics—the still unformulated Grand Unification Theory linking all the elemental forces with speed and mass in a single elegant equation. They were all goals in the endless attempt by Piranypa to understand and control the universe for their own interests.

The Tjukurpa and The Law established and explained all the laws of existence to the Anangu. Unlike the Piranypa, Anangu sought to understand and obey their Law for the best interests of the universe, of which they were an integral part.

The stories of the Tjukurpa were memories, complete in detail and design, passed through generations of spirits and humans to the living. Every man and woman who learned them brought the past into the present, and lived with them simultaneously into the future, until it became part of the great present, all determined and ordered according to the Law.

Much later, Robert tried to explain it to Heinrich.

"Remember when I was a kid and I asked you why is there time?"

"No." Heinrich smiled, shaking his head. "What did I tell you?"

"You said it was to stop everything happening at once. I thought that was a pretty elegant way of explaining it."

Heinrich chuckled. "That doesn't sound like me."

Robert grinned at him. "It was you, Dad. In the Tjukurpa, everything happens at once and not at once. All the stories we learn are part of us. When we see them or follow their lines across the country, we're literally living in the past and the present at the same time. The past is guiding us, and teaching us how to live in the present. It's like a memory. What's your favorite memory, Dad?"

"Oh." He laughed quietly. "There are so many of them. The day we brought you home. The night you talked for the first time. So many of them."

"Another one."

Heinrich looked into the distance, unreeling the years, and smiled wistfully. "The night I met your mother." He realized the irony of that, seeing an overlay of images from the cold office of a government adoption official, and from a college dance in Adelaide before the war. "The night I met Giselle," he added, self-consciously. "She was the most beautiful girl I had ever seen."

"It's right there, isn't it," Robert said, "the memory."

"Oh yes. As if it happened yesterday."

"Well, the Tjukurpa is like that. Except we see it as if it happened today. In the now."

Robert recalled the entire conversation in an instant. He glanced at Malu and at his son, Walkalpa, riding silently in the back seat of the Land Cruiser. In the same overlaid instant, Robert saw his memories of playing with Walkalpa as a boy limping beside him on the desert, spotting prey with his penetrating eyes, waiting for Robert to notch his spear into his miru and bring down the animal.

In the same instant, he swept through a host of memories as if he had flashed a laser through layers of filaments, each a complete memory.

In that same instant, he saw the depth and breadth of the filaments, of all the creation tracks he had learned and preserved as the Story Keeper, just as the spirit of Tjilkamata the echidna preserved all the stories of the Tjukurpa.

And in the same instant, he saw the body of Ilyi, the teenaged girl betrothed to him when they were both babies. There was blood on her thighs and her neck was twisted unnaturally. He saw the women cleaning the body and preparing it for burial. He saw the man who had raped and killed her, a Tjanpi man, of the Sandhill Dreaming. He was also a teenager, a year younger than Robert. The elders had sentenced the Tjanpi man to an ordeal by spearing, and they summoned Robert from the city for it. The offense was against his betrothed and he was obliged to throw the first spear.

The ordeal lasted from sunup to sundown. The Tjanpi man stood on a wide basin running between two low sandhills. Thirty yards away, Robert and four of Ilyi's closest male relatives stood with their spears. Each man in turn threw a spear at the Tjanpi man, who tried to evade it. The ordeal would continue until the man was speared once, or until the sun set. If he avoided the spears during the day, he still did not escape punishment: at sundown, he would be held down, and while the elders watched to see all was done according to The Law, the point of a spear would be pushed completely through the main muscle of his thigh and withdrawn.

Only then was the sentence complete. As the sun passed over its zenith, Robert could see the Tjanpi man was becoming exhausted. Throughout the morning, he had been able to see each spear coming, and easily evade it. At intervals, they had to recover their spears, while the Tjanpi man waited patiently for them. There was no sense of malice. He was undergoing his sentence and they were carrying it out according to The Law, preserving the fabric of the Tjukurpa. After each completed volley, the men wordlessly picked up their spears with a clacking of wood, and returned to their firing line. Robert saw his shadow at his feet, no wider than his shoulders as the sun passed overhead. By then, the men had already thrown at the Tjanpi man more than two hundred times. Robert gauged the range to the man, notched his spear into its miru, and drew back his right arm, holding his left out straight, alongside the fire-hardened wood. For an instant he locked eyes with the Tjanpi man, and felt a visceral connection with him, with the man's controlled fear, and deeper, with the knowledge of his crime. Robert felt his body galvanize as if the spear was alive, as if it launched itself in a smooth flow of muscle and throwing stick. The spear barely shivered in the air, rising fast and quiet along its trajectory and dipping down smoothly, impaling the Tjanpi man through the chest. His eyes were still open when the men reached him, lying on his side with the lance through him, its tip wet and making a small arc in the sand as he tried to breathe. He looked at Robert and bared his teeth in pain. The peculiar sense of connection seemed to hold between them, as if their spirits changed places, then reverted back to their original bodies. A shudder went through the Tjanpi man as he died. All this Robert recalled in the same instant of overlaid memories.

In the Tjukurpa, the Wirruntjatjara believe, when the spirits had returned to Uluru along their creation tracks, they went to a secret place near the monolith and held a huge inma, a ceremony of singing and dancing. Only the creation spirits were allowed to the inma. They brought with them their tjurungas, the sacred boards and stones inscribed with the symbols of their dreaming. The tjurungas were the embodiment of their spirits, so hallowed that all who were not initiated were forbidden to even look at them. Any woman or child who saw such a tjurunga, even by accident, must be killed at once. A warrior named Tjilkamata was jealous of the creation spirits and their deeds, and crept in to watch their inma. They were recounting their dreaming stories, and in the darkness, Tjilkamata listened to everything they said, and saw the symbols on all their tjurungas. Then Tjintirtjintirpa the willie wagtail bird discovered

Tjilkamata's hiding place and he was seized and sentenced to an ordeal by spears. When the spirits threw their spears, all of them found their mark until Tjilkamata's body was riddled with long brown lances. To try and escape, he burrowed into the sand at the base of an anthill, until only the spears in his back stuck out of the ground. After the sun set, Tjilkamata came out of the ground, and sought to avenge himself. He cast the spirits into a deep sleep and when they awoke, they could remember nothing of their creation tracks or their songs or their dreamings. They wandered through the desert weeping in grief and desperation, lost from their own past and families, trying to find their stories again. Their crying was so woeful that Tjilkamata took pity on them, and one by one, he Sang each spirit, returning to each of them their dreaming and creation songs. When she saw what happened, Wanampi called all the spirits together. After they had been purified by smoke, Wanampi brought Tjilkamata into the center. "For breaking the taboo on the first inma, you were rightfully sentenced to an ordeal by spears," Wanampi told Tjilkamata, as the spirits pressed around. "You were wrong to make them forget their dreaming. But you showed remorse when you saw what you had done, and you have restored their creation songs and dreamings to the last detail. Henceforth, you will be the Story Keeper. But to remind you of your original wickedness, you will always carry the spears in your back, and you will only find your food in anthills. You will be known as Tjilkamata of the Spiny Anteater Dreaming."

This, also, Robert recalled in the same instant that he perceived all the other images, separate and synchronous. He was Tjilkamata, the keeper of all the songs and all the dreaming tracks converging on Uluru, a living registry of all the knowledge stored in the stones and sand and water holes of the Rock. Throughout his life, as he returned to Uluru each year for the inmas and initiation rites, more knowledge was passed to him.

The Land Cruiser roared westward toward Uluru, with Robert, Malu, Lungkata, Tjitutja, and Walkalpa riding in silence, contemplating their mission, feeling their entrance back into their own country, and the desperate sounds of grief rising from the stones and hills and dunes around them, echoing through the timeless dimension of the Tjukurpa.

As he saw the outline of Uluru grow larger through the windshield, Robert unstrapped his electronic wristwatch and buried it out of sight and mind in the pocket of his trousers.

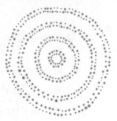

CHAPTER 19

THE GULFSTREAM LANDED SMOOTHLY at Alice Springs airport, rolled out past a line of Australian and U.S. military aircraft, and turned onto the taxiway that led to the BIRD Aviation hangars where a black limousine was waiting on the tarmac.

It was only the third time Andrew Bird had returned home to Australia in nearly twenty years. The first time, he remembered, there was no limousine, only chanting picketers who mobbed the entrance to Richmond air base denouncing baby killers and fascists, and hurling plastic bags of human waste and animal blood at the buses carrying troops returning from Vietnam to a condemned home for heroes where the doors were shut, the windows shaded, and veterans were shunned as pariahs. He stayed four months, growing his hair and a beard, dining with his mother in the evenings, and restlessly prowling the streets through the night with a lethal anger that he barely kept in check as he watched the faces of soft young people who knew nothing of the world beyond their own petty diversions and pathetic depravities. He spoke only twice to his father, unable to bridge the chasm opened through years of Owen's absence from the great sandstone home, and widened by all that Andrew could not unknow from his journeys into the night with Keith Bliss. He answered an advertisement for a newspaper reporter in Hong Kong, and in the swashbuckling atmosphere of the island, he was hired by telephone within a week.

Now the Gulfstream braked to a stop near the long black sedan, and Andrew looked out the porthole to see the woman who had met him on his second return to Australia. Then he had been filing radio reports for the BBC from Cambodia when Agnes Horstmann telephoned with the news that his mother had been found in the back seat of her Bentley with the engine running, inside the garage of the sandstone. His lasting image of his mother was the one that found its way to a tabloid wire service from the lab of the police photographer who, once the exhaust fumes cleared, recorded Isabel Bird sitting primly in a navy Dior suit and matching pillbox hat with its dark gauze covering her precise makeup, her sad eyes staring sightlessly through the glass screen that separated her from the empty chauffeur's compartment and the world she finally chose to leave. "It's simply awful, Andy. Your father was in London. He's devastated," Agnes told him when she met his jet in Sydney. "I've taken care of everything."

Now as Andrew came down the stairs of the Gulfstream into the smiting heat of Alice Springs airport, he saw Agnes Horstmann step out of the limousine to greet him with a warm smile, mantled with the power of the sole confidante to Owen Bird that his mother—for all her impeccable grace and poise—could never manage to wear.

"Mark's in Alice Springs," Heinrich reported to Grace Morgan as he hung up the telephone. "I've told him all about your concerns and plans. He suggested you wait here with us for news. But"—he raised his hand as Grace's eyes narrowed—"I've told him how insistent you are, and he's invited you to visit him at his mission. It's very near Robert's country."

"Good." Grace's voice was businesslike. "When can I leave?"

"When Mark returns to Lake Amadeus. That's the name of the mission."

"When's that?"

"A day or two."

"Then I can fly up and wait for him. What's the nearest town?"

"Yulara, next to Uluṟu," Heinrich said. "But I think it will be wiser to wait."

"May I use your phone? I'd like to check the airline schedule."

"Really, Grace, I understand your eagerness to get there, but I wish you would wait for Mark to get back."

"Perhaps you could drive her up," Giselle said from the doorway.

Heinrich looked at her in astonishment.

"You could be up there in a day," Giselle continued. "Heinrich knows the area very well, dear. He can help you avoid blundering off into the desert. It's so easy to get lost there."

She smiled sweetly at her husband and realization dawned on him. But Grace was watching them both closely and she sighed in resignation.

"And you can keep me from interfering with whatever Rob's doing up there." She smiled, and her voice softened. "All right. You win. When do we leave?"

"Andrew. Thank you so much for coming," Owen Bird stood in the center of his hospital room, braced with a walking cane in his good right hand, the left silk sleeve of his long tailored dressing gown hidden in the white triangle of a sling that supported his arm and its fiberglass cast. He looked determined, resolute. "Have a good flight?"

Andrew Bird took in the perimeter of flowers and the banks of computers and television equipment crowding toward the large articulated hospital bed near the windows.

"I slept most of the way," he said, crossing the room, unsure for a moment of what to do—he and Owen only ever shook hands in greeting: one now gripped the heavy cane, the other hung from its sling. Owen reached out to embrace his son, something Andrew had never seen him do in the past. They hugged self-consciously, navigating Owen's injuries and a relationship that had only ever been brusque and formal. "Agnes said you were paralyzed."

"She wasn't lying to you. Grab a chair," Owen indicated the reclining armchairs circling a large round coffee table to one side of the room. Agnes pressed a button for a steward.

"What's the situation?" Andrew settled into custom padded leather with electronic controls in the armrest.

"What's Agnes told you?"

"She says you're in danger. I told her to hire a security company."

"I told him we've done that," Agnes said.

"Sounds like you finally took something that might bite you," Andrew said.

"I suppose this amuses you," Owen said.

"No, it pisses me off that you sent out an SOS to pull me away from my job, just because you finally pissed someone else off enough to frighten you. That does not amuse me. And it pisses me off that after all these years of ·

avoiding me, you suddenly want to get warm and fuzzy because you're running scared. Next time you want to throw your weight around, remember
how afraid you are now. And, by the way, don't . . . ever . . . pull strings on me
the way you did yesterday. I've stayed right away from your life, just as you
always wanted. Stay out of mine."

Owen glowered silently, waiting for his son to finish.

"One," he replied finally, "I've never run scared in my life. Two. Getting
Atlanta to release you was just a returned favor from someone there who owes
me much more. And three. I've always wanted you to join me. You can have a
directorship any time you say so. It's you who've wanted to alienate yourself,
Andrew, not me."

"Let's not go down that road. If you'd cared as much for your family as you
did for . . ." Andrew glanced at Agnes. " . . . your business, you'd still have a
family."

"Why'd you bother coming?"

"Agnes told me you were paralyzed."

"I was . . ."

" . . . and that this was urgent."

"It is," Agnes said. There was a knock at the door and she went to let the
steward in.

"Tea? Coffee? Breakfast? Dinner?" Owen asked. "What time zone are
you in?"

Andrew ordered breakfast.

"So. What's the situation?" he said after the steward left.

"I've changed my mind about something I acquired," Owen replied. "I
want to send it back."

"Call UPS."

Owen smiled slowly, examining his hands. He looked directly at his son.
"All right, Andrew. I've fucked something up. I want to fix it. I'd like to keep it
within the family."

"Play the heart card, eh?" Andrew's voice was harsh. "Family."

Owen shrugged his eyebrows.

"You turned out all right, despite everything."

"What's it involve?" Andrew ignored the attempt at reconciliation.

"Taking a package down to Ayers Rock."

"You're serious?" His anger rose. "That really is a courier's job."

"Not exactly. There may be some risk involved."

"All right." Andrew settled into his chair. "Let's hear all of it."

"I've got someone who can explain it better than I can," Owen said. "He's on the way over. Incidentally, he doesn't need to know any more than I tell him."

≈

"Walkabout!" Rooster Wilson's eyes narrowed in disbelief at the young cook standing on the ground below his cab window. He had driven nearly three hundred miles straight through from Erldunda, past the Ayers Rock/Uluru reserve where the macadam ended, and onto the corrugated dirt road that ran for another one hundred and thirty miles west to the settlement at Docker River. Rooster had barely parked his rig in Docker River before he heard the bad news.

"They can't go bloody walkabout!" he cried, hoarse from too many cigarettes and no sleep. "I've got a bloody truck to unload."

"Well, pet, y'better jump to it, hadn't yer," Astrid Joyce said. She was a month shy of thirty, and a veteran of kitchens and mess halls across the Outback, and she took no nonsense from anybody. "They've all gone bush on men's business, eh. Any men left are moving cattle up before the rain, aren't they."

Rooster cast a bloodshot eye over her.

"And don't be lookin' at me like that neither," she warned him. "I've got too much work of me own to be droppin' everything and unloading a truck, now then, haven't I."

She thought Rooster's veins were going to explode across his face. He went dark red, working his jaw and battling to control his temper. She turned and walked smartly back to her kitchen before a storm of curses erupted in the cabin of the Mack, and raged on long after she had closed the door behind her.

≈

"Padre! Thanks for coming. This is my son, Andrew."

Mark Hansen watched Andrew Bird turn to greet him. He could see the resemblance to his father, the same set of the shoulders, though taller and leaner than Owen, and with a similar steady gaze.

"I understood you were in the Balkans," Mark said as he shook Andrew's hand warily.

"He came home to help me with this . . . situation."

"That's nice," Mark said.

"I've told him he has a chance to save a big mob of people," Owen said.

"How's he going to do that?" Mark couldn't understand how a television journalist could contribute anything here.

"By returning the stone."

"I see," Mark said, then shook his head. "Owen, you can't do this."

"And why not?" Owen's voice dropped.

"You send him back with the tjurunga and you're as good as sacrificing him."

"Then that would be very Christian of me, wouldn't it, Padre."

"What are we up against?" Andrew returned to his armchair and tilted the footrest up. He closed his eyes and ran through a relaxation mantra, focusing himself on the answer.

"Tell him, Padre."

"Your father stole . . . rather he arranged the theft of something extremely valuable from a tribal group called the Wirruntjatjara."

"No surprises yet," Andrew said.

"They believe they will die if it's not returned, and they may have already killed three suspects so far."

"What are the police doing?" Andrew asked.

"Fuck-all," Owen answered. "We're not involving the police."

"How are you going to hush up three murders?"

"Because they're not murders," Mark replied. "They were Sung to death."

Andrew opened his eyes and smiled. "Go on."

"There is reason to believe the Wirruntjatjara will send a kudaitja to kill your father."

"That's why you called?" Andrew turned to Agnes.

"Agnes thinks you're the only one who can handle this."

"So if it's not returned," Andrew said to Mark, "what are we up against?"

"If they call in a kudaitja he'll be accompanied by a sorcerer."

"Go on," Andrew said.

"The kudaitja," Mark cautioned, "has one critical advantage over his adversaries."

"Really?" Andrew closed his eyes again. "And what's that."

"He will be invisible."

Six men walked soundlessly through the low scrub around Uluru. They were led by the man from the deep desert, Kumanara, who bore the name of the dead, and who was waiting for them at Uluru when they arrived from Erldunda with Robert. Behind him came Tjitutja of the Dingo Dreaming with a heavy burlap sack. Malu of the Red Kangaroo Dreaming followed, hefting two new hunting spears with long fire-tempered wooden shafts, and tipped with razor-sharp stone blades. Walkalpa the sorcerer brought four leather pouches, the cured and stretched scrota of red kangaroos, containing separately red ocher and white clay powder, a ball of black sticky kiti, and a number of stone tools and talismans. Despite his deformed foot, Walkalpa of the Emu Poison Bush Dreaming moved efficiently with a rolling gait across the ground where, three decades earlier, he and young Robert had been forced to run bleeding and terrified on the first night of their initiation. Robert and Lungkata of the Blue Tongue Lizard Dreaming brought up the rear, carrying kangaroo hides, cured and rolled tightly into packed cylinders, bound with leather thongs and sealed with black kiti.

A quarter of a mile from the north side of the monolith, the ground became heavily bearded with shoulder-high mulga. The men stopped a short distance from three large boulders, each the size of a small truck. They stood quietly for a long time, listening. The only sounds they heard were insects and the rustle of lizards foraging through the sand. To the west, they could see clouds beginning to bank into the sky. Kumanara took the burlap sack from Tjitutja, and placed his hand on the Dingo Dreaming man's chest. Then Tjitutja turned and moved away through the scrub.

They watched him disappear into the high mulga. When Tjitutja was gone from view, Kumanara walked toward one of the boulders. He seemed to sink into the ground as he went. The others followed him, disappearing down a throat of rock that swallowed them deep into the earth. They felt their way in darkness, running the tips of their fingers along the rock walls enclosing them. The fissure snaked downward for more than two hundred yards, then opened out in a stone cavern. They could smell water. Even with night vision, they could see nothing. The darkness was complete.

A loud smack broke the stillness, then another and another as the five men clapped their hands, calling out to the water, «Waṉampi! We are coming!» Kumaṉara felt his way across the rock floor until his feet splashed into the pool. It was almost lukewarm, and difficult to feel in the darkness. He opened the burlap sack Tjiṯutja had given him and spread kangaroo meat along the rocky edge. Unseen ripples splashed lightly against the rock.

«Wai, Waṉampi, we are coming to you,» Kumaṉara called, walking further into the water. A hand touched his shoulder, as Robert followed him in, leading Walkalpa behind him, then Lungkata and at the tail end Maḻu. The air was so black they could barely tell where the warm artesian water rose against their skin. They felt for the presence of Waṉampi the Rainbow Serpent deep in the pool, trusting her to let them continue in.

Kumaṉara used both his hands to feel ahead until he touched a crevice in the rock, below the surface.

«We are coming in, Waṉampi!» he called into the void. Then he took a deep breath, and with his hands on the lip of the submerged opening, pulled himself beneath the water and deep into the crevice.

Moments later, the last of the five men disappeared below the surface, and were gone from the rock chamber. Their ripples had barely settled when something large surged through the water and up onto the stony edge and with a loud slash of jaws devoured the raw meat.

Four stewards served rounds of filet mignon and steamed baby vegetables on gold-edged porcelain plates. Owen made small talk with his son and Mark and Agnes, waiting for the servants to leave. When they were alone around the linen-draped table, assembled and laid with remarkable efficiency by the stewards, Owen's mood changed.

"Start at the beginning, Padre. This is fascinating."

Mark picked up his gold knife and fork and felt the tines and blade sink through the tender steak. He was calm, resigned, ordering his thoughts to recall all he had learned and gathered in four decades in the Dead Heart. He plumbed the landmark research done by the great anthropologists Professors Roland and Catherine Berndt. He mentally reviewed his own meticulous investigations with the Wirruṉtjatjara on Lake Amadeus.

"The kudaitja," he began, "hunts with a ngangkari, a sorcerer."

"Start with him, then."

"The sorcerer? I don't know who he is."

"Tell us what you know."

"About sorcerers."

"Take your time," Andrew said. "From the beginning."

"From the beginning. It begins with a woman's dream."

She had awoken abruptly on the sand, with her dingo clutched to her belly. The dog jerked awake, his ears up, staring into the cold desert night. She was young and lovely, barely out of girlhood, and the first thing she saw in the glittering river of stars overhead was the constellation of Aliti, the Wattle Dreaming spirit, for whom she was named. She closed her eyes and saw the thing again, something enormous, sliding over itself. Aliti trembled and buried her fingers in the dingo's winter coat.

Her husband came out of his hunter's sleep, alert. Apart from their loin strings, they were both naked, huddled back to back, between their dogs and two small sleeping fires. In the starlight he could see across the camp, where other bodies lay between sleeping fires, huddled with dingoes and children on the ground. He peered beyond the faint haze of smoke, past the low windbreak of stacked mulga branches, but there was only the night on the desert, and the sounds of small animals scuttling through sand and spinifex. Aliti's husband was named for his birth totem, Malu, the Red Kangaroo Dreaming spirit. Malu's two dingoes were on their feet, their tawny coats red with dust, their hackles up, as they scanned the camp.

Malu watched his young wife silently.

"I saw a baby," Aliti whispered. "It's entered me."

"When?"

"Now. In my sleep."

"Remember everything."

"I'm afraid."

"Remember everything."

Malu slid back into shallow sleep. His male dingo turned three times, licked Malu's face, and dropped back against him on the sand. Its mate settled at Malu's ankles.

Aliti remained awake. When the spirit of a new baby arrived from the world below the ground, and took up residence in its mother, it brought her clues to its identity in a conception dream. In the morning, she would have to recount all of it.

Aliti watched the tribes of stars crowding the sky. Every point and cluster of light marked the story of a spirit on the great journey from Creation. Finding her totem up there was like seeing herself, clearly defined with her eternal family.

Like all inducted girls, Aliti had been tutored by elder women to notice every detail of the conception dream: to remember if the unborn child was standing, sitting, or lying; and what features of rock, water hole, sand, scrub, or animal appeared near it. These revealed the spirits and characteristics that would define the child's totem, and its path into adulthood. She might never be told what the images meant, but The Law demanded she report them accurately, so the elder men could properly interpret them.

Aliti remained awake through the night, examining the dream. In the starlight, she watched wives and daughters rise to stoke their sleeping fires, then return to the broken nap that is the most rest a tribal woman can hope for.

In the morning, weary and still afraid, Aliti told her husband everything. She said the spirit who appeared to her was a boy, standing at the southern side of Uluru. The child was standing in the ancient clump of walkalpa, emu poison bush. Hunters use it to drug water holes along the emus' grazing routes. The tall flightless birds can easily outrun a kangaroo, and a man is no match for their speed, but an emu drugged with walkalpa staggers in a daze, unable to escape the hunters' clubs.

When Aliti told him their unborn child's left foot was deformed, Malu's face remained impassive. Such babies do not survive in the desert. Then, Aliti described the huge, dazzling creature writhing around their child's feet and coiling back into Uluru. Malu was silent for some time. Then he questioned her carefully, making her repeat all of her dream. When she finished he told her to say nothing more, and sent her off to join the women.

Later in the morning, Malu went hunting. His dingoes flushed a goanna up a desert oak. The big black and yellow lizard was nearly six feet long. Malu killed it with his throwing club, and in the afternoon, he carried the goanna and a smoldering firestick out of the camp with the elder men. They walked far into the desert, to a distant ridge, then up a long secret gully to a sheltered ring of stones. The elder men made a fire at the center of the ring of stones, then covered it with green eucalyptus branches, and walked through the aromatic smoke to purify themselves. As the sun went down, they sat on the ground within the *ring and focused their minds with the chant for this ritual, each man clicking the rhythm with his throwing sticks.*

The fire burned to glowing coals. Malu thanked the spirit of the dead goanna, then turned its lower intestine inside out and discarded the waste, leaving the goanna correctly cleaned, with its organs intact. He used his throwing stick to clear back the coals at the edge of the fire, exposing a strip of baking sand, and laid the goanna on it. Soon the men heard it sizzling and popping beneath the sand, and a mouthwatering aroma wafted from the mound. The embers cast a red glow over the men, and sent their shadows veering high across the walls of the gully. The choice side pockets of fat were removed from beneath the ribs and passed to the senior elder. Then the baked organs, muscles, and remaining fat were shared out according to each man's status and totem.

As the men ate, Malu related every particular of Aliti's conception dream.

The elders confirmed Malu's suspicions about his young wife's unborn baby. The enormous, brilliantly colored snake wrapping itself around the child's feet was Wanampi the Rainbow Serpent, the mother of creation, and maker and guide of ngangkari, sorcerers. Wanampi clearly protected the boy growing in Aliti's belly. The crippled child would not perish, instead he would be born with exceptional gifts. But any relief Malu and Aliti might enjoy was overshadowed.

A ngangkari forsakes all to serve Wanampi and the Law of creation, the Tjukurpa. A ngangkari is a protector and guide of his people. He is profoundly respected, and for the same reasons, gravely feared. His powers are so great that merely staring at a ngangkari will cause the viewer to fall ill. The ngangkari is blessed and doomed to travel through life in the rich company of spirits, but unloved and isolated by his own people.

As they journeyed across the desert, Aliti's breasts and belly grew. She worked as hard as any of the women, heading out with them each sunrise to scour the desert for the grass seeds, flowers, larvae, honey ants, and small animals the signs and creation stories led them to. As she grew larger, the women watched her more closely, nodding approval as her body showed it was ready to make milk.

When she was close to term, the women took Aliti far away from the main camp. No men, boys, or unmarried girls were allowed to follow or watch or listen. In the shade of some river red gum trees, the women prepared the ground, and lit a fire. They positioned Aliti for the birth, and when the crown of the head appeared, the women warmed their hands at the fire, and held the emerging baby, singing to it, welcoming it into the world. When they saw his feet come out, they fell silent. The tiny left foot was cruelly twisted inward.

The eldest woman seemed unperturbed, and gently cleaned him as she directed the remainder of the birthing ritual, strictly observing each detail of medicine and magic. The severed umbilical cord was fashioned into a loop and placed around the baby's neck to protect him from evil. All other traces of his birth were burned on the fire to stop any sorcerer from recovering them, and using them to lay curses. Then the women placed a green branch on the fire, and passed the baby through its thick eucalyptus smoke to purify him.

The women brought Aliti food while she nursed him. She had no knowledge of the men's business that deciphered the clues in her conception dream. And she fell in love with the baby the moment he was placed on her breast. Even with his deformed foot, Aliti saw he was beautiful. He was named Walkalpa, of the Emu Poison Bush Dreaming, and at first, old women muttered approval when they pinched his fat, and saw how healthy he was. But soon they stopped touching him, and Aliti felt a deep dread slowly uncoiling inside her, sliding over itself through the few, fleeting years of his childhood until the night her son, Walkalpa, was seized, and borne away by the monsters who make boys into men.

Mark waited until the stewards returned to serve coffee and departed again before he continued.

"Aboriginal women dream about their children from conception. If the dream suggests the child may be destined to become a sorcerer, he will go through the usual rituals of manhood. Sometimes the sorcerer may be female, in which case she will enter into women's business rituals. But usually it is male. He will be apprenticed to a respected practicing sorcerer, and by a process of testing and ceremony, be prepared for a visitation by the supreme creation spirit called Baiami. At a chosen time, the young candidate is taken to a sacred ground with his guardian and Baiami appears, with eyes of fire, producing liquid quartz crystal, like water, that enters the child.

"Baiami instructs the child on the use of quartz crystal, and Sings a piece into his forehead to give him X-ray vision. Baiami also takes fire from his own body and Sings it into the child. Then he takes a sinew, called a maulwa cord, and Sings that into the child. The boy is then taken to a water hole, accompanied by sorcerers, to receive his power. At the water hole, he is blind-folded and left alone. Wanampi, the Rainbow Dreaming Serpent, rises from the water hole and swallows the boy whole. Some time later, the other sorcer-ers return, and feed Wanampi, who vomits the boy into the air, as a baby reborn as a sorcerer. The elder sorcerers place the child in a ring of fires and he grows at once into a man.

"Small discs of pearl shell, called maban, are placed in his joints and ears and jaw to give him supernatural powers. Finally, he submits to a confirma-tional ritual, in which the initiated elders of the tribe throw spears at him. The weapons bounce off him, proving he is protected by the maban discs, and he begins his role as a fully ordained sorcerer and protector of his people and the Law.

"The ngangkari is invested with great powers to enforce the Law. To speak to spirits, to heal the sick, and exorcise the possessed, to see beyond life and death, to lay and lift curses, and to evict the souls of grievous offenders by pointing a splinter of human thigh bone at them, and Singing them to death."

Mark looked from Owen to Agnes to Andrew. They were sitting forward in their armchairs, watching him closely.

"If the elders decide that a particular crime must be punished more . . . forcefully," Mark said quietly, "it is the sorcerer, the ngangkari, who summons a suitable warrior. A transformation ceremony is conducted to change him into a kudaitja, a ritual assassin, to carry out a more violent execution."

Tjitutja of the Dingo Dreaming loped steadily through the scrub from where he left the five other elders toward the north face, the male side of Uluru. Partway along it he saw the long narrow pole of rock, a fertility site called ngaltawata, more than two hundred feet high, leaning up against the monolith and fused to it at the top. In the Tjukurpa, the Mala hare wallaby men came to ngaltawata for initiation rituals. The Wintalka mulga seed people from Docker River had invited the Mala men to a ceremony there, but the Mala men refused to go because they were conducting their own men's business. In anger, the Wintalka people called up a dingo demon spirit called Kurpan, and sent it to attack the Mala people. Kurpan howled in from Docker River slaughtering Mala women and children on the female, southern side of Uluru. Then the monstrous spirit charged around to the northern side to attack the Mala men, but they escaped with their ngaltawata pole by dragging it up the side of the rock and over the top.

Tjitutja could still see the red stains up along the rock where Kurpan had savaged the Mala people. He saw the holes and grooves up the side where the men had made handholds to escape over the summit.

The rock walls of the cave he entered were still red with splattered Mala blood, and pieces of their bodies, turned to stone, were still strewn on the sandy floor. Tjitutja made a fire and squatted close to it, and first smoked himself with eucalyptus, then with growing anticipation of the forces he was about to unleash, he began the ritual to summon Kurpan once again from his demonic lair.

The water moved down in chilled currents, seizing the five submerged men with a desperate urge to struggle to the surface. But there was no surface above them, only water and rock. They propelled themselves by pushing along the rock with their feet and free hands. The kangaroo skin bundles bumped along the rock ceiling of the tunnel. Robert felt his lungs searing desperately for air. The men lost any sense of up or down, only forward. There was no indication the tunnel was curving up until they burst into a second chamber. Robert surfaced with an explosive gasp, and heard the others panting loudly until they recovered their breath, still immersed in absolute darkness, feeling rock beneath their feet. The air smelled of stone.

Kumanara waded up the sloping floor, feeling his way along the low wall. They were still deep in the belly of Wanampi, but climbing now, as the thin fissure arced gently upward. Silently, the men made their way up the tunnel, feeling their way again with their fingers. Robert traveled with his eyes closed, unable to see any better with them open, and more attuned to the rhythms of Wanampi singing in the rock. They made slow progress for some time, then the air began to change.

They could smell cool dry earth through the metallic cleanness of stone. Then they felt the tunnel disappear and were standing on fine sand. They heard Kumanara searching for something at the mouth of the tunnel. They heard the sound of a straight firestick being notched into its baseboard and rotated swiftly between the palms of his hands, then the rustle of fine strands of dry stringybark.

In a few minutes, out of the blackness, they saw a tiny soft glow of heated wood appear like a distant nova on the ground in front of Kumanara. He was still invisible in the dark, but as the glow grew brighter, they began to see the silhouettes of his foot, holding the baseboard in place on the ground, and the firestick standing in a notch on its surface, rotating one way, then the other at high speed. They saw his fingers drop the dried ball of stringybark around the glow, then the firestick began its whirring again, accompanied by the fast rasp of skin over skin, as his palms spun it.

The glow spread through the fibers as Kumanara blew gently on the tiny fragments of light. Then there was a tiny pop of flame and he held it in his hands and stood up, rolling the fibers in his palms to keep them burning.

The tongues of fire lit his face, as he breathed life into it. The darkness ebbed away from him, and he followed it to a circle of charred stones. The others followed him with their bundles. He placed the ball of fibers at the center of the circle, coaxing the flame. Robert and Lungkata broke open the kiti seals on their hide bundles and took out slim, dried twigs, and sturdier short branches as thick as their wrists. The fire was very small, but quickly cast a soft light around them. Their eyes, after such extended darkness, saw every detail of the enormous cavern they had entered.

It was nearly forty feet in diameter, rising to a rough dome that was more than forty feet high. The floor was packed earth, and showed no trace of the randomly dispersed bones and droppings that generations of bats and birds and predators usually left in such places. It was as if the creatures of the desert avoided it. But more eerie than the absence of earthly life was the silent horde of painted creatures surrounding them.

The entire circumference of the cavern, lit by the wavering firelight, was a gallery of all the spirits of the Tjukurpa. The paintings were breathtaking, done and refurbished by generations of artists who were obviously familiar and intimate with the shapes and forms of the creation spirits. There were the figures, in classical Anangu X-ray style, of Kalaya the emu and Mala the rufus hare wallaby and Malu the red kangaroo, Tjintirtjintirpa the willie wagtail and Liru the poison snake, and Luunpa the red-backed kingfisher and Lungkata the blue-tongued lizard. Kuniya the python appeared with her eggs on her head on a wall opposite Liru, separated as were all the others from their individual enemies and taboo spirits. Tjilkamata the spiny echidna was painted standing apart from them, watching and listening, remembering everything, preserving all their stories and songs. Spaced among the creatures were outlines of spearheads and boomerang-shaped throwing sticks, and the hands of elder warriors, each painted by artists who filled their mouths with a slurry of red ocher mud and blew it in a fine spray over the object to be silhouetted. These blown outlines recorded the passage over thousands of years of elders who came to this inner sanctum to serve the Law.

The only shape that seemed to observe no taboos of separation was a magnificently drawn creature that slithered around the entire circumference, touching each of the other spirits with her giant, sinuous coils.

She was Wanampi the Rainbow Serpent, who went into the earth at Uluru, leaving her mark in the water hole on top of the Rock, a thousand feet above this cavern where she slept.

Walkalpa went to the base of one wall and returned to the fire. Set in the ground in front of him was a large tjiwa, a grinding stone. There was a groove along its center, made by a tjungari, the small round stone used to pulverize the seeds of grass and mulga and wakati into flour. On the tjiwa he placed the large black ball of resinous kiti he had brought with him. Beside the kiti, he laid a tjularrka, a surgically sharp blade of basalt rock. He made another trip to the wall and returned with three wooden bowls, each the size of two cupped hands. He set them on top of the tjiwa. One of them held the white powder of ground pipe clay, and the other the red ocher, to be mixed into ceremonial body paint. The third bowl remained empty.

The men's voices rose to fill the cavern beginning a low circular chant, singing the Law through each stage of the ritual. Walkalpa stood again, leaning to one side to accommodate his deformed foot. But in the firelight, surrounded by the spirits of the Tjukurpa, Walkalpa no longer looked like a crippled man. His eyes blazed with an unnatural intensity. His twisted foot emphasized his separation from ordinary men. He bore the unusual initiation scars of the Emu Poison Bush Dreaming. At the side of his loin string hung a small leather bag with a thong drawstring, containing the stones and bone slivers of his craft. Wanampi raised his arms above the men, and his shadow was thrown up on the curving wall behind him, flaring across the paintings with all the energy of the most powerful sorcerer.

In his own cave, Tjitutja stared into the flames of his fire, surrounded by the remains of the victims of Kurpan's ancient killing raid. His chanting resonated off the walls and reached far beyond the boundaries of sound and space, across the desert toward Docker River, where the demon spirit stirred in its sleep, opened its eyes, and raised its great muzzle from its paws and smelled the scent of new prey.

In the cave of Wanampi, in the depths of Uluru, Robert lay on his back staring at the paintings rearing from the walls toward the dome. Walkalpa squatted beside him, completing the last line of painting on Robert's skin. From forehead to toes, his body was covered with the intricate fine lines of the spiny anteater totem, Tjilkamata. Walkalpa's body bore the complex red ocher and white clay paint of the Emu Poison Bush Dreaming. The three other men also bore the patterns from head to foot of their dreaming spirits. When Walkalpa completed the final paint stroke with his possum hair brush, Robert rose and sat on the ground again.

The sorcerer removed from its hiding place the tjurunga of Wanampi, wrapped tightly in a kangaroo hide, and bound with thongs made of tendons. He blew quickly on it, sending a puff of fine dust into the air. When he unwrapped it, he found a long wide quartz slab the size of a man's forearm, and polished until it was like a curved prism, refracting the firelight over their faces.

Beside it was a small thin roll of hide, and inside it, Walkalpa found two small red stones, each the size of the joint of a man's finger: these were the eyes of Wanampi, the left one to see physical things at a great distance, the right to see spiritual things.

Robert took the sealed bundle he had brought into the cavern, wrapped tightly in kangaroo hide and secured with kiti and tendons. He unrolled the skin in front of him. A small compressed stack of emu feathers inside it began to expand to their normal size. There were more than forty of them, each nearly eighteen inches long, from the point of the quill to the tip of the vane, opening in soft, gray, downy layers.

The men's chanting changed rhythm, to a mesmerizing drone that dulled their minds to the pain that was about to come. With quick, violent wrenches, the five of them methodically tore out hanks of their own hair, and began braiding it into lengths of fine string. Each man drew the pain in his scalp into himself, into his chanting. They twined the hair in their fingers, pausing frequently to take the ball of kiti from the grindstone, soften it over the fire, and pull the wound strands through it. When each hair string was complete, it was passed to Walkalpa. His fingers, trained on cat's cradles, and refined in ritual, flew over the braids, forming them into a small intricate net, secured with kiti. When it was made, he began a second one. The two nets were each large enough to slip over a man's foot. Both of them had a hole in the top for the ankle, and a smaller one at the tip.

As Walkalpa worked, Robert took the two hunting spears and dismantled them, unbinding the tendons holding the stone flake points to their shafts.

It took Walkalpa more than an hour to complete both nets. Finally, he looked up from his work, and nodded to Robert, who passed the feathers around the circle. Walkalpa took each one, and trimmed its quill off with the basalt blade. Using the softened kiti as a sealant, he wove the emu feathers into each net. His fingers moved deftly. When he finished, he placed on the flat grindstone in front of him a pair of emu feather slippers, oddly shaped, but perfectly matched in skill and craftsmanship. The net and sealant and tightly woven feathers made them sturdy and waterproof, save for the peculiar small hole, at the outside toe of each slipper.

Robert passed the stone points of his two hunting spears around the circle to Walkalpa. As they came to each man, he put the stone point in his mouth, then took it out and passed it on. Walkalpa began rebuilding each spear, and fitting it back into its notch at the end of the shaft. He bound them firmly with new tendons, sealing them with kiti.

He took a small leafy branch that was still damp from the tunnel and threw it on the coals of the fire. A rich smoke rose up, thick with the smell of eucalyptus. Walkalpa held the slippers and the two spears in the smoke, watching it coil over them, and out around the men, as they chanted to it, calling it to purify them.

Then the singing stopped.

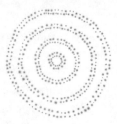

CHAPTER 20

"THE ANANGU BELIEVE a kudaitja can see his quarry over hundreds of miles," Mark Hansen said, "and cover vast distances on foot at phenomenal speed."

Agnes watched Owen. He was listening intently. She never doubted his courage, but she knew from the effect his dreams were having on him that something deeply disturbed him. She had no idea what it was, but she believed it was stalking through everything Mark described. It exasperated her, to know she may be hearing it, even seeing it as Mark spoke, but she was unable to identify it, as if it occupied a separate world in front of her, completely invisible to her. She wondered if the priest might actually be in league with the sorcerer. That she would not tolerate, and she would do anything to protect Owen.

"There was the case of an Aboriginal man named Alfred Quinn," Mark continued, "who killed his father-in-law and was followed by a kudaitja man for more than two thousand miles. The remarkable thing is that Quinn fled from Darwin to Western Australia, then to Adelaide by plane, then by car to Mount Craigie. Nevertheless, he says the kudaitja followed him within a matter of days. And Quinn's brother claims the kudaitja speared Alfred through the heart, but an autopsy found no wounds. Officially, he died of heart failure. His brother says he was told otherwise by some elders who wanted him to know tribal justice had been carried out."

"All good for headlines, Padre. You're talking to a publisher. Will any witnesses talk? Did anyone see any spears?"

"No. But in 1971, on Groote Eylandt, there were definitely spears. The mining company that runs the island has it on record. I've read the account. A man named Peel was transferred to the mainland after he found three ceremonial spears impaled in his pillow. He was white. There were claims that Peel raped an Aboriginal woman on the island. I've been told the kudaitja was the woman's uncle. He was a highly regarded spear man. He could hit a packet of cigarettes at a hundred yards."

"This Peel escaped, I take it," Agnes said.

"He committed suicide in Darwin two weeks later," Mark answered quietly.

"Hardly the kudaitja's fault." Owen's voice was harsh and Agnes appraised him, remembering the garage where she found his wife, Isabel, in the back seat of her Bentley, in a navy Dior and pearls, elegant and lifeless.

"Has anyone ever charged a kudaitja with murder?" she asked.

"There's no record of one even being caught. But ritual killing certainly isn't considered murder by tribal communities."

"It's premeditated murder!" Owen said sharply, and Agnes studied him more closely.

"They don't see it that way," Mark said. "Are you familiar with virtual reality? Yes? Telepresence? It's the next advance from virtual reality. The operator acts through the program or machine, as if he had become the device, not just a controller of it. A kudaitja acts in the same way for the avenging spirit."

"Just following orders," Owen said snidely. "Convenient."

"A kudaitja doesn't have that luxury," Mark answered. "He has no choice. But he is bound by rituals to insulate himself from the deed. He is protected from personal guilt because he is acting in proxy for the spirits who are discharging the Law. In preparation for the execution, the assassin is transformed by body paint and disfigurement, to represent his body being taken over by the avenging spirit. The word 'kudaitja' means 'the changed one.'"

"Owen's right," Agnes said. "The man's still a murderer."

"Not always a man," Mark said. "On occasion, a woman's nominated to be the assassin. She is called an illapurinya."

"So he's a lone assassin," Owen said, glancing at the camera. "Hard to stop."

"He's not alone," Mark answered. "The sorcerer travels with him."

"So there'll be two of them?" Owen asked.

"Yes. The sorcerer sees where the kudaitja cannot."

"Any more men than that?"

"Just those two."

"How do they work together?"

"It begins with the ceremony to create the kudaitja. The sorcerer makes special shoes for him and smears the kudaitja's killing spears with a secret concoction."

"Poison?"

"I can't say, Owen. But I suspect not. It's to make the spear find its mark."

Agnes closed her eyes, then looked up to the ceiling, warding off images of Owen being speared.

"Then what," Owen pressed on.

"They put the emu slippers on the assassin, then they deform his feet," Mark replied, "to profoundly change his connection to the earth. It makes his tracks impossible to follow. Then the sorcerer and the kudaitja put small stone tjurungas in their mouths to give them strength and vision. Now, the kudaitja is invisible. Until he's changed back, the only ones who can see him are his sorcerer, and his victim, at the moment of execution."

"And what is this thing," Owen kept his voice level, "that they do to his feet?"

The five men rose and walked quietly to the side of the cavern, where Wanampi's painted jaws opened as if to grip the boulder. Malu flexed his powerful shoulders and began rocking the stone until it rolled back to reveal an irregular opening, nearly three feet high, and wide enough for a man to enter. They felt the air move and saw the smoke from their fire waft toward the hole.

Walkalpa picked up the emu slippers and the two red stone tjurungas, the eyes of Wanampi, and disappeared through the hole. Robert followed him at a distance, carrying the two hunting spears. Behind him, Malu and Lungkata brought up the rear. The hole was eight feet deep, and came out into a narrow ravine, slashing up through the center of Uluru. The bottom sloped up steeply, and was strewn with scree crumbling from the sandstone walls, and dirt accumulated by centuries of wind and sandstorms. The men heard Kumanara rolling the stone back into place, sealing himself alone inside Wanampi's cave, leaving them outside, in the crevasse carved by the Rainbow Serpent.

Walkalpa began climbing toward the summit of Uluṟu, moving carefully to favor his twisted foot, and to protect the emu feather slippers for Robert's final ritual.

ⵊ

"Geez, Rooster, you look like shit," Astrid announced. "You ought to get some sleep before you go anywhere."

"No time, darlin'," Rooster replied. His enormous satisfaction at unloading the rig's three trailers into the Docker River warehouse was overborne by exhaustion. "I've gotta make a mile before the rain comes. Forecast says tomorrow morning it'll move in. I don't want to be stuck on the dirt when it gets here."

"Plenty of time, pet. Besides, it hasn't rained here in years." Astrid raised her chin toward the horizon. "It's just empty clouds. Nothin' in 'em."

"You want to look after me here in a flood?"

"Don't get your hopes up. You oughta get some shut-eye, but before you leave." She eyed him sharply. "You've been rattlin' haven't you?"

"'Course not," he lied.

"Don't come the raw prawn with me, Rooster. You look like you're bleedin' from every orifice. Get some sleep, before you hurt yourself."

He calculated his driving time back to the paved road at Kata Tjuṯa, near Uluṟu, and shrugged. Despite the drugs, he felt he could sleep twice around the clock.

"If I leave about an hour before sundown," he said, relenting, "I can be back on the bitumen by morning. Would you wake me?"

"No worries. You're being smart, pet."

Rooster turned to climb up to the sleeper box behind his driver's seat, then looked at her slyly. "Ya wouldn't like to join me?"

"Don't be a bloody mug. You couldn't handle me. I'd kill you."

"Be worse ways to go, darlin'."

"Just get in yer dog box. I'll bring you a cuppa tea when I wake you."

When she came from the house to Rooster's rig three hours later, the air had grown cool and the clouds had moved farther over the western quarter. Astrid was barefoot and she could feel the dust, as fine as talcum powder, covering the parched ground. She banged on the driver's door but there was no reply. She opened the door and looked inside, then climbed up into the cabin, smelling the foul stink of body odor and dust and diesel oil. The curtain to the dog box was drawn and she pulled it aside and heard him snoring. She shook his shoulder, and he stopped snoring, but she couldn't wake him. He smelled putrid. She shrugged and climbed back down and shut the driver's door gently. If he was this exhausted, she told herself, it was better for him to stay there. She went inside and set her alarm to give him another hour's sleep. He'd be furious, she was sure, that she'd let him sleep to sundown, but she'd make him a fresh pot of tea and send him off with some dinner. He'd still make it down the dirt road and reach the bitumen by sunup, and the sleep would do him more good than harm.

ꭗ

Walkalpa led them up the Uluṟu crevasse. The steep path was bordered with hardy rock fern, and hair-leafed nardoo, and low ruby saltbush. Overhead, through the long slit of the ravine, they could see dark clouds churning in. The sound of wind gusting over the Rock carried down to them like the irregular panting of an enormous animal at the mouth of a cave.

Body paint made them resemble four horrific spirits, rising from the bowels of Uluṟu toward the rounded skull of its summit. They crested the ravine beside the Uluṟu water hole, narrow and deep, where Waṉampi's foot indented the sandstone. Its shape made it resistant to evaporation from smiting heat and desiccating winds. The crown of the Rock was more than a mile long, curved like a bow along the northern rim, and distinguished by deep clefts and inlets on the opposite female side. At first sight, it appeared bare: an impermeable stone desert, elevated in the heart of a larger wilderness. Closer scrutiny revealed small sparse clumps of grass and occasional stunted, hardy trees that grew out of sand-filled clefts, protected by the stone and nurtured by condensation that formed at night, even in dry weather. The dried trunks and branches of small dead trees poked out of crevices, or lay bleached and cracked on the stone.

ꭗ

"So they'll come from Ayers Rock, Padre?"

"The ceremony will most likely be conducted at Uluṟu."

Owen glanced at his son. Andrew barely blinked.

241

"Very good." Owen smiled warmly at Mark. "Very enlightening. Thank you, Padre. And you've convinced me. The stone will be returned. Now, I don't want to hold you up any longer. I know you have a long trip in the morning."

Mark rose from his chair. He felt he was being dismissed, of no further use. He nodded awkwardly to Andrew and Agnes and went out the door without acknowledging Owen's parting call.

"Safe journey, Padre."

As the door closed behind Mark Hansen, Owen turned to his son.

"What do you make of it?"

"Hocus-pocus," Andrew said.

"So, you'll do it?"

"I can take the stone back. Drop it off where you say it was found, stay away from invisible men, and bug out."

"They get their stone back, no need to stay mad." Owen didn't mention the check. "Everybody's happy. I appreciate this, Andrew."

Andrew looked at his father and ran through a mental litany of all the things he should say in response. He had an image of the photograph of his mother, prim and lifeless in the back of her Bentley. Emptiness. He felt manipulated by Owen and Agnes to go on what appeared to be a selfish and petty mission, all in the name of family. And he resented his first reaction, the simplest truth of Occam's razor, anchored deep inside the vault of memories of a small boy who wanted only to please his father enough to have him around. Andrew shrugged nonchalantly.

"Piece of cake," he said.

They were more than a thousand feet above the desert and Walkalpa, Malu, Lungkata, and Robert knew they were viewing the world as Wanampi saw it when she first stood here. It was an hour before sundown, and long shadows fell across the red plains, casting the ocean swell of sand dunes into sharp waving lines. They saw the straight lines of the blacktop road threading in from the main highway beyond the horizon, and twisting west toward

Docker River. They could see the low rooflines of the Yulara resort village, tiny from their altitude, lying to their north in the heavy mat of surrounding scrubland that petered out toward the red dunes. Dark clouds lay along the western horizon, and small banks of dark cumulus scudded low overhead.

The men sat beside the water hole in a state resembling transcendence, opening their minds to the rhythms and harmonies of the Tjukurpa. The sandstone around them was red with desert sand and pocked with the scorched blast marks of lightning strikes. A burst of wind swept over the summit, tossing dust and grass stalks and a small pink bud of Sturt's desert rose, tumbling them along the red stone and onto the pool, where they floated across its rippling surface.

Willy-willies coursed over the plains below them in tall red columns of dust, careening across the ground, then spinning into empty air like marauding spirits materializing, then vanishing into space.

The men felt a powerful tingling on their skin, prickling the roots of their hair, and spreading rapidly over their bodies, then they were blinded by a blue and white flash that exploded in crackling thunder around them. They felt the ground quake, and shook their heads to stop the ringing in their ears. Slowly, their vision came back, marred by jagged vertical lines whenever they blinked, the brands made by the lightning bolt on their retinas. They smelled the sharp bite of ozone, the breath of Wanampi. They saw a small stretch of rock, charred by the blast and still smoldering where the Rainbow Serpent set foot once more onto Uluru.

Walkalpa limped over to the blast area. A jagged shank of dried wood smoked and popped, all that remained of a dead bloodwood, disintegrated by the lightning strike. Walkalpa gripped it firmly and snapped it off at the roots. He swung it in a circle at arm's length, fanning the smoldering tip until small flames licked along it. He picked up the few dead twigs strewn around it, brought them back to the water hole, and set them into a shallow slit in the rock, protected from the lifting wind. The smoke encompassed the four men in a purifying cloud.

They sat on the sandstone between the fire and the edge of Uluru water hole, with Robert between Lungkata and Malu, facing Walkalpa. The sorcerer slid the emu slippers onto Robert's feet. Each of his little toes protruded from the hole in the side of its slipper. Malu and Lungkata seized Robert around the shoulders and held him firmly by the ankles.

Walkalpa stared at him intently, then without a word, he leaned forward and took a powerful grip on the little toe of Robert's left foot. With a violent wrench, Walkalpa dislocated it sideways.

Excruciating pain erupted through Robert's bones and sinews, but he made no sound. He looked at his toe, mangled and swelling quickly to lock the slipper on to his foot. Malu and Lungkata tightened their hold on him, and Walkalpa grasped the little toe of his other foot and dislocated it. Robert felt heat sear through his toes and thighs and belly, and with it a powerful change rode through him. He felt himself shifting through a blazing membrane. On one surface, he was Robert Erhard, scientist, designer and guide of robotic creatures bound for other planets. On the other, he was Tjilkamata, of the Spiny Anteater Dreaming, keeper of all his people's primal stories and songs. He drifted like a slow-moving whirlwind, churning from core to rim, feeling himself cross the membrane from one identity to the other and back. He felt emptiness at his center, and into its space, he sensed another presence, the avenging spirit of Wanampi striving to take possession of him. He felt himself dying. To save his people, he knew he must sacrifice all of himself to the greater force of the Rainbow Serpent, but every part of his being struggled to survive, to resist the invasion. The battle between his instinct and his force of will wracked his body and spirit

Malu and Lungkata watched Robert convulse in agony on the stone. Walkalpa remained impassive, well aware that his friend's ordeal of submission and transformation into the Changed One could endure far into the night.

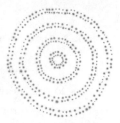

Chapter 21

OWEN PUSHED HIMSELF AWAY from his bed and walked steadily across the room toward Agnes.

"I'm amazed." She stood against the window, beaming at Owen and the physiotherapist walking beside him. Outside, the sun was beginning to settle onto the horizon.

He laughed. "Not bad for a bloke who wasn't supposed to stand again."

"That's very good, Owen," Dr. Andrews said. "But let's not push it."

"It's miraculous," Agnes said.

"All thanks to young Kennedy," Owen replied. The physiotherapist and duty nurse tried to help him back to his bed, but he shrugged them away. The fiberglass cast with its magnetic inserts was the only visible sign of his accident. "That drug he ordered up made the difference."

"Methylprednisolone," Andrews said. "You're right. You might still be on your back without it."

"It'll take more than a fucking buffalo," Owen muttered. "Or anything else."

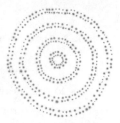

Heinrich Erhard walked painfully around the car and stretched. His back hurt and his joints ached. The Erldunda service station was ablaze with fluorescent lights. He uncapped the fuel tank on the car and inserted the nozzle. Grace was sound asleep in the passenger seat.

They'd shared the driving up from Adelaide, taking a full day and a night to reach Erldunda. After he filled the tank, Heinrich planned to book them into two motel rooms and sleep until late morning, before making the final leg out to Lake Amadeus.

But when he came back from paying for the fuel, he found Grace wide awake, walking around the car, insisting on taking over the wheel again and pushing on through the night. Heinrich wanted to argue, but she was relentless. He was beginning to feel this journey was slipping out of his control.

꙳

The whirlwind moaned through the empty tunnels of Robert's dream. He saw Heinrich and Giselle Erhard reaching for him. He saw the ridges of scars along his father's fingers and remembered the gentle strength of his hands holding him safe as a child. He remembered Giselle's perfume and cried out as she faded away with the wind. Walkalpa sat motionless on the rock at Robert's side, watching his friend's ordeal. Robert felt an immense gravity drawing him violently through empty stone passageways.

He smelled another woman, comforting, warm, safe, Maureen, singing to him inside the clattering shadows of the boxcar. He saw the Kalaya man watching from a distance, and recognized his birth father, the constant benevolent presence in his boyhood dreams. He heard the singing change in pitch, perplexing in both its familiarity and strangeness, computer code, streaming through his dream in a harmonic whine of commands and answers, directing his creations onto the plain on their bodies of circuitry and camera eyes, as he slipped inside the virtual presence of their images and sounds until he was them, extending his insect legs onto the distant ground, even as he knew it was an illusion. He groaned aloud as the tunnels through his dream buckled and tore, and he realized they were his own vessels and nerve fibers, wrenched with the force of Wanampi's relentless will to occupy him.

He felt his identity disintegrating, felt the part of him that was Robert Erhard evaporating until only his birth spirit remained, that of Tjilkamata of the Spiny Anteater Dreaming. That too was dissipating and all he could sense was movement, as if he had been reduced to a single atom, drawn into the overwhelming presence of Wanampi, a mote in the flux of a black hole at the center of the universe.

⁂

In his cave at the base of Uluru, Tjitutja of the Dingo Dreaming watched his fire burn low as he sang. He sang as the first dingo spirit sang in the Tjukurpa, conjuring life out of the void of space, filling it with the red dust around him and transmuting it with his chant into the shape and form of his dreaming. His song continued without pause as he dropped another branch into the coals and watched flames climb smokily around it, and deep inside their coiling light he saw the distant figure of Kurpan the demonic Dingo Dreaming spirit responding to his call, rising out of the darkness onto its great paws, turning three times, sniffing the night air, then heading out in a slow loping trot along his creation track from Docker River.

⁂

"Fucking useless bitch!" Rooster Wilson yelled. "I said to wake me an hour before sundown!"

"You watch your fucking mouth!" Astrid screeched back at him. "If you weren't so fucking beaned up on those fucking rattlers, you'd have fucking woken up when I fucking woke you, wouldn'tcha!"

She stalked back to the kitchen, leaving Rooster fuming inside his rig. The setting sun lit deep banks of storm clouds with red and gold fire halfway across the sky. Astrid heard the explosive sound of the diesel firing up, and the air brakes coming off. Above the roar of the truck, she could hear him still cursing loudly, all the way out of the settlement toward the Uluru turnoff.

Rooster Wilson kept the rig at fifty miles an hour, banging over the deep corrugations in the dirt road. Outside, the wind blasted dust and tumbling spinifex across his path. The sides of his three freezer vans, empty now after unloading at Docker River, were like taut sails. He could feel the buffeting of the wind through the steering wheel.

When he saw the first spatters of rain on his windshield he began cursing again. Between blasphemies, he prayed he would make it off the dirt before the storm hit. But in less than a minute, he saw his headlight beams closing in on him, as if he were driving into a translucent wall. Whatever was out in front of him seemed to be swallowing his lights, sucking them into a dark pit.

The wind hammering against his windows was changing to a sinister hiss. In his drugged state, he thought it was rain, and he turned on his windshield wipers. But it was worse than rain. Silhouetted against his waning headlights, he saw the blades sweeping across the glass in front of him, piled high on each pass with fine orange-red sand.

Rooster gave out a long demented howl of exhaustion and desolation. It was no hallucination. He slowed the rig, steered her onto the near shoulder of the road, and shut down the engine. Running the diesel in a sandstorm would clog the air filters and fill the intake valves with dirt. It was more destructive to an engine than water.

Rooster heard the cooling diesel clicking under the hood, and the hiss of sand blowing against the cabin. He banged his head on the steering wheel, swearing violently and sobbing with frustration. The noise of the wind and dust grew louder. He had seen sandstorms strip the paint off a truck in three hours. He worried the trailers were too light now to withstand the force of tons of windblown sand slamming into them. He killed the spotlights to conserve power, and watched the beams of his headlights blanketed by flying sand, plunging him into darkness.

Then through the unearthly shriek of the storm, Rooster heard a dingo.

The shapes stood at the foot of Owen's bed and stared through him. He came awake in a body as immobile as lead. He recognized the three ghostly figures closest to the bed, drawing the heat from his body so completely that he felt his veins hardening into ice, and a coldness so intense it burned through him like molten stone. He couldn't breathe to shout for help. The duty nurse was less than ten paces away, but even his eyelids were paralyzed.

He felt hysteria shaking him from the inside, but his heart kept beating steadily, nowhere near the tachycardia that would set off his monitor alarms. He groaned inwardly with the searing pain of the cold, and the terrible knowledge of what was coming.

He saw Teddy Gidgee and Russell King and Oscar Woolie raise their hands to their mouths. He was aware again of a fourth presence standing behind them in shadow, someone who filled him with even more dread than the three specters spitting their teeth into their hands, and surveying him from their dark, sightless eye sockets and hurling their blood-slicked enamel onto his bed.

All his life, Owen had resisted fear with unswerving bravery. Now he wanted to give in to it, to let the panic take him and make his heart race, to trigger the cardiac alarm. He hovered between courage and cowardice, willing himself over, but his survival instincts were too well conditioned to let him weaken.

Then the fourth figure moved out of the darkness and into clear view.

"You don't have to go through with it, Mark," Alistair Steele said.

"It'll be all right. Everyone has a right to be buried in his own ground, even a criminal."

"They're just accomplices, and we both know it." Dr. Steele pointed to the ceiling. "The real criminal's up there."

"He still thinks he's above all this."

"It'll catch up with him sooner or later."

"He would deny that. He thinks he can return the stone scot-free."

"Arrogant bastard."

"He said he was a hero. And he is right, there. We make heroes of men like him."

"You think he's in danger?" Dr. Steele asked quietly.

Mark looked through the office door into the morgue. The stainless steel autopsy tables were hosed down and spotlessly clean under the harsh fluorescent lights. In the chill darkness behind the doors in the coldroom wall, the bodies of Oscar Woolie, Teddy Gidgee, and Russell King lay on their slabs, awaiting their last journey.

"Yes he is," Mark said. He finished his rum. He hoped it would help him sleep before he returned at dawn to load the three bodies for Lake Amadeus. "And he thinks he can do something about it. He has no idea yet what he's up against."

Owen stared past the three dark shapes to the fourth, who had moved into view at the foot of his bed.

Slowly it raised its hands and spat its teeth into them, then appraised Owen with sightless eyes and flung the teeth onto the bed. They struck like bullets.

His heart lurched violently, pounding against the walls of his chest, launching the cardiograph past the danger line and triggering the alarms.

He labored for breath, unable to tear his eyes away from the fourth specter. It stood motionless beside the shades of Teddy and Russell and Oscar. The ugly mangled gash of its mouth curved slowly upward into a death's-head smile. Owen heard nurses running toward him, and the hoarse sound of his own cries. The fourth figure was himself.

Robert/Tjilkamata screamed, and Malu and Lungkata recoiled in alarm, covering their ears with their hands. Tjilkamata's back arced up from the stone in a convulsion that made his spine creak and his muscles and tendons stand out like power cables. Walkalpa sprang to his feet. Tjilkamata's body remained bowed back in its impossible curve, then they heard his vertebrae crackling.

A sheet of lightning exploded between low clouds overhead, freezing the four men in luminous blue light. The blast deafened them, drowning Tjilkamata's cry in a roll of thunder. Malu and Lungkata stared as Tjilkamata writhed smoothly out of his contorted arc, and slithered upright, rearing from the ground and swaying hypnotically between them. He swept his eyes over them, and Malu and Lungkata saw him begin to fade, drift back into focus, then disappear completely from their view. Only Walkalpa could still see him.

Tjilkamata swung his head around, and the sorcerer looked directly into his face, but instead of seeing the calm gaze of his boyhood friend, Walkalpa found himself peering into the thin lethal eye slits of the Rainbow Serpent.

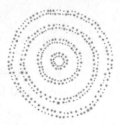

CHAPTER 22

ROOSTER WILSON HEARD THE DINGO above the roar of the sandstorm. He had ventured out of the cabin with a flashlight, on the leeward side, to relieve himself, and even with the truck blocking the wind, the fine stinging sand flayed his skin. He saw he was still passing blood, but all thought of that danger vanished when he heard the animal in the storm. He scrambled back into the cabin.

A giant dingo stared at him from the engine hood. Its enormous head was lowered, and its bloodshot eyes pierced the windshield. Its great jaws lolled open, exposing yellow fangs as sharp as knives. Its golden fur stood upright along its hackles, its eyes burned with a demonic light, and it panted steadily as it watched Rooster, the appearance of a smile curling along its gaping jaws.

The dingo raised its head high into the wind and howled, vibrating the truck. Rooster clapped his hands over his ears and clamped his eyes shut but the baying reverberated inside his skull. He pulled the chain for the air horns, but no sound came out; they were clogged with sand. The dingo leered through the windshield and Rooster feared it could shatter the glass with a casual swipe of its massive paws.

He hit the starter, and heard compressed air turning the big diesel over. Nothing. The dingo watched him silently. Rooster hit the starter again and sobbed aloud with relief as the engine roared.

"Fuck orf!" he yelled. The dingo didn't respond, but Rooster was relieved to have found his voice again. "Fuck orf, yer mongrel bastard!"

The storm beat wildly around him, reducing visibility to a few feet in front

of the rig. Rooster turned on the spotlights and slipped the gearshift into first
and eased forward, alert for any warning sounds or vibrations in the trailers.
The dingo didn't waver. The rig creaked and whined as the wind battered the
empty freezer vans but Rooster kept her moving forward, straining to see the
road, alert for drifts of sand. He didn't want to lose sight of the track and stray
into the desert. The dingo kept its footing on the hood.

"Piss orf! Get orf me fuckin' truck!"

The great paws remained firmly planted.

The rig pulled onto the middle of the road and gathered pace, driving the
speedometer needle steadily around the dial. The dingo braced itself, reared
its head back, and howled into the storm. Rooster jammed the accelerator
down and answered back with a wailing litany of blasphemies that barely
sounded human.

"Go with God," Dr. Alistair Steele murmured, and raised his hand in
farewell.

Inside the Land Rover Mark Hansen recalled ancient exiles to a mytho-
logical necropolis, doomed to wander the halls of the dead for all time. He
was familiar with the abundant legends of the eternal ferrymen and escorts of
the dead, from the deserts of Egypt to the stone cities of the Andes, and from
the dawn of the Tjukurpa, who accompany newly departed souls to the after-
world, for a fee ranging from a single coin to coitus with his spirit passenger.

In the back of the vehicle the three coffins were roped firmly to the
mounting rings in the floor. Mark had the air conditioner running cold. With
luck, he would be at Lake Amadeus by late morning. Weather forecasters
were predicting that the coming storm was the long-prayed-for drought
breaker, and Mark planned to reach the mission well before it. He had roused
Dr. Steele two hours before dawn to be sure he beat the rain home.

He waved back, watching the doctor mouth the blessing, then eased the
Land Rover up the ramp from the morgue and into the last of the night.

On the summit of Uluru, Walkalpa and his companions looked west
across the darkened plain far below them to the distant bank of cloud that

rose twenty thousand feet into the fading shroud of night. There was a pale orange cast to the wall of cloud rolling slowly toward them, a towering tidal wave of churning dust driven over the desert ahead of the rainstorm. Sheet lightning glimmered through its massive cliffs of sand and cloud, and tall willy-willies of red dust separated from the front and wound over the desert like pillars of fire.

In an instant, the rim of the rising sun rose above the edge of the world.

The dawn light flashed across the continent and into the eleven-hundred-foot-high rock, creating a mind-bending effect over the western desert. While the sun remained below the crown of Uluru, its shadow spanned the plains between its base and the rapidly advancing sandstorm. On each flank of Uluru's shadow, north and south, the dawn light grew brighter, defining its outline as the serpentine tail of Wanampi. The men watched the interminable shadow intently for what they knew was about to happen.

As the sun came level with the top of the monolith, the shadow appeared to flicker, then rays of light shot over the dome, flashing across the water hole and out to the horizon. For each fraction of a degree the sun rose past the dome, the shadow of Uluru shortened, withdrew from the storm and raced in over the ground at spectacular speed, twenty miles in an instant, ten in the next, then five miles, then a thousand yards, one hundred yards, then ten, until it slowed and stopped four miles out from the monolith. A mathematician could have explained the phenomenon with the trigonometry of light and the tangent of the angle of incidence. The watching elders knew better. They knew it was Wanampi slithering in from the storm base, through her cave beneath Uluru, up the crevasse to her water hole on the summit, and into the one whose body and spirit she had fought through the night to possess.

"Minga!" The pilot pointed to the mass of Uluru turning slowly like a red planet beneath the circling Gulfstream. Tiny black dots moved unevenly down from one end of the monolith. "Aboriginal word for ants."

Andrew Bird leaned forward between the two pilots to see. The scale of the moving dots below disoriented him. They resembled tiny black insects scaling down a steep narrow path of slopes and steps for a thousand feet from the summit to the ground.

"They're tourists," the co-pilot said. "The rangers are getting them off the Rock before the storm moves in."

Andrew sensed something just outside his vision. He scanned the summit that stretched for more than a mile from the patrolled area where tourists climbed, to the farthest end, off limits to visitors, where a small water hole reflected the gathering clouds.

"Go around again," he said.

The captain nodded and the jet continued its slow orbit at fifteen hundred feet, and Andrew focused on the summit water hole, where his instincts told him to search. But every time he scanned the rock around the edges of the pool, the light seemed to shift, making dark shapes look like bodies that changed to shadows whenever he looked directly at them. On the third orbit, he shook his head, still troubled, and told the pilot to land at Yulara's Connellan Airport.

Andrew returned to one of the big leather armchairs that lined the passenger cabin and tightened his seat belt. Agnes had booked a Range Rover rental to be waiting for him at Connellan. He could drive the tjurunga out to the drop-off, and be back on the jet within three hours. He eyed the heavy package, flown in overnight from Owen's private gallery in Sydney, secured now in bubble wrap inside a tennis bag, and strapped to a seat across the narrow aisle.

Rooster Wilson was doing eighty miles an hour when he outran the sandstorm. The Mack burst out of the soaring maelstrom of dust and flying vegetation, and thundered over the corrugations into daylight. He was still on the dirt road, but far ahead he could see the low rock domes of Kata Tjuṯa, and beyond them, Uluṟu. He was hoarse from shouting, and barely able to keep his eyes open. He peered out at the hood of the truck. The monstrous dingo had disappeared. He whimpered with relief, and eased back on the pedal, but as soon as the truck slowed, the beast materialized on the passenger seat, its jaws bared in a low snarl, swamping Rooster with its foul breath.

He rammed his foot down on the accelerator, sobbing, and the road train charged forward again. The dingo fixed its terrible eyes on him, then slowly turned its head to watch the road racing beneath them. In the drug-hazed shadows of his exhausted brain, he knew the creature was still in control of his rig, and was steadily taking over his mind. Rooster didn't realize he was screaming again.

Andrew signed for the Range Rover and thanked the girl, who handed him the keys and map. She was so excited she could barely speak clearly, and that made her embarrassed and stumble over her words even more. He resented the deferred fame of his family name, but she bumbled on until he couldn't help laughing, assuring her everything was fine, and autographing her business card. When he checked in the rearview mirror, he could see her still standing on the tarmac, clutching the card and staring wide-eyed from the BIRD colors on the Gulfstream tailplane to the Range Rover rolling out through the gate and onto the narrow Lasseter Highway running south past Yulara and Uluṟu to the junction that ran west to the dropoff point and on out to Docker River.

On the summit of Uluṟu, the painted elders watched fork lightning march across the desert. The jagged electric arcs resembled the twisted legs of a supernatural creature stepping onto the earth. They felt the temperature dropping and heard the wind howling from the heart of the storm.

"Kurpan," Walkalpa said. The others nodded solemnly. Tjiṯutja of the Dingo Dreaming had done well, calling up the avenging spirit from Docker River. "Kurpan is coming."

Rooster Wilson wailed incoherently above the roar of the diesel, racing the storm that reared far into the sky behind him. The rig's high beams and halogens blazed like infernal eyes erupting from the dust and lightning. The speeding road train was nearly two miles away and closing on Andrew Bird when he saw it and glanced at his speedometer. He was driving the Range Rover at a little over sixty miles an hour. He slowed to fifty-five, easing farther left of the broken white line that divided the road into two narrow lanes. The rig appeared to be weaving over the center line. Andrew heard the feral wail of its air horns growing louder.

"Stupid bastard," he breathed.

The road shoulders were graded dirt with a deep culvert on each side. Andrew lowered his speed to fifty, and relaxed a little when he saw the rig move back to its left-hand lane. It was half a mile away now and approaching with a combined speed of more than one hundred and thirty miles an hour. He kept the Range Rover far onto his left side of the lane, and began speeding up, now the rig was no longer hogging the road. It was less than three hundred yards away when he saw it veer onto the center line again.

Andrew took his foot off the pedal and touched the brakes lightly, ready to pull onto the shoulder. The road train swerved over the line toward him.

Two hundred yards; three seconds.

One hundred; two seconds.

Andrew could see the high steel bull bar aimed straight at him. Above it, in the cabin of the rig, the driver seemed to be screaming hysterically. Fifty yards. There was no room for the Range Rover to pass on the left shoulder. Andrew jerked the wheel hard to the right, across the path of the rig, toward the open shoulder. The gap narrowed and was gone.

The Mack's bull bar slammed the rear of the Range Rover with an explosion of metal and glass, and spun it completely around to face the way it had come. The seat belt and airbag saved Andrew from crashing into the windshield, but it couldn't stop the force of the spin that smashed his head on the roof pylon. His hands were hurled from the steering wheel, and the vehicle flipped over with a bang, blowing out the windshield, rolling twice, crushing its roof as it tumbled down the shoulder of packed dirt, and came to rest on its driver's side, creaking and hissing in the bottom of the gully.

The rig roared on down the highway at more than eighty miles an hour. Rooster Wilson was oblivious of the crash. All he wanted was to escape the creature occupying his cabin. Outside, the fiberglass front left fender of the rig banged along the road, torn away by its impact with the Range Rover. The automatic tape deck cued Midnight Oil, and "Beds Are Burning" thundered from the speakers. Rooster was deaf to it.

He raced on down the highway toward Uluru, accelerating again where the road veered sharply left to Yulara. But the Mack barreled straight ahead, aimed at the looming monolith. The entire road train became airborne, plowing off the highway and over the rim of the gravel embankment. Its drive axles screamed as they left the road. The rig dropped four feet through the air and hit the dirt in a cloud of red dust, lurching forward as the drive wheels bit again. It tore through a clump of mulga and straight into a low sandhill, decelerating from more than seventy miles at an hour to zero in two yards.

Because of the deteriorating weather, rangers had closed the park sites to visitors at Uluṟu and Kata Tjuṯa since early morning. Nearly half an hour passed before a ranger drove by and saw the rig. She radioed a sighting report, and parked near the deep gouges in the shoulder where the road train left the highway. There was a path of debris to the wreck: a spare wheel torn from its mounting, scattered fiberglass body panels, an unraveled length of yellow nylon cargo rope, and the entire side panel of the rear trailer, cleaved away when it turned over and plowed across the ground.

When she reached the wreck, the ranger found the cabin demolished, but no sign of the driver. Midnight Oil blared from one speaker. Bedding and clothing from the dog box had been blasted through the curtain into the cabin, strewn across the seats and dashboard. The windshield was completely blown out. She checked inside the dog box but found no sign of life. She hit the eject button on the tape deck. Silence descended save for the clicking of metal from the diesel engine, embedded in the side of the sandhill. Her eyes tracked over the floor beneath the driver's seat, covered by white pills scattered from a shattered bottle, then she heard groaning. She searched the cabin again, but found no one. The noise sounded hoarse, barely human. She stepped out of the cabin and looked up the face of the sand hill in astonishment.

Rooster Wilson dragged himself into view on top of the dune and stared down at the trail of devastation that had been his rig. He was covered in bleeding lacerations from the top of his head, down his chest and belly to the tops of his feet, from being ejected through the windshield like a spear from a miru, on a clean trajectory that grazed over the crest of the dune and down the gentle slope on the other side. Through a haze of rattlers and shock, Rooster hauled himself onto his elbows and tried to focus on the ranger, staring back at him in disbelief.

Rooster shook his head slowly, and groaned with pain. But when he looked furtively around him he realized he could no longer see nor hear the terrifying beast that had driven him to destruction.

The ranger's eyes widened as she watched the ghastly, blood-covered face of the driver split in a hideous grin. And the smile never wavered when she drew herself up and announced in a stern voice, "You are one lucky fool. And you are under arrest."

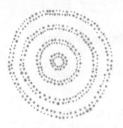

CHAPTER 23

MALU AND LUNGKATA SAT IMMOBILE on the summit of Uluru, listening to the spirits prowl across the desert on bolts of lightning and micro-tornadoes. Further out, the sandstorm rose like a moving range of cliffs, their peaks impaling the storm clouds, their foothills obscured by a churning mist of red dust. The elders heard the rolling thunder of rain clouds moving in behind the sandstorm. The desert was cast in pale gray-green light, and beneath the sporadic sorties of lightning and willy-willies, all natural life seemed to have become still, waiting.

Far down on the highway, the elders watched the flashing red and blue lights of an emergency vehicle racing from Yulara toward the strewn wreckage of Rooster Wilson's rig. Farther out, in the low, brush-hugging skyline of the resort village, a fire truck rolled out of its street, switched on its lights and siren, and picked up speed toward Uluru. The elders looked west of the mangled rig, at the small shape of the Range Rover, lying below the road in a gully. There was no sign of movement.

A pair of willy-willies funneled down from low cloud near Yulara, broke away and wound across the plain toward the airport. To the elders watching from the top of Uluru, they were like the legs of a giant whose body was hidden by thunderheads, striding down the main runway and casually kicking over aircraft, lifting them off the tarmac in bursts of turbulence, and hurling them back down to skid into each other, and career into the terminal building in a peal of shattered glass and screaming tourists. The elders watched more flashing lights swarming toward the chaos, weaving to avoid bodies and fleeing survivors who dotted the area like ants.

They saw other movement farther west, ahead of the advancing sand-storm, of animals fleeing, not the high winds and lightning, but something more dangerous that was spreading rapidly along the flat plain. The spirits were taking up their positions across the desert. The sirens of fire trucks and ambulances wailed over the plains and up to the watching elders on the monolith, a counternote to the deep baying of a dingo, rising and falling in the buffeting wind and the boom of thunder.

In his cave at the base of Uluṟu, Tjiṯutja of the Dingo Dreaming drifted in the void, his eyes closed, listening to Kurpan howl above the debris of the road train. Tjiṯutja heard the sound change as the Dingo Dreaming spirit turned for home, racing west in its great loping gait past the overturned Range Rover, and disappearing back into the storm, its mission complete.

Grace Morgan was already south of the Yulara turnoff when she heard the sirens, and saw in her rearview mirror a small procession of fire trucks and ambulances race out of the resort village and turn north, away from her.

"We must have just missed something big," she said.

Heinrich looked over his shoulder at the receding vehicles. "The airport's back there."

"Plane crash?"

"I don't see any smoke. This storm's moving in fast though."

"How much farther to the mission?"

"About forty miles. We'll make it before it hits."

"Oh my, look at that," Grace pointed toward the trail of wreckage of Rooster Wilson's rig, and the flashing lights of the fire truck and ambulance. "All hell's breaking loose out here."

They both stared as they passed, the frozen images of the fire truck spray-ing foam on the truck's diesel tanks, a park ranger and an ambulance crewman examining a man covered in blood who sat at the base of the low sand dune that seemed to have devoured the front of the rig, a fireman run-ning from his truck, waving both his own crew and the medics back to their vehicles for another emergency. The scenes slipped past the car as Grace fol-lowed the highway through its sharp right-handed curve and straightened out due west, toward the turnoff to Lake Amadeus Mission, and beyond that the domes of Kata Tjuṯa, pointing toward Docker River buried behind a towering wall of churning sand that rolled in from the horizon.

"Sandstorm," Heinrich said. "They can last for days."

But Grace wasn't listening. She was straining to see past a trail of torn fiberglass strewn along the road ahead, toward four deep gouges in the dirt shoulder that ran off the side into a gully, where she could just make out the outline of a wheel, spinning slowly in the rising wind.

The Range Rover lay on its driver's side in the bottom of the gully. The roof had caved in, between the pylons that held the rear door hinges. Grace scrambled down the steep embankment toward it. She could see someone crammed tightly behind the steering wheel. The windows were blown out and a trail of shattered glass glittered from the embankment to the wrecked vehicle.

"Are you all right?" Grace called. She crouched in the bed of the gully, and peered in through the jagged gap where the windshield had been. "Hi. Can you move?"

"G'day." Andy saw her sneakers and the legs of her jeans first, crossing the sand near his head. He tried to smile when he saw her face come into view, but pain stabbed through his skull. Fork lightning crackled a mile away, then slammed into the ground like an artillery shell. Grace cringed, aware at once of the mass of metal so close to her. A cool gust of wind blew down the gully, lifting dust around them. "Not enough to get out. I'm stuck in here."

Grace could see he was pinned between the steering wheel and the back of the driver's seat, and jammed in from above by the collapsed roof. The pylon between the two side doors had saved his head from being crushed. His shoulder rested on the sand in the shattered driver's side window.

"Do you think you have any injuries?" she asked.

"Got a whack on the head. I don't think I've broken anything. I'm just stuck, that's all. Door won't open. Trapped."

A kangaroo came bounding down the gully. It was a big red, more than five feet high. It swerved past them, bounding eastward, pounding the sand with its great narrow feet. Grace watched its huge tail dipping behind it like a pendulum, never touching the ground. Heinrich reached the bottom of the gully, and watched the fleeing animal thoughtfully, his face impassive.

"Do you think you can squeeze out of there?" Heinrich said.

"I'd have done it by now if I could."

Heinrich ignored the reproach. "Maybe we can help you."

"I can't move my head. And I can't get my legs out from under the steering wheel. I can feel my feet, but I can't shift them. The roof's got me stuck."

A long sheet of lightning arced above them. They saw low, heavy clouds scudding in from the west. There was a clean smell of rain on the wind, cool and fat and dangerous. They heard a scuffle in the scrub above the gully, and saw two yellow goannas, each more than four feet long, burst out of a hole and dart away running high on their thin legs, chins up, tails weaving. Grace shuddered at the sight of them. They disappeared in the same direction as the kangaroo.

"I think we're going to need help," Heinrich said. "There's a fire truck back up the road. I won't be gone long."

"We're not going anywhere," she answered, and smiled at Andrew. "I'm Grace Morgan."

"Andrew Bird. Nice to meet you. Thanks for stopping."

They heard the car starting up and turning around, then driving off. Grace suddenly felt extremely isolated. A few moments ago she felt safe, traveling with someone who felt like family. Now she was alone, twelve thousand miles from home, in the middle of a desert with a total stranger trapped inside what could only be described as a huge lightning conductor, and a storm coming in. Thunder crashed overhead.

A gray wallaby bounded down the gully, racing toward Uluru.

"Something's got them going," Andrew said.

"Lightning?"

"Maybe. Do you remember how far back the fire truck was?"

"Only a few miles." She heard him trying to free his legs, but he was completely trapped.

"Could you look in the back for a tire lever or something to pry open the door?"

"Sure." Grace went to the back of the vehicle, feeling foolish for not thinking of it herself.

Andrew heard her scream, once, twice.

"What's the matter?"

"Snakes!"

Grace recoiled up the side of the gully as two long black snakes slithered toward them.

"Where are they?" Andrew kept his voice level, twisting his head painfully to see.

"Gone," he heard her call behind him, as she peered through the shattered rear window.

"See anything?"

"No." She crawled inside the back, picking through broken glass.

"There's a tool compartment back there."

"I think I see it. But everything's pretty beat up. The lid's jammed tight."

"Shit!"

"What?" Grace looked up and felt a cold tendril of nausea clutch her stomach. She could see through the upturned vehicle, past Andrew, to the sandy bed of the gully outside, where reaching toward them, no more than six inches wide, was a long flat finger of brown water, swirling and foaming at the edges and moving fast.

Andrew recognized the deceptively subtle vanguard of a flash flood, and fought to control himself. Was this how he was going to die? Aware all the way? Options! Control. What were the options?

"Any sign of your friend?" he called.

Grace was amazed he was so calm.

"I'll go look."

She scrambled up the side of the gully, and surveyed the empty highway. Wind lifted blasts of sand against her skin. She smelled rain. No sign of any vehicles. Perhaps the fire truck had left. Perhaps Heinrich was driving back to town for help.

"See him?" Andrew's voice came faintly up through the gusts of wind. Grace looked over the edge. The water had reached the Range Rover and was spreading past it down the gully. A scrap of conversation came back to her, about how the doomed astronauts on the *Challenger* had been running through their SOPs, standard operating procedures, during the entire time it took them to plummet into the ocean after the explosion. Never give up. Never, never, never give up. What are my priorities? Grace made herself stop and list them. Tools. Something to roll the vehicle upright? Impossible. Something to pry the driver's door open? Tools again. Something to pry the tool compartment open. She scanned the road for a branch, a piece of metal, anything.

"Hang on!" she called and sprinted back up the road to the debris torn off in the collision.

Torn sheets of fiberglass skidded and spun in the wind. Her eyes fell on a twisted length of bumper bar, too slim to have come off the rig, perhaps wrenched off the Range Rover. She ran to it, and heaved one end off the ground. It felt remarkably light. She hauled it up the road, and scrambled down the embankment with it, and splashed into water that swept around her sneakers.

"I've got something!" she called to Andrew.

"Whatever it is, move it!" The water was running around the crown of his head and covering the top of his shoulder. Grace crouched beside the driver's window and looked for a leverage point.

"If I can lever your seat back, maybe you can slide out through there."

"Just do it!"

She tried to ignore the water swirling over her feet and slid the end of the fender between the driver's seat and the roof pylon, using the column as a fulcrum. With a mighty heave, she leaned on the fender, and fell full length into the water as it doubled over.

Andrew strained to see her, dragging herself out of the shallow current.

"What happened?"

"I'm sorry, I'm sorry," she called. "It was plastic. I thought it was metal. That's why it was so light."

"Stay cool," he said, feeling the water rising around his forehead. He wanted to scream, to tear at the metal, the way sailors trapped in holds tore at steel bulkheads until their nails ripped away and bone showed through their fingertips. "You hear me?"

There was no answer, then she was kneeling beside him.

"Heinrich's back!"

Andrew felt relief flood through him, but it was fleeting. A small branch floated in through the windshield frame and grazed his face.

"Get him down here now!"

She disappeared and Andrew heard her calling out and imagined this was how people thought when they were taken to mass graves, knowing what was coming, aware they were going to have time to think about dying violently before it happened. Is this how he was going to go, before he was finished? A man appeared beside him, holding a tire lever.

"There's someone else coming," Heinrich said. "Grace is going to try and stop them. Let's get you out now."

Andrew strained to keep his nose and mouth clear of the water. He heard metal scraping as Heinrich tried to wedge the tire lever into the door. He tried to fan hope, to hold on to his self-control, but the water was rising perceptibly faster now, with more debris spinning on its surface. He heard the tire lever skid over the door panel with a dull squeal of metal. He stared up at the noise and thought he was already losing his mind, that his would-be rescuer was already scrabbling at the metal until he mutilated himself. The hands that gripped the tire lever and tried to wedge it again into the door jamb had no fingernails.

He heard Grace calling again, but the water was almost over his ears now and he could only hear the sound of the flood climbing around his head.

"He's stopping!"

Heinrich didn't dare look up from his task. The Range Rover's doors fitted so snugly and securely he couldn't budge the door. The water rippled against his ankles.

Andrew felt himself losing control. His lungs hovered on the verge of spasm and his muscles felt ready to convulse in terror or go weak with fear. Never, never, never give up. He thought it was the sound of his own thoughts, but he realized it was the girl again, leaning in through the windshield

"He has a four-wheel-drive. Don't give up now. Never, never, never give up."

But her voice disappeared behind the rumble of the water covering his ears and splashing over his nose and mouth. Andrew reached around with his free hand and pinched his nostrils tight. He knew if he started coughing, he would drown like a diver. Never, never, never give up. He tried to twist his head up just once more, to take one final lungful of air before he went under for the last time. So this was how it was going to be, he heard the detached observer inside his mind, the one that calmly watched all he did. This was the way he was going to die, aware of it, and aware of being aware of it, not like the targets he slipped up on in the darkness with Bliss, shadowing in so close he breathed in rhythm with them, moving the wire onto them so smoothly that they were already dying as he lowered their bodies to the ground. This would not be so easy, this was going to be very nasty down to the last. He twisted his back and neck upward, breaking free of the water for one agonizing contortion, gasping in as much air as he could inhale, then felt his fatigued muscles fail as his head went below the surface again, and his ears roared now with the water, and the pounding of his heart. He felt his lungs begin to burn as he used up all his oxygen. He felt streams of air escaping his lips as he tried to hold it in to the end.

He felt something pressing against his mouth, and wondered if this was the start of the delirium of drowning. It felt like a kiss! He felt a hand slide behind his head to hold the kiss firm. He felt a tongue try to pry his lips apart and he recoiled. It must be delirium. He opened his eyes, and through the muddy water, he saw her face pressed to his, her eyes open, trying to open his mouth. She was trying to breathe for him! He would have to exhale first! He would have to make himself completely vulnerable to drowning before he could inhale her breath. And what if she disappeared just as he did that? He turned his head away from her, and she saw a long stream of bubbles erupt from his mouth. Then he turned back, pinching his nose, and she pressed her mouth over his and he sucked in warm air, keeping their lips sealed against each other. He closed his mouth and nodded and she was gone, and he was alone again, as alone as Isabel in the back of her Bentley, all air gone. Then she was back, her hand behind his head again, waiting for him to release his used air, and breathe in hers.

Andrew's life shrank from an epoch running from birth to death, down to a single breath, then the next, and the next, each an act of faith. Through the roaring of the flood, he heard metallic sounds, rattling underwater, the running sound of cable tightening around a door pylon. He waited for his next breath, and this time, after she filled his lungs again, she held her hand over her mouth, signaling him to do the same. Then she was gone again, and he was alone, clamping his hand over his mouth and nose, waiting for . . . he had no idea.

He was completely unprepared.

His world shuddered, rocked, then wrenched violently, rotating through ninety degrees. He felt water surging around him, so strong it threatened to tear his hand away from his mouth. His lungs burned and he fought to keep his head from ramming against the pylon and roof. There was a massive crash in his ears, and the Range Rover slammed onto its wheels, punching the air out of his lungs, but holding firm, pulled upright by a steel winch cable that snaked from its anchor point on the passenger side pylon, and up the embankment to the electric winch bolted to the front of Mark Hansen's Land Rover.

Andrew vomited floodwater. He smelled it in his nose and lungs as he
coughed violently and gasped for air. When he looked up again, he was staring at the dark churning sky, his ears filled now with the sound of Grace Morgan shouting in triumph, and Heinrich and Mark calling to each other as
water poured out of the cabin. He heard himself laughing now, and went into
a spasm of coughing, as water splashed into his lungs, laughing as he gasped
for more air, feeling her leaning in through the window and hugging him
wildly. Then Heinrich Erhard was craning in over the hood to talk to him
through the empty windshield gap.

"We're going to reattach the cable and tow you out. When Mark signals,
put the gear stick in neutral."

"Got it," Andrew said. His throat ached, and he went into a coughing
spate again. "Thank you," he called, between spasms. "Thank you, thank
you."

He glanced up the embankment and in the cramped space of his trap, he
waved to Mark Hansen, behind the wheel of the Land Rover, controlling the
winch. He watched Heinrich unhook the cable from the window pylon. The
water was up to their thighs now, and Grace and Heinrich gripped handholds
along the side of the Range Rover, fighting against the current.

"Get up the bank," Andrew called to her over the sound of the water. "I'm
fine now."

Grace nodded, and inched her way around the Range Rover, holding the
cable firmly as she waded out of the current and up the embankment. She
turned and smiled at Andrew. She could see the water rising rapidly now.
Floating branches and clumps of scrub clunked along the Range Rover as
they were swept past.

Heinrich manhandled the cable through the flood around to the rear of
the vehicle. He took a deep breath and went under, feeling in the current for
the rear axle. The flow dragged at him, and he had to hang tight to the fender
with his free hand while he tried to secure the cable to the axle.

The rear right side was bent and holed from the collision with the rig.
Jagged metal yawned where the Mack's bull bar slammed through it, and the
right rear wheel housing was compressed hard onto the tire. Heinrich felt the
oxygen drain out of his lungs, and struggled to the surface, releasing his hand-
hold. The surge of the flood hurled him out from under the car.

Grace screamed as she saw him being washed away. Andrew felt the
Range Rover shudder in the torrent. If it rose enough on the water he knew it

would float and tip in the current, beyond help this time, and after escaping a grisly death once, he would certainly drown this time.

The cable went taut, and Heinrich pulled himself to his feet, grasping the hook firmly with both hands, bracing himself against the torrent, and pulled himself back to the Range Rover. Again, he reached down to hold the bent rear fender, took a deep breath and hauled himself back underwater. He felt for the rear axle again. He passed the hook around the axle and snapped it back onto the cable. As soon as it was fast, he gripped the fender and cable, and let the current carry him back out. He staggered, trying to find a footing. The water raged up to his waist and he clung grimly to the cable, fighting his way ashore.

Andrew felt the Range Rover shudder once more as the flood began to lift it. The images of overturning, and being trapped beneath the water swept back again. He forced them away. He saw Mark Hansen signal him to put the gearshift in neutral. Andrew moved the stick and felt the vehicle roll along the bottom and buck on the current. The cable came taut around the rear axle and Andrew saw the world spin as the Range Rover was buoyed up and swept out to the end of the line. Water poured in through the smashed rear window, and over the seats, surging around his chest and out through the windshield. He heard the loud twang of the cable straining against the weight of the water, and heard the roar through its steel filaments rise as it began hauling him in. If the cable snapped now that the crash-damaged vehicle had logged so much water it would be impossible to stay upright.

The groan of the straining winch vibrated down the cable, and changed pitch. At the Land Rover, Mark Hansen heard the warning sounds of the electric motor overheating. He knew he should stop the winch and use the engine in four-wheel-drive to haul Andrew out of the flood. But if he stopped it now, the overweighted Range Rover could take on more water and snap the cable or pull his own vehicle off the road shoulder. He revved the engine to keep generating power for the electric motor, and let the winch continue.

The two vehicles shook with each vibration along the taut cable. Mark saw smoke rising from the electric motor as the Range Rover inched toward the edge of the gully, and hit the embankment with a shudder. The winch motor screeched, but the Range Rover was coming up out of the current, and onto the muddy slope as the vibrations became more violent.

Mark felt his Land Rover jolt forward and checked that the hand brake was locked on. The Land Rover lurched again. Grace leaped up the slope away from the shuddering cable. The roadway was breaking up under them! The movement changed the tension in the cable, and the Range Rover, overflowing with water, slewed on the gully slope. Andrew was watching the flood move farther below the nose of his vehicle when it swung sickeningly and he instinctively jammed the brake pedal to the floor. Only one wheel locked, and the straining cable spun the Range Rover and sent it tumbling onto its side with its hood resting on the foaming waterline. Andrew groaned in pain. The twisted steel pillars and roof that imprisoned him battered him as he rolled. The last sound Andrew heard before he lapsed into unconsciousness was the whine of the winch cable vibrating like a piano string.

Mark was thrown across the passenger seat as the edge of the roadway collapsed beneath him. With Andrew's vehicle on its side, anchoring the cable, the winch pulled Mark's Land Rover to one side. He tried to reach the winch kill switch on the instrument panel, but his pitching vehicle slung him onto the floor, stunning him. The winch wound on, stripping paint and metal from the side of its cable drum and lifting the Land Rover onto two wheels above the side of the gully. Mark saw a flash of lightning through the windshield above him as he was thrown under the dashboard, then he was falling into the roof as the vehicle rolled down the gully, turning completely twice before it crashed into the underside of the Range Rover.

Grace heard metal tearing and glass shattering as the Land Rover tumbled, then she watched in horror as she heard another sound more organic, of wood splintering as three coffins shot from the back of the Land Rover onto the muddy wall of the gully, blasting off the lids, and exposing the bodies inside.

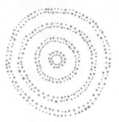

CHAPTER 24

WALKALPA STOPPED and raised his head. He and Tjilkamata were midway down the side of Uluru, taking a route well away from the carved steps and chain handholds of the Tourist's Climb. Far above them, on the summit of the monolith, Malu and Lungkata kept vigil beside the water hole. Somewhere below, Tjitutja was hunched over his fire, watching Kurpan's journey home. Walkalpa listened for some time, staring into the distance toward the area of the collision between the rig and the Range Rover, then resumed his descent, treading carefully over the steep scree and sand. The sorcerer felt the small red tjurunga, the left, spiritual eye of Wanampi, cold and hard beneath his tongue. The right, physical eye, he had placed in Tjilkamata's mouth.

When they reached the base, Walkalpa and Tjilkamata turned west, moving swiftly across the sand, smelling the change in the air that buffeted them. Walkalpa moved tactically, letting the ground and scrub protect him from view, extending his senses beyond himself, allowing the power of Wanampi to guide them. They kept a brisk pace, falling comfortably into a rhythm they had kept for hours at a time when they hunted together over the desert as boys.

They moved in silence across the plain. On the sand behind them was a line of clear imprints of Walkalpa's left foot and the small dragging line of his right. But there was no track of anyone else traveling with him.

Owen Bird walked back across the ward.

He lowered himself into his armchair, beaming at Agnes and his physiotherapist.

"We'll be out of here," he announced, "and home tomorrow."

"I don't know if Dr. Andrews will agree to that," the physiotherapist said.

"We'll see," Owen said quietly. "I feel even better than I did before all this."

A telephone rang, and Agnes answered it.

"It's Dr. Kennedy," she said.

"Tim!" Owen grabbed the phone and laughed. "Perfect timing, son. I've been up and around all morning. Thanks to you, young fellow. What can I do for you?"

Tim Kennedy heard the exhilaration in Owen's voice and hesitated before answering.

"I'm in the radio room, Mr. Bird. All hell's breaking loose down at Yulara."

"What's happened?"

"There's a major storm moving in there. It's blown over a couple of planes at the airport. Your jet's been totaled."

"Crew all right?"

"I don't know. They're still treating casualties. Four people are dead. I thought you'd want to know."

"Of course. Thanks, Tim. I want to know about the crew."

"I'm afraid there's more, Mr. Bird."

"Go on."

"Your friend Reverend Hansen's radioed in from a car accident."

"Is he hurt?"

"He wasn't in it. But they've got real problems there. There aren't enough rescue vehicles to get to them, and there's more trouble on the way."

"Tell me?"

Agnes recognized the expression that swept the exuberance from Owen's face as he listened to the answer.

"All right, Tim," he said. "I'll take care of it from here. Thanks for telling me."

He hung up.

"I have to go. Drive me out to the airport will you?"

"What's wrong?" Agnes said.

"Mr. Bird," the physiotherapist pleaded, "I can't let you leave without doctor's permission."

Owen ignored her.

"Andrew's rolled his vehicle. Mark Hansen rescued him apparently, but they're trapped outside Yulara by flash floods. There's been a hell of a storm down there. The Gulfstream's totaled. No news on the crew. The airport there's shut down."

"Then send the police out to get them." Agnes's voice was urgent. She knew what Owen was thinking.

"They're tied up. I have to go."

"You have to stay here, Owen. Let our people take care of it."

"We can't contact our people down there."

"Owen, please don't."

"Mr. Bird, you can't leave until Dr. Andrews says so."

Owen was throwing off his dressing gown.

"Be quiet, woman." He glared at the physiotherapist. "I'm grateful for all you've done. Now, help me get dressed. Agnes, call the hangar. Time to kick the tires and light the fires. I want the Bell fueled. Long-range tanks."

"I can't do that, Owen."

"Call them, Agnes. I don't want any arguments."

"Then I'm coming too," she said.

"Why?"

"Because I'm afraid."

He threw his dressing gown on a chair.

"Of what? Bogey-men?"

"I know what you've been going through with these dreams," she said. "I've never seen you like this. I don't want you to go."

"It's all bullshit, Agnes. I've never dodged anything before."

"I know, Owen. That's why I'm afraid."

He stared at her. "What's that mean?"

She heard a voice, her own inside her head cry, *Don't say it! Never say it!*

"I'm afraid of losing you," she said.

The physiotherapist watched Owen's shoulders slowly sag, and the hard lines of his face relaxed in a way she had never seen.

"I can't not go, Agnes," he said gently.

"Then I'm coming with you."

She watched him watching her, aware that for the first time he was seeing through the mask she had so carefully maintained for more than forty years. She felt exposed, vulnerable, no longer in control, and she knew he knew it.

"So be it," he said quietly. "Now make the call."

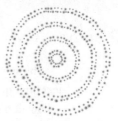

CHAPTER 25

WATERFALLS PITCHED A THOUSAND FEET down the sides of Uluru gushing off its gray stone summit and plummeting past deeply folded curtains of rock, and yawning caves veiled in mist. Clouds hugged the long peak, cold and white, coiling and billowing across the surface of the water hole where Malu and Lungkata kept their vigil for Tjilkamata and Walkalpa. The two men sat beside the sodden embers of the fire. They were soaked by rain and chilled by cloud that whirled in behind it, but they barely noticed.

Their eyes were closed, their minds floating, following the sounds of Wanampi storming over the desert. And something else. Through the roll of thunder and the hiss and rumble of cataracts falling into space far below them, they heard another sound, pitched high and clear, like the keening voice of a great flying creature, moving very fast, outside the cloud.

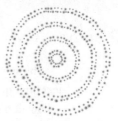

The Bell 222 banked steeply around the end of Uluru, bursting through tendrils of cloud and mist that trailed to the ground as lank and pale as the hair of ghosts.

"There's the highway," Owen said calmly. Agnes leaned forward in the co-pilot's seat next to him, to see. The microphones on their headsets were voice-activated.

"Look at the size of it!"

She stared at the boiling cliffs of the sandstorm towering twenty thousand feet high no more than twenty miles away and rolling closer. They both wore yellow rain slickers from the aircraft's gear locker. They bumped through turbulence from the leading edge of the storm, but the helicopter held the turn smoothly, the twin Allisons singing in harmony through the first flurries of rain.

Owen watched the artificial horizon tip past fifty degrees and trimmed the pitch of the blades with a light touch on the collective lever in his left hand. The hydraulically assisted controls required barely any pressure through his injured arm. The ASI showed they slowed to one hundred four miles an hour in the turn. Owen tapped a code on the small keyboard beneath the navigation computer and sucked at his teeth as the power plant data scanned onto the screen. They had enough jet fuel to make the nonstop flight from Alice Springs, but they would need to load more in Yulara for the return leg.

Agnes watched the ground whip past the starboard windows in the turn, feeling every part of her pulled downward by G-forces.

"Crash at one o'clock," Owen said. "Six miles."

"I see it," Agnes answered, looking down at the path of smashed trailers and scattered debris leading to Rooster Wilson's wrecked Mack, embedded in a sandhill. "And there's the other one, off the road. In the gully."

"Seen," Owen confirmed. "Good work."

"Oh my heavens, they've both crashed." Agnes leaned forward and her harness unreeled with her.

"The report said only Andy crashed," Owen said, puzzled as the tiny shapes of a man and a woman moved around the green Land Rover lying uphill from the white Range Rover. Beyond the Land Rover they saw Heinrich Erhard's car parked beside the road. "It's something else."

He selected the general service frequency for the transceivers fitted in most Outback homes and vehicles in the Red Center.

"BRD to Mark Hansen's Land Rover, do you receive?"

Static blasted in their headsets with every lightning strike out on the desert.

Owen repeated the request, but there was no answer.

He lined up on the wrecked four-wheel-drives and brought the helicopter out of its tight turn thirteen hundred feet above the ground. The earth rolled back below them and the hulking shape of Uluṟu swung into view on their right again, streaming water, like an immense gray head rising from a misty ocean. A field of clouds boiled in a turbulent blanket barely a hundred feet above the Bell's rotors.

Agnes screamed as they plunged two hundred feet in a downdraft before Owen flew them clear.

"You all right?" He grinned at her. She could see savage triumph in his eyes now he was the hunter again, not the target.

"I'm fine," Agnes said tartly, annoyed she had screamed.

"We'll put down on the road above them," he said. He was tracking up the highway, a thousand feet above it. Streaks of light rain trailed up the curved windshields. Lightning slashed from the low cloud to the plain around them.

"We're cutting it a little fine for fuel," he said, surveying the wall of sand rearing into the clouds ahead of them. "We'll put down, load them on, and lift out. It'll take no more than five minutes, tops."

Agnes nodded, watching the road.

Then the world turned blood red.

Grace and Heinrich pulled layers of glass away from Mark Hansen's shattered windshield. He eased himself painfully out through the gap they made, feeling the glass crunch under him.

"You frightened the life out of me," Grace said as Heinrich Erhard helped him up.

"I frightened the life out of me." Mark winced and stood painfully.

"We're far too old for this." Heinrich was beginning to shiver. "This was supposed to be a relaxing reunion for two old men."

"You two old men were fantastic," Grace said.

"We should get you into dry clothes," Mark said to Heinrich. "There are some in my bag, if we can find it in there. How's our friend?"

His Land Rover lay on its side against the chassis of Andrew's Range Rover. The flood roared through the gully below it, licking around its battered metal. Mark's head throbbed and he had grazed both arms climbing out.

"He's still trapped," Grace said, indicating Andrew's vehicle.

The radio in the Land Rover crackled and they heard Owen Bird's voice calling.

Mark reached in through the gap he'd just left and found the microphone.

Heinrich watched for a moment, shivering inside his drenched clothes, then followed Grace down the bank to the Range Rover, to try and free its driver.

It was raining lightly, red-orange drops that had fallen twenty thousand feet through the front of the sandstorm turning to mud on the way down. Heinrich and Grace edged their way down the slope to Andrew's vehicle. Above the sound of the water, they heard the whine of a helicopter, buffeted by gusts of wind as the foothills of the sandstorm rolled over them.

The rain was dark orange now, streaking them with long fingers of mud and painting the two vehicles the color of the deep desert.

Grace looked up, toward the landing lights of Owen Bird's Bell 222 hovering in, nine hundred feet above the highway.

Muddy clouds coiled forward from the front of the sandstorm like a lazy fist, and engulfed the helicopter, cutting off the beams of the landing lights as casually as a hunter pinches off entrails.

꙳

"Mud!" Owen said curtly. The windshield turned dark red, then they were flying blind, under a rapidly thickening layer of paste. "It's solid mud!"

He checked his instrument panel.

"No problem," he said, smiling grimly at Agnes. Then his eyes snapped back to the instrument panel. "IFR."

There was a loud crack above them, and a dying wail of engines, like an animal mortally wounded.

The helicopter rocked giddily.

"We've lost an engine!" Owen called, watching the data displays for the jet turbines go red.

A rapid staccato, like machine-gun fire, rattled above them, then the second jet engine died.

They fell from the sky.

꙳

Tjilkamata barely felt the ground beneath him. His mind flowed like a questing organism far beyond his physical boundaries. He saw clearly the landmarks of the Tjukurpa spirits, the indentations where they slept, and the mounds where they had gone back into the earth. He felt the clarity of universal knowledge beyond the chains of information he'd learned laboriously since childhood, from Anangu elders and Piranypa teachers. It was so familiar it seemed it was forever part of him but was only now moving into focus. He heard the voices of his ancestors, like the sound of distant water, flowing through lives and deaths and back into life in the tides and currents of an infinite river, drawing all existence into its course.

He was traveling in the most powerful part of its current, closing fast with his targets.

⚡

Agnes felt the sickening lurch downward as the helicopter went into free fall. They became weightless, floating against their harnesses.

"Clogged intakes," Owen said. His voice was controlled, responding to a discipline grooved into his brain in fighter school, but his reason fought against it. They were blind and without power. Agnes dug her nails into her thighs, certain they were about to die.

"Autorotating," Owen said. "Hang on. We'll use the blade to brake us in."

His hands moved swiftly over the instruments, through the emergency checklist for autorotation, lowering the collective lever on his left to the limit, decreasing the pitch of the blades in split seconds until their angle of attack was zero and Owen saw the rotor RPM gauge fall at once.

The helicopter rocked as it dropped through the air, and he eased back on the vertical cyclic lever between his knees, changing the plane of the spinning blades until they sped up again, raising the RPM needle.

The hands of the analog altimeter unwound wildly. They were surrounded now by the eerie absence of jet noise, and the rush of air turning the rotor blades with the increasing speed of their fall.

Owen eased the cyclic forward and their airspeed and descent rate moved outside the lethal Dead Man's Curve that governs autorotation. They felt their weight surge back as the blades bit the air and began to slow their dive.

"Seven hundred feet," Owen said aloud. The descent indicator showed they were falling fourteen hundred feet a minute.

The windshield wipers could only smear the mud like thick blinding paint.

Owen reached up with his good right hand and wrenched his side window back. Muddy air roared into the cabin. Outside he saw the flash flood stretching farther across the desert.

"Open your window." His voice filled Agnes's headphones. "You're going to have to line us up on the road. Stick your head out!"

Agnes didn't hesitate. She leaned into the howling slipstream and tried to see the road but her eyes filled with a swirling mist of mud and she cried soundlessly in frustration into the gale and collapsed back in her seat, blinded.

"BRD, this is the Land Rover." Owen glanced at Agnes and flipped the radio to intercom. She heard it too, hissing into her headphones while she tried to wipe the mud from her eyes. "BRD, this is the Land Rover."

"This is BRD, whoever you are, we're autorotating. We have less than twenty seconds to land. Guide us onto the road. Call left or right. Over."

"You're too far left," came the reply. "No! Right! Your right, not mine. You're too far to the right of the road."

Owen watched the altimeter drop through five hundred feet, and banked to port, then straightened out again.

Standing beside his Land Rover, Mark Hansen saw the helicopter veer to its left, across the road and above the floodwaters raging along the other side.

"Too far, BRD." He gripped the microphone, watching the dropping aircraft respond. "You're twenty, no, about fifteen meters to the left, your left of the road."

Four hundred feet. The wipers were groaning against the mud, thinning it to an opaque veneer that was still impossible to see through.

Owen eased the cyclic to the right and straightened up.

"Almost over the road, BRD. Go three meters to your right."

Three hundred feet.

Owen glanced out his side window and saw freeze-framed details of trees in flames from lightning strikes, standing in sheets of water like giant firesticks with their gaunt flares reflected on the flood spreading steadily across the plain.

Two hundred and twenty.

"You're drifting, BRD. Your tail's coming around!"

"Which way?" Owen barked into his microphone. One hundred and fifty feet. Cold gritty rain smacked through the side window. Owen wondered fleetingly if a crash landing would paralyze him again, before he banished the image.

One hundred and eighty feet.

"To your right!"

Owen eased his right foot on its pedal, and watched his heading needle creep two, three, four degrees.

"Other way!"

One hundred and thirty feet. The blazing trees glimmering across the water were clearly visible out the starboard window.

Owen eased his left pedal down, three, four, five, six, seven, eight degrees.

"Good, BRD. You're lined up."

Ninety feet.

Owen eased the cyclic back to flare the rotors, slowing their airspeed and lifting the nose. The altimeter was still dropping too fast.

"Brace! Brace! Brace!" Owen's voice was steady and urgent, and Agnes crossed her arms over her chest and doubled over against her seat belt.

"Fifty! Brace!"

"You're turning again, BRD! To your right!"

Thirty. The floodwaters out the starboard side rushed toward them.

Owen eased down on his left pedal.

"More!"

Owen pressed his left foot farther and raised the collective swiftly, abruptly increasing the rotors' angle of attack, making them bite the air harder, grabbing lift.

The rear of the Bell's skids slammed the edge of the roadway and swerved over the mud-slicked macadam, with a deafening squeal of metal, slewing to one side and pitching them hard against their harnesses, tipping up on one skid, its blades snicking the ground in a blaze of sparks.

Owen felt fire shoot up his spine as they hit, then he was deafened by the crash and shrill voices shouting in his headset.

The main rotors buckled into the road, and the helicopter pitched over, shuddering as the blades disintegrated, thrashing the ground, sending their honeycombed shrapnel slashing through the air. The windshields imploded in a shower of muddy slivers. The cabin bucked violently as the amputated blades battered themselves on the road, warped the main shaft, and tore the jet engines from their mountings. Owen and Agnes heard metal groaning and tearing around them, and saw light flash above them as the roof assembly ripped open, with pieces flying away as they careened along the road.

Grace and Heinrich watched spellbound from the base of the gully where they had almost pried open a gap in the driver's door large enough to insert a tire lever and force the locking assembly using the jack from the Land Rover. They gave a running commentary to Andrew, still wedged inside, waiting to be set free.

Above them, Mark gripped the microphone and recoiled against his over-turned Land Rover, watching the skidding aircraft batter itself into pieces as it screeched toward him. An elbow of twisted rotor blade whirled through the air toward him, like a hunting kali, and thrummed over his head for forty yards before hitting the water with a mighty splash. A plume of sparks flew up beneath the fuselage, illuminating the two bodies inside the shattered canopy, held fast in their seats by harness. The bodies pitched violently side-ways as the helicopter jerked left and stopped, hissing and creaking less than twenty yards from where Mark pressed himself against the chassis of his vehi-cle, frozen by the deafening noise of the crash rushing toward him. He shook himself alert and ran toward the two people hanging in their harness inside the mangled fuselage, aware of the sparks and smoke and the sharp smell of aviation fuel rapidly filling the air.

Walkalpa and Tjilkamata were completely still, staring far across the plain toward the highway. They were in shoulder-high mulga when they heard the whine of the helicopter turning at Uluru, then the uncanny silence when its jet engines stopped in midair, followed by the sounds of the crash.

Motion. Balance. Harmony.

The spirits were with them.

The two men moved off again in silence.

Wanampi the Rainbow Serpent had delivered the last of their quarry, now it was time for her to purify the killing ground.

"Anyone hurt?" Mark saw Owen hanging against the starboard bulkhead and window, which were now on the ground, his face bleeding from cuts from the shattered windshields. Agnes hung above him, her hands to her face, staring at the wreckage that held them.

"Agnes?" Owen peered up at her.

"I think I'm all right. Hello, Mark." She sounded dazed.

"Get her down first," Owen ordered, struggling with the release on his harness. His right shoulder was bruised from hitting the bulkhead and his left hand felt numb.

Mark clambered in through the jagged gap in the windshields and stood up beneath Agnes, bracing his feet around Owen, who lay wedged beneath him.

"Lean on my shoulders," he told her, "and release your harness when you're ready."

"Thank goodness for slacks," Agnes said dryly. He felt her grip his shoulders and braced himself to take her weight, reaching up for her waist. Then she turned the release and dropped awkwardly into his arms.

They heard an explosion as fork lightning blasted the road behind the helicopter.

"Out!" Owen barked beneath them.

"Are you all right?" Agnes crouched beside him.

"Get out of here, Agnes!"

"Not without you," she said firmly.

"Out! Mark'll help me. Go on!"

"No! Not without you."

"Smell that?" Owen grunted in pain as Mark released his harness and he settled onto the ground. The smell of jet fuel was becoming overpowering.

"Then we'd better hurry with you too," Agnes said.

Owen glared at her. "You're a bloody stubborn hag."

"I need to be."

She and Mark helped Owen to his knees.

"Can you stand?" Mark asked.

Owen took a deep breath and nodded. They stood each side of him, bracing him as he struggled to his feet.

"Out!" Owen's voice was a growl through clenched teeth.

Mark kicked away the lower shards of windshield and they muscled Owen through the gap and onto the road as the helicopter sizzled and creaked around them.

"Move!" Owen staggered between them, and they manhandled him away from the wreckage, ten yards, fifteen, twenty.

There was no explosion, just a low *whooom!* as the jet fuel ignited and they were hit in the back by a hot blast of searing air. They didn't look around until they were fifty yards down the road.

A long trail of jet fuel had leaked along the road behind them, burning brightly as it meandered over the macadam like a brilliant, fiery snake.

The helicopter was enveloped in thick black smoke that billowed in the gusting wind. Bright red and orange fires roared through the cabin licking around the engine housing, and buckling the airframe with their intense heat. When fire reached the external tank, it withstood the flames for a few seconds, then disintegrated in a loud explosion that spun the helicopter around and severed the tailplane, sending it skidding along the shoulder of the road, gouging a track down the bank of the gully and coming to rest a car length from the Range Rover. It happened so fast, Grace and Heinrich barely had time to react before a cloud of steam erupted from the floodwaters where the smoldering tip of the tailplane splashed beneath the surface.

Up on the road, roiling black smoke blanketed the entire crash site.

"Where's Andy?" Owen shouted.

"Down there!" Mark pointed down the gully, where smoke coiled down in dark fingers and swirled around the Range Rover, merging with the steam still hissing from the submerged end of the tailplane. They saw Grace and Heinrich manhandling the driver's door open, and a hand reaching out of the cabin.

Owen pushed himself away from Mark and Agnes and limped through the smoke, down the embankment toward his son. Agnes and Mark followed him, scrambling and sliding down the slope until they reached the Range Rover. Grace climbed onto the upper side of the vehicle and helped Andrew struggle out. They both stood on top of the battered doors, hugging each other. Heinrich and Mark and Agnes watched them from the bank.

"She saved my life," Andrew called down to them, draping an arm around Grace's shoulders. "She was terrific. Dad, say hello to Grace Morgan."

There was no answer.

Andrew turned to see why, and Grace felt his body tense next to her. She saw where he was looking, and the others on the ground turned too.

Owen Bird stood quite still, his face blank, his lips working steadily, opening, then closing, opening, then closing, opening, closing, but no words, no sound at all came out.

They followed the direction of his gaze and saw for the first time, against the gully wall behind them, side by side in their upended coffins, the rigored bod-ies of Teddy Gidgee, Russell King, and Oscar Woolie. Their mouths were gap-ing black cavities, their lips contracted tightly inward making them appear toothless, while tendrils of blood-red rain streamed over their open eyes, which were rolled back in their sockets and showing white, staring sightlessly at Owen.

✎

Walkalpa watched the distant smoke swirling around the road and into the gullies on each side, purifying all it embraced.

Tjilkamata ranged a little ahead of him, moving light as air over the ground, reading the creation tracks that snaked beneath them, analyzing the data in their stories, letting them show the proper path into the killing ground.

✎

"Owen," Mark said quietly. "Are you all right?"

Owen wheeled angrily on him. "What the fuck are they doing there?"

"It was the accident," Mark said. "They were thrown out when the Land Rover rolled."

"You should have fucking covered them!"

"Owen, we've been pretty busy."

"Cover them up!"

Mark looked bewildered.

"Owen, we're all soaked, and very tired. We should get under cover and into some dry clothes. These three aren't going anywhere."

"Suit yourself," Owen snarled. "I'll do it."

He strode toward a coffin lid lying where it was hurled several yards from Oscar Woolie.

"Hang on," Andrew said, climbing painfully down from the top of the Range Rover. He helped Grace down, then went to help his father recover the first lid. Grace watched them fit it back on the nearest coffin, then begin searching for the remaining two. She looked along the bank for them, and saw instead the long gouge marks made by the tailplane. Something in its deep groove in the embankment caught her eye. She walked over to it and bent down to look closely. There were half a dozen of them, lying in the orange mud. She picked them up, one by one, and spread them on the palm of her hand, turning each one with her finger. She heard the four men fitting the lids back on the coffins.

Agnes came down to join Grace.

"Mark's radioed for help," she said, looking at the objects in Grace's hand. "But the emergency services have their hands full in Yulara. The airport's been devastated. It'd be different if we had someone with serious injuries. We'll just have to wait until they're ready to send someone. Those are pretty."

"They are, aren't they," Grace said, holding them out on the flat of her hand.

"We'll set up some cover for the night," Owen said behind them. "Up there on the road."

"There's a tarpaulin in the Land Rover," Mark said. "We can rig a lean-to."

"Good. And we'll need whatever warm gear we can salvage," Owen said curtly. It was a good thing, he thought, they'd both put on slickers in the helicopter.

"I'll see what I can find in the vehicles," Mark said. Heinrich went with him and Andrew wandered over to the two women, carrying the tennis bag he recovered from the Range Rover. He was puzzled by his father's behavior, tense, nervous, completely out of character. It made Andrew uneasy. He reasoned Owen might just be suffering aftereffects of surviving the crash. Andrew wondered if Agnes was going through the same thing.

"These fell out of the tailplane," Grace said, showing him the objects in her hand. "They look like colored glass."

"I think they are," Andrew said. "Agnes, did you hear anything like machine-gun fire in the chopper?"

"Yes we did." Agnes looked surprised. "Just before we lost the engines."

"Sounds right," Andrew said. "I've seen these before. Different color. Different country. But the same thing. Sand and rain get sucked into the intakes, they're superheated inside the engines, melted into these slugs, and blasted out the back."

"That'd be the sounds we heard when we lost power," Owen said, coming down the embankment. "Glass being fired out the exhausts and into the tailplane. Let's have a look."

He held his hand out, and Grace tipped the smooth glass pellets into it. The fused red mud had cooled to a brittle white glaze.

Owen felt them hit his hand with a faint clatter, and stared at them for an instant before hurling them away with a startled cry. They landed on the muddy embankment, and lay there, pearl white and streaked with red, like freshly extracted teeth.

Half a mile away, Walkalpa squatted in the trough between two low sand dunes. He felt the hard stone of the spirit eye of Wanampi between his tongue and palate. He could feel the presence of the stolen tjurunga very close now. He sensed the spirit of the thief, discordant, at bay, frightened but still threatening. And he felt another entity, smooth, focused, dangerously well disciplined.

Tjilkamata was alert to it too, along with the sense of someone else, who shouldn't be there.

Walkalpa remained motionless, watching the highway, aware of Tjilkamata moving away from him like a wisp of air.

Owen stared at the glass pellets in the embankment. His fear made him angry. He was tired of being afraid. He reminded himself that all his past fears had been external, capable of being overcome, face-to-face. This new terror was inside him. His anger faltered, and fear rose through him again like floodwaters. He strode up the embankment, and the others made their way up behind him.

"Let's get the tarpaulin up," Owen said, "and rig a shelter."

"We can salvage the seats out of the vehicles," Mark said.

"Good," Owen said, glad to be busy. "We'll get a fire going and dry everyone out."

"It's so bleak and gray," Agnes said.

"That's what happens in a fucking storm," Owen answered.

"No, I mean Ayers Rock," she said, looking down the highway at the monolith, rising into cloud. "It's gray."

"It's the dust," Mark answered. "The sandstone in Uluru is gray, but the dust makes it red."

"I always thought that was its natural color, red," Agnes replied.

"Nothing out here is ever what it seems," Mark said.

Agnes kept staring down the highway at it, and hugged her slicker more tightly around her.

"We have company," she said quietly.

Andrew came alert, moving silently up beside her.

Two hundred yards down the road, he saw a black figure painted with intricate red ocher and white clay patterns and carrying two hunting spears. The man stood still, watching them silently.

"Anyone know who or what he is?" Andrew asked, his voice low.

"That's ritual body paint," Mark Hansen said. "I can't see what he's carrying."

"Look at those designs," Grace breathed. "He's beautiful."

"Spears," Andrew said to Mark. "Painted. Barbed."

"Ceremonial killing spears," Mark responded softly and glanced at Owen.

"What is he?" Andrew asked.

"A liability," Owen said. Behind him, Heinrich was watching the distant figure intensely.

Andrew turned to Owen, one eyebrow raised in a question.

Owen nodded in reply.

"He's gone!" Agnes said. She glared at Mark. "He's the one you were talking about, isn't he."

"No," Mark answered.

"He's the kudaitja, isn't he?" Agnes's voice shook.

"You said he'd be invisible, Padre," Owen said. "Not very invisible is he?"

"You're in grave danger, Owen," Mark said.

"What's going on?" Heinrich asked. "What are you all talking about?"

"Then," Andrew said, ignoring him, "we should be proactive."

"How do you think you can do that?" Mark said.

"Prick him, and he'll bleed," Andrew said, remembering the first time he heard Keith Bliss recite Shylock's challenge to Salarino, "'If you prick us, do we not bleed? If you tickle us, do we not laugh? If you poison us, do we not die? And if you wrong us, shall we not revenge?'"

The word "revenge" slid around his mind, taunting him, reminding him he wasn't the one who was wronged, nor was Owen, rather to the contrary. Andrew felt a niggle of doubt, and drove it out of his mind.

"What do you have in mind?" Mark asked, aware that Heinrich was watching the conversation with intense curiosity.

"If they're going to attack, we're sitting targets," Andrew said.

"We could get in the Land Rover," Agnes said.

"More of a sitting target," Andrew said. "Once it gets dark, it'll be worse."

"What are you all talking about?" Grace asked. "Do you know that guy out there?"

"Ask Reverend Hansen here," Owen said.

"I can't say who he is," Mark said.

"You wouldn't be thinking about keeping anything from us, would you, Padre?"

"It doesn't matter," Andrew said, casting his eyes around for potential weapons. "We still need to be proactive."

"Will someone tell me what is happening here," Grace said.

"Someone is trying to get to Owen," Agnes told her.

"That guy in the paint?" Grace asked.

Agnes nodded. "And someone else."

Grace saw Andrew walk over to the Land Rover's winch cable. It was made of dozens of fine steel strands, twisted around a core. Andrew picked it up with both hands, bending it like a hairpin. He straightened it out, then bent it again in the same place, repeating the movement quickly until the cable became warm at the bend.

"Well, Padre," Owen barked as his son worked on the cable, "are you keeping secrets from us?"

"I've told you everything I know, Owen."

"What did you tell him?" Heinrich asked.

"Owen here has taken something that doesn't belong to him," Mark said, avoiding Heinrich's eyes.

"I paid for it, Padre . . ."

"And the people to whom it belongs desperately want it back."

"What is it?" Grace asked.

Andrew didn't look up from the cable. "See for yourself, Grace. It's in the tennis bag."

Grace saw the bag on the ground beside Andrew. Something stirred deep inside her, a sense of enormous danger. She moved toward the bag.

"No!"

The shout startled them all and they spun around to stare at Heinrich. He stood staring at the bag, clenching and unclenching his hands.

"Don't touch it, Grace!" he ordered.

Grace stopped in her tracks. Andrew lowered the cable and examined Heinrich with new interest.

"What do you know about this?" Owen demanded.

"Heinrich's an old friend," Mark said quickly. "I've told him your story."

"What do you know about this, Heinrich?" Owen's voice dropped.

"Nothing."

"What brings you out here?"

"He and Grace are visiting me, Owen."

"Is that true, Heinrich?" Owen crossed the space between them to bring his face inches from Heinrich's.

"Yes."

"Grace?" Owen didn't take his eyes off Heinrich. "Is this true?"

Grace saw Heinrich's hands clenching and unclenching, and suddenly she knew. She didn't know how she knew, but she was certain of it.

"Grace?"

"She doesn't know anything about this," Heinrich said.

"But you, my friend do, I think," Owen said smoothly. "Don't you? You know that fellow out there? Who is he? Who's he with? Where are they?"

"Owen." Mark put his arm between the two men. Owen gently pushed him away.

"Who's out there, Heinrich? Tell me. Where are they?"

Heinrich had an image of men running through jungle, and white cranes unfolding their wings on a wooden table, and felt his knees go weak and nausea stir his stomach.

"Where are they now, Heinrich? What are they doing?"

"Maybe you'll tell me," Andrew said quietly.

Agnes saw him slip away and return a few moments later.

Owen grinned savagely at his son and stood aside.

"Who's out there?" Andrew asked. "Who are they?"

Heinrich felt his knees shaking, but he stood his ground.

"Tell me." Andrew's voice was barely audible, patient, dangerous.

"Stop this!" Grace took Heinrich's arm and stood with her face in front of Andrew's. "I saved your life down there."

Andrew stepped back, startled.

"You're right," he said. Then he smiled slowly at her. "Besides, it doesn't matter what our friends here know. The best defense is offense."

He turned and she saw what he was carrying in his right hand.

"All of you should stay here in the center of the road. Safety in numbers."
To his father, Andrew said, "I'll be back soon. Keep an eye on the bag."

Then he dropped down the embankment, with the steel wire in his hand, coiled neatly with each end wrapped and secured firmly around a brass coffin handle.

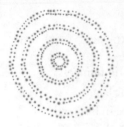

CHAPTER 26

«A PIRANYPA IS COMING OUT,» Walkalpa said over his shoulder. The sorcerer squatted in the cover of a clump of mulga and watched the road three hundred yards away. He spoke without looking back at Tjilkamata.

Tjilkamata heard the words like clear streams entering a murmuring flood of voices. He was no longer conscious of his arms or legs or eyes or ears. He was no longer aware of being Robert or Tjilkamata. He was in a river that was everything, and nothing. He was pure awareness, physical and spiritual, guided by powers as subtle and strong as gravity. His two killing spears felt weightless in his fingertips, as light and sharp as clear thought.

He was a flowing junction of all the knowledge he had ever acquired, surrendering himself to it with the humility of utter self-discipline. He heard the creation spirits Singing down all their ancient pathways, into him, into Wanampi.

He was their instrument.

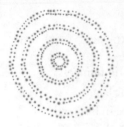

Andrew inhaled lightly through his mouth and nose, absorbing every sound and taste and smell until he felt himself blending with the landscape. He began filtering out the roar of the flood down the gully beside him, seeking other sounds through it. As he melded with his surroundings, he began looking for anomalies, shifts in the feel of the ground and air and life around him. He scooped more mud across his bare skin. He was becoming part of the ground and air. He extended his awareness beyond himself, seeing in his mind his own life-force moving far beyond him, alert for any other presence. He knew he would feel it soon, even as it reached for him.

First contact would begin long before he moved into visual range.

⚡

Walkalpa rubbed the spiny leaves between the heels of his hands until they broke into strands like cigarette tobacco. They smelled pungent.

"Antidote" was not a term he would have used for the leaves. By themselves, the fine strands he rolled into a ball and stowed in a leather bag on his waist string were highly toxic. The bag was small, a third of the size of his fist, made from the scrotum of a malu, red kangaroo. The leather was durable, chewed and stretched and seasoned until it was soft, and tied at the neck with a narrow thong.

In the Tjukurpa, it was a Malu man who seeded the ground and made the bitter leaves grow, as a warning to his relatives of the more dangerous poison growing nearby.

⚡

Andrew smelled the rain on the air, and something fainter behind it. Bruises from the wreck were hardening around his skull and right shoulder. His head ached and nausea stirred his stomach. The joints of his arms and legs felt weak and he had an overwhelming urge to roll into a fetal ball and go to sleep. But he understood these symptoms of fear and flight, and instead centered himself, and focused his energy into his belly, his hara, where all his power resided.

His breathing became deep and slow, and he visualized great strength flowing from the storm into his bones and muscles. When he exhaled through his mouth, he felt all his weakness and fear flowing out. He opened the edges of his mind again, letting it drift out beyond him, searching for sound and smell and sign and spirit, until he sensed what he was looking for.

He moved low down along the gully, just above the waterline, barely touching the ground beneath his bare feet. Overhead, the gray afternoon light washed away hard shadows, softening the lines of the ground. When he found the track, his senses leapt forward, like a hound over a warm scent. He could see fragments of bare footprints running ahead of him. Andrew knew no man could pass here without leaving spoor. There was no magic. He breathed lightly, casting ahead over the tracks. He had traveled more than three hundred yards down the gully when he saw the figure far ahead, beside a clump of mulga that had grown down through the gully in the drought and was now partly submerged.

Andrew only saw him when he moved. The man was painted, and appeared to be squatting at the edge of the torrent. His spears lay on the ground beside him, away from the water. Andrew smiled to himself. The sound of the flood would cover his approach. He could float in and take the man before he even sensed he was there. He changed his hold on the wire. *Come in like a germ,* he thought. *Before they know you're there, become them, like a silent plague turning their own breath against them.*

Andrew felt light as air, breathing down the bank of the gully, sliding in with the sound of the torrent, feeling the man's vulnerability, easing himself into it. He was in close now, shadowing the man down to the water, breathing in along his spine. He felt the wire uncoil, his ears hummed with the feel of it, an old familiar urgency to do it now. His fingers closed around the contoured brass handles.

He was in close enough now, feeling his reflexes smoothly lifting him. He hesitated for an instant, then raised the wire to strike when he felt the man move inside his reach, rising and turning to face him, smiling with fat billowing cheeks. Andrew's mind dislocated as the man turned inside his reach. In the last instant, Andrew realized it was he who had been infiltrated. The painted man had led him here, willing him along his patently clear track, letting him move in close, open and vulnerable at the moment of attack. The man blew out his cheeks like an ocher painter, blasting a fine spray of slurried emu poison bush from his mouth. Andrew inhaled in surprise, barely feeling the mist surging into his lungs, coating their membranes, penetrating the cells and capillary walls, feeding their toxin into his bloodstream.

Walkalpa watched the Piranypa stagger. He stepped back, a limping pace, and heard the brass-handled wire hit the ground. The Piranypa stared at him in astonishment, fighting to stand. Then his feet buckled and he collapsed onto mud.

Walkalpa dropped to his knees beside the gully and took huge mouthfuls of water, rinsing it between his cheeks and spitting it onto the ground. He took out the ground spiny leaves from his waist pouch and chewed them methodically. The emu poison bush had only been in his mouth for a few seconds before he blew the spray into the Piranypa's face, but he could already feel the distinctive numbness it produced along his cheeks and tongue. The spiny leaf fibers contained the acidic molecular chains of an organic stimulant, a direct chemical antidote in his nervous system. He drank more water, welcoming the pungent sting of the ground leaves on his throat and stomach. Then he placed the spirit eye of Wanampi back in his mouth, and looked down at the Piranypa. He had no animosity for the writhing white man. Walkalpa knew this killer was no less a creature of his instincts than a common desert scorpion.

He took a stone blade and made a short deep incision inside both the Piranypa's thighs. Walkalpa picked up his spears and set off in his limping gait along the gully to where Tjilkamata was waiting.

In a moment, Andrew would begin to regain his senses, but the incisions would require direct pressure from both hands to stem the flow.

Walkalpa knew that the Piranypa could never pursue them like that.

It was all the advantage they needed.

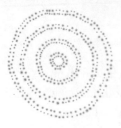

CHAPTER 27

Agnes and Grace sat in the middle of the road on one of the passenger seats salvaged from the Land Rover. Mark and Heinrich had stretched the tarpaulin from the back of the overturned vehicle, forming a lean-to. They were both cold and tired. Agnes could see Owen pacing along the road shoulder above the gully. She stood up to join him.

Grace was watching a line of ants marching resolutely up from the gully, onto the drying red mud covering the road. The tiny insects resembled a miniature army of explorers on some foreign landscape. She thought that a curious image, watching them file past her feet, obeying their secret codes and instructions.

"Andrew's been away a long time," she said to Mark, who was pacing between the seats and the smoldering debris of the helicopter.

Agnes must have stood up too quickly. She felt dizzy, and looked down at the tennis bag at her feet where Owen had left it, and the ground appeared to shift beneath her. Everything seemed far away. She had the sensation of swaying into a gap between reality and illusion.

Something was traveling in from the desert, barely out of sight, but moving with a sense of purpose.

✦

Owen scanned the bank of the gully in the direction his son had taken. He turned and saw Teddy Gidgee, Russell King, and Oscar Woolie gazing through him from the edge of the water.

He felt a numbing cold descend on him, and felt himself walking slowly down the embankment toward the water, past the three upright coffins. He moved in a dream, turning slowly to see why they were empty while their occupants stood at the water's edge, staring sightlessly at him. He saw the lids propped against them, each beside its gaping empty casket. Owen turned back to confront the three figures, laboring as if his body had turned to lead. Teddy Gidgee, Russell King, and Oscar Woolie had disappeared.

In their place were two painted men.

Agnes came to the shoulder of the road and saw an Aboriginal man covered in white and red patterns standing silently in front of Owen. He appeared to be unarmed. She felt another presence too, but could see nobody else.

She hurried back to the tarpaulin, snatched up the tennis bag, and carried it down the side of the gully.

"This is what you're looking for," she called.

The painted man looked up as if he expected her.

"Here." She raised the bag and reached into it.

The man's eyes blazed fiercely and he held his hand up to stop her. She hesitated and dropped the bag. Something moved toward her with enormous force and she heard Owen call, "No! Take me!"

Walkalpa watched the Piranypa woman with the eye of Wanampi in his mouth, and could see she carried the tjurunga. He heard her call to him, "This is what you're looking for," and saw her reaching for it. Any woman or uninitiated man who looked at it would have to be killed. He held his arm up to stop her, and saw her drop the bag.

Owen saw Tjilkamata streak up the bank to catch the bag as it fell.

He saw the other painted elder gesturing to Agnes.

"No!" Owen heard his own voice from a long way away. "Take me!"

Tjilkamata seized the bag and turned back down the slope. The part of him that was Robert understood that Owen was offering to sacrifice himself for the woman, but the discovery was a small fleeting instant in the kudaitja's consciousness. The part of him that was Tjilkamata of the Spiny Anteater Dreaming was gauging how much she had seen. There would be no choice if she saw the stone. Both personalities registered as distant voices in the presence of Wanampi directing the kudaitja toward Owen.

Owen saw the kudaitja advancing on him, the painted totems on his body glowing and writhing with brilliant colors. Owen tried to focus on them but their outlines kept changing. The patterns on the man's black skin pulsed with all the hues of the rainbow, expanding far around him into the shape of a giant creature with spines as sharp as spears radiating into the sky. The light dazzled Owen, filling his mind, blocking out all else, and overwhelming all his defenses. He struggled to call out to the kudaitja.

He watched the sorcerer hand the kudaitja a spear pulsing with energy, and look up at Agnes.

"No," Owen heard his voice sucked into a void around them. "Not her. Take me."

The lights emanating from the kudaitja were blinding him. The spear glowed above his head as the kudaitja raised it and with a mighty heave, hurled it downward. Owen felt the spear drive into his chest, exploding the breath from his lungs as if he had been hit by a train. He buckled forward, but the kudaitja lifted the blazing haft, forcing Owen upright. Owen tried to cry out, but all his muscles were paralyzed. There was only the agony of the barbed spear impaled in his heart.

The kudaitja leaned on the shaft, working it from side to side, opening a huge gaping wound in Owen's chest. Owen stared, his mouth open, unable to utter a sound. Pain surged through him like molten steel, searing his nerve endings, sending the signals screaming to a brain that would not respond.

The wound was so wide now, Owen could see the outline of his own heart inside the bloody cavity, with the head of the huge spear buried in it. He staggered, fell to one knee, then collapsed onto his back, too stunned by pain to make a sound.

He saw the other figure materialize next to the kudaitja. This one glowed with the white-and-ocher-colored patterns of a sorcerer, running the full length of his body where they seemed to split and refract. They seethed over the sorcerer, blasting Owen with every color of the spectrum, warping from the man's deformed foot, up around his legs and belly, and coiling over his scarred chest.

Agnes cried out as Owen fell. She did not see the kudaitja or the spear, only the sorcerer bending down as she scrambled down the slope to Owen and threw herself beside him with her head on his chest. She felt his body convulsing violently, heaving up under her cheek as if he was being savaged by a creature she could not see.

Owen felt her clutching him, then the kudaitja put his foot beside the wound, braced himself, and hauled the spear out. Owen's body was jerked up by the force of it, and he heard the deep sucking sounds of the weapon's cruel barbs being hauled out of the deep gash in his heart. He saw the sorcerer kneel beside him, placing the bag with the tjurunga next to him.

With a mighty effort, Owen brought his good hand up and covered Agnes's eyes to stop her seeing the stone.

"Forgive me," he groaned.

Agnes raised her head and looked into his eyes. She saw agony and something else that she had prayed to see since the first day she met him, when he carried her things across the tarmac. He was looking for her. She felt him looking for her as he searched her eyes. Then he closed his hand over her face, blocking out all light.

She pressed her lips against his hand, and felt his body convulse again.

Owen felt the spear wrenched from his heart, and saw it blazing brightly in the hands of the kudaitja, who stepped back, casting his shifting lights over them as he made way for the sorcerer.

Tjilkamata heard Owen ask forgiveness, but there was no place for that under The Law. Now there was only recovery, restoration, retribution.

Walkalpa moved with the grace of an enormous snake, reaching past the Piranypa woman and striking forward with his hand deep into the maw of the thief's chest, driving down to the chambers of the heart.

From the roadway, Grace saw Agnes kneeling over Owen, and the same painted man from the road moving over him. She saw no one else, but she was struck by a vivid recollection of the live pictures from space she had watched less than a week ago, of two astronauts chasing down a satellite and opening it up to reach into its heart and restore service.

Owen watched the sorcerer's hand enter and open inside him, revealing a brilliant white sliver of quartz. With surgical precision, the hand embedded the sliver in the heart wall. Numbing cold, as cruel as fire, expanded around the quartz. The sorcerer withdrew his hand, leaving the quartz inside, sucking the heat from each cell until it was dead, frozen solid, and leeching the heat from the next. The cold expanded rapidly inside him, chilling his flesh layer by layer.

"There's nothing to forgive, Owen," Agnes said. She felt his hand fall away and saw the sorcerer pressing on Owen's chest.

Walkalpa closed the wound, sealing the quartz inside. Then he folded the tjurunga into himself, hiding it from all view, and rose and stepped back. Owen's eyes flickered as he watched the sorcerer and kudaitja looking down at him. The sorcerer fixed him with a gaze as black as space, drawing out all light.

Walkalpa and Tjilkamata watched the quartz extinguish the life in the Piranypa thief's body.

Agnes saw the light go out of Owen's eyes.

She felt him go still, and laid her head on his chest, whispering, "Oh, Owen. Oh, my Owen."

Mark and Heinrich heard Agnes call out and ran to the shoulder of the road. They saw her kneeling over Owen, beneath the lifeless gaze of the three corpses.

But they saw no other living soul, apart from two animals climbing away from the floodwaters. The two clergymen looked at each other for an instant. Understanding flashed between them like desert lightning. Secrets. Powers beyond power. The two animals disappeared down the gully, a spiny anteater waddling swiftly along the edge of the water, followed by a brilliantly colored snake.

Tjilkamata and Walkalpa traveled over the plain toward Uluru. Around them, thousands of ghostly figures appeared, the spirits of all their ancestors, parting to welcome them. Balance. Harmony. Flow. Tjilkamata moved quietly beside the sorcerer, through the multitude, over the songlines that defined each of them securely and completely in the current of the Tjukurpa and its Law. He was still a kudaitja, a changed one, and until he returned with Walkalpa to the cave beneath Uluru to be transformed back, he remained dislocated, between the world of spirits and the dimension of humans.

The spirits flowed around them with the murmuring sounds of a great river as he and Walkalpa walked toward the monolith.

Far ahead, low clouds rolled over the summit of Uluṟu, lit by a glowing arc of brilliant colors that curved across the sky and onto the red desert like the magnificent coils of a great serpent.

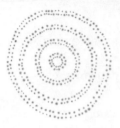

CHAPTER 28

AN AIR FORCE HELICOPTER sent to patrol the flood zone answered the emergency call before sundown. It carried Agnes Horstmann and Andrew Bird and the body of his father out to the hastily cleared runway at Connellan Airport outside Yulara. From there they were airlifted on a RAAF Hercules back to Alice Springs. Heinrich Erhard drove Grace Morgan on to Lake Amadeus Mission with Mark Hansen.

"You've come this far," Mark told her. "I think you should finish your journey properly."

He installed them in two spartan guest rooms, each with an iron bed and shelves loaded with yellowing Everyman paperbacks. They spent much of their time sleeping. In the evenings the three of them sat on squatter's chairs on the veranda, drinking rum and watching the profusion of stars roll slowly overhead. They talked about journeys and navigators and astronomy and life and death.

On their third morning at the mission, Grace and Heinrich were informed by Mark that an old Anangu man had arrived and was asking to speak to Pastor Erhard.

Grace watched from the veranda when the old man appeared and Heinrich greeted him like a respected friend. The old man had skin as black as gunmetal and he was dressed in cast-off clothes, and a pair of ill-fitting shoes with the toes protruding through holes in the leather. He led Heinrich across the dry brown lawn to a pair of garden chairs beneath a shade tree, away from the main building, and out of earshot. The two men talked quietly through the morning.

Grace sat on the veranda trying to read one of Mark's ancient paperbacks. Occasionally, she looked up to see the two men watching her. Then they would turn away and continue their conversation.

Shortly before lunch, Heinrich came up the stairs of the veranda and sat on a chair next to Grace. She did not see the old Anangu man leave.

"Robbie will be back in the morning," Heinrich said.

Grace lowered her book, and closed her eyes, unable to speak.

Heinrich waited for her to open them again.

"Are you sure about him?" he asked.

She nodded. "Yes."

"When Owen and Andrew were questioning me at the crash site," Heinrich said, "I was watching you."

"What did you see?"

"I saw the moment you realized what was really happening out there."

She nodded silently.

"I was remembering," she said eventually, "why you told me the story about how Ashima died. You did something you didn't want to do because of duty and honor. That's when I knew what Rob was doing here."

"You're sure about him, then?"

"Yes." She smiled at him. "I trust him completely."

"Enough not to have to know everything?"

"Is that what you and the old man were talking about?"

"Some of it. Malu's an old friend. I've known him since Robbie was a boy."

"If you're talking about men's business, yes. I trust him enough."

Heinrich nodded. "He's a lucky man." He looked out over the brown grass toward the shimmering dry flats of Lake Amadeus. "We'll pick him up tomorrow."

Grace and Heinrich drove out to the camp early the following morning. It was already very hot.

As they got out of the vehicle and waited, they saw Robert, wearing slacks and an open-necked shirt and loafers, standing a short distance away with five Aboriginal men who were dressed in old clothes and battered hats. Two of them were shoeless, including a tall, gaunt one with deep penetrating eyes and a sinister-looking one with a cruelly deformed foot. The fifth man

Grace recognized as the old one who had come to talk to Heinrich the day before.

She saw Robert place the palm of his hand on the first man's chest. The man did the same to Robert, and they both spoke solemnly in a language Grace could not understand. Robert repeated the parting ritual with each of the five men, and across the baking ground, Grace heard catches of words, alien, poetic: Tjilkamata, Tjitutja, Lungkata, Kumanara, Walkalpa, Malu. Then the five men turned and walked away, and Robert came toward her, carrying his travel bag, smiling.

"Can't get away from you, eh?" he said as she came into his arms.

"You should be so lucky."

"I am." He held her at arm's length and looked at her closely. Then he reached into his pocket and took out his watch and strapped it back onto his wrist, and said, "Ready to go home?"

"Houston?"

He nodded and she pulled him to her and held him, with her eyes closed. When she opened them and looked over his shoulder, she saw the air shimmering in a heat haze out to the horizon, and five flickering shapes moving away over the desert, like tongues of fire.

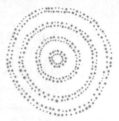

Acknowledgments

I wish to thank Dr. Brian and Patricia Ford, my parents, for introducing me as a child to the richly complex cultures and stories of Australia's Aborigines. Brian Ford's enthusiasm for history and anthropology was the catalyst to the founding of the Miles Museum.

I am enormously grateful to my agent and manuscript editor, Robbie Anna Hare of Goldfarb & Associates, Washington, DC, for her unfailingly wise advice and assiduous editing throughout. And to Ronald Goldfarb for his insight and counsel. The final rewrites over a year were made possible by the enormous hospitality of James Lindsay, Robbie Anna Hare, Larry and Laurie Checco, and Catherine Wadley, to whom I am lastingly thankful.

My enduring thanks go to my attorney, Paul A. Mahon, of Mahon, Patusky & Rothblat, Washington, DC, whose generous and meticulous literary critiques, advice, and cheerful encouragement, at all hours have been indispensable.

I am grateful to Andrew Fisher, Larry Checco, David Franken, Gary Steele, and Annabelle Brayley for their invaluable editorial advice. I am especially grateful to Lori Butterfield, for her detailed critiques and encouragement. I could not have completed this book without Victoria Hansen's support, patience, and edit notes, for which I will always be thankful.

I am grateful to those at Simon & Schuster who have worked on this book, especially my editor Chuck Adams and Editor in Chief Michael Korda for their valuable advice, and Associate Director of Copyediting Gypsy da Silva, her remarkably industrious copy editor Fred Chase for his painstaking attention to detail and accuracy, and intern Brenna McLoughlin for her careful and enthusiastic checking of the final stages of proof.

For technical advice, I wish to thank Maureen Natjuna of the Liru Poison Snake Dreaming, and her husband Peter Kanari of the Mutitjulu Community, Uluṟu; Steve Byrnes, Operations Manager, Royal Flying Doctor Service, Alice Springs; Mario Moldoveanu, author of the Protocol for Accident & Emergency, Alice Springs Hospital; former Royal Flying Doctor Toby Ford MB, BS; Doctor Oscar Mann MD, FACP, FACC, FCCP, Georgetown University School of Medicine; Nurse Margaret Allen, Mater Hospital, Sydney; naturalist Peter King; biologist Neil Hermes; and instructor Bob Pagett, of Bankstown Helicopters.

I am deeply indebted to Professors Ronald and Catherine Berndt, anthropologists and authors of *The World of the First Australians*. I greatly appreciate Prof. Catherine Berndt's encouragement.

I wish to thank my mentor, teacher, and friend Lee Robinson—eminent writer, producer, director, and chronicler of Australian history—for his encouragement, wisdom, and guidance.

Finally, I wish to express my enduring gratitude to the Anangu of the Central Australian desert, especially those elder men and women who guided the final reading and editing of the creation stories, camouflage stories, and rituals recounted here. I remain indebted to them for their advice and generosity to me in the desert.

Peter Shann Ford
Toowoomba, May 2000